Dark Temptation

IMOSHEN TURNED TO HIM, pride blazing in her eyes. A smile of triumph curved her lips.

The T'En had done it again. She'd reached into his mind and invaded his thoughts.

He flung her hands away.

"Don't ever do that again!" Even as he spoke he registered the confusion in her eyes. She didn't understand his anger. A sheen of unshed tears made her eyes glisten and he realized he'd hurt her.

She'd offered him a vision of the future and he'd thrown it aside. Damn her!

Damn her beautiful, trembling mouth.

He had to kiss her. It made no sense. He ignored the small, quiet part of his brain that warned him not to give in. One kiss would never be enough. Instead of heeding common sense, he let the need that had been steadily building within his body guide his actions.

He caught her to him, capturing her lips with his. . . .

BROKEN VOWS

Book One of

THE LAST T'EN TRILOGY

CORY DANIELLS

Bantam Books

New York Toronto London Sydney Auckland

BROKEN VOWS
A Bantam Book / Published in association with Bantam Australia,
a division of Transworld Publishers, Australia

PUBLISHING HISTORY
Bantam Australia edition published 1999
Bantam paperback edition / July 1999

First published in Australia and New Zealand in 1999
under the title, *The Last T'En*, by Bantam Australia,
a division of Transworld Publishers, Australia

ISBN 0-553-58097-3

Published simultaneously in the United States and Canada

Bantam Books are published by Bantam Books, a division of Random
House, Inc. Its trademark, consisting of the words "Bantam Books" and the
portrayal of a rooster, is Registered in U.S. Patent and Trademark Office and
in other countries. Marca Registrada. Bantam Books, 1540 Broadway, New
York, New York 10036.

PRINTED IN THE UNITED STATES OF AMERICA

OPM   10 9 8 7 6 5 4 3 2 1

To D, who always believed in me.

BROKEN VOWS

ONE

GENERAL TULKHAN STRODE the halls of the Stronghold, triumphant. But even though the last of the T'En royal family had surrendered he experienced no thrill of victory. His father, the Ghebite King, was dead.

Shattering glass broke his concentration. Heart pounding, he spun around. Nothing.

According to the terms of surrender he had promised there would be no wanton destruction. Senses strained, he made out the muffled sounds of jeering male voices a little way down the passage. Scuffling noises were followed swiftly by a man's frustrated yelp of pain.

Tulkhan cursed in three languages. He had forbidden his soldiers the rights of conquest. There was to be no looting, no women. It was hard on the men who had followed him so faithfully. They expected no—they deserved—the rewards of victory but Tulkhan had granted terms, and besides, he wanted to study the renowned T'En culture and that meant preserving it wherever possible.

Suppressing his annoyance, he strode toward an ornate set of double doors as he heard one of his men shout a warning followed swiftly by a dull thud and more curses.

Throwing the doors open he took in the carnage— smashed pots, exposed scrolls and the overwhelming stench of preserving fluid. Two of his men stood with their backs to him, restraining a woman. Three of his Elite Guard circled the captive, nursing various injuries.

Tulkhan immediately dismissed the possibility that the haggard old man in the corner who was watching all of this with bright eyes could be the cause of this mayhem. It had to be the female his men were attempting to subdue. He cursed silently. It wasn't like his Elite Guard to disobey an order.

"Halt! What is this?"

An ominous silence descended on the room. His men looked almost sheepish. For an instant amusement pierced Tulkhan's irritation, but he did not reveal it.

"A veritable hellcat, General," one man ventured.

With a flick of his wrist Tulkhan signaled the Ghebite guard to turn the captive toward him and prepared to be lenient. He could afford to be magnanimous, his army was victorious.

But this was no ordinary captive. His guards restrained one of the legendary T'En. Jolted, Tulkhan swallowed. His instinctive revulsion warred with his innate curiosity.

The female was a pure T'En—in his own language an accursed Dhamfeer—a dangerous alien creature with mysterious powers.

Disheveled but defiant she glared at him, her torn bodice revealing small, firm breasts which rose and fell with each short breath. But it was her unnatural gaze which captivated him. The old superstitions were true. The eyes of a pure Dhamfeer were dark as red wine, red as the blood which ran in a rivulet from her swollen lips down her long neck and over her high breasts.

He should have been repelled, for she was the antithesis of a Ghebite woman.

Instead of a rich coppery sheen, her flesh was as white as milk. A fine tracery of blue veins ran underneath the skin's surface like marble. Absently he wondered if her skin was as flawless to stroke as that silky stone. His fingers tingled in anticipation of an exploratory touch.

Riveted by the sight of the Dhamfeer's milky flesh, streaked red by her own blood, Tulkhan felt his body respond. A rush of lust which was equal parts fascination and fear gripped him. Shocked, he licked dry lips. Never had he known such an immediate reaction.

By all that was holy he should be repelled by this Dhamfeer! She was not even a True-woman. According to the Ghebite priests, women possessed weak, inferior souls. Tulkhan smiled grimly. He was sure the priests would declare that this female Dhamfeer possessed no soul. After all, she was little more than a beast.

Yet if so, why did he read intelligence in her strange eyes?

Taking a deep breath, he put theological questions aside and considered the situation. He had personally viewed the remains of several half-breed Dhamfeer during this campaign but never come face-to-face with a live specimen. To see one who was not only very much alive, but so obviously pure Dhamfeer reminded him that this was a foreign land, until recently ruled by the legendary T'En.

He shuddered, suddenly aware of a strange scent which made his heart race. It was not the taint of fear—having been soldiering since he was seventeen, he knew that intimately. This scent was rich and slightly musky. Suddenly he felt an overwhelming urge to lose himself in its source.

With a start he realized it was coming from the Dhamfeer. Why didn't she fear for her life? Why did she respond to threat with this heady, sensual scent?

In a flash of insight he recalled the survival instincts of a little marsupial, a native of his homeland. When threatened by its natural predator, this creature gave off a scent which mimicked the mating scent of the predator. In the resulting confusion the marsupial had a chance to escape. Instinctively he sensed that the Dhamfeer was trying to protect herself by seducing him.

"Stop that!"

She blinked, confused. "Stop what?"

Tulkhan cursed under his breath, unable to explain. How could he prove his suspicion? Who would believe him when his explanation presupposed that the Dhamfeer could control her scent?

Just what *could* the Dhamfeer do?

Superstition held that one of her race could possess a True-man such as himself with the sheer power of her will.

The hardened soldier in Tulkhan shrugged this aside—a great deal of nonsense was said about this almost mythical island. They'd said it was impregnable and he had proved them wrong.

Command meant never revealing weakness, and years of experience came to the fore. Stifling his disquiet, the General turned on his men. "So it takes five of you to subdue a mere female!"

They wilted under the attack, resentfully eyeing the ground.

The Dhamfeer smiled and he caught a glimpse of her sharp white teeth. He realized she was enjoying the guards' discomfiture, the hellcat! He itched to wipe that sly smile from her face, to subdue those defiant eyes and see that proud chin fall.

Superstition also said that the eyes of the Dhamfeer could ensorcell you. Tulkhan held her wine-dark gaze, meeting those feral eyes with a challenge of his own.

Nothing! He experienced no tingling apprehension of ensorcellment. Even better—for an instant he thought he read a flicker of fear, quickly cloaked.

Having proven folklore wrong, Tulkhan assessed his captive. This Dhamfeer was very young. Her own people must have considered her too young to fight or she would have died at their side on the battlefield.

He grimaced—how barbaric of these people to train women for their regular army, and condone their slaughter on the battlefield!

The Elite Guard waited with bated breath as the conquering Ghebite General confronted the last of the T'En royal family.

Imoshen met General Tulkhan's eyes, desperate not to reveal how he unnerved her. She'd heard he was a freakish giant, bigger than a normal Ghebite warrior. But seeing him in the flesh was startling. His massive dark form dominated the room. She had to look up to meet his eyes and this annoyed Imoshen. Being pure T'En, only the tallest of Truemen could look her in the eye and she hadn't realized till now how much she enjoyed looking down on people.

But it was more than that. This Ghebite General looked utterly alien in his flamboyant war finery. He'd removed his crested helmet to reveal dark, sweat-dampened hair which clung in fine tendrils to his broad cheekbones. With his strange, coppery skin and obsidian black eyes, he was the antithesis of her own kind—extrinsic, unknown and unknowable.

But what unnerved her most was the sharp intelligence she perceived in his calculating dark eyes and the cynical twist to his mouth. Here was a man who believed in nothing, who would stop at nothing.

As she held his gaze she realized he was studying her, assessing her. A prickle of fear moved over her skin. This Ghebite was too clever for her liking. She feared perceptive intelligence in an invader more than brutality.

Worse. She was his captive! Her heart sank, but she would not reveal her weakness to him.

Instead, she raged at the ignominy of her position—to confront her captor like this, restrained and half naked! But she would not grovel.

If only she had heeded the Aayel's advice. Not so long ago she had been unwilling to face the reality of their defeat. If only she could go back and retrace those impetuous steps which had led her to this!

Imoshen's six-fingered hands closed in fists of rage. "I hate him! I—"

"*Imoshen!*"

With a guilty start she turned to face the Aayel. Her great-aunt had received this title on her hundredth birthday. As the Aayel she was a living repository of their society's shared history. It was an honor for her family, a minor branch of the royal line who were second cousins to the Empress.

Where were her kin now? Murdered on the battlefield by that man? White hot rage ignited Imoshen. Her gaze flew to the plains beyond the Stronghold's walls. She raised the far-seer and peered searchingly through it.

There he was, the Ghebite General, resplendent in his barbarian battledress. A defiant crest of red feathers topped his helmet, rippling in the breeze. Linked plates of armor emphasized his broad shoulders. Long tendrils of his dark hair had come loose from his plait. They lifted in the breeze, twining around the strong column of his throat.

Even from this distance, the farseer enabled Imoshen to make out the severe planes of his arrogant face, burnt to a coppery sheen by the blazing sun of his northern homeland, Gheeaba. It was a word to strike fear in the hearts of peaceful people everywhere.

The General sat astride a magnificent black destrier, a massive creature trained to trample the enemy beneath its hooves, ready to die for its master. Imoshen grimaced. She had heard his men were happy to die for him too. It was said he inspired this devotion.

"Barbarians!" Imoshen hissed.

"Come here, Shenna." The voice was soft. But Imoshen knew that even though the Aayel used her pet name, it was a command.

Slapping the farseer closed she slipped lightly off the windowseat and padded cat-light across the bare boards. The Aayel despised the trappings of luxury. According to her they were a symbol of weakness, a sign of how the royal House of T'En had succumbed to indolence and infighting, making it ripe for invasion by the northern barbarians.

"The Ghebite General stands on the field with his army and demands we open the Stronghold gates, Aayel." Imoshen's throat was tight with emotion. Logic told her that for the General to have come this far her family must be dead. Even the Emperor and Empress who had led separate armies in a pincer attack, a last-ditch attempt to crush the invaders, must have failed.

All lost!

Other than the Aayel, every relative she had lay dead, fallen between the Stronghold and the coast.

A vision of a bloodied battlefield swam before her mind's eye. Sickened, she saw the carrion birds pecking at the flesh of the dead, heard the screams of the horses dying and the moans of the wounded.

Was it a true Seeing, or all her too vivid imagination? Imoshen did not know. The Aayel was the one who had the gift for scrying. Imoshen's gift was the more mundane but useful ability of hastening healing.

"If only our mainland allies hadn't deserted us!" Imoshen's hands closed in fists of frustration. "I don't understand. The Empress sent for their aid in plenty of time."

"*Why* does not matter."

"It matters to me!"

The Aayel sighed. "I am old and cynical, Shenna. I have seen too much. True, the southern kingdoms have not honored the treaty of alliance, but it is not surprising. Fair Isle is small and richer than they. Gheeaba stretches across the north of the mainland like a great canker, growing more powerful with every country it absorbs.

"Meanwhile the southern kingdoms withhold their support. They watch and wait to see if Fair Isle will fall. Whatever happens they cannot lose. If we stand against the Ghebites it halts their southern march and leaves us weakened, eager to accept our allies' help on any terms before the Ghebites renew their attack in the spring. Think of your lessons."

"How can you talk of history when the General stands at our gates, demanding our surrender?"

The Aayel smiled. "One day this will be history. But listen!" She caught Imoshen's hand in her own six-fingers and held her gaze with faded, wine-dark eyes.

Below them in the courtyard Imoshen could hear the fearful moans of the people who had fled before the invaders, retreating within the Stronghold's walls.

"Imoshen, heed me! To have come this far the General must have conquered all resistance. We can expect no aid. We must surrender the Stronghold."

"There are still the southern nobles."

"A handful of stubborn men and women. But they are no use to us here, today. We must surrender."

"The church? Surely they will—"

"Protect us?"

Imoshen tried to interpret her great-aunt's expression and failed.

"If the Ghebite General knocked on the door of the basilica itself, do you think the Beatific would pause to consider for more than a heartbeat before turning us over?" the old woman demanded.

"But the Beatific is head of the T'En Church, which reveres our gifts. We are the last of the pure T'En, sacred vessels of—"

"Pretty words, Imoshen. But think! The Beatific is a True-woman, unlike you and me. If the church lived up to its vows I would be the Beatific, not her. No, the church is for True-people, while we are nothing but inconvenient Throwbacks to an earlier time." The Aayel hurried on before Imoshen could draw breath to argue. "We are on our own. We must surrender the Stronghold."

"No!" Imoshen gasped, outraged. Her head spun as her perception of the world tilted from its axis. "This Stronghold has never fallen. What right has the Ghebite General to march his armies across our lands and take by force what is ours?"

"The same right our ancestor had six hundred years ago when she marched across these fertile lands and defeated the simple farm folk to lay claim to Fair Isle—the right of might."

Imoshen's skin went cold with the logic of it. She had never thought of her namesake's acquisition of this island as anything other than a glorious victory. That it had been an invasion which stripped True-people of their ancestral homes and rights was an unwelcome revelation.

The Aayel nodded wisely, her pale face like parchment. Imoshen felt those old, thin claws tighten on her hands, saw the Aayel's faded eyes glow.

"It is hard to be marked as different, I know. You could be the child I was never allowed to have." Fondly, she stroked Imoshen's long hair. "The blood of the first T'Imoshen runs as strong in you as it does in me. Mark the signs—the silver hair, the six fingers, the garnet eyes. But over six hundred years our people have interbred with the locals, our language and culture have interwoven with theirs and we have lost our fierce will. We have grown content, ripe for plunder. This Ghebite General is only doing what the first T'Imoshen did, bringing fresh blood to a fertile island.''

Imoshen shook her head, blinking back tears of fury. She could not see it that way. This was her home, her people, and she would die for them.

''Better to live and protect them!'' the Aayel insisted, reading her thoughts. She glanced to the door as the sound of booted feet marching on stone and the jingle of metal heralded the arrival of their own Stronghold Guard.

''Will you do a scrying to see if the Stronghold can stand against him?'' Imoshen pleaded.

The Aayel waved this aside impatiently. ''It is never so precise. Besides I need no gifts to see what logic tells me will happen.'' She fixed Imoshen with her sharp eyes. ''The General will offer us Terms. We would be wise to accept. At least we will have something to bargain with. If we force him to lay siege to our Stronghold and take it by force he will punish our defiance by systematically killing all who oppose him.''

Imoshen bowed her head in acknowledgment, but resentment burned in her as her great-aunt signaled that she would meet with the defenders to hear the Ghebite's terms.

Retreating to the window embrasure, Imoshen picked up the farseer again. A compulsion which was equal parts fascination and revulsion drove her to study the True-man who had destroyed her world and stolen her future.

General Tulkhan was the first son of the Ghebite King's second wife. Imoshen sniffed disdainfully. Wife! That word smacked of slavery. What could you expect of a culture where men had more than one bond-partner and called them ''wives,'' not equals?

These barbarians had complicated family lines. Being the first son of the second wife, the General had not inherited the kingship when the old king had died during the spring campaign. Instead the first son of the first wife, Tulkhan's younger half-brother, had assumed the title.

Young King Gharavan followed the main army at a more sedate pace with his own contingent of men, consolidating the General's rapid victories. This much Imoshen had heard. Rumor ran wild concerning the Ghebite General, his cunning, his prowess in battle.

But she could not discount any of it, for General Tulkhan was here at the gates of her Stronghold. He had defeated Stronghold after Stronghold. Often with a lesser army he had met and surrounded opposing forces in the fields and vanquished them. If half of what she'd heard was true, Imoshen had to conclude that he was a brilliant tactician.

It was said that the men who served under the General adored him, that he had led a charmed life, working his way up through the ranks on ability, not connections. Loyal to the old king, he had subjugated nations, collected bounty and annexed countries all in his father's name.

Creeping southeast across the mainland like a plague year by year, the Ghebites under the young General's leadership had advanced steadily, devouring all resistance in their path. Through brilliant strategy and, Imoshen suspected, tactical errors on the part of her complacent blood relatives, in one short season General Tulkhan had defeated the T'En. He was on the brink of ultimate victory. Fair Isle, the center of T'En culture and learning, was within his grasp.

Once he had captured the last great Stronghold he would ride into the capital and the citizens, with nothing more than their city patrol to protect them, would lay down their arms and the jewel in the crown would be his to lay at the feet of his half-brother, King Gharavan.

From this fertile, strategic island General Tulkhan could command the trade routes of the world just as Imoshen's people had done for six centuries.

Studying the rows of men standing at attention in orderly ranks, she had to admit that despite their constant battles and enforced marches they looked fresh and their pride was obvious.

Closing the farseer, Imoshen swallowed uneasily. She did not relish her position. It would have been better to die on the battlefield than live a captive.

She bitterly resented her parents' decision not to allow her to fight alongside them. Though she had been trained in the arts of war, they had considered her too young to fight.

She had offered to travel behind the army to serve as a healer, but her elder brother and sister had objected. Imoshen had not been surprised. She knew them well enough to understand that though they loved her with one breath, they resented her with the next. This war was their chance to win honor and recognition on the battlefield, to outshine her.

They had not found it easy to watch her outgrow them in size and ability. And when her T'En gift for healing surfaced during puberty they had withdrawn even further, excluding her from their social life with cruel taunts and whispered jibes.

Imoshen knew she had been more of a burden than a blessing to her family. A Throwback daughter who was forbidden to take a bond-partner could not hope to advance the family's power through a good marriage.

Even now, her face grew hot as she remembered the last time she had spoken with her family. She had turned on her siblings in a rage, accusing them of not caring about the men and women who served them. If they did, they would take her along because of the lives she could save, the suffering she could ease. But no. All they cared about was their own advancement!

After that outburst her parents had banished her from the strategy meetings. So their parting had been strained with resentment on both sides and now they were all dead. She could never take back those words, or make amends.

Imoshen didn't know how she felt. So much had happened since spring. This war had come upon Fair Isle like a storm at sea, sweeping all before it. It was four hundred years since the T'En had led an army into battle and that had been to quell local resistance to T'En rule. Since then her people had relied on threat and coercion, otherwise known as diplomacy. The Aayel was right—her people had grown complacent.

But not Reothe. Her betrothed had sailed south and east

discovering new trading routes, returning with knowledge and riches.

A cold hand closed around Imoshen's heart. She fought a wave of nausea as the realization struck her—Reothe must be dead, too.

Impossible! He was so alive, so intense. Her heart raced with the memory of him.

Her family had been honored when Reothe chose to ally his line with theirs. But when he made it plain he wanted Imoshen and not her elder sister her parents had balked, for Reothe was a Throwback like herself, exhibiting all the T'En traits untainted by the blood of True-people. Everyone knew pure T'En women did not bond, that the church expected them to be celibate in honor of the first Imoshen's celibacy.

T'Imoshen the first had decreed that the T'En males, both pure and part, and all part T'En females were to take bond-partners outside their own people. The policy had been designed to assimilate the invaders with the native population of Fair Isle. It was an old law which had been followed without question until the T'En race was spread far and wide but was diluted to a point where it was almost negligible.

T'En Throwbacks from these unions were so rare everyone had thought the Aayel was going to be the last pure relic of their race. That was until Reothe's parents announced his birth but, unlike Imoshen's arrival, his hadn't been so unexpected.

His eccentric, first-cousin parents were a tolerated oddity. Their fascination with everything T'En was considered in bad taste.

After years of infertility the birth of a pure Throwback son was seen as retribution. When they retired from court life to live quietly on their estates and raise the child, their extended family was relieved.

All this she had overheard. The child Imoshen had missed few of the nuances of adult conversation. Anything she had failed to understand had been thoroughly explained by her sister, who never missed an opportunity to make sure Imoshen understood her place.

She'd always felt her parents could not understand why

they had been blessed, or cursed, with a Throwback. All her life she had been an object of fascination, distrust and derision.

She had never expected to take a bond-partner.

But Reothe had anticipated everyone's objections. He had brought with him a document of dispensation signed by the Emperor and Empress, witnessed by the Beatific. Relieved, her parents had given their consent for Reothe to approach Imoshen.

Assuring Imoshen it was a good alliance, they had pointed out that she and Reothe were second cousins, both related to the royal family. And with two voyages mapping new trade routes to his credit Reothe already had a reputation for brilliance and daring. He would go far.

She had not been so sure. Something about Reothe made her senses quicken with a presentiment of danger. It had all happened while the Aayel was away at Landsend Abbey serving the church in her official capacity. With no one to consult, Imoshen had been forced to make a decision.

She recalled how she had last seen Reothe striding toward her, his fine silver hair lifting in the breeze, his piercing wine-dark eyes fixed on her. It was an eerie sensation, seeing a male mirror of herself. Had he experienced the duality of their people? He must know what it was like to be both loved and feared.

Imoshen had longed to let her guard down. All her life she had been a barely tolerated outcast in her own family. Even the Aayel had kept her at a distance. In Reothe she hoped to find a kindred spirit. If so, why didn't she trust him?

Was she unnerved by his Otherness? How absurd, when she was as pure T'En as he!

But he was different and it made her wonder if the people she lived with found her as unnerving as she found Reothe.

A shift had occurred over the six hundred years since the first T'Imoshen and her explorers set foot on Fair Isle. Where once the vanquished people were the underclass, recognized by their language, their religion, their slight frames and golden skin, through interbreeding and the interweaving of everyday life the T'En had grown to be one with the locals, just as the original inhabitants had assumed a fierce loyalty to their once-invaders.

It was odd, Imoshen thought. She had never regarded her people as invaders but innate honesty forced her to admit the truth.

The Ghebites' primitive chanting carried on the wind. The men were singing a deep, repetitive passage which stirred her blood despite herself.

Yes, she could sense their virility, their passion. No wonder they drove the complacent and overfed T'En army before them. Sated with life's pleasures, her people had been no match for the primal hunger of the battle-hardened Ghebites.

In other circumstances she might have admired the vitality of these barbarians. Imoshen had studied the tactics of mainland invasions. Unlike many of her peers, she had learned the ancient T'En art of armed and unarmed combat, as well as diplomacy of state.

Her brother and sister had teased her, contemptuous of her old-fashioned dedication to knowledge for its own sake. But Imoshen felt more at home immersed in the ancient manuscripts, communing with long-dead people, than dealing with the sly smiles and whispers of her peers. While her brother looked for recognition with his poetry and her sister prepared herself for the acid frivolity of court life, Imoshen retreated to the library and read of old battles.

Having heard the many tales of the Ghebite General's tactical brilliance, she was curious to get a closer look at the man who had subdued the warring northern kingdoms, allied Gheeaba to the Low-lands and then in one summer campaign conquered Fair Isle, once thought impregnable.

Raising the farseer, she located General Tulkhan again, the Ghebite standard billowing behind him. His commanders gathered around him, gloating over the Stronghold's surrender, no doubt. Imoshen's lips curled with contempt, for she did not see one woman in the ranks. So it was true. The Ghebite males shut their women away from life.

Instead the warriors bonded to each other—the Ghebites believed it made for a fiercer fighting unit. Ghebite women were either wife-slaves or a harmless diversion for their males.

She had heard they kept their wives and daughters in seclusion to produce sons, that Ghebite women were merely instruments of birth. The males ran their barbaric society and look where it had led them: on a pointless path of destruction, acquisition of territory for its own sake!

Imoshen tensed. Anger threatened to consume her. It was a sad day for the T'En, reduced to Ghebite rule. She was no man's slave. The Ghebites were fools if they underestimated the women of Fair Isle.

Wincing, she felt heat flood her cheeks as she heard the Aayel accept the Terms of surrender. Against her will Imoshen's gaze was drawn to the tableau. Having delivered the General's message, their own Stronghold Guard stood with despair written clear in their faces. The men and women she had trained beside now faced defeat with her.

". . . and in return for a bloodless victory," the Aayel was saying, "General Tulkhan must appoint someone to meet with me and discuss the welfare of our people. There will be no looting, no wanton killing, or we will defend this Stronghold to our last breath."

The old woman's dark eyes flashed fiercely and hope surged in Imoshen. Defeat was ignoble, but if they could rescue some honor from this surrender . . .

When the defenders had gone, the Aayel beckoned Imoshen. She came forward, head held high, rebellion in her breast.

"You are the last pure T'En. I am old, but you hold the seeds of the future. If you die, our line perishes. Now is not the time for heroics, Shenna. Keep quiet, attract no attention."

Imoshen would have spoken, but her great-aunt silenced her. "I will negotiate an honorable surrender. The fields are ripe with crops which must be harvested or the winter snows will find us all starving. Already, from here to the northwest coast the land lies black and ruined. Unless we move now famine will stalk us this winter. Go, and heed my warning. I rely on your good sense!"

Her great-aunt's aged hand trembled as she lifted it in the T'En sign of blessing, causing Imoshen a stab of guilt. The light touch of the Aayel's sixth finger brushed Imoshen's forehead.

Impulsively she caught that hand between hers. "I will heed your words, but—"

"I know it is hard, Shenna. You are my sister's daughter's child yet you are more mine than theirs. I thought I had years to watch over you but now . . . There is much I wanted to tell you, only your parents would not have it. They wanted to ignore the pure T'En in you—"

They were interrupted by anxious Stronghold servants and the Aayel dismissed her. So Imoshen was left to wander, angry and heartsore. It was bitter to have confirmed what she had always suspected. Her family had tried to deny what she was.

Throughout the Stronghold the inhabitants went about their tasks in trepidation, unsure whether the General would honor the terms of surrender. They came to Imoshen—some merely touched her hair or her sixth finger in passing, others asked for verbal reassurance.

The irony of it made her smile. In good times they had barely tolerated her but when they felt threatened they turned to her!

She had to cloak her own fear and mistrust to bolster the courage of her people but she was practiced at this. All summer, as word had come of defeat after defeat, she had lived a lie of reassurance while she watched her world crumble. Since spring her life had veered off course and changed direction irrevocably.

She should have been taking her formal vows with Reothe in the coming spring, creating history as the first pure T'En female to take a bond-partner, a pure T'En male. Imoshen shivered.

Banishing her betrothed's intense eyes from her memory, she stood at the window of her tower room to watch a different, unwelcome history unfold. The Stronghold's inner gates opened and the General entered astride his black warhorse, flanked by his commanders.

The people watched sullenly as their barbarian conquerors filed into the courtyard without a drop of blood being shed.

General Tulkhan was followed by his Elite Guard, who oversaw the laying down of arms.

Impotent rage seared Imoshen as she stood at her tower window. The autumn sun sank, cloaking her in its red glow, staining her with the unshed blood of their ignoble surrender. And she hated General Tulkhan with all her heart.

Shut away from everyone, she brooded, feeding the fires of her anger until shrill cries of excitement told her that the General was making his way to the formal chamber to meet the Aayel.

Imoshen knew she was supposed to remain out of sight, but she wanted to hear the terms, to judge the man for herself. So she slipped a cloak over her shoulders and joined the scurrying workers in the stairs and corridors of the conquered Stronghold.

Truly, she meant to follow the Aayel's advice and hold her tongue but as she entered the passage leading to the Great Library she heard a terrible commotion.

Impulsively, Imoshen tiptoed quickly down the passage and slipped into the library. All the knowledge of the Stronghold was stored there, along with treasures, treatises on herbal cures, plays, and profound philosophies, held in trust by the Keeper of Knowledge.

Before Imoshen could take in the chaos around her, the old scholar threw his frail body between the barbarians and his charges. Already the Ghebites had broken open several earthen jars and tipped the oil on the stones to expose the ancient scrolls to the air. When they broke the seal of the next jar the Keeper cried out in dismay. The Ghebites laughed raucously.

A flash of fury ignited Imoshen. These men were animals!

One lifted a glass jar of preserved organs and smashed it on the floor. The pungent aroma of its preserving fluid filled the air. Where it met the oil a slow fusion occurred, hissing and fizzing menacingly—two vastly different substances in contact with one another, destroying each other. Was it an omen foretelling the fate of her race, as the T'En met the Ghebites?

The largest male snatched up another precious canister and prepared to break the seal.

"Cease!" At Imoshen's command he stopped. The men looked at her, startled. "You must stop the wanton destruction immediately. The knowledge in this room has been collected over—"

They recovered and laughed. Imoshen strode toward the nearest soldier, who held the old man, and cuffed him across the head as she would an errant stable boy. Though she was only seventeen she looked down on the man. "This is an outrage! Release the Keeper of Knowledge. Have you no respect?"

The Ghebite and his partner released the old man. Leering, they turned on Imoshen, who instantly realized her mistake. Both men were armed. But they ignored their weapons, seeking instead to grab her.

She ducked under the arms of the first and swung her foot at his knees, sending him to the floor. The second caught her shoulder, but instead of pulling away she went with his strength, darting inside his guard to elbow him in the ribs and jerk her head back into his face. His nose broke with a satisfying crunch.

These were both simple moves learned in early childhood by those who revered the old ways. A female might not have the muscle of a male but she had speed and could use her enemy's own strength against them.

The Keeper of Knowledge gave a shrill laugh, which spurred the other three to attack Imoshen again. She knew the odds were against her. The floor was littered with broken pots and glass, and covered by a thin film of oil. She had little opportunity to maneuver.

Experience told her the only way to fight superior odds was to place her enemies so that they impeded each other and were reduced to attacking her one at a time. With this in mind she stepped back toward the shelves and kicked the first in the knee. He went down cursing.

Her aim was to disable. It felt good to take action after the idleness forced on her since spring.

One of the men yelled something and the other two tried to encircle her. She saw their intention and charged the man between her and the door, but her foot slipped on the oil-slick floor and he caught her. She'd only just broken away from him when the other two were upon her.

Furious, she twisted and writhed in their grasp—all silent rage. Twice she drew blood with her sharp teeth. One cursed and a fist caught her in the mouth. She tasted her own sweet, salty blood.

Two of the men succeeded in pinioning her arms and the others, all nursing various injuries by now surrounded her, keeping beyond range of her kicks. Their expressions told her they were intent on exacting revenge. Imoshen knew her situation was desperate.

One tore the neckline of her gown, baring her breasts. She felt her nipples tighten on contact with the cold air and heated looks.

They laughed. Outrage roiled in her belly—and cold dismay. It had been an eager, throaty laughter which made her skin crawl. So it was true, these Ghebites raped captive females. Such an act was an abomination to her people.

"Barbarians!" she hissed.

The nearest balled his fist.

That was when the General himself had entered. She writhed under his calculating gaze, caught at a disadvantage. She wanted to rage defiantly at him, but already her impetuous actions had cost her her dignity. Imoshen knew she must not anger this barbarian. If he chose, he could order everyone in the Stronghold put to the sword and nothing or no one could stop him.

Channeling her fear, she tried to think clearly. She could not afford to allow her anger to take over. This was war—she had to use every weapon she had. The Aayel claimed everyone had a weakness. She had to find the General's.

Meeting his eyes, Imoshen made her stand.

"According to the terms of surrender . . ." she swallowed—how it galled her to use that word—"there was to be no wanton destruction. I found these fools smashing the pots which preserve our most ancient parchments. I call on you to honor the Terms and preserve this knowledge. Our people have a saying, 'Knowledge knows no loyalty. It is the tool of the wise.' ''

She let the words flow, but her mind was concentrating on what lay behind his penetrating gaze. Focusing on the man, she tried to read any nuance in his expression, any unguarded thought that might reveal his weakness.

It was said that sometimes in moments of great stress, the pure T'En could call on their gifts to see into another's heart, but she could discern nothing from this Ghebite. His face was guarded, like the too-black eyes which hid his thoughts from her. He was physically different from any of the men she had known, but something in her recognized his type. He was a soldier, a man of action used to command, physically and mentally disciplined.

The Elite Guard waited to hear their General's response.

Tulkhan shifted, irritation eating at him. He didn't need this girl-woman to tell him his duty, to lecture him on the Terms of Surrender. What rankled him most was the knowledge that she was right. His men had been in the wrong. He would have to discipline them.

Already he had confronted an aged crone—the Aayel they called her—who seemed to think she would be representing her people to negotiate terms. Once he would have laughed outright, but many years in foreign countries taught him to hold his tongue and watch.

His own men had snickered, for in Gheeaba an old woman past childbearing age was good for nothing but minding the babes or feeding the dogs.

Tulkhan experienced a painful flash, a memory of his old mother hobbling around the royal courtyards, dodging blows. How proud she had been of him. Yet he had never acknowledged her, even when he had felt her glowing eyes on him. And she in turn had not expected so much as a kind word from him in passing. Then, during one of his numerous summer campaigns she had died, unmourned, buried in a communal grave for the fever victims.

After all this time he thought he'd forgotten, yet the sight of the proud old Aayel had reminded him of his mother. Though he did not know why when his mother's demeanor had been that of a servile dog waiting to be kicked, as was appropriate for an old woman who had no value to society.

Yet when the Aayel spoke, these odd people had blanched and watched with fear in their eyes as though she might strike him down with her withered arm. Did they know something he didn't? A quiver of disquiet moved through him. The Aayel was a Throwback, pure Dhamfeer.

Now he faced another of these Dhamfeer women, one who had taken on five of his Elite Guard in defense of an old bag of bones and a library of knowledge.

It amused him, though he was not about to show it.

"Who are you to lecture your captor?"

"Release me."

He stiffened, irritated by her demand. To give ground was to show weakness, but his men had been in the wrong, so now was the moment for compromise. He nodded to the members of his guard. "Release the Dhamfeer and no more destruction—"

"They can help the Keeper of Knowledge restore the manuscripts," his captive interrupted, in the tone of one used to giving orders.

He knew she had to be one of the royal line, yet he'd been eliminating them as he did battle, first the Empress and Emperor, then their heirs. Who was this Dhamfeer? Even the Emperor and his kin had looked more like True-people than she did.

The guard stepped away from her. She tossed her head and shrugged her shoulders as if to rid herself of the imprint of their hands, but she made no move to cover her breasts, making him wonder if what they said was true—Dhamfeer women did not know modesty because they considered themselves above True-men, allowing none to sully their perfect, pale flesh.

Heat suffused him. It was also said if the Dhamfeer chose to take a lover they were insatiable, that a True-man could die trying to satisfy one. Again his soldier training surfaced. Superstition and nonsense. He wanted answers.

"Very well," he demanded. "Who are you?"

A prickle of excitement moved over his skin as he noted fury flaming in her wine-dark eyes.

"I am T'Imoshen," she said, giving herself the T'En title which translated roughly as princess in his own language.

Lifting her chin, she held his eyes defiantly. A well-bred woman of his race would have looked down out of deference, especially an unmarried female.

Tulkhan stiffened. She had claimed the prefix T'. It was a sign of the royal house which meant this vixen was directly related to the Emperor—by rights he should have her killed.

A member of the royal household would foster insurgence, and provide a figurehead for the rabble to congregate around in the event of rebellion, even a female.

"Imoshen," he acknowledged, intentionally ignoring her title. She was too sure of herself, he needed her more malleable. If he was to use her, he had to frighten her. Deliberately rude, he nodded to the man at her side. "Lock her in with the old crone, the one they call Aayel."

He caught a flicker of triumph in her carefully schooled features. Was she pleased because he had ordered her locked away with the old woman or was she pretending to be pleased? He didn't know. He didn't understand any of these people, least of all a Dhamfeer Throwback.

Tulkhan felt his mouth tighten in a grim line of annoyance. Privately he might find her unsettling, but he must not show a moment's indecision before her, or his men. To maintain command he must always appear to be in command.

He would have to decide what to do with her. Killing a female did not bother him. He had seen what these females were trained to do in battle and he would order her execution without compunction.

But after nearly eleven years with the army he was beginning to feel that he had seen too many deaths. He was sick of the stench of destruction. More importantly, he could make use of this Dhamfeer. She was his direct link to the cultural treasure of this island. But he wanted to see fear crawl across her features, he needed to see it. With a flick he indicated her cape on the floor. "Cover yourself, woman."

She bent down and lifted the cape, a little smile playing around her swollen lips. As though it made no difference to her, she swung the cape over her shoulders and pulled it closed. Then she stepped forward before his men expected it so that her face was near his, her eyes level with his mouth.

She was much bigger than a woman of his race, as tall as a tall man.

Her six-fingered hand closed on his bare forearm. He had a flash of cool white fingers pressed around his coppery skin.

Her strange eyes fixed on his, searching intimately. He felt . . . naked.

Again, he caught that foreign scent on her skin, not unpleasant but carnal. It sliced through his civilized exterior, through his educated mind to the primal male in him, eliciting a rapid response from his body, a response so immediate it unnerved him.

His physical vulnerability was a revelation and he hated it. Tulkhan had not been unnerved since his first campaign. Irritation flashed through him so that he had trouble distinguishing her words.

"I see an old woman." She grimaced as if in pain and Tulkhan went cold to the core. "The fever troubles her—"

Before she could finish the soldiers jerked her away from him, cursing her and apologizing profusely to him.

"Fools! If she'd wanted to kill me I'd be dead by now!" he snarled, aware that her other hand had been only a finger's breadth from his ceremonial knife.

Her comments had to be a trick, a lucky guess. Yet, honesty forced Tulkhan to admit she had dipped into his mind and plucked an image of his mother—not as he had ever seen her, since he had been leading the army in another country when she died—but as he imagined the old woman had lain, alone, unloved, dying, with no one to mourn her passing.

Guilt surged through him. He hated the Dhamfeer

woman for stealing the image from his mind, for using it to pierce his defenses. All his life he had prided himself on his control; even in the heat of battle he assessed the odds, the enemy's capabilities and his own men. Next to the king his word was absolute.

Now, looking into her pale face, he faltered, but he could not afford to reveal his trepidation. She must never know he feared her, and his men must never suspect this chink in his armor.

The Dhamfeer frowned, her eyes widened and she asked as if genuinely confused, "Why did they refuse the old woman medicine to ease her passing?"

General Tulkhan's mouth went dry—it was his private torment. If he had been there, if he had shown one shred of feeling, he would have insisted they treat his mother, but it was the custom not to physic the old women. Only a girl or a woman of childbearing age would be treated. The old females must live or die depending on their strength.

"Take her away!" he snarled.

The Dhamfeer stepped back, surprised by his tone. Even his men flinched.

Furious, he gestured. *"Out!"*

Head held high, she walked past him as though the men who stood to each side of her were there to serve her, not to imprison her.

Defiant Dhamfeer!

Tulkhan fought an urge to grab her slender throat and crush her defiance. He longed to see her at his feet pleading, as he had crushed the defending armies. He had dealt with kings and noblemen. He had seen honorable defeat and cowardly defeat but he had never feared his captive before, and he felt a sudden loathing that went bone deep.

She defied him on every level, made him question his very concept of himself. Only once before had he been forced to question his place in the world. When his half-brother was born and his position as the king's heir was supplanted, General Tulkhan had seen his erstwhile mentors withdraw their support. Human nature was fickle, he discovered. As leman-son any chance of inheritance had died with the birth of his half-brother. He had no rights, only those which he took and held.

Swallowing this bitter knowledge, he had chosen to walk alone, to make his own future.

As a matter of political necessity he gave lip service to the Ghebite religion. He had sworn fealty to his father, the king, and striven to prove himself. He had fought with great honor in his father's name, but still the old man had died without saying those words Tulkhan longed to hear.

Every time he returned triumphant to present his father with the news of another victory he had looked for that particular expression in the old man's eyes. But the king had died without acknowledging him as anything more than the son of his concubine.

When this campaign was over he would swear an oath of fealty to the new king, his half-brother, but he silently raged against a system that acknowledged a man's birth and not his worth.

In his heart Tulkhan called no man master.

In the deepest recess of his being he recognized that same defiant quality in the Dhamfeer woman, and he had to admit a certain reluctant admiration.

It could not be easy to find oneself a captive, confronted by the victor.

The Dhamfeer were an ancient race. They had come out of the rising sun six centuries ago and taken this land of the True-people by force. They'd made use of written language and created art and music when his ancestors were still eating their enemies' hearts to bolster their courage.

Much was whispered of Dhamfeer powers, their ability to read minds and to see the future. How much of it was true Tulkhan did not know. A good tactician did not reveal the extent of his power and he had assumed it was all bluff, until now. After all, their armies had not outwitted him on the field of battle.

Yet she had plucked a long-buried image from his mind!

"Give the Keeper of Knowledge the aid he needs," the General ordered, as though he wasn't dizzy with the implications of what he'd just learned.

He stepped into the long hall and went to a narrow window. He could not deny the evidence—his skin crawled with the knowledge. She had touched him and with that contact, delved into his thoughts and pulled out an image. He felt violated, more frightened than the first time he had faced death on the battlefield. Because his mind was private, his only sanctuary.

His tutors had filled him with the lore of his homeland and the strategies of great battles. In the years he had traveled with the army he had kept an open mind, learned all he could about his enemies. Knowledge knew no allegiance, knowledge was power. Damn her, she was right!

His Dhamfeer captive had invaded his mind and laid open his vulnerable self—he should kill her.

A strange shudder passed over his body at the thought. In his mind's eye he saw his old mother lying on the mat, suffering in silence.

The image came more clearly to him than ever before. Was it a true Seeing? He tried to bury it as he had done repeatedly in the last few years, but the Dhamfeer had exposed it and in doing so she had laid open his hidden grief.

Tulkhan gripped the window frame till his shoulders ached with tension. Moisture gathered in his eyes. Eyes that had witnessed countless deaths on the battlefield burned with unshed tears for a mother he had loved but had never acknowledged.

In Gheeaba a man had no time for tears—they were a female weakness. The Dhamfeer had defied him. She had emasculated him!

He had to kill her!

The Aayel's surprisingly strong hands closed on Imoshen's arm, stopping her when she would have risen to leave with the other women.

They had the use of a wing of chambers but effectively they were prisoners in their own Stronghold. The other women retreated to dress for the evening meal. The Aayel had said they were to be very formal, to carry on as if they were not living on a knife's edge.

When the connecting door closed on the last woman Imoshen prepared for the worst. She felt her cheeks grow hot. Had the Aayel heard about her meeting with the Ghebite General?

She had no excuse. Her impulsiveness had led her into trouble, again. Imoshen opened her mouth to apologize but the Aayel spoke.

"We haven't much time." Her voice rustled like dry leaves on paving stones. "We need to find this General Tulkhan's key."

Imoshen felt a rush of excitement. The Aayel was talking about using her gift. And it wasn't a simple scrying either!

Imoshen knew that despite the Terms they faced execution. It would only take a small shift in some factor, perhaps something they could not predict, for the General to justify their deaths.

"What will you do? Can I help you?"

The Aayel's garnet eyes fixed on Imoshen's face. "No, better not. I want you out of the way. If I'm worried about you, it will break my concentration. Contrary to what is rumored the T'En gifts aren't very powerful. You can heal a little and I can scry imperfectly.

"If I maintain body contact and concentrate very hard I can sift a True-person's mind to find their deepest fear, their secret wish—the key to controlling them. It is not easy and the General might resist. He strikes me as a man who is used to keeping to himself. He is no fool, Imoshen."

"I know that." She eyed the Aayel resentfully.

The old woman squeezed her arm. "Go, get dressed. I want you looking very regal tonight. We are the last of the T'En and must look the part. Appearance is everything to the susceptible."

Imoshen nodded and touched her lips briefly to the old woman's forehead. But in her heart she raged against the unfairness of it. She wanted to be there to see how the Aayel used her T'En powers.

Resentment burned in her. Her parents had forbidden the Aayel to teach her about her T'En heritage, condemning her to suffer all the subtle slights and indignities of her accidental birth and none of the advantages.

Imoshen had to know how the gifts worked. She wanted it so badly she could taste it. Well, her parents were dead so their strictures no longer counted. In the changed future she would have to rely on herself and whatever skills she had, which meant she had to learn all she could about her T'En gifts. Grimly determined, Imoshen chose to disobey her great-aunt.

Rather than waiting for the maid to return from fussing over the other women, Imoshen dressed quickly. Choosing one of the fine skull caps made of wired metal and inlaid with pearls, she brushed her hair then set this circlet in place so that the large pearl drop hung centered on her forehead. It was the sort of headdress she would normally have worn on a special occasion. The Aayel was right, it did help give her confidence.

Then she slipped her feet into the soft-soled boots and scurried back to the connecting door, making no sound on the polished floor.

A screen of scented wood stood to one side, blocking her line of sight, but it offered the perfect cover to prevent the room's inhabitants from seeing her open the door a crack. The General was already there, speaking with the Aayel. Imoshen caught her breath.

His low voice with its faint Ghebite accent rumbled to a stop as the Aayel interrupted.

". . . be best if you interfered as little as possible with the running of the Stronghold."

He muttered something short and sharp. "My men have been campaigning since spring. They expect their rights of plunder. You are in no position to lay down—"

Suddenly the Aayel gave a cry. Heart thudding with concern, Imoshen pushed the door open and stepped forward to peer over the screen. She was in time to see her great-aunt gasp and clutch the wall for support, but her fingers slipped. The old woman fell headlong into the barbarian's arms.

Tulkhan cursed as he caught the old woman. She was so light, nothing but a bag of bones. What should he do with her?

"Barbarian! What have you done to her?"

He whirled around to see the Dhamfeer girl running across the room toward him. She was no longer the untidy feral wench who had confronted him in the library, but a graceful princess dressed in rich brocade and pearls. Yet she was no less dangerous, he reminded himself.

"Nothing. She collapsed—"

"Browbeating her, no doubt!" the Dhamfeer snapped, placing a hand gently on the old woman's forehead. She gave a soft grimace as if stung and pulled back, rubbing her hand thoughtfully. "Bring her through here." Gesturing imperiously, she led the way through a door to what he surmised was her own bedchamber. "Sit here, before the fire. No. Don't put her down, you must hold her upright."

He resented her tone. "Why?"

"I am the healer. Do you want her life on your conscience?"

Tulkhan sank onto the seat before the empty fireplace. He didn't want the old woman dying in his arms. Even if he had done nothing to cause the old one's death, rumor would have him blamed for it and this would make his task more difficult.

The old hag was held in high esteem by the people of the Stronghold. The least he could do was cooperate with the Dhamfeer healer, but he would not let his guard down.

Imoshen was only a female and apparently a mere girl at that, since she was not married. But was she truly girl or woman? By Ghebite standards she could not be given the title of woman until she was of marriageable age. Surely she was more than fifteen summers?

Then why wasn't she married like a Ghebite girl? Of course, she was pure Dhamfeer—untouchable. Perversely, he felt a surge of defiant lust for what he knew he could not have.

He put the thought aside and concentrated on the situation. Foreign customs never ceased to amaze him. The men of Fair Isle treated their women with a strange mixture of license and contempt. Revering them one instant, then sacrificing them in battle the next.

If the Dhamfeer had been a Ghebite girl he would have considered her harmless but he had learned not to make snap judgments. His every instinct warned him to be on guard against this heathen healer.

He studied Imoshen's concerned face as she examined the old woman. Strange, the Dhamfeer were not beautiful by Ghebite standards. Their faces were too narrow, their cheekbones too high and features too pointy. Yet there was something about the girl's face that fascinated him. Was it the contrast of her pale skin and wine-dark eyes?

Abruptly she glanced up, meeting his gaze.

He swallowed, his heart thudding uneasily. Tulkhan saw the knowledge in Imoshen's eyes. She had felt it too. It was hard to define the sensation—a metallic taste on his tongue, a tingling which made his skin crawl, his teeth ache and his temples throb.

A seed of panic stirred in his belly. "What's happening?"

Imoshen licked her lips. "It is the T'En gift you feel. I . . . I am seeking the source of my great-aunt's weakness."

He nodded, gritting his teeth. The sensation was unpleasant. It felt like a ruffling of his senses, much the way a cat might feel if someone rubbed its fur against the grain. He swallowed, forcing his tense throat muscles to work.

Imoshen poured water into a bowl, sprinkled herbs on the surface and dampened a cloth, using this to sponge the old woman's temples and wrists.

It didn't appear to do much good, but the sensation of discomfort persisted so Tulkhan thought she must be working on two levels.

"What is wrong with Aayel, girl?"

"Not Aayel, *the* Aayel. It is a title, not a name," Imoshen corrected. "And I have a name. You know it. I give you leave to use it. As for what ails the Aayel, it is old age. She had her hundredth birthday the year before I was born."

It was on Tulkhan's lips to deny this, but the simple way the Dhamfeer girl spoke told him she believed it, so it was probably true. In Gheeaba fifty was considered old.

He concentrated on the healer, Imoshen—she gave him *leave* to use her name. How condescending of her! In any case, he did not trust her. Who knew what trick she might try? But she seemed focused on the Aayel.

Tulkhan shifted to ease the muscles of his shoulders. The Aayel was light, but he was tense.

Interesting, if they weren't stoned to death by their own people the Dhamfeer could live for a century! His own father had been considered an old man when he had died at fifty-three. He left behind him only two sons, but his seven daughters by his first wife and two lemans had married well, extending the royal family's network of support throughout the Ghebite aristocracy.

Tulkhan grimaced. For there, too, he had failed to win his father's approval. He had not been able to cement the alliance of his only arranged marriage. It had been annulled by custom, three years from the date it began when his wife produced no children. He had refused another marriage fearing . . .

The old woman stiffened in his arms. Immediately the unpleasant pressure behind his head eased.

"She recovers?"

Imoshen nodded, letting the cloth fall into the bowl.

Gently, Tulkhan eased the old woman off his lap, propping her against the back of the deep chair. He crouched at her side to observe her. The Aayel was awake and aware, even if she seemed a little bewildered.

"How did I get in here?" she demanded feebly.

He patted her thin shoulder. "You passed out, old one. I carried you in."

The Dhamfeer healer came to her feet. "You may leave now. Whatever you were discussing can be put off until tomorrow. I will escort the Aayel down to the great hall. It will ease the fears of the Stronghold if you join us at the table and break bread with us."

Tulkhan also rose. He was growing used to the way this

Dhamfeer girl simply assumed command but it still annoyed him.

"No. I will be back to escort you both down to the great hall."

She inclined her head, as though this wasn't important. He left having had the last word but it didn't give him any satisfaction.

Imoshen walked the General to the door then shut it after him. She turned back to her great-aunt, hardly able to contain her excitement.

"I thought he would never leave! What did you learn?"

The Aayel smiled, her eyes as bright as a bird's.

"Well?" Imoshen prompted, secretly amazed by the old woman's ability to assume a misleading cloak of feebleness while being as sharp as a finely honed blade.

The Aayel frowned at her with mock severity. "You deliberately disobeyed me, Shenna!"

"Yes. And just as well I did. Not only could I feel it, but he felt it when you used your gift. I had to pretend it was me seeking to heal you."

The Aayel waved this aside and rose, but she wavered for a moment. Instinctively, Imoshen offered to support her.

"What is it, grandmother?" she asked, using the term of endearment.

The Aayel laughed. "Foolish child. I am old. I overextended myself. But you were right, you did distract him for me. He was so busy watching you, making sure you weren't playing some trick on him, that he wasn't worried about a frail old crone. He dismisses me as an old bag of bones."

Imoshen had to smile.

The Aayel patted her arm. "He is a clever man but he is trapped by his own culture. He is hardly able to believe you are a threat to him. And since I am not only female but old as well, he disregards me altogether."

"Foolish man," Imoshen purred, delighted with her great-aunt. "So, what did you learn?"

The Aayel straightened, stepping away from her. "I must dress for dinner."

"Why won't you tell me?" Imoshen called to her retreating back.

"You will know soon enough."

"When will you teach me how to do that trick?"

The Aayel spun around to face her, dark eyes snapping fire. "It is not a trick. The gift is never to be taken lightly. I have seen what can happen when a pure T'En oversteps the mark. I was twelve the last time one of us was stoned. And the Beatific of that time ordered that I witness it. I shall never forget!

"The rogue T'En male stood in the courtyard and held my eyes, held me captive. I had no defense from him. He sifted my mind freely, seeking something. I . . . I never understood what he wanted but I felt every stone that hit him. I felt his agony, his fury and despair. I died with him that morning, stoned to death, and I have never trusted a male T'En since. I—."

"Is that why you refused to meet with Reothe?"

The Aayel looked away. "I can tell you now that he is dead. T'Reothe was . . . dangerous. Your betrothal to him was a mistake."

"If you believed this, why didn't you tell my parents?" Imoshen demanded, unable to stop herself. "Why didn't you warn me? Why didn't you teach me the ways of the T'En, even if my parents forbade it?"

The Aayel took several paces forward, her dark eyes flooded with anger and grief. Her fierce expression made Imoshen fall silent.

"I can see it in you, all restless fire. You wonder why I never rebelled? Why I followed the edicts of the church?" She gestured sharply. "How can you stand there and judge me? You cannot know what I have witnessed. I grew up living in fear for my life. Nothing, not royal birth, not the Empress's favor, could have saved me from the power of the church, had the Beatific declared me a rogue!"

Imoshen bit her lip. "I am sorry. But that was almost a hundred years ago. It is not like that anymore. Besides, everything has changed now. The church is as much a victim of the Ghebites as we are."

The Aayel nodded slowly. "True, the rules have changed. But we must make our own." She paused to study Imoshen critically. "Try not to look too 'Other.' The General finds your differences disturbing."

Imoshen snorted but nodded.

Once her great-aunt had left to dress, she used the bowl of useless, sweet-smelling herbs to bathe her flushed face and neck. For some reason the Ghebite General made her feel gauche. When confronted by his calculating gaze, her instinct was to attack, and she could tell he didn't like it. So he found her unnerving? Good.

If the truth be told she found the General equally unnerving. But considering that he held the Stronghold and all of Fair Isle in the palm of his hand, the less she irritated him the better.

Imoshen vowed to be on her best behavior—her life depended on it. But the thought of pandering to the whims of a barbarian Ghebite filled her with rebellion.

Two

IMOSHEN WAS INTRIGUED. Why had the Aayel woken her
so stealthily? The night candles had been doused long
ago and she had fallen asleep after enduring a painfully
tense meal at the General's table.

The household servants who waited on the Aayel and
herself were asleep in the antechamber. Imoshen's great-aunt
drew her aside to the windowseat where they sat in a patch of
moonlight.

The Aayel's voice was low, intense. "He believes he
must have you killed."

"You did a scrying without me?"

"No—"

"You read it when he touched you? I saw how you pretended to stumble when you rose from the table. What
secrets did you discover when you touched him?" Imoshen
gave a disgruntled sigh. "I took his arm when he escorted us
down to the great hall with the intention of trying to touch
his mind but I felt nothing!"

The Aayel patted her shoulder. "It is not easy to Read a
person. Don't be discouraged. I've had years to hone my
skills. I did get an insight into the Ghebite General when I
touched him, but no, I did not Read him.

"This time I used logic, Shenna. I am old and in his eyes
useless. You are young and even though 'only' a female"—
her voice grew rich with laughter—"you could be used to
unite those loyal to the old empire."

"But I—"

The old hand clasped hers, willing her to silence.

Heart hammering with the injustice of it, Imoshen held her tongue.

"Don't despair, there is hope. He came to see me again after you retired tonight. He came on an excuse, but he was looking for you. He's drawn to you . . ."

"I despise him!" Imoshen leapt to her feet and silently prowled the length of the room. What could she do? She felt trapped.

She could feel the Aayel watching her thoughtfully. It irritated her.

"A strong emotion moves you," her great-aunt acknowledged. "But listen, time is short. If we are to survive you must think with a clear head and make difficult decisions which will require great fortitude to fulfill—"

"I will do whatever I must!" Imoshen strode back to the window eagerly. Her hands clenched and unclenched. How she wanted to take action! "Show me the way and I will follow it without fail—"

"No matter how hard it may be?"

She grasped the old woman's hands. "I will not fail you. I will not fail the T'En blood that runs strong in me."

The old woman nodded and walked stiffly to the recessed cabinet. She used her personal key to unlock it. Imoshen felt a stirring of hope as she watched the Aayel remove different medicaments.

Her great-aunt knew them by touch and by smell so she did not need to light a lamp, which might have given them away. Imoshen had learned her herbal-lore from the Aayel who, though she did not have the gift to hasten healing, was a veritable fount of practical knowledge.

Imoshen darted eagerly across the room to join her. Already she felt optimistic. "A slow, debilitating poison? I will find a way to slip it to him."

"No."

"Much better," Imoshen nodded. "A quick-acting poison which mimics a natural illness."

"No."

"Then what?"

"Hush and listen. You know your medicaments. What's this?"

Imoshen sniffed and concentrated. She wanted to please the Aayel and show that she had learned her lessons well. "A . . . woman's herb, it has something to do with the bleeding cycle. It's not for inhibiting fertility—"

"No. It brings on fertility."

Imoshen's lips formed a question but she held it back, fearing the answer.

As if her silence was expected, the old woman continued speaking in a voice that was no louder than the rustle of leaves in an autumn breeze. "This must be taken each night for fourteen days to bring the body into cycle. Remember this whatever happens—"

"What do you mean?" Imoshen's skin went cold, her voice rose.

"Hush. The General leads through the loyalty of his men. He must show himself to be all-powerful and without doubt, but he is a True-man with all the human frailty that a man possesses. He must cloak his weakness, just as you must hide your thoughts when you have to take a path you may despise to achieve your ends."

"I don't understand you!' Agitated, Imoshen turned and walked to the window. "I wish the General had never come to invade Fair Isle! Oh, why did our armies fail? We had the numbers, we had—"

"We had grown arrogant in our complacency. Hubris is fatal. Humility is a painful lesson."

"Hubris, humility—what have these to do with it all?" Imoshen muttered, resentfully. Was the Aayel mocking her?

"If you live long enough you will understand."

Imoshen grimaced. That was a cheerful thought!

She sank onto the padded window seat with a sigh. Her fingers clasped the casements as she turned to look up to the twin moons.

The smaller represented woman; the larger, man. They performed a dance around each other, sometimes one was in the ascendant, sometimes the other. Then four times a year on the cusp of the seasons both moons would fill the sky with a blaze of light so bright that night was almost as clear as day, bathed in silver.

Soon it would be that time, the time of the Harvest Feast, of ancient rites the people still performed after six hundred years of foreign lords, a time when the T'En performed ancient ceremonies dating back to the customs of their homeland.

Imoshen flinched, recalling her history lessons.

The first T'Imoshen had ordered their ship burned to the waterline so that none could desert her and flee back to their distant homeland. That took courage. It was a hard decision which had forced them to succeed or die trying.

Pride surged through her. She could be as unflinching as her namesake if need be.

"Here it is." The Aayel recalled Imoshen's attention and offered her a small stoppered decanter and a vial. "Pour out this much each night and drink it when you retire."

"What would you have me do, Aayel?" Imoshen's hands closed in fists on her knees. She made no move to take the small measuring vial. The dark liquid glistened. Its pungent smell stung her nostrils, making her stomach churn.

The old woman looked through the window. "Double full moon, a propitious time. You are blessed. You must convince the General to send his men out into the fields to assist the farmers to harvest the crops. Our people have made great sacrifices for us. On the farms there are few able-bodied people, mainly the very old and the very young.

"The food must be harvested and stored in our central granaries, from whence you will dole it out. Hundreds, even thousands, will come down from the north, pitiful and starving. There may not be enough to feed everyone, but you must share it fairly, between our own refugees and the barbarians as well as the locals."

"What are you talking about?"

"Survival. Drink this."

"No."

A silence grew between them. Imoshen could hear her own pulse rushing in her head. She felt sick at heart.

"Isn't there another way?"

The old woman's voice was implacable. "You have no choice. You must ensure your survival. Tulkhan means to kill you. He must or you will become a figurehead for rebellion. To save your life you must lie with him and conceive a child, a son. You know the way to ensure the babe's sex."

"Lie with the barbarian!" Imoshen swallowed hard. Must she compromise her principles to live?

Would General Tulkhan even want her? She shuddered, recalling how he had stared at her with cold, calculating eyes. He was not a foolish youth driven by the first flush of lust.

"Even if I did somehow trick him into planting his seed, why would that stop him from killing me?"

"Listen! I question and I learn, you must do the same. Knowledge is power! General Tulkhan has no son. The Ghebites place great significance on having a male heir. If Tulkhan is to hold this land he must take it into his heart, into his bed, to become one with it. You represent the land, you are the last of the T'En. If you and he are joined you will be the mother to the future heir."

"But from what I've heard the king is young. He will have heirs of his own."

"The king has dominion from here across the mainland to the north as far as Gheeaba. He must maintain control over all of this and ensure his conquered lands remain loyal. What has been won by might can only be held through forethought. Remember your lessons."

"Yes. But the General despises me!" It was a cry from the heart. "I see it in his eyes."

The Aayel closed Imoshen's cold, reluctant fingers around the glass vial and raised it toward her lips.

"Fourteen nights in a row you must drink this and, on the last, trick him into planting his seed."

Imoshen's blood rushed to her head. She felt herself go hot and cold as she considered the steps she would have to take. She had never lain with a male. For most of her life it had been taken for granted that she would never do so.

She had never told of her secret shame, how Reothe had come to her before their formal betrothal and suggested they go riding. How innocently, because she had never known anything but circumspect treatment from the males of the Stronghold, she had gone with him.

The memory of it still made her cheeks burn, for she, who previously spurned all males, had been captivated by Reothe.

He had challenged her to a race across the plains, then along the forest paths. She'd let her horse have its head and matched him, leap for leap. She never could resist a challenge. When they had dismounted, panting with excitement, the blood was singing in her body.

He'd challenged her to perform the formal defense—offense maneuvers with him, but it had been a ploy. He'd abandoned the standard responses and tricked her, blocked strikes. When she realized he was playing with her, she grew angry. He'd proved that though she knew her moves she could not defeat him physically.

Finally, he'd laughed at her outraged expression. She'd struck him while he was off guard, knocking him to the ground. When he looked up, his expression told her she would pay for it.

She'd turned and ran, almost mounting her horse before he pulled her from it. He'd tripped her and pushed her to the mossy ground. She'd fought him fiercely. But she hadn't intended to hurt him so she hadn't used the blows to his eyes or throat which might have freed her. Still, she had made it clear with the force of her resistance that she was not giving in.

At last, panting with exertion, she ceased to struggle and looked up at him. Despite her intention not to cause him harm she saw that his lip was bleeding and she experienced a ridiculous pang of guilt. But it was the intensity of his expression which unnerved her. She had never seen naked desire written clearly on a man's features before.

When his lips claimed hers she remained still, unsure. She tasted his blood on her tongue, experiencing the velvet softness of his lips for the first time. It felt strange.

He explored her mouth with tantalizing little touches that left her wanting more. His breath, his scent and his essence enveloped her, imprinting him on her. A sweet languor stole surreptitiously through her limbs.

Curious, she had returned his touch, surprised by a savage surge of desire which claimed her consciousness. Suddenly lost, she had forgotten herself in his embrace, forgotten all caution. Seared by a passion she did not know existed, she gave herself up to sensation.

When their lips parted she had moaned in protest.

He could have taken her then, but he hadn't. He had laughed, a wild, passionate laugh which both frightened and fascinated her. And though she could tell it cost him, he had held back.

It seemed he was pleased with her response to him.

It was then he revealed that he'd always intended to make her his. A formal request to bond with her fell falteringly from his lips and she'd agreed without prevarication, surprising herself by the surge of heat which flashed through her body. His eyes had widened, as if he sensed her response, and he had smiled.

At that moment she realized Reothe did not intend a cool, political bonding, but a bonding of the blood, of the soul.

Looking back, Imoshen decided he must have sensed a sensual liability in her. Maybe it called to him and he had recognized it for what it was—a wild, wanton streak. He had deliberately passed over her elder sister, who by rights should have been bonded before her. He had come to the Stronghold prepared with the dispensation which allowed him to break six hundred years of custom and take her for his bondpartner.

During their formal betrothal ceremony, Reothe had touched her and she him, they had shared their scents and mingled their blood symbolically, for the approval of the witnesses.

This was the sum total of her experience with men. Because she had been born a Throwback, destined to live a celibate life like the Aayel, no man had shown an interest in her. The idea of dying chaste had not bothered her. She could not understand the way her sister and friends eyed the young men of their acquaintance. Her own reaction to Reothe's touch was a shock. He appeared to have awakened something in her.

Imoshen licked her lips. Before the betrothal she had not received the same formal training as her sister.

Once she was betrothed she began new instruction. Other young people of a comparative age and social level had started lessons years earlier to prepare them for the pleasures of bonding. She had to make up those lessons to train her in the arts of lovemaking. These sessions did not hint at the depth of sensation she felt in Reothe's embrace, and they had certainly not prepared her to undertake the seduction of a Ghebite barbarian who despised her.

Imoshen shuddered.

"Drink," the Aayel ordered. "You have it within your power to supplant the barbarian's victory with a victory of your own, to blend our blood with his, to rule through him and his son."

The glass vial felt cold against Imoshen's lips. It smelled strongly of herbs she'd never had reason to use. What choice did she have? It was not her way to accept her fate calmly, bowing to the inevitable. She would fight it every inch of the way. Even if it meant this!

She held her breath and drained the vial in one gulp. It burned all the way down, finally forming an intense ball of heat in her belly.

Imoshen closed her eyes. She'd made her decision. It was begun. She would turn surrender into victory!

Fire surged through her veins, a passionate conviction. She felt an awareness of her body, a tension which coiled within her. Was it a presentiment of what she intended for the General?

The next morning Imoshen sought him out. Somehow she had to ensure her survival for another thirteen days and during that last night she must seduce General Tulkhan. The knowledge weighed heavily on her.

In the cold light of day she did not feel so confident.

Pausing in the courtyard entrance, she watched him talking to his commanders. She studied the way they interacted. They were all seasoned veterans, some younger, most older than he.

It was obvious from the timbre of their voices and the way they stood that they deferred to him, not just because of rank or his freakish size but out of respect. In their eyes he had proved himself. She would do well to remember that.

Whatever she might think of him and his coarse barbarian ways, he had proved himself to his peers.

She would not approach him until the men parted, for to accept the advice of a female would demean him in the eyes of his men. Imoshen felt a little smile tug at her lips. Already she was learning to think like a Ghebite. As the Aayel said, to know your enemy is to know how to manipulate him!

She did not want to weaken the General's position. It would force him to make a show of strength, perhaps force him to sacrifice her to shore up his hold on the command.

General Tulkhan threw back his head and laughed.

Imoshen shivered. The men echoed his deep-throated laughter.

For an instant she experienced an unfamiliar pang—they shared a camaraderie. On the battlefield they were equals. Yet when the General looked at her she read his reaction despite his guarded expression. He despised her.

Resentment burned in her breast and all her good intentions were forgotten as she stepped into the morning sunshine.

The men parted and the General spun on his heel, his cloak billowing. She noted how his sharp eyes scanned the courtyard. Imoshen knew instinctively that he missed nothing.

A shiver of awareness crept up her spine. He was a dangerous animal and she had to seduce him, trick him into spilling his seed in her. Suddenly she was very aware of her body in a way she had never been before.

The bustling courtyard surged around the General. His soldiers were victorious but forbidden their rightful plunder. Consequently, they laughed too loudly, swaggered too much

and looked threateningly on the frightened people who had
sought shelter within the Stronghold. The Stronghold
soldiers stood by unarmed and resentful, bristling at each
unspoken threat. Amid all this ran geese, ducks, dogs and
small children. The place was packed with humanity, brim-
ming with tension.

Tulkhan inhaled the rich autumn air, savoring the scent
of wood smoke. This fertile southern island was so different
from his homeland where it would not grow cold for several
small moons yet. Already he could feel a chill on the air, and
it quickened his senses with a strange anticipation.

He stiffened as the Dhamfeer stepped from the shadows.
Her silver hair held an unearthly radiance in the pale early
morning sunshine. When she lifted her chin and met his eyes
he felt his body tense in response. His heart rate lifted a
notch as if anticipating battle.

There was no mistaking it, she meant him to see her. She
was approaching him here where any of his men might see.
Had she no shame, no fear?

She gave none of the signals of deference a Ghebite
woman would have given when approaching a high-ranking
male. Her rudeness was sure to irritate his men on his behalf.
Tulkhan understood she did not know his country's customs
and so did not know any better. Obviously, she considered
herself the equal of any man. She would never have grown so
bold in Gheeaba. Any sign of independence would have been
beaten out of her. Strangely enough that thought caused him
a moment's disquiet.

As she strode toward him, he could not help but admire
the very boldness that set his teeth on edge. Yet, for her own
protection he should lead her away, find a private place
where his men could not observe her lack of respect.

Again he felt an inexplicable surge of desire. Obviously
he had been without a woman too long to respond this way to
a female, especially a Dhamfeer—a creature learned men
regarded as less than human.

Less than human she might be, but the intelligence
which gleamed in her feral red eyes was unmistakable and

dangerous. His mouth went dry as he sensed her anger, held in tight control.

When she stepped within what was considered polite speaking distance he caught a faint hint of her scent.

There was no doubt about it. He would have to find one of the Stronghold women and bed her tonight—anything to rid himself of this need, this unnatural longing for the Dhamfeer woman.

Inclining her head in a gesture which was the nearest she had come to deference so far, the Dhamfeer met his eyes, yet another unintended insult. "I would speak with you, General."

Tulkhan stiffened. She accorded him his title but her face revealed no deference and her body shouted a challenge to his. What trickery did she plan?

"Speak."

She glanced about, wishing perhaps to go somewhere private—perversely he decided to confront her here in the midst of the bustling courtyard. Let her show him what she made of it!

"In thirteen days it will be Harvest Moon—"

"The conjunction of the moons—"

"Yes. It takes several weeks to harvest the grains. Normally at this time we would be midway through it, preparing for our Harvest Feast. I don't know what it is like in your homeland, but here winter can come on rapidly. Soon the snow will lie thick on the ground and the days will grow short. If we do not fill the storerooms with grain my people, your people—everyone—will starve before the thaw.

"The fields between here and the northwest coast lie ruined and the farm animals slaughtered."

He tensed. "A traveling army must eat—"

"And empty fields mean little resistance from hungry people. I know!" She eyed him narrowly.

A frisson of danger danced across his skin as he sensed her animosity. She did not defer to him. She met his eyes, met his challenge. Her mind was as sharp as his and he resented having to acknowledge it.

"You think like a man!" It annoyed him.

Her eyes widened, then narrowed. "And *you* think like a Ghebite!"

What did she mean by that? Why did she invest it with such mockery? He had the uncomfortable feeling that he had not bested her in that exchange and he resented it. "Make your point, Dhamfeer."

She flinched. Good. He had meant the name to be an insult. He wanted to unnerve her.

But she continued in a measured tone. "Even your Elite Guard must eat and the lands from here south to the coast are the only untouched fields where the grain hangs heavy, spoiling to be harvested. We can't afford to lose this harvest but the farmers are reduced to the very young and the old. They cannot bring the crops in.

"You must order your army out into the fields to help harvest the grain, thresh and winnow it. The harvest must be brought in here to be stored, for in no time those survivors from the north will come here pleading for food. We must be able to feed our own people, your army and the refugees—"

"We?" He bristled. She stood there, telling him what to do without deference to her position as the representative of a conquered people. But as much as he resented her tone, he knew that she was right. He did not know the climate of this southern island and during his long campaigns he had learned the folly of not listening to those who knew the locality.

"Your men grow restless. Only this morning I had to stop one of them from raping a kitchen maid."

"It is the custom for the conqueror to take the women. It is their right of conquest."

"It is uncivilized. By the terms of our agreement—"

"Your surrender, you mean!"

Her wine-dark eyes flashed with rage and color stained her pale cheeks. He could see her chest rising and falling under her thin garment, visibly reminding him of her high, milky white breasts. He felt his body react instinctively and scorned his physical response.

Why, she was hardly a real woman by Ghebite standards, tall and scrawny instead of small and rounded! What was wrong with him?

The silence stretched between them and the clamor of the crowded courtyard seemed to fade as the moment hung in the balance.

Imoshen had seen the blaze of desire in his eyes, followed by the contempt he felt for her. The desire boded well for her plans, if only she could get past his disdain. With an effort of will she dropped her voice and continued with a calm she did not feel. "By the terms of our surrender your men are to respect our property and our people. Your men have been well disciplined for the most part, but they grow restless."

"This is a poor excuse for a victory, no victory feast, no rights of conquest—"

"Debauchery!"

"Rights of conquest."

"I won't argue!" Imoshen reined in her composure with difficulty.

Tulkhan smiled. It was as close to losing her temper as he had seen her come. It pleased him. He wanted to see her lose control, to see her plead.

He had to goad her. "What do you call this?"

She flashed him a look which said she knew what he was doing and chose not to respond to his taunt.

"I am here only on behalf of my people and yours. Your men need activity, we all need the grain. Occupy them with a task, have them bring in the harvest. With your army on the move it could be done in half the usual time. By custom we would hold our Harvest Feast on the night of conjunction, let this be your victory feast. Thus they will have their victory celebrations without engendering ill feelings—"

A girl screamed as she ran into the courtyard, her long golden-brown hair matted with blood from a cut to her forehead, her budding breasts bared.

Blind fear filled her face. She took in the crowded Ghebites, and fled in terror as several soldiers lurched after her. In no hurry to catch her, they were enjoying the chase.

With a moan of despair she staggered toward the General and the Lady of the Stronghold, falling at Imoshen's feet.

"Lady T'En, save me. I am bound till the harvest-feast—"

She gasped as Imoshen impatiently pulled her to her feet.

"Don't plead! Stand tall. You will be safe with me." Imoshen pressed her fingers over the cut in the girl's forehead to stem the blood, but her eyes sought the General's, offering an unspoken challenge. "According to the people's religious beliefs they must abstain from pleasures of the flesh while they are harvesting the grain to appease the gods." She did not add that this abstinence culminated in the Harvest Feast, where the peasants indulged in ritual intercourse as a way of giving thanks and ensuring the fertility of the fields the following spring. Theirs was an old religion, a religion of the earth.

Instead, she held his eyes and nodded toward his men who had come to a sheepish, resentful halt. She was sure he could read her unspoken words—so this was what his Elite Guard had been reduced to?

"Explain!" he snapped and the men blinked, swaying slightly.

It was obvious they'd been drinking. They were nothing but Ghebite barbarians. Rage flowed like fire through Imoshen's veins.

Let them argue their way out of this one, Imoshen thought with relish. If the General was an honorable man, as he professed to be, he had to chastise his men. Yet, she realized he might hesitate to do so in front of her, for his men would resent her witnessing their dressing down. She should slip away.

As though the outcome of the interchange did not concern her, Imoshen led the girl away to treat her wound.

As she entered the darkness of the doorway she heard the General bellow, using the soldier's coarse cant. A smile escaped her. They were rough men and they understood rough treatment. It was only as she escorted the girl back to her chamber that Imoshen realized the General spoke her tongue. That meant he was fluent in at least two languages— he was not an uneducated man. Had he deliberately learned their language before attempting the invasion? If her guess was right it suggested a cold, calculating mind, and a determination to succeed which made her shudder.

How was she to seduce this strange man?

Pushing her own troubles to one side, she took the reluctant girl to her chamber to treat her.

"Bring me fresh water," Imoshen ordered and turned to the girl. "What are you called?"

"Kalleen, but please don't."

Imoshen hesitated. The girl was typical of her people, small with warm golden skin and eyes the same shade of light hazel. At this moment she appeared intensely embarrassed because one of the royal family was caring for her.

"Nonsense." Imoshen snapped. "You are in need. It is my place to serve the needs of the people." When her servant returned with a bowl of water Imoshen sprinkled purifying herbs in it and rinsed Kalleen's cut. As she worked, it occurred to her that she had been learning the healing arts at the Aayel's side since she was a child, yet she had only brushed the surface of the old woman's knowledge. She was lucky her T'En talent was for healing. It was so practical.

"If I'd had a knife I'd have gutted them, one by one!" the girl muttered.

Imoshen snorted. "If you'd had a knife you'd have been dead. The General's men are battle-hardened veterans, not farm boys out for fun!"

The girl sniffed as though unconvinced.

Imoshen smiled. She supposed Kalleen was her own age or a trifle younger. She could sympathize with her sentiments.

Rising, she went to the camphor wood box and removed the hidden panel. Selecting a small, well-balanced knife, she returned and offered it to the girl.

She swallowed eagerly and rose, her deft brown fingers closing around the handle.

Imoshen gripped Kalleen's narrow wrist and tilted her hand so that the blade angled up. She positioned it just below her own ribs.

"There, like that. Strike for the heart," Imoshen advised. "You will only have one chance, make it count."

The girl's eyes widened but she nodded.

"And wear it like this." Imoshen shifted the brocade panel of her tabard to reveal her own knife, strapped to the front of her thigh. The central seam of her loose pants was open, allowing her easy access to the weapon. "For quick access. Speed may mean the difference between life and death."

Kalleen's golden eyes shimmered with understanding.

Imoshen let the panel drop and turned to clear away her healing possets. She felt the girl's eyes on her and looked up.

Kalleen slipped the knife inside her sleeve for safekeeping and caught Imoshen's free hand in hers.

"Lady T'En—you give me back my pride," the girl whispered, kissing Imoshen's sixth finger.

At little later Imoshen heard the General's voice in the courtyard below, ordering his men to prepare to move out. So he had taken her advice to heart.

The Aayel sent Imoshen a speaking glance.

She felt dizzy with relief. Their gamble had paid off. She had distracted him from ordering her execution and relieved the tension in the overcrowded Stronghold by finding a fruitful task to occupy the invaders.

With his army out in the fields harvesting the crops and delivering the grains to the Stronghold their winter food source was secure.

It was a small victory, but Imoshen was determined it would be the first of many. All she had to do now was remain in the background and avoid the General for the next thirteen days.

Unfortunately, that was not to be.

Imoshen paced the storerooms overseeing the cleaning and preparation for the influx of grain. When she heard the approach of booted feet on the stone a shiver of fear overtook her.

The Ghebites rounded the corner and stopped. She knew they were Tulkhan's Elite Guard because they wore his personal insignia.

Her own Stronghold Guard and servants straightened. Again she felt that undeniable tension. Her people had surrendered, but they had not accepted their defeat. The ignominy of it seethed beneath the surface, needing only a spark to bring it to flame and open rebellion.

The General must be aware of it, too.

"Lady T'En. General Tulkhan requests an audience." The young soldier who spoke obviously found it hard to be civil. He would not meet her eyes and though it was phrased as a request, Imoshen knew it was an order.

She wiped her hands on the smock she wore over her gown and undid the ties, placing the pinafore to one side.

"See to the other storerooms and stop all rat holes. I shall expect it done on my return." The order was unnecessary as her people knew their job but she must appear in control, just as the General must maintain that aura of command. She turned to the soldiers. "Where is the General?"

"With the one called Aayel."

"*The* Aayel. It is a title, not a name," she corrected instinctively. "It translates as Wise One. You may escort me."

Thus she strode before them, aware that she had outmaneuvered them. What was meant to be the escort of a prisoner had become an escort of another kind.

What did Tulkhan want? Imoshen refused to let fear undermine her composure. She would take her cue from the Aayel.

When she arrived General Tulkhan was standing before the fire, hands clasped behind his back. The Aayel, as befitted her great age, was seated stiffly in her hard-backed chair. Imoshen had noticed that in the presence of the Ghebites, her great-aunt continued to affect a physical weakness which was misleading. This amused her, but she hid her smile.

At the sound of her approach, the General turned. "Pack your traveling kit. I'm taking you with me."

"But my place is here, looking after my people—"

"Exactly. If my men ride up to these farmers very likely they will run into the woods and hide. I need their cooperation so I'm taking you with me as ambassador. You know the farmers' dialect, they'll trust you."

Imoshen's eyes flew to the Aayel, who gave an imperceptible nod of encouragement.

She drew breath. It was unexpected, but he was right. "In that case. We will visit the nearest village and speak to the head family there. They can send runners to the outlying farms."

The General nodded and it was agreed. A shiver of anticipation moved over Imoshen's skin. She had meant to keep away from him over the next thirteen days but now she would be in his company, forced to socialize with him, bedding down in his camp each night. She would have to tread very carefully. But maybe she could turn this to her advantage.

The rest of the afternoon was spent packing and preparing their escort. That night Imoshen took her draft as the Aayel watched.

Wincing at the taste, she sealed the decanter. It was their first chance to speak freely.

Imoshen wiped her mouth with the back of her hand. "You put the idea in his head?"

"No, he came to me. He is no fool. I merely suggested one of us would make a good ambassador. He chose you because I am so old and frail."

Imoshen chuckled, then sobered as the old woman clasped her hand.

"You will be with him day and night, Imoshen. It is a chance to observe him. He's proud and he does not like to rely on others, but he is also a practical soldier. Learn, ingratiate yourself with him. Hush. I'm not finished. Go as far as

Landsend. From there the Abbey can send out messengers, they will be trusted. The southern highlands raise little grain. We can not rely on them for food.

"Once that is done you must return here in time for the Harvest Feast."

Imoshen nodded. She saw the logic of it, but she still felt sick at heart. Would the simple folk view her as a traitor, aiding the invader?

There was an almost imperceptible noise from behind the hangings. Both the Aayel and Imoshen stiffened. With a deft flick, Imoshen slipped her hand under the panel of her tabard and retrieved her dagger. Padding softly across the stone floor of the chamber, she positioned herself in front of the tapestry.

The Aayel nodded. Imoshen tugged the hanging from the wall, dragging their eavesdropper forward by one arm. With the ease borne of years of practice, she twisted the spy's arm behind her back and held the dagger to her captive's throat.

"A traitor?" Imoshen hissed.

The Aayel stepped forward to view the eavesdropper. A strange expression flitted across her face. "I don't think so."

"Never, my Lady," Kalleen whispered fiercely. "I am yours. Let me serve you. I want to go with you. I know the farmers, they're my people."

The Aayel nodded and Imoshen released her. The girl fell to the floor and kissed the tapestried hem of Imoshen's tabard.

"Oh, get up!" Imoshen impatiently pulled her to her feet.

Kalleen tilted her head, obviously surprised by the Lady T'En's outburst.

Imoshen felt a reluctant smile tug at her lips.

"My mother despaired of ever teaching me court protocol," she confessed.

Kalleen laughed. "Protocol could not make the goose boy Emperor."

Imoshen did not know what to say. The household servants knew their place, unlike this impudent girl from the fields.

"How true!" the Aayel observed dryly. Imoshen met the old woman's eyes above the girl's head. The Aayel approved of Kalleen. "Go and get some sleep. You leave at dawn."

They set off into the rising sun, riding at the head of a small army. The smoke fires of the morning meal hung on the still, cool air. To the east the rolling hills fell away to meet the distant sea.

Imoshen felt a reluctant surge of excitement. She knew her position was perilous but she couldn't cower forever, and she couldn't contain her natural exuberance for life.

Soon she would see the ocean again and visit the villages on the road to the Abbey. Joy filled her at the thought of once again seeing the beautiful port of Landsend. She tried to feel resentment, told herself it was shameful that she was forced to do this as the ambassador of the invader—in reality a prisoner whose cooperation was "requested"—but her naturally buoyant spirits wouldn't allow her to feel downcast.

Far above on the Stronghold ramparts she knew the remaining Ghebites watched the main body of their army file away into the morning mists. A large force remained to keep the Stronghold secure.

General Tulkhan urged his horse to one side and let the procession flow past. He had placed the Dhamfeer in the thick of the army in case an attempt was made to free her. There were still rebel bands wandering the plains, remnants of the once mighty T'En army who refused to accept the surrender.

The Dhamfeer was astride her horse, riding loosely in the saddle accompanied by the little serving girl whose forehead still bore the wounds of yesterday's attempted assault.

The Aayel had explained to him the reason for the people's abstinence at this time and he had informed his men to restrain themselves until the feast, where according to custom they would be able to indulge themselves freely. It amused him to think that Imoshen had chosen not to tell him the form the Harvest Feast celebration took.

But this religious forbearance meant he'd had no chance to take his release with a willing woman and he shifted in the saddle, only too aware of the tension in his body. At his signal the Elite Guard who escorted the last member of the T'En royal family parted, allowing him to weave his way to her side.

Apart from his uneasiness with the Dhamfeer, all was going well. Tulkhan expected any day now to greet a messenger who bore the news that the capital had fallen to his half-brother, King Gharavan. T'Diemn lay two days' journey west on the River Diemn, which provided safe harbor to oceangoing vessels of the mainland, just as Landsend provided safe harbor for those from the eastern archipelago.

Imoshen looked up, her face bathed in pure, early morning light and he was suddenly taken aback. She was so young and at that instant so transparent. She glowed like a child with a treat.

The air echoed with the rhythmic jingle of the horses' saddles and bits, the soft mutter of the men and the early morning cries of the birds. It was utterly peaceful, belying the tension which brooded beneath the surface.

Imoshen wondered why the General had fallen in beside her. He gave an odd, reluctant grin and she felt herself smile.

The Elite Guard fell a little behind them, only Kalleen remained stubbornly at Imoshen's side. They rode in silence, amid the sense of excitement which came with an army on the move.

"I wish to learn the farmers' speech. From what I've overheard it has much in common with your tongue," General Tulkhan announced. "You will teach me."

Imoshen felt a flash of annoyance, but even his high-handedness could not deflate her good spirits this morning. She chose to be amused.

"Our tongue is a hybrid of the two, not the original High T'En we first spoke. It evolved to facilitate commerce between the T'En and the locals," Imoshen said. She always enjoyed tales of the past. "You speak our tongue very well, General. I gather you learned it from our trading partners on the mainland to the west. Surely you don't make it a habit to learn the language of every nation you conquer?"

He cast her a swift glance and she gave him a bland smile, determined he should know she might be his captive, but she would not be his slave.

The General laughed.

Tulkhan's reaction was so unexpected Imoshen stared at him.

Heat flooded her body, coloring her cheeks.

"It's no hardship," the General told her. "I have a gift for languages. When I take a country I stay long enough to establish a regional governor, garrisons, ensure the smooth running of the colony. Gheeaba supplies the administrators, which leaves me free to take the time to learn the customs of the new culture."

"What of your own home, Gheeaba. Don't you miss it?"

He was silent for a moment and she thought he wouldn't answer.

"There is nothing for me there."

"But the old woman who died?" She could have bitten her tongue.

He frowned and shifted in the saddle, his eyes meeting hers fleetingly, unwillingly. Imoshen realized she'd found the chink in his armor and she knew instinctively that he didn't like revealing his weakness. It was lucky she had attempted to read him or she would never have discovered his hidden guilt.

Suddenly he kicked his mount's flanks and rode forward at an angle. The troops parted for him so that in a few moments he was out of the column and galloping toward the outlying scouts.

Imoshen ground her teeth, annoyed with the General for being so proud and with herself for not minding her tongue. She was supposed to be insinuating herself under his guard yet with one unwary comment she'd lost any ground she might have gained.

All day Imoshen watched General Tulkhan surreptitiously. She had time to observe the easy way he rode and how he used the strength of his powerful thighs to guide his black destrier with barely perceptible signals. As he rode, he held his head so proudly, his long dark hair streaming behind him. He was a magnificent male, she couldn't deny that.

But he was also a warmongering, arrogant Ghebite barbarian who held her life in the palm of his hand. Worse still, she'd alienated him, for he did not come near her again.

When she caught his dark gaze as he galloped past to speak to those bringing up the rear with the supply wagons, she felt a shiver of anticipation. But he made no move to acknowledge her.

In the late afternoon they entered the first village. The inhabitants had come out of hiding to meet the invaders, silently watching the procession advance on the village square with a mixture of apprehension and curiosity.

News of the General's arrival had preceded them. An army this large could hardly travel without being noted. There were few able-bodied women who weren't laden down with babes. Mothers stood with their little ones at their sides and the old men and women watched from seamed faces. There were no young men.

The Ghebites remained mounted, filing out to each side of the small village square. Their horses shifted restlessly, sensing water and feed nearby.

When they reached the square, the Elite Guard moved apart, clearing a path for the General and Imoshen.

As she rode up, considering how she should handle this moment, Imoshen sensed that the villagers were wary but reassured by her arrival.

General Tulkhan met her eyes. Before he could tell her what to do she urged her mount forward. Careful not to appear threatening, she swung lightly from the saddle. Out of courtesy to the farmers she chose to approach them on foot, so that they did not have to crane their heads up to look at her.

Her confident stride gave no sign of her thudding heart or the sickly fear in her belly—fear that they would spit on her for siding with the invaders, for betraying her people, for surrendering when the Stronghold could have held out for days, maybe even into the winter. She made the sign of deference used when approaching those of great age and greeted the Elders of the village, an ancient bonded couple.

She could tell the villagers were pleased to see their Elders treated with the proper respect. Then Imoshen began her explanation, slipping quite naturally into the patois of the people. She found its sweet lilting sound soothing because it reminded her of her childhood nurse.

The old man and woman exchanged glances. Smiles of relief lightened their faces as the purpose of the visit became clear. Imoshen realized her fear of rejection was unfounded. These people were realists. They needed the grain harvested so they would accept help.

Did they really care who ruled, so long as the rulers were just? Imoshen wondered. It was a sobering thought.

Acting as interpreter for the General, she learned the number of men the village and surrounding farms would require to bring the grain in then prepare it in time for the Harvest Feast. Several pigs had been slaughtered in their honor and it would have been discourteous to leave. The villagers wanted to entertain them.

Tulkhan chafed at the delay but understood the political necessity of accepting the villagers' hospitality. He ordered his men to pitch the tent for Imoshen. He would bed down in the open with his men as he always did. It was a necessary part of his command strategy to forge and strengthen the bonds of brotherhood.

As soon as Imoshen's tent was erected, he observed a line of villagers and many others he suspected had been hiding out in the woods or had come in from nearby farms making their way to her. Some who entered were obviously ill and left carrying little bags of herbs. At one point he saw Imoshen's maidservant open the tent flap to throw out a bowl of bloodied water.

So the Dhamfeer was carrying out her heathenish healings. No word had been sent out. It appeared to be a custom, almost a service the villagers expected of her.

He sent for a man he trusted, Wharrd, a commander who was renowned for his ability to set bones and sew flesh on the battlefield. Together they approached the tent. The people watched them warily, but held their ground. Small children clung to their mothers' legs and a boy lifted his puppy into his arms.

Tulkhan's skin prickled unpleasantly as he touched the tent flap and there was a metallic tang on his tongue. It reminded him of the time Imoshen had healed the old woman. He knew enough of unseen powers from his travels to realize that something more than simple healing was going on here.

Without waiting for a welcome he tossed the flap open and strode in to find Imoshen crouched beside an old woman. They were both peering into a dull mirrored surface which held a thin film of water—scrying. The maidservant moved forward to prevent him from interrupting, but Tulkhan signaled her that he was no threat and she stepped back.

Silence stretched within the tent. Only the murmur of voices outside, the distant shouts of his men as they relaxed around their camp and the sounds of animals as they settled for the night filled the air.

When the vision faded, Imoshen lifted her eyes from the water's surface and a great sadness rushed through her. Even with her poor skills she knew it was hopeless. It had been the same as her own vision when she had searched for her family. The pain cut just as deeply. This sort of task required an effort of will and openness which left her no protection from the emotions of those she served. The old woman looked at her hopefully.

She was aware of the General and another person watching, but ignored them. Taking the old one's hand, she said gently, "I am sorry, Grandmother. The one you seek will not be returning."

The old woman's shoulders sagged, then she straightened. She nodded once and rose stiffly, pressing a bag of dried herbs into Imoshen's hands. It was not the custom to pay for the T'En's services, but a gift would be welcomed.

The old woman shuffled out and Imoshen rose to her feet, feeling dizzy. "Yes?"

Since puberty she had assisted the Aayel at the seasonal cusp festivals, but she had never had to bear the burden of the healings alone. Her gift was small and her skill with it raw. The effort drained her. If only the Aayel were here now! She needed her great-aunt's keen observations, the wisdom gathered from over a century of life.

As Imoshen fought the ache in her chest, her throat closed painfully and tears stung her eyes. When she tried to pour a drink of honeyed wine her fingers shook so badly, Kalleen came to her side protectively. The young woman took the jug from Imoshen's hands and poured it. Imoshen nodded her thanks, glad her back was to the General so he could not see her weakness.

Greedily she gulped the sweet liquid.

"My man Wharrd is a bone-setter," Tulkhan announced without preamble. "He will assist you."

It was not a request, it was an order! Imoshen turned, her face flushed with the heat of the wine and a surge of anger. She met Tulkhan's eyes and saw that he knew she didn't want help. She looked her unwelcome assistant up and down. He was a grizzled campaigner, a capable man who at the moment appeared very uncomfortable. Her contrary nature made her feel a flash of understanding.

She put her wine aside. "I need no assistant, only the privacy of—"

"You are wearing yourself out. We must travel tomorrow. Wharrd will help you."

"Very well." Imoshen knew that now was not the time to argue. The General was determined to outmaneuver her. For now she would tolerate his spy at her side. She straightened and gestured to the flap. "You may leave. Send in the next one."

She knew the General hated it when she told him what to do, but as he had achieved his goal of foisting an unwanted observer on her, he carried out her order good-naturedly, which succeeded in annoying her further.

She eyed the one called Wharrd. Despite her resentment

of him she must make the most of it, must somehow turn this to her advantage. General Tulkhan would learn not to cross her.

A woman entered with a small girl who held her arm at an odd angle. At a glance Imoshen knew it had been dislocated at the shoulder and had not been put back properly. She flinched, imagining the pain the child had already endured. Then she smiled grimly. This was a chance for Tulkhan's spy to earn his keep. Using her voice to soothe the woman and child, she directed the mother to sit down with the child on her lap and gently removed the little smock to reveal the child's deformed shoulder joint.

As she talked, Imoshen crushed and burned a pungent herb. Inhaling the herb would help them to relax. She knelt to wave the smoke toward the mother and child with a small fan, speaking all the while, weaving a spell of enchantment with her words. The Aayel had told her it did not matter what you said, only that you built up a feeling of trust with the one you sought to help.

When this was done, Imoshen put the bowl of cinders aside and took the child's hand, holding her gaze. Calling on her gift, she impressed her will on the child, eventually inducing a state of waking-sleep. Over and over she repeated that the child would feel no pain. The mind was a powerful thing. She had seen people undergo excruciating procedures and not feel the pain as long as they believed they wouldn't.

Rising swiftly, Imoshen placed a hand on the mother's shoulder and nodded to Wharrd. "This is where your superior strength is useful."

He nodded grimly.

Doubtless he had sawed off wounded soldiers' legs as they screamed in agony. He was a hardened veteran, but he seemed reluctant to touch the trusting child. She stared drowsily at him, her wispy golden head tucked into her mother's chest as Imoshen's soothing chant continued to weave its spell. Imoshen understood his reluctance, but it had to be done.

He wiped his palms and grasped the child's arm, pulling it out sharply. There was an audible click as the joint landed back in place but no scream from the child, only a look of mild surprise.

The mother gave a soft gasp.

Imoshen waved Tulkhan's spy aside and knelt to strap the little arm against the child's torso. She gave the mother some advice, sending her away with herbs which would help the child sleep that night.

It pleased her to know the little girl would now live a normal, useful life. This was the joy of her gift. Imoshen closed tired eyes, thinking how lucky she was. She could hear Kalleen thanking the woman for some eggs and escorting her out.

Weariness overcame her, bringing with it a faint nausea. She knew she was taking on too much with these healings, but the people expected it of her and she could not let them down, not when they had been let down so badly by the Emperor and Empress.

Imoshen felt a tentative touch on her upper arm. Startled, she opened her eyes to see Whaard, his eyes wide with awe.

"The child didn't scream. She didn't even wake," he whispered.

"No."

He went pale. "Magic?"

"No." Imoshen shook her head. "It is a skill I was taught. With the herbs to aid concentration I coax the patient into a sleep-like state. While they are suggestible they can be told they won't feel pain, or even that they will not lose too much blood. It saves much suffering."

His eyes widened and he licked his lips eagerly. "What must I give you to teach me?"

"Nothing," Imoshen answered, then smiled at his surprise. His urgency did not stem from greed. Instinct told her it came from his nature. This man was a true healer, serving his general as best he could.

She repressed a shudder.

How could a healer choose soldiering as his vocation? How could he inflict pain and loss of life when in his soul he wanted to ease suffering? She touched his hand, feeling the conflict in him. With joy she realized she could ease it. "Simply watch and learn."

He dipped his grizzled head to kiss her hand. A rush of embarrassment flooded Imoshen. She didn't want to become involved with this Ghebite warrior yet already she could feel a bond forming. Her fingers brushed his gray hair.

"Please don't. There must be things you can teach me." With a tug she urged him to straighten and held his eyes. "I am only the Aayel's student in herb lore. I am sure we can learn from each other."

There was no chance for Tulkhan to speak with the Dhamfeer. He had wanted to discuss their plans and begin his language lessons, but she was occupied until the food was prepared, then courtesy meant he had to join her at the long plank tables set up in the square to partake of the feast.

His supply wagon had provided part of the food but his men mingled freely with the villagers. He only hoped as the music began and the dancing that his men remembered his rule and did not force the women. Diplomacy was not a foot soldier's strong point.

Some of his men were to be billeted in the simple houses, others would go out to the farms on the morrow. Many had been traveling since their early teens fighting on behalf of their homeland so this would be a change. How would they react to simple farm life?

All around him the villagers celebrated and so far his men had not offended anyone. He began to relax.

This was not his home but strangely enough Tulkhan felt a tug of recognition. Though the music was unfamiliar the feeling around the fires was oddly seductive. It spoke of a day's honest, hard work and the reward of home and hearth. It was so long since he had been back to his homeland it took him a few moments to pinpoint the sensation. Then he acknowledged what he felt was a rush of homecoming.

What surprised him was Wharrd's reaction to the heathen healer. He had expected skepticism, at least resistance. But the Dhamfeer seemed to have won over one his most trusted men in a single afternoon. Tulkhan encouraged his sense of irritation to fester. He did not want to feel at home here. This was not Gheeaba. It was a deceptively peaceful island which would turn on him the moment he faltered. He could not afford to reveal weakness.

Music lilted on the chilly night air and flickering firelight lit the people's happy faces. The same firelight danced over Imoshen's narrow features, warming her pale skin, making her wine-dark eyes pools of mystery. He caught her watching him several times and each time he felt a sense of unease, as if he was being sized up.

Once she raised her farmhouse cup to him in silent salute, and sipped as though it were fine crystal. He returned the salute, amused and intrigued. Was she acknowledging the success of their plan, or mocking him because she had won over his bone-setter?

He did not know what to think and her mystery both annoyed and fascinated him.

The farmers called forth their storyteller who regaled them with a long and involved tale. Tulkhan had time to study the people. They wore their best clothes. No rags here, but ornately embroidered vests and bodices. He saw fine examples of carved wood and pottery so elegantly turned and painted it could have graced a Ghebite lord's table.

This was a prosperous island where even the simple farmers enjoyed good food and wine, and took the time to create things of beauty. There was much he could learn from this culture.

Long before the festivities showed signs of dying down Tulkhan noted that Imoshen made her excuses and slipped away. She seemed tired, paler than usual. Tulkhan observed the way the people touched her shyly, stroking her sixth finger for luck.

What must it be like to live in a land where legends walked among men? Tulkhan shuddered. The mainland stories of Dhamfeer powers varied from place to place but some of the rumors had to be based on truth. He had already experienced Imoshen's insidious mind-touch. Logic told him he should keep well away from her.

After Imoshen was gone he felt restless. The scene seemed less intense and much less interesting once she was no longer there to explain a song or translate a question.

Tulkhan rose and stretched. With no real destination in mind he left the table and found himself wandering away from the noise into the darkness and toward the welcome glow of the tent, illuminated against the trees by the light of a single candle.

He paused. Through the thin walls of the canvas tent he heard her singing softly. She was alone, her maidservant having joined in the fun.

He watched the Dhamfeer's silhouette on the tent's wall as she stripped, unaware of the effect she was having. Her hair fell like a curtain, obscuring the line of her pert little breasts and the curve of her hips and buttocks.

True, she was tall and scrawny for a woman, but somehow it didn't matter. He liked the length of her legs, her slender waist. It made it more tantalizing to know that her perfect pale flesh was considered sacred, too precious to be desecrated by the sweaty touch of a lustful male.

Tulkhan shifted, aware of a sudden tension in his body.

Innocent of any guile, Imoshen turned with natural grace to pour a drink and drained it before dousing the single candle.

Tulkhan stood in the quiet of the night as the sound of music drifted to him, laced with shouts and laughter.

He suddenly ached to go to her. Imoshen was his by right of capture. Yet he knew she had never surrendered, and would never surrender in any sense of the word.

Every conversation she'd ever had with him reinforced her resistance. It was a tangible wall between them. The hardheaded realist in Tulkhan sneered at his traitorous body's demands. Did the Dhamfeer tempt him because she was unattainable?

He knew by all that his Ghebite priest had taught him that he should not feel this physical pull. Yet, it made his mouth go dry and his body burn. The soldier in him said she was all woman, whatever her race, and her body called to his.

Tulkhan ground his teeth. He despised himself for his

weakness. He would not let his flesh rule his mind. Frustration boiled in him. How he despised her for bringing him to this!

Desperately he turned and stalked off, determined to burn off his desire—only to find himself back at her tent a short while later. Equal parts rage and fear filled him. Had the Dhamfeer bewitched him? Was his soul no longer his own?

THREE

WITH AN EFFORT of will Tulkhan held firm. One small, sane part of him did not believe Imoshen, who after all was only a female and a mere girl at that, had cast a spell on him. This tug was simply too physical.

It disturbed him to find the demands of his flesh threatening to outweigh his rational mind. All his adult life he had prided himself on his control. He had simply gone too long without a woman. It was affecting his judgment.

Eventually he won a hollow victory.

The hard ground was cold comfort, especially near dawn when a chill mist stole over the land. Perversely, Tulkhan rejoiced in the discomfort. He had to purge his body of its unruly desires. At the first hint of dawn he stripped and bathed in the village pond, much to the amazement of the few villagers out doing their early chores.

There was a frost on the ground and the water was bitterly cold, forcibly reminding Tulkhan that this was not his northern homeland. For a moment he felt nostalgic, recalling the thick-walled houses and a sun so bright that the light hurt your eyes.

The cold might have put out the fire in his body, but it did not cool his temper. His men felt the sharp edge of his tongue that morning as he rounded up those who'd slept overlong after their night of drinking and dancing.

It annoyed him to find Imoshen already mounted and waiting, her breath misting in the fresh dawn air.

"Lady T'En," Tulkhan acknowledged as he approached her, maneuvering his black destrier to her side. He saw her eyes narrow warily. He never addressed her by her royal title. "It is obvious you haven't made a practice of camping."

"No, when we traveled my family and I stayed in lesser noble houses," she replied cautiously. "Why, what have I omitted to do?"

"Nothing, if it was your intention to display yourself to my men last night." Her shocked expression was a balm to his irritation. Tulkhan plunged on. "The next time you disrobe, put out your candle first, then you will not cast your shadow on the tent wall for all to see. Unless it was your intent to entice my men—"

"You know very well it was not!" Her eyes flashed red and he knew he'd pierced the polite facade she maintained to keep him at bay.

His accusation was unjust and he was secretly pleased that he had been the only man to witness her innocent display.

Imoshen flushed delightfully to the roots of her pale hair. "It won't happen again, I can assure you."

She went to urge her horse past him, but he caught the bridle and pulled it closer so that their thighs were pressed together. She glared at him, her lips white with fury.

"It had better not happen again because my men are due their rights of conquest. I've told them to wait till Harvest Feast, but with you flaunting your body before them I cannot answer for their deeds. They might forget you're a precious Dhamfeer, sworn to celibacy, and recall only that you are a woman!"

For an instant he caught a flicker of fear in her eyes, quickly cloaked, and regretted baiting her.

But she lifted her proud chin and fixed those exotic eyes on him. "The females of Fair Isle aren't compliant Ghebite women fit only for breeding sons! I'm more woman than any of your barbarians could handle!"

With a flick of her reins she freed the mare's head and

forged past him. Tulkhan watched Imoshen's stiff, straight back, his heart pounding with the intensity of their exchange. She was magnificent. She hadn't backed down, hadn't deferred to him. Instead she'd met him with a challenge of her own and he did not doubt her boast for a moment.

Irritated by the turn of his thoughts, he cursed and pressed his knees to his horse's flanks. His men were in formation, waiting. He stood in the stirrups and bellowed the signal to move out. As he watched the column file from the clearing of the village he found he had to consciously force his hands to relax their grip on the reins.

There she went, infuriating Dhamfeer!

Honesty made him admit no one but he had seen her disrobe so innocently and enticingly. No one but he had ached for her, torn between duty and desire.

What was wrong with him? Never in all his years campaigning had he let his emotions rule his head when dealing with the enemy. And Imoshen was definitely the enemy. He only had to look at her to see her differences. She was one of the feared and revered Dhamfeer, as the children's rhyme went.

But she was no nursemaid's invention to scare naughty children. This Dhamfeer was all too real. He shuddered, recalling how she had plucked a thought from his mind.

Tulkhan compressed his lips in annoyance and vowed not to let the Dhamfeer pierce his guard again. He would be polite but distant. The gods knew he had enough responsibilities to occupy him without creating complications by acting on his base physical desires.

Imoshen rode away from the General without so much as a backward glance. Crude barbarian! He had enjoyed baiting her.

She was furious with herself. Her shoulders ached with tension. She could still feel his eyes on her, but she refused to acknowledge him.

What had possessed her? The General must think her a wanton creature, boasting like that. She, who had never lain with a man, who had only theoretical knowledge of the procedure, claiming to be more woman than any man could handle! Her cheeks flooded with heat as she recalled her ridiculous challenge.

She hadn't even been particularly good at her studies! It had all seemed a little bizarre to her when she had looked at the illustrated texts.

She pressed the back of her hand to her mouth, appalled at the implications of her boast. Why, she had all but challenged him to bed her!

Was she any better than the Ghebite women she had so cruelly mocked? She had to admit she planned to trap the General, bait him with her body and steal his seed. The conception of a child should be a joyous event, shared by bondpartners. Shame flooded Imoshen, for she planned to steal General Tulkhan's son and use him as a tool to save her own life.

Just then Tulkhan galloped past her, rounding up the last of the men as the column moved out. She felt her eyes drawn to him, despite herself.

What if the Aayel was wrong?

What if he thought nothing of his own flesh and blood? Would he order her execution, knowing she carried his unborn child? Could he be so inhuman?

She didn't know.

The Aayel's gift was scrying, interpreting what she saw and reading people. Imoshen could only trust in the old woman's advice and hope. And she vowed to keep a rein on her tongue when next Tulkhan spoke to her.

But when Tulkhan did join her it was only for his language lesson and he was scrupulously polite. Imoshen found it easy to instruct him. He was a fast learner, quick to pick up the nuances of the language. She would do well to remember that.

The short days passed uneventfully, and each village they entered wanted to entertain them. Minor noble families vied to outdo their neighbors in providing hospitality. They shed more and more men as they progressed, leaving groups behind to bring in the crops. Everywhere they went the locals consulted Imoshen with Wharrd at her side. The man even slept on the ground at the entrance to her tent, much to Tulkhan's irritation.

His plan had backfired. Instead of inserting a spy he had provided the Dhamfeer with a willing servant and lost one of his most trusted men.

They were only a few hours' ride from Landsend when Tulkhan called for a pause to take lunch. They were skirting an expanse of hilly country covered with virgin wood which, according to Imoshen, took days to traverse if you were lucky enough to reach the other side. The men eyed fearfully the encroaching forest warily.

Like the thickly wooded ranges of the southern highlands this forest was ancient and for the most part untouched. It was said ancient spirits roamed the thickly clustered trees, unfriendly spirits which took a human toll from those who passed through their domain.

More superstition, Tulkhan cursed impatiently, as he signaled his troops to stop. He knew the value of presentation. He ordered his men to clean their weapons and deck themselves out in full regalia, so that when they marched into Landsend that afternoon they would be an impressive sight.

They had stopped in a pleasant glade. Great shafts of autumn sunlight fell through the canopy, illuminating the silver trunks of the trees which ringed the clearing. As the men ate, the camp grew quiet and the vast silence of the deep, virgin forest seemed to absorb every man-made sound.

Imoshen wasn't hungry. She felt restless and strangely uneasy. She looked around the clearing. The midday sun was brilliant but gave little warmth.

Kalleen was teasing Wharrd and, as usual, he was trying to outdo her. Imoshen listened absently as they compared the kinds of food their countries considered delicacies.

The girl snorted as he described how a mainland beast with a single horn would be killed solely so its horn could be crushed into a powder believed to help men maintain their sexual potency.

If he thought to embarrass the farm girl he failed, for she

winked at Imoshen and asked innocently, "Of course a man like you would never have need of that horn's medicine, now would you?"

For once Wharrd had no reply and Kalleen preened, having won that encounter.

Imoshen found it confusing. The Ghebite men were quick enough to talk of their prowess with women, but confronted by a woman who would talk of such things, they became offended. It was not at all like the court where the Empress and her friends recommended each other's lovers.

Not that she had belonged to that circle. Her family had preferred the quiet of their country estates and held old-fashioned values such as fidelity between bond-partners. She hated to think what they would say about her plan to seduce the General and steal his son.

Imoshen stood, arching her back, and decided to stretch her legs. She wasn't planning to wander too far away, but then she caught the scent of a familiar herb and on impulse followed her nose, intending to pick some leaves to bolster her supplies. Then she noticed the heart-shaped leaf of a plant renowned for treating conditions of the heart and another which was ideal for bringing down fevers and protecting against the poisons which could take root in a wound.

As she picked the leaves she hummed the little songs the Aayel had taught her to use when selecting herbs. She twisted the leaves neatly upon themselves and tucked them inside her jerkin to keep her hands free.

Pleased with her find, Imoshen didn't pause to wonder why the locals hadn't come by to collect herbs so near the main path to Landsend. She supposed the plants had survived this late in the season because this was a northern slope and caught the sun for most of the day.

Around her the insects hummed, filling the air with their busy song. She came to the top of a small rise and carefully picked her way down the slope, through waist-high ferns surrounding the massive trunks of trees which rose above her like the columns of a great building. She could no longer hear the occasional comment from the Ghebites or the snicker of their horses.

The ground sloped away and in between the cleft of two great rocks a bracken-cloaked spring seeped from the ground, pooling in small rock ponds as it made its way downhill.

Pleased, Imoshen picked up her pace. This was excellent, just the place she needed to find the moss which aided the healing process. She got down on her hands and knees and crawled amid the bracken, turning over the smooth river stones, searching out the best specimens. She was careful to leave some moss so that it could regrow.

Imoshen followed the little stream downhill between the rocks. Despite the shafts of autumn sunlight the cold was intense near the water's edge. The brook grew wider, spreading into a pool bordered by large rocks.

It was so good to escape the Ghebite General's presence. For days she had been on her best behavior. The villagers and minor nobles expected her to be the Lady T'En, a healer who could advise them, while the General treated her with aloof indifference. But his gaze, when he thought she wasn't looking, devoured her. She had been so controlled and circumspect, never acting without thinking of the consequences.

It wasn't natural for her. Here she could let her guard down and delight in simply being herself.

Unplaiting her hair, she massaged her scalp, feeling the faint warmth of the sun seep into her skin. The cool water tempted her but she wasn't foolish enough to strip. The cold would be intense and, besides, the General might send one of his men to bring her back.

Imoshen sighed. The Aayel would be pleased with her, she was behaving with great maturity. Still, it couldn't hurt to paddle her feet. Slipping off her boots, she dipped her toes in the pool. The cold was fearful but it was also invigorating, so she splashed some on her face and drank from her cupped hand.

Feeling suddenly vulnerable, Imoshen looked up.

A presentiment of danger made her mouth go dry. She had the distinct feeling that someone or something was watching her. Instinctively, she froze and strained to hear.

Her heart thudded in her chest. A prickle of fear lifted

the hairs on the back of her neck. It was not the earthy, natural response to danger she'd felt when she first confronted the General. This was an eerie, preternatural instinct.

Listening intently, she could not discern the faintest sound from the men in the glade. Even the knowledge that if she were to scream they would hear and come crashing through the undergrowth brought her no comfort. Instinct told her that their hearty barbarian ways could not protect her from what threatened here.

She had teased the General with old tales about special places where ancient spirits dwelled, spirits which predated even the locals. Her old nurse, long dead now, had told tales of a dawn-people who predated the golden-skinned locals and worshipped a race of Ancients.

Fleetingly, Imoshen wondered if it was an eternal cycle. Fair Isle was taken by force and settled, then the invaders were absorbed by the island. So that they in turn were subjugated by new invaders. The thought made her head spin, but she had no time for such questions.

Something was threatening her here and now.

She had heard rumors of places the locals avoided in the deep woods, places of power—evil, greedy power—but she had dismissed these stories as superstition. They were traditionally associated with the hot springs where steam seeped from the cracks in the stone.

Slowly Imoshen rose to her feet. There was definitely something here, and her T'En senses told her that this something was not friendly. She wished it were a product of her imagination.

Tightening the laces on her jerkin to keep her herbs safe, Imoshen bent and hastily retied the straps of her boots without dropping her apparently casual gaze about the pool. As yet there was no physical evidence to back up her terrible sense of foreboding. Finally, she straightened and shaded her eyes against the sparkle of the autumn sun on the pool's surface. Get away from here, her instinct screamed.

She backed away from the pool but the feeling did not ease, instead the space between her shoulder blades ached. Slowly, she turned to face the unseen threat.

Her eyes widened as she took in a patch of bare earth where nothing grew. It was surrounded by tall, slender-trunked trees which towered over her. The trees and bracken grew right up to the bare circle but from that point nothing flourished, not even a weed. Instinctively she knew it was a sacred, accursed place where innocent blood had been shed—no seed could take root on such soil.

Bordering the empty patch was a circle of low, worn stones. Her heart lurched as her theoretical knowledge confirmed what her senses had known all along. This was not a natural phenomenon—it was an ancient site where the dawn-people had worshipped.

Imoshen focused, trying to pierce the veil of time. This was not her skill, the Aayel would have been better at it. She frowned in concentration, her heart thudding erratically. At first there was nothing but the writhing squiggles in her mind's eye, then a brooding darkness gathered. Distant voices grew closer, chanting, bringing with them the unmistakable scent of fresh blood.

A hand closed on her shoulder. Imoshen gasped, reacting instinctively. Clenching her fist, she brought her arm up and swung the point of her elbow back to catch her attacker in the midriff. Even as she darted forward she heard a grunt of surprised pain. There was only one way to run—across the clearing—so she did.

A man cursed.

She felt the impact of her running feet on the bare earth through the thin soles of her boots. She caught the scent of her attacker. It was familiar but the need to escape dominated all thought.

The impact of a heavy body knocked her off her feet. Flying forward, she flung her hands out to take the force of her fall. Even as she hit, she attempted to writhe out of his grasp, but he had her upper thighs wrapped in his arms. His heavy chest pressed on her buttocks.

The chanting grew stronger as the darkness closed in on her. The smell of blood was nauseous, overpowering.

They had her!

"Imoshen, it's *me*!"

She twisted, desperate. A flurry of images filled her mind—blood, death, a great power grown old and vindictive.

Because she was pinned she couldn't reach the knife strapped to her thigh. Arching her back, she tried to bring the back of her skull into contact with his face, to smash his nose.

"Imoshen, it's Tulkhan. Stop!"

The General?

Panting, she froze. The confusion faded from her mind. She'd panicked, the Ghebite meant no harm. Or did he?

"General?"

Her voice hung on the air as she lifted her upper body and twisted beneath him. Grudgingly, he released her, letting her slide from under his weight. She was aware of the hard planes of his belly and thighs.

Relieved to escape him, she raised herself up onto her knees to catch her breath. He remained crouched before her, watching her thoughtfully. She could still feel the imprint of his body on hers and a strange languorous feeling of longing.

Blood on the stones. Passion in the voices.

A surge of excitement flashed through her. Imoshen gasped and licked her lips. She saw a flicker of awareness in his coal-black eyes. He felt it too, for all that he was a Trueman.

For an instant the victor and vanquished faced each other in the center of an older, greater power, grown malevolent with the passage of time.

Tulkhan had felt the ridge of a hidden knife on Imoshen's thigh as she slid from underneath him. He knew if she could have retrieved it his life would have been forfeit. The Dhamfeer had been a heartbeat away from slitting his throat.

Until now he hadn't known she carried a knife. He should punish her for concealing a weapon. His heart raced at the thought of taking her in his arms, exacting payment for all the tortured nights he had lain awake wracked with his need for her.

"*No!*" she spat, about to spring to her feet.

But before she could, he tackled her, driving her backward onto the dirt.

She grunted, the air knocked from her lungs.

With her body pinned beneath his he felt the hard ridge of her knife. She sucked in a painful breath and writhed furiously, trying to slide from beneath him, forcibly reminding him of both her feminine curves and the knife. He must not let her get to it. Fury darkened her T'En eyes to a mulberry black.

She wore the blade strapped to the front of her left thigh. How did she get to it? It would be useless unless she could reach it quickly in an emergency.

Slowly, his hand traveled beneath her tabard. The panel of brocade material offered no barrier. His mouth went dry with longing. He felt the soft material of her leggings. Then near the warm flesh of her inner thigh he found the cunningly hidden slit in the fabric. Beneath him her body quivered with tension. He felt the silky smoothness of her skin. With a flick he released the catch and pulled the knife from its sheath, bringing it out into the light between them. It felt hot in his hand, hot from her body.

She struggled convulsively, but he tightened his hold, pinning her to the ground. He thought he caught her faint womanly scent on the knife.

"Was this for me?" His voice sounded strange.

"This is a very bad place," she whispered.

He hesitated. What was she talking about? Her eyes were wide with fear. He could smell it on her skin.

Why?

His body tensed against the unseen threat. Was he reacting to her fear, or to an outside source?

Tulkhan didn't know. He only knew that despite the heat of the knife, which burned into his hand like a brand, and against all his better instincts, his body ached to bury itself in her.

Her wine-dark eyes searched the clearing and she flinched at what she saw, but when he looked around there was nothing, just emptiness and a few old stones.

"We must leave here, General."

Her voice came to him from a great distance, ordering him about yet again! He had an overwhelming urge to take the knife's sharp point and part the strings of her jerkin, slice through the fine linen of her shirt. He wanted to see the pale rise of her breasts. Since that first time he saw her held captive by his men, bloodied but not bowed, he had wanted her.

If he were to lower his head, he could bury his face in her soft feminine curves, inhale her unique scent. A savage surge of desire gripped him. He had the knife, the superior strength and she was his by right of conquest.

Her lips drew back from her teeth and her eyes narrowed as if she knew what he was thinking. Instinct told him she would fight with the last breath in her body. Tulkhan knew then that he would have to kill her before he could subdue her.

His free hand sought her breast beneath the material and encountered something else. A puff of heady herbs engulfed them both. Inhaling the sharp, pungent scent, he winced. It stung his nostrils, clearing his head.

What was he thinking?

He had never forced himself on a woman. They were always willing, only too willing, for all the good it did him.

Shocked by the path his thoughts had taken, he sat up slowly to crouch on his heels. It cost him dearly to pull away from her. He felt as if an invisible cord joined their bodies, reeling him ever tighter to her. So fierce a pull must be sorcery.

She also came to her knees, drawing closer to him. Her hands closed over the knife in his. Deftly and without apology, she pressed her fingers into his thumb, breaking his hold. He didn't resist as she slid the knife from his hand and calmly replaced it in its sheath. He caught a flash of white thigh before the tabard fell back into place. He fought a convulsive urge to lick that flesh.

"It's the rocks." Her voice was a warm breath caressing his skin.

Rocks? He could only make sense of her words through a supreme effort of will. His whole being was focused on the raging need in him—a need so violent it had nothing to do with casual dalliance. What possessed him? He had to break free of this compulsion.

"Rocks?" He forced himself to follow the arc of her arm as she gestured and noticed the worn stones in a circle around them.

"Blood on the rocks," she hissed.

Why was there a tremor in her voice? Tulkhan watched uneasily as she dipped inside her jerkin to pull out a handful of leaves, crushing them between her fingers. Again the spicy, sharp scent flooded his senses and his thoughts focused.

Her troubled eyes held his, willing him to listen. "It is older than the locals, ancient and hungry for our bonding, our blood—"

"Imoshen!" She had never seemed more Other, more Dhamfeer, to Tulkhan than at that moment, yet he still desired her. This was wrong. It went against all his natural instincts. Shuddering violently, he fought for control. The force of his need frightened him. Was his raging desire fed by an outside source? The idea was unnerving and repellent because he hated to think his actions had been dictated by an unseen presence. Shocked, he forced himself to concentrate on what she was saying.

Her fingers bit into the tense, corded muscles of his forearms. He could see Imoshen was terrified. A surge of protectiveness banished the primal violence which had threatened to overwhelm him.

"We have to get out of here. Come, General."

"There . . ." His voice was a croak. He had to swallow before he could continue. "There's something here?"

"It lured me here." Intense, dark eyes held his. "It nearly invaded you, but you resisted it. I think the moment is past."

In a lithe, circling movement she came to her feet, eyes searching the clearing. The length of her thick hair fanned out as she moved.

She extended her hand in a friendly, boyish gesture which seemed odd to him considering his behavior had been less than brotherly. But he rose, brushing the dirt from his knees and thighs.

"So we're safe?" He was irritated with her, with himself, and he didn't know why.

She was right, there had been some force acting through him. No matter how much he might desire her, he would never have contemplated forcing himself on her.

"I'm not like that," he said.

She cast him a swift, calculating glance and once again he was aware of her intelligence and her perceptiveness, of what wasn't said between them.

"Let's go, while we can."

He laughed but the sound was hollow on the still air.

Imoshen strode across the barren ground and he fell in behind her. When she came to the stones, she made several signs on the air and whispered something under her breath, then crushed more of the leaves on the ground.

Tulkhan watched all this with a certain skepticism.

But when they stepped between the worn stones he realized with a jolt that the soft sounds of the deep woods hadn't pierced that fell circle, for now those sounds rushed in on him.

He stiffened, recognizing the scent of an animal—a rank, fetid scent. A predator was close, very close. There was no breeze so the beast could not disguise its presence by standing downwind.

They had escaped one threat to face another, but at least this one could be defeated with a man-made blade.

Imoshen stopped. Suddenly, she, too, recognized the scent of danger—a wildcat on the prowl.

"What is it?" Tulkhan's voice was a whisper in her ear.

"A hunter. It won't attack while there are two of us, unless it's desperate. But it is very close and it is watching us."

She was glad of the General's presence. Imoshen didn't question why she knew she could trust him to protect her back, she simply accepted it. Once again she drew her knife. "Watch behind, I'll watch ahead."

They walked uphill, striking away from the brook toward

the rise beyond which they knew the others waited. The beast kept pace with them, only falling back as they entered the clearing where the horses shifted uneasily, showing the whites of their eyes. Several of the handlers were whispering soothingly to calm them.

The return of General Tulkhan and his captive was greeted with relief and some ribaldry. Their extended absence had been marked. The men were amused, tolerant. Imoshen's hair was hanging loose, filled with bracken, her clothes dusty and disheveled. Tulkhan was also dirt-stained.

The General escorted her to her horse, ignoring the jibes. The men were ready to move out. As one of the foot soldiers passed Imoshen the reins she saw a knowing smirk in his eyes. Her hands tightened convulsively, but she restrained herself because she noticed the man's expression when he met the General's eyes.

With a jolt she understood the Ghebites' amusement and it gave her an unwelcome insight into their world. They thought their General had been bedding her, too eager to restrain himself. Imoshen's cheeks stung with heat.

Didn't they know pure T'En women were sacred? She would never consider bedding a man for idle enjoyment.

Didn't the Ghebites despise the Dhamfeer? Yet, the men were not offended. It appeared that despite her Otherness she was female enough for them to tolerate the idea of their General lying with her.

Tulkhan held her gaze, his dark eyes sparkling with amusement.

She gritted her teeth and swung into the saddle. Tulkhan gave her a rueful grin and she realized he was not only aware of her chagrin but he was enjoying it. She could feel a fierce blush coloring her cheeks. With all her being she wanted to wipe that arrogant masculine gleam from his eyes. Instead, she lifted her chin and held her head high, daring anyone to comment.

The General might be grinning now, but she knew better! He had almost raped her at the insistence of an ancient force. She was lucky those herbs had been tucked into her jerkin. Their pungent scent had helped clear his head and she'd been able to use the moment to distract him.

But honesty forced her to admit it had been the General's willpower which had conquered the unseen force and freed him. As much as she wanted to, she had not been able to help him. Frustration filled her. Unlike the Aayel, who could scry the future and read anyone, Imoshen's T'En powers were weak. Only once had she sifted a conscious mind and that was when she was first confronted by the General.

Then she had been in a heightened state of awareness, fearful for her life. It had been an almost unconscious act of self-preservation. If only she had more control over her T'En side.

Tilting her head forward, she caught her hair and began to braid it.

"No." Tulkhan grabbed her nearest elbow. "Leave it loose."

He raised his hand and drew his fingers through the first part of the braid, separating the strands. Her scalp tingled with the slight tug. His hand traveled the length of her hair and came free with a small piece of brown bracken. Laughter lit his eyes as he held it up for her to see, then tossed it aside.

"Your people expect you to look like the T'En princess you are," he told her.

She opened her mouth to argue but it was true and he moved away, satisfied that she would obey him though it galled her to do so.

Kalleen's saucy eyes met Imoshen's and the serving girl curled her top lip, silently giving her opinion of men, the General in particular. Imoshen had to smile.

She stole a glance in his direction, watching as a soldier helped Tulkhan into his battle regalia. She should despise the Ghebite General but she had to admit he had all the makings of a leader. For one, he looked so fine in full battle dress. She had to admire his easy stride, the grace of his body as he swung onto the back of the black war horse.

The column moved out and it was a relief when they finally left the forest. Soon they were riding into a cool breeze, sharp with the salty tang of the sea.

Tulkhan held his cape around him and ignored the chill in his exposed hands on the reins. His men had never traveled this far south before and the cold this early in the autumn boded badly for the winter.

"So." He shifted in the saddle. "If the farm folk see the twin moons as a mother and child, what do the T'En see them as?"

He knew the answer but he wanted to hear the Dhamfeer's explanation. She never missed a chance to lecture him on the superiority of her culture and he never missed a chance to confound her with his knowledge of other cultures.

"As a man and woman," she replied, plucking a long strand of silver-blond hair from her lips and tossing her head. Obviously she enjoyed the bracing sea breeze. "Like man and woman, the moons vie for supremacy, first one is in the ascendancy, then the other. Their relationship is strongest and thus at its most powerful when both shine freely; so it is with a man and woman.

"While there are things one does better than the other, they are strongest when they can stand side by side, equal in each other's eyes." Her fierce wine-dark eyes met his and held. "I will call no man my master!"

A shiver moved over his skin. He found a laugh. "Neither will I!"

She laughed, then eyed him narrowly. "I've heard your people see the moons as two half-brothers who battle constantly for supremacy."

"Yes." He shifted in the saddle. "One is the son of the first wife, the other the son of the second. Both want the father's love, so they try to outshine each other."

"Are they not equal?"

He grimaced. He was the king's eldest son, but his mother had been the second wife, not the first taken to consolidate political power. So his younger half-brother, Gharavan, was now king. But he had known this would happen ever since the boy was born. He had seen the marked difference in his treatment once the king's first wife produced a male heir. He had known then who his true friends

were and since that day he had learned enough of human
nature to be grateful for that early lesson, cruel though it had
been.

As leman-son Tulkhan had no birthright. His General's
rank and the respect of his men had been earned and he was
proud of this. "The first son of the first wife inherits the
father's property, while the second gets nothing."

"What if the firstborn was a daughter?"

He snorted. "Females don't inherit."

"Why not?" Her eyes flashed violent red.

He knew how to irritate her and shrugged casually.
"They just don't. They don't own property, they don't sit on
council . . ."

Imoshen laughed, startling him. "Then Gheeaba is the
poorer for that policy, because you lose the skills of half your
people!"

She urged her horse forward and galloped a little ahead.
He stared at her shoulders, admiring the way she rode the
horse. Damn her, she'd done it again. Honesty forced him to
admit she was probably right. If he could feel disinherited,
how did his elder half-sisters feel? He hardly knew them.
They'd been married to consolidate his family's position during the long years he had spent on the campaigns.

Imoshen urged her mount forward, pleased to have gotten the better of Tulkhan. He was looking far too fine and
pleased with himself in his battle regalia. She understood
why he had ordered his men to dress for their arrival at
Landsend. His army made an impressive spectacle, none
more so than the General himself. But she was on edge after
what had happened and she didn't want to ride too near him.

She thought she recognized a rocky outcropping and
urged her horse toward it. The Elite Guard parted for her,
used to her conversations with their General, her coming and
going freely. Several had consulted her on matters of old
wounds which hadn't healed properly.

Imoshen leapt from her mount, tied the reins to a low
bush and ran to the top of the outcropping. The view was just
as she remembered it. From where she stood the ground fell
away, a checkerboard of rolling grain fields and winding

lanes which led to the port of Landsend. In the distance she could see the magnificent abbey that dominated the bluff and overlooked the bay. The horizon was an endless blue. Somewhere beyond that eastern ocean was the original home of the T'En.

She was looking at history—Landsend, where her namesake, Imoshen the First, made landfall.

Inhaling deeply, she rejoiced. The ozone made her heart race. The stiff sea breeze pressed her clothes to her body and filled her lungs.

She sensed the General at her side and pointed.

"There it is!" She had to raise her voice to be heard over the sea breeze. "See the wharf and beach. That is where the first T'Imoshen ordered her ship burnt to the waterline. She had a much smaller army than yours, made up of the old and the children. They were explorers, looking for wealth and knowledge.

"Within a generation the T'En had captured the whole island. Sporadic uprisings occurred for around two hundred years, but we brought culture, music, art, written language, medicine and science to this land."

She turned to him, pride blazing in her eyes. A smile of triumph curved her lips.

Tulkhan knew then that Imoshen would never yield to him. Beauty lay spread out below them, but he did not see it. He stiffened, stung by the implications of her comment—she considered him a barbarian.

"What have your people done since then?" he demanded. "Grown lazy and self-indulgent?"

"While the T'En ruled, no one, not even a landless drifter, lived in fear or starvation. If anyone, male or female, was wronged they could bring their grievance before the church to be heard. There was justice for all."

Tulkhan tensed as she caught his hands in hers, fixing her glittering eyes on him. "You've bested our army—I'll admit that, General, but don't throw out what is good. Keep the best, build on it. Be a leader with vision!"

He searched her eyes, startled by her vehemence. True, in the rare idle moment during his many years of campaigning he had compared the way different kingdoms drafted and enforced their laws. The weak gave their loyalty to the strong for protection and in doing so gave up their freedom.

But Imoshen was talking justice for all regardless of gender or social status, an individual's right. Tulkhan's head reeled at the concept.

"Fair Isle is renowned for its culture, the music, the arts—"

"The decadence!" Tulkhan bit back. He would not let her compare their homelands and call him a barbarian by default.

Imoshen's hands tightened on his. "Discard the bad, build on the good. Gather the greatest minds in Fair Isle . . ."

"I have met great thinkers on the mainland, too. Men who were working on medicines, men who turned their far-seers to the night sky and others who designed machines to do the work of ordinary men."

"Then invite them to Fair Isle. Knowledge knows no master, knowledge is power!"

As Tulkhan stared into her upturned face, a vision of Fair Isle's future swamped him. Was it possible to eliminate disease, free the farmer from endless toil, and create an island where the weak did not fear the strong?

She lifted his hands to her breast. "You *do* see it!"

He flinched.

The Dhamfeer had done it again. She'd reached into his mind and invaded his thoughts. He felt defiled.

Revulsion flooded him. He flung her hands away. Fury goaded him to inflict the same measure of pain on her. Catching her by the upper arms, he shook her, pressing his fingers savagely into her flesh.

"Don't *ever* do that again!" he growled. Even as he spoke he registered the confusion in her face. She didn't understand his anger. A sheen of unshed tears glistened in her eyes and he realized he'd hurt her.

She'd offered him a vision of the future and he'd thrown it aside. Damn her!

Damn her beautiful, trembling mouth.

He had to kiss her. It made no sense. He ignored the small sensible part of his brain which warned him not to give in. One kiss would never be enough. Instead of heeding common sense he let the need which had been steadily building within his body, guide his actions.

He caught her to him, capturing her lips with his.

She tasted so good. Her skin was soft, her mouth hot. The curves of her slender body pressed against his. He felt her quicken under his touch and recognized her raw and uninhibited reaction. Her ragged breath fanned his face, her hands caught his neck as she strained against him. She was an innocent wanton. The thought inflamed him.

Drunk on sensation, he felt like laughing till he heard a silken whisper in his mind. Tulkhan registered her unspoken plea for more. He froze. She'd done it again—she'd invaded his mind!

He broke the contact abruptly, thrusting her aside. As he pulled back he noted her flushed face, her lips swollen by his kisses.

"Get on your horse, Dhamfeer!" But his hands held her close, pressed to his body, thigh to thigh.

She blinked. He realized that she didn't understand his abrupt change. Was it possible that she didn't even know she was doing it? Were her abilities intuitive, rather than controlled? The analytical part of Tulkhan's mind put this thought aside for future consideration.

A ragged cheer broke from the Elite Guard. It surprised Tulkhan. Their embrace must have appeared spontaneous and passionate to his men, who were too far away to have caught the undertones.

He met Imoshen's eyes, saw her cheeks flush.

Sliding his arm around her shoulder, Tulkhan turned her to face the men, who cheered again. He felt the first stirring of resistance and when Imoshen would have shrugged free of him, he tightened his grip.

Still grinning, he hissed, "Never disappoint your people, Imoshen! Didn't they teach you anything?"

She turned into his embrace and caught his face in her hands. "More than you think, General."

This time when she kissed him the unexpectedness of it ignited his passion, bypassing all logic. His body was ready for hers.

Then snap, her teeth closed painfully on his bottom lip before she pulled back, Dhamfeer eyes alight. Stunned, he released her.

Laughing, she jumped lightly to the ground and freed her mount's reins.

Tulkhan tasted his own blood on his tongue. The pain was nothing, but the challenge baited him. Damn her vow of celibacy. He would have her, and she would beg him for more!

They rode into Landsend as the sun set. Tulkhan had timed it perfectly for the sun gilded their polished armor and weapons. A curious populace escorted them up the winding rise to the Abbey, cheering. It appeared the purpose of their visit was already known. Good news traveled fast.

Though the Dhamfeer was his captive, she was greeted with honor, almost reverence, by the Abbey scholars, reminding Tulkhan forcibly that Imoshen was the last of the T'En.

The Abbey leader, the Seculate, was a woman who wielded the power of her office with quiet authority. Again, he was reminded of Fair Isle's differences. In Gheeaba a woman would never have commanded a man, yet here the male priests not only listened attentively to the Seculate's every word but they scurried to do her bidding.

The troops were housed in the township itself, only the Elite Guard were quartered within the Abbey. Tulkhan remained outwardly impassive, but he was on edge. If she planned treachery, the Seculate could have them all murdered in their sleep and leave his men leaderless.

Yet the more he saw of these people the more he was impressed by their culture, their architecture and by their reverence for knowledge. Their meal was simple but delicious and they were entertained in the courtyard by music and obscure plays which he found hard to follow. He would have much preferred to follow Imoshen when she withdrew with her maidservant.

The sounds of revelry drifted up the stairwell as Imoshen and Kalleen made their way to their chamber.

Imoshen noticed how Kalleen tilted her head to catch the noises from the courtyard. She realized the poor girl would rather be out there joining in the fun than helping prepare a bath, so she dismissed her. Kalleen didn't need to be told twice.

In the bath chamber Imoshen stripped.

Ha, she thought, let Tulkhan pretend to be unimpressed by hot running water! Even she was impressed. The Stronghold did not indulge in such luxuries. For the first time she wondered why the church, devoted to serving the T'En, should allow its members this kind of luxury. A niggling worm of disquiet troubled her. The Aayel's talk of the Beatific returned to Imoshen.

But the Beatific was far away in T'Diemn and she was here in Landsend.

Imoshen sank into the water, reveling in its heat. She washed her hair with scented soap. It was a luxury to be clean. After delaying as long as she could she climbed out and dried herself.

Taking her time, she inspected the bruises caused by her fall when Tulkhan tackled her. Her heart still thudded when she recalled how her life had hung in the balance.

Yet, for a moment when they looked out over Landsend she'd felt he shared her vision. She'd seen the leap of understanding in his eyes. Then he had thrust her aside. Just when she thought there was something more to him, he had proved her wrong.

As for that kiss!

Her lips tingled and her body thrummed with the memory. She had to admit he had moved her, but the man was such an odd mixture of scholar and barbarian! He could learn a country's language before invading it, then be forced to cloak his surprise when he saw the Abbey Seculate was a woman.

What must he think of her!

Imoshen stalked from the mosaic-tiled bathing room into her chamber. Tightening the drawstring of her nightgown under her breasts, she knelt in front of the fire, enjoying its warmth. Methodically, she spread her hair over her fingers to dry it.

She would not think about him.

Yet, the General had withstood the effects of that ancient evil. He'd pretended scorn after their encounter but she sensed he'd been unnerved, even a little frightened by what he'd experienced. She had been truly afraid for a moment, afraid that he would attack her, that she would have to fight for her life and it wouldn't have been him she was fighting. Imoshen tried not to dwell on her strange reluctance to hurt him.

Somehow Tulkhan had found the strength of will to throw off the ancient power's domination. Her hands slowed as she finger-combed her hair. She could tell he disliked being out of control. He was truly a man of rational thought, a man ahead of his time, ahead of his own people. Not that he wasn't a barbarian, she amended, then grinned, aware of her twisted logic.

The Aayel had said he was a man trapped by his own culture. The General could barely believe her great-aunt was a threat to him. From what she had overheard, Imoshen knew the Ghebite religion regarded the ''Dhamfeer'' as less than human. Though Tulkhan was a contradiction, a soldier who strove to learn he was still a product of his upbringing. He would have been taught to despise the T'En and their innate powers, that must be why he feared her. Imoshen frowned.

She was still his captive, for all that the Seculate had presented her with this room and had asked her to perform the ceremony over the meal tonight.

Yet Tulkhan feared her?

She shook her head wearily. Too much had happened.

The fire was warm and she spread her hair to dry, running her fingers through the thick waves which hung past her waist. She wouldn't think about him again.

Perversely, her mind presented her with a picture of General Tulkhan watching her during the meal tonight. Twice she had caught him staring, his gaze calculating, weighing. She knew he didn't trust her, she was too well liked by the people. Her life hung by a thread. Imoshen shivered, despite the fire. Yet, the desire in Tulkhan's eyes had been real enough tonight. There had been no mistaking his intention when he kissed her.

A soft click made Imoshen turn. Her heart thudded uneasily in her chest. As she scanned the room, she saw a panel beside the fireplace eased slowly apart.

Light-footed, she darted over to the traveling bag and drew out her knife as the panel opened. A figure stood in the darkness of the secret passage.

Imoshen lifted the knife, prepared to use it. Should she throw and risk missing a fatal blow or wait till she could aim for the attacker's heart?

A soft chuckle made her skin prickle.

Reothe stepped into the dim glow of the firelight. He was dressed in battle gear but had discarded his armor, leaving only leggings and chest leather. His slender, sinewy arms were bare and his narrow, intelligent face watched her closely. The fine silver tendrils of his hair glistened in the firelight as he moved toward her, one side of his mouth lifted in a mocking smile.

"If you mean to use that knife throw it now, because I'll disarm you if you let me get within arm's length," he warned.

"This knife isn't for you." She found his assurance annoying, but her body reacted to him as it had once before. What was it about him that made her heart race and her head swim?

She let the knife point drop with an odd reluctance and he smiled, his eyes brilliant pools in his pale face.

"You don't seem surprised to see me? Did you guess I'd survived?"

"Hardly. General Tulkhan—"

"Tulkhan? That northern usurper?" His harsh tone made her wince. Suddenly he stepped nearer, still not touching her, but close enough for his breath to stir the fine hairs on her forehead. "I've been thinking of you. Imagining you.

We would have been bonded this spring if the Ghebites hadn't invaded. Now I'm a renegade, my estates forfeited and you're a captive—but I've come for you.''

Imoshen swallowed, trying to concentrate. His scent was achingly familiar, reminding her of the day they took the oath of betrothal—how his eyes had consumed her, how he had promised to bond to her and no other.

Reothe represented her people, her loyalty was to him and her family, her land. Wasn't it?

He lifted one long hand and pulled undone the drawstring at her throat so that the neck of her garment loosened and slid over her shoulders to hang below her breasts, where the second drawstring held it in place. She heard his sharp intake of breath and felt her skin tighten. Her nipples hardened under his gaze. A wanton heat suffused her, confused her.

When he spoke his voice was deeper, thicker. ''I've lain awake in the fields, hidden in caves and imagined you like this, imagined claiming you. You gave your word and I gave mine. I've come for you.''

''What, now?''

''Now! You must come away with me. I'll take you south. I have followers who are loyal, contacts in the southern kingdoms who will help me raise an army as well as friends on the islands of the archipelago. Come spring we can return to retake our island. We'll drive these Ghebite barbarians out!''

Imoshen's head swam. She hadn't considered raising an army of mercenaries. Was it possible to retake their land, to fight at Reothe's side?

He snatched her hand and took the knife. Lifting its sharp blade to his lips he kissed it.

Imoshen swallowed. No, he couldn't mean to make a formal bond here and now.

''With my blood,'' he breathed and slit his left wrist, the one nearest his heart. ''I vow to bond only unto you, Imoshen of the T'En.''

She stared dumbfounded as the blood oozed from the

cut, gathering momentum. He lifted her left hand. Suddenly she knew she didn't want this.

"No."

"Yes." His voice was implacable. "I made a promise to your family, to you."

She gasped as the blade cut through the flesh of her left wrist and he pressed the two wounds together.

"By the joining of our blood, by the breath in my body, I cleave to you." His fierce eyes held hers. He gave their bonded wrists a little shake. "Say it. Say the vow. I have a boat waiting in a hidden cove below. We can escape through the passage to the sea—"

"I can't do it!" The words were torn from her.

"Why not?"

"I can't leave them now." Imoshen felt a rush of heat take her as she thought not of the people who trusted her but of General Tulkhan as he listened so intently to her language lessons. "If I go now the people will think me false. They will revolt and the Ghebites will turn on them. The harvest will fail, blood will stain the fields and starvation will stalk the snows. Better I stay and be the General's prisoner, a guarantee of their behavior, than leave them to their fate."

"Farmers?" he repeated incredulously. "I'm offering you a chance to retake our lands, to drive the Ghebite General and his army out."

"More fighting, more bloodshed and what will the people eat? Will you war till not a house stands, till weeds cover the fields because no one is left to plow them? No!" She wrenched her wrist away and grasped it to stop the flow of blood. She needed to bind it and take something against the poisons getting into her system.

"We made a vow."

"In another world. When my family lived and—"

He grabbed her around the waist, lifting her off her feet, so that she felt his hard thighs against hers and how much he wanted her.

"I made a vow," he ground out. "I don't go back on my word, Imoshen."

"I can't do it. I pledged my word to the General, the people trust me, they depend on me."

"Your word to General Tulkhan?" He gave an odd, strangled laugh. "What is the word of a captive? What choice did you have? You aren't bound by it. Our vow stands true, it is of an older making."

She watched the blood from her wrist trickle down across the muscle of his shoulder so that it appeared he was bleeding. He was probably staining her gown. Her breasts pressed against the leather of his jerkin and she could smell his unique male scent. Her head spun with an intoxicating passion. What was it about Reothe that called to her? Was it because he was one of her own kind?

His voice changed, softened. "You want me, don't deny it. Come away with me now."

Before she knew he meant to, he lowered his head and inhaled her scent, a ragged groan escaped him. His involuntary moan made her body shudder, then his lips were on hers and it was like the other time in the woods, only this time she was as good as naked with nothing but a thin gown fixed under her breasts. He did not restrain himself, he devoured her.

Did he hope the force of his passion would convince her, obliterate all but his will?

His passion frightened her, ignited her. His scent was so familiar, all the things she had learned about him before returned as if some deep inner truth were being confirmed.

"Imoshen," he breathed her name, his lips on hers. "You can't stay here."

"I can't leave my people." This time it was a plea for understanding. "They need me."

He uttered a groan and let her weight slide down his body till her toes touched the ground, then he released her and stepped back. She could see what it cost him to maintain his control. Right at this moment her body raged against her mind.

"You have a hard head, Imoshen."

"I must—"

"What about your heart? The honor of your family?"

"I . . ." she swallowed. "Practicality guides me. Honor is useless if you're dead and . . . and I have no heart."

He nearly laughed. "A lie. Very well. I will come again."

"No! They'll catch you and kill you!"

This time he did laugh. "I'm going now, but I'll be back—and next time I'll claim you and take you with me!"

He caught her wrist and pressed it against his, reaffirming the bond. His eyes held hers.

Imoshen felt her body yearn for him, but she refused to succumb to the power of his will. "I haven't taken the vow."

"I have. I knew you were meant for me when I saw you in the palace. Then when I came to the Stronghold last autumn I felt it in my body and you did too."

"No, no I—"

"Don't bother to deny it." He lifted her wrist to his mouth and she thought he was going to kiss her wound, but he closed his eyes. "Seal flesh."

Then ran his tongue across the torn flesh.

A flash of heat stung her and she snatched her hand from his. There was a new pale pink scar on the fine white skin of her inner wrist where the wound had been.

She gasped. "How did you do that?"

His wine-dark eyes which were so like hers, held her gaze. "There's much I could teach you. We're the last of our kind, we can't let our line die out, we can't let the knowledge and the gifts die with us."

He lifted his own wrist and held it to her face. "Heal me."

"I . . . I can't—"

"Nonsense. You can do it. Heal me."

Tentatively she caught his hand, feeling the bones, the strength in him. She turned his wrist to her mouth and touched the tip of her tongue to his wound, tasting his blood as she drew along the torn skin. In her mind's eye she saw the skin closing, sealing. When she looked again, a fine pale scar closed his bonding-wound.

"It's healed!"

"It will never heal until you lie with me and complete the vows. I still bleed, but you can't see it, Imoshen."

This time when he lifted her face she knew he was going to kiss her and she found a strange reluctance grip her. His mouth was firm, his tongue tasted of blood and she knew he must be able to taste his blood on her tongue. She felt a surge of fear. Suddenly, he was a feral creature, implacable and alien.

She was afraid of him. What else could he do? Did he know what his body did to hers? Obviously he had recognized it long before she did. She didn't like being at a disadvantage. It was frightening not knowing the extent of another's ability, not knowing if they were manipulating you.

In a flash the thought came to her—no wonder Tulkhan feared her.

Reothe pulled away from her. His eyes narrowed and she knew he had sensed her thoughts.

She opened her mouth but hesitated as his lips set in a hard, implacable line.

"What double game are you playing, Imoshen?"

"I . . . nothing." She felt at a loss, a child caught in an adult's game. "I seek only the best for my people."

Noises in the hall alerted them. There was so much left unsaid. The door creaked on its hinges.

Reothe gave her an intense look which promised this was unfinished. Then he darted through the narrow panel, ducking his head to pass into the passage. The wood slid shut.

Imoshen pulled up her gown and kept her back to the fire to hide the bloodstains from his bonding-wound. She could still smell his scent on the air, on her skin, but her maidservant wasn't so sensitive. Imoshen could tell Kalleen was weary as she gave her pithy opinion of the Abbey, of Wharrd.

She offered her services to Imoshen who refused, saying she wanted to sit up a little longer. Kalleen curled up on the low bed at the foot of Imoshen's bed. Within minutes she was fast asleep.

Thoughtfully, Imoshen dropped her gown to the floor

and studied the bloodstains on the small of her back where Reothe had held her. She lifted the material to her face and inhaled his scent.

He was her other self. Her loyalty should be to him and to her family, to regaining the kingdom, yet she could not abandon the people of Fair Isle. She was torn—she'd given her word to General Tulkhan.

Her word? She had also given Reothe her word and all but made the vow of bonding. What was wrong with her? Opposing loyalties clawed at her. She felt as if she would tear in two. What could she do? She tossed the gown into the fire and watched it burn, the flames casting shadows across her naked, pearly white flesh.

It seemed symbolic—the burning of her innocence. She knew whatever path she took one of the two men would grow to hate her, and one of them would die.

FOUR

IMOSHEN LIFTED HER hand and looked at the wound on her wrist. Reothe had been right. She had healed him after he had done the same for her. She would not have thought it possible. Perhaps that type of healing would not work on True-men and women, perhaps it was only effective because of their racial affinity?

Frustration gripped Imoshen. Because her parents had kept her birthright from her, forbidding the Aayel to instruct her in T'En ways, there was so much she did not know and Reothe did. He'd had longer to hone his natural skills, but healing had always been her gift. His skill surprised her.

Was he more gifted than she? The Aayel's fearful voice returned to Imoshen as she described how she had witnessed the stoning of the rogue male T'En. He had captured the Aayel, invaded her mind and forced her to experience his pain. His death had nearly been hers. How cruel he had been. Imoshen felt anger on behalf of the twelve-year-old child her great-aunt had been. She might sneer at the Ghebites but she must not forget it wasn't so long ago that her own people had practiced barbarism.

Her great-aunt had had good cause to fear that rogue T'En male. Now Imoshen understood why the Aayel had chosen to absent herself during Reothe's visit.

Did the Aayel have a good reason to fear Reothe? Surely not.

Imoshen shivered. She would not rest until she knew the

extent of Reothe's gifts and how to defend herself from him. He had all but read her mind! She hated knowing her thoughts were open to him.

Was that how the General felt?

Her hair was almost dry. Feeling strangely distant, she separated the long strands and began to plait them together. As she did, a flicker of firelight reflected on the knife blade, attracting her eye.

Imoshen flushed.

Reothe had challenged her to use it, knowing she wouldn't. He had risked his life to come back for her. She owed him something. Yet his intensity frightened her. When he held her, she couldn't think clearly.

Was he trying to force his will on hers by subtle use of his powers? Her skin went cold at the thought.

Had her confusion been caused by the strength of his gifts and not by her natural response to him? Had he chosen her from the first because she was susceptible to him?

Being a Throwback she had searched the Stronghold library for works which predated the first T'Imoshen's invasion of Fair Isle. But there was very little information on the T'En. What she did find was too obscure to be useful.

It appeared that there had been great workers of the T'En gifts in their ancient homeland, but the histories were strangely silent on exactly what these gifts had been.

Yet the Aayel had said the T'En gifts were poor, unreliable things, that those who used them unwisely faced the wrath of the church—their church—which was supposed to revere the T'En.

Imoshen shuddered, recalling the Aayel's eyes as she spoke of the stoning. The horror of that event had stayed with her for over a century, coloring her actions for the rest of her life.

Anger flashed through Imoshen and she directed it toward the long dead Beatific who had ordered the Aayel to witness the stoning. She understood that it had been a precautionary measure to ensure the young Aayel's cooperation, but the consequences were far more damaging to a young child. If its purpose was to ensure that the T'En would remain repressed, then it had succeeded.

Was the church protecting the people of Fair Isle from the T'En? Imoshen shivered. Suddenly, she felt very alone.

All her life she had been an object of curiosity. The people were both fearful and fascinated by her. It had been a burden she bore with growing resentment. But perhaps the True-men and women had good reason to fear the T'En? She did not know. So few Throwbacks had been born, only two in the last one hundred years . . .

No, it was all a fabrication of her overtired mind. She was no monster and neither was Reothe. They might have small useful gifts, but these benefited True-man and T-En alike. Her priority was to ensure her own survival under a barbarian invader.

Imoshen kept her own counsel while at Landsend Abbey. She performed her duties, but remained aloof from Tulkhan and the abbey seniors because she knew for Reothe to have access to the abbey's secret passages one or more of the abbey leaders must know of his presence, the Seculate herself might have sided with her betrothed.

Did they despise her, consider her a traitor?

Was she a traitor?

The return journey was made swiftly. Already, loaded wagons of grain were wending their way to the Stronghold to be stored and cataloged. Imoshen knew there was work ahead of her.

The easy companionship which had developed on their ride out was gone. Tulkhan's Elite Guard watched her closely. Had they heard a rumor of Reothe's visit? Was she condemned without trial? Imoshen didn't know what to think.

Should she have run away with Reothe when she had the chance to save her own life, even though it meant deserting the people who trusted her? Again, Imoshen had no answer.

They entered the Stronghold late one afternoon on a cool, autumn day which held a foretaste of the winter to come. When the Aayel came out to greet her, Imoshen tried to mask her disquiet but her great-aunt sensed it. General Tulkhan did not exchange one word with her as he rode off to the stables with his men.

"You're chilled to the bone. Come inside, Shenna." The Aayel led Imoshen to her chambers where the servants waited.

It was all so normal, so soothing—an illusion. But Imoshen let them fuss over her, glad to relinquish all responsibility this once.

The Aayel dismissed the women then sprinkled healing herbs in the hot water. While Imoshen bathed, she sat and watched.

"It did not go well?"

"It did at first. I learned a great deal. He is not a stupid man."

The Aayel gave a snort. "So, you discovered that!"

"But he's stubborn and he hates . . . no, fears me."

"So he should. You could be the death of him and the downfall of his hold on Fair Isle."

Imoshen gnawed her bottom lip. Should she tell the Aayel about Reothe and the dual tug of the familiar against the unknown? She desperately wanted the Aayel to confirm that she had made the right decision. Imoshen stole a look at the wizened old woman. Would she look like that in a hundred years from now?

She almost laughed—she should live that long!

The Aayel watched her, silent, weighing but uncritical. It was reassuring.

"I've been taking the potion," Imoshen said.

"I know. I can see it in you. You're blooming with health, with fertility. Perhaps that is why the General is distancing himself from you. He fights his instincts."

Imoshen grimaced. She was not so hopeful. Her instincts were totally confused. Duty and the General, or duty and Reothe?

As she stood and took the drying cloth from her great-aunt, the old woman's hands brushed hers.

"What has Reothe to do with this?" the Aayel demanded suddenly.

Imoshen opened her mouth to lie but she couldn't. Instead, she lowered her voice. "Reothe entered the Abbey. I believe he has a supporter or two there. He came to my room. He . . ." She felt suddenly vulnerable because she did not understand her confusion. Why was she drawn to him? To hide this she dried herself vigorously. "He wanted to bond with me. He tried to perform the ceremony, but I wouldn't give him my vow, wouldn't flee with him.

"I told him I had to stay for the people. He said I was betraying them by not leaving with him to help raise an army to retake Fair Isle. But I had to refuse. It tore me in two!" She tossed the cloth aside, lifting her hands to the Aayel in supplication. "I've been going over and over it. One moment I think I have failed the memory of my family, yet I feel I cannot fail the people. Please, tell me—did I do right to refuse him?"

The Aayel ran her paper-dry fingers down Imoshen's cheek. "He is very gifted, that Reothe." Her sharp eyes held Imoshen's. "What do you feel?"

"I don't know!" She turned and walked away from the Aayel toward the fire. The warmth attracted her, but she also used the movement to cloak her intimate feelings. She hardly dared admit to herself this secret yearning for Reothe. It seemed a weakness because it made her vulnerable to him and she could not afford to let anything but cool, rational thought guide her decisions, not if she was to survive this crucial time. "He calls to something in me, but he frightens me."

"Your instincts are good. I knew his parents, their parents and their parents. There is bad blood in his family, a brilliance, but also an unsteadiness. It sometimes surfaces in the pure T'En. His mother and father were first cousins. They were scholars of history. I know despite the concerns of their family they bonded to keep the blood pure. They risked social stigma to bring Reothe into the world. I suspect that is why he wants you, you're so obviously of the pure race.''

Was it true? Was that the only reason Reothe wanted her? Would his body call to hers with such ferocity of purpose if it was only a logical choice? Instinct told Imoshen his need for her went deeper than logic.

She dropped her nightgown over her head and pulled the drawstrings. "You didn't answer me. Who should have my loyalty, my betrothed who wants to rekindle a war, or the people who want only a chance to live out their lives free from war? And what of General Tulkhan? He is the invader, yet I have given him my word. Reothe said a vow given under duress is no vow at all, that my betrothal promise to him is of an older making. I want to do the right thing but . . . Tell me, what should I do?"

Imoshen turned hopefully to the Aayel. Surely her great-aunt would vindicate the decisions she had made?

"There are no easy answers, child." The old woman poured the potion. "You must survive, concentrate on that. You are blooming. Drink."

Imoshen downed the fluid. Was there a visible physical difference in her? Her breasts had grown more sensitive. She felt impatient with those around her and during their tour of the villages she had caught herself watching General Tulkhan when he moved through the ranks, when he prowled around the fire circle. She liked the way his body moved and she couldn't help recalling how he had pinned her to the ground, his arms around her thighs, his weight on her.

Imoshen gave an impatient snort.

She had one desperate gamble, one throw of the dice in another three days. Maybe her heightened sensitivity, the slight change in her scent, the slight ache in her core were all her imagination, and the potion wouldn't work. Then what would she do?

Imoshen returned the empty vial to the Aayel. "I want you to try a scrying. I must know if I am doing the right thing!"

The old woman sighed. "It doesn't work like that. It's never that simple—"

"I must know. This is tearing me apart."

Imoshen stiffened as the Aayel signaled her to lower her voice. The old woman sighed. "Very well. Bring me my scrying platter."

She hurried to obey.

When she returned Imoshen knelt at the old woman's knee, her heart pounding. What would she learn? Would she see herself with Tulkhan or with Reothe? Should she lead her country into war, or keep the peace with the Invader at a price almost too steep to bear?

The Aayel scooped up a handful of the scented bath water.

"Bath water?" Imoshen wrinkled her nose.

"It's your future," her great-aunt muttered dryly.

Imoshen lifted the knife she had selected for this purpose and pricked her finger, adding two drops of her own blood. She had noticed any working of the gifts was stronger if blood was spilled, and the more you gave of yourself the more you got back in return.

The Aayel stiffened.

"I have to know," she defended her actions. "I don't care what the price is."

"Don't be too quick to make that claim, Shenna," the Aayel muttered, swirling the water around on the plate to mix the blood. "You don't know the price the gifts may demand."

Imoshen tensed. Did she read some hidden knowledge there? Was the Aayel hinting that the gifts had more potential than she had previously claimed? An unwelcome thought came to Imoshen.

Had the Aayel deliberately kept a deeper, more potent form of knowledge from her in an attempt to control her?

"Take it."

The Aayel interrupted her brooding. Automatically, Imoshen accepted the scrying plate. "Me?"

"It's your scrying, your future. Take responsibility for it."

Controlling her instinctive resentment of the implied criticism, Imoshen concentrated as she tilted the scrying platter this way and that, observing the thin film of water which covered its surface.

Nothing! She was useless.

No. She had to know. Gritting her teeth, Imoshen peered through the film to the platter's reflective surface, searching for a form, a hint. Nothing.

"What do you see?" she asked the Aayel.

"What do *you* see?"

"Me? I am no good at scrying—"

"And never will be, if that's the attitude you take!"

Stung by her great-aunt's tone, Imoshen focused. At first she only saw the glint of candle flames distorted by the thin film of water in the shining metal of the platter.

"Bring to mind what concerns you. Guide it," the Aayel whispered.

Imoshen nodded. She had to know if her decision was the right one.

Her heart lurched as the General's broad features appeared. His coppery skin darkened, flushing with anger and exertion. He grimaced and dodged as someone struck at him. In rapid succession more and more figures attacked.

"They'll kill him!"

"What do you see?" the Aayel pressed.

"The General. He's being attacked in a narrow hall. They look like our people." Imoshen gasped as one of the assassins leapt forward shouting a name. "Reothe!"

"Is Reothe there?"

"No, they attack in his name."

"Assassins?"

Imoshen shuddered, water slopping onto her nightgown.

The Aayel took the platter and tipped the remaining water into the tub. She used her apron to dry the surface. "So."

Imoshen felt cheated. "But I don't know any more than I did before!"

Her great-aunt shrugged. "Now do you believe me? Scrying is not an exact science. Concentrate on what you do know. The General desires you—"

Imoshen made a noise in her throat. "He hates me—"

"He wants you. I can see it in him. True?"

She nodded reluctantly. "But he also hates and fears me."

" 'Twould be worse if he were indifferent." The old woman seemed pleased. "You must seduce him three days from now when we host the Harvest Feast. You know what the people will want that evening, a formal consummation."

"No!" Imoshen was shocked.

The Aayel shrugged philosophically. "It is an old custom and most cultures have something like it to ensure the fertility of their fields the following spring."

"But we've never taken part in that side of the festivities. We left it to the people to choose the male and female to consecrate the—"

"So?"

Imoshen folded her arms. "I won't do it. I . . . I've never even lain with a man!" She flushed. "I wouldn't know what to do!"

Birdlike, her great-aunt tilted her head. "You've had the lessons—"

Imoshen snorted helplessly.

Suddenly the old woman gripped her arm, eyes intense. "Don't live a life bounded by fear like I did. Seize the moment."

Imoshen licked her lips reluctantly. "Tell me how to go about it."

The old woman gave a hoot of laughter. "You ask me? By law I had to remain celibate or risk death."

"Didn't you . . . I mean, weren't you tempted? Did you never love someone enough to—"

"Risk death for the love of a man?" the old woman mocked.

Imoshen watched her great-aunt and wondered what memories caused the bitterness in her voice.

"Maybe I was too comfortable, too timid to risk everything for love. But you . . . you have nothing to lose and everything to gain." The Aayel gripped Imoshen's hand. "This is your great gamble and you will only get one throw of the dice. If the General suspects you are manipulating him he will react badly."

Imoshen shuddered. She did not need her great-aunt to spell out what she meant. "Very well. But all I have is theoretical knowledge. I am not very experienced. Should I lie with—"

"No!"

"It was only a thought. I will never succeed in seducing him. He despises me." Imoshen felt her face grow hot.

"He burns for you."

"He has a strange way of showing it!" she snapped, feeling cornered. Resentment seared her. She wasn't ready for this. Life had been simple before General Tulkhan and his Ghebite army invaded.

"What if he rejects me?" Imoshen whispered.

The Aayel said nothing.

Imoshen felt her body flood with heat. General Tulkhan cast a wall of indifference between them, yet she would be lying if she did not admit to sensing his attraction to her. As much as she hated to admit it, the same reluctant desire for him burned in her.

"Listen not to what he tells you, but to what his body says," the old woman advised her and would say nothing more.

Everyone had pitched in to bring in the grain before the snows came. The harvesting was nearly over. The weather watchers forecast an early, bitter winter and already there were frosts in the hollows of the morning.

With most of the army out in the fields those who remained behind in the Stronghold were busy cleaning out the grain stores and performing the usual winter preparations.

Ten times a day the Stronghold servants came to General Tulkhan asking directions. His own men waited to be told their tasks. Trained from childhood in the arts of war, he suddenly faced the task of ordering the lives of a thousand people, administering to the needs of a small civilian army.

He found himself constantly referring to the Aayel and to Imoshen, who had been raised for this responsibility. Indeed, the Dhamfeer seemed able to keep a dozen strands of thought in her head, to know instinctively which tasks needed priority, much as he would have done on the battlefield. He saw her as a general in times of peace. Before he knew it, she was his right hand, running the Stronghold and half his Elite Guard.

Tulkhan watched with a growing sense of satisfaction as the wagons rolled in, heavily laden with grain. In the courtyard his men were working side by side with the people and the Stronghold Guard.

He was surprised by the pleasure this simple yet vital task provided him. In the past he had left the day-to-day tasks to underlings. He'd moved on once a nation had been conquered and his curiosity about their culture had been satisfied. His administrative involvement had gone only as far as selecting places for forts and garrisoning them. Intent on taking the next country, he'd been happy to leave the holding of the conquered lands to the administrators appointed by the king.

Now he realized that to conquer was one thing, to hold was another.

He turned toward the stairs. When the Stronghold was built six hundred years ago, access to these storerooms, which were designed to double as prisons, had been through a hole in the ceiling and a ladder. But over time the inhabitants of the Stronghold had sacrificed defensibility for practicality. He had seen evidence of similar compromises over and over during his inspection of the Stronghold.

The walls of the original circular keep were three times as thick as a man was tall with no windows or doors on the ground floor. It had been designed primarily to repel attack, with only the third and fourth floors set aside for living quarters. But as the Stronghold grew, its role became less vital and it was reduced to one tower of many. Once the T'En hold on Fair Isle was more secure the defenders had enlarged the Strongholds, joining outer walls with battlement walks to the keep, and reducing its defensibility. However, all of these battlements between the towers could still be isolated by dropping the collapsible walks which circled the towers, so that if one section of the Stronghold's walls were breached

this area could be cut off and the threat from attackers mini-
mized.

Tulkhan had made a point of studying the defenses of
every country he traveled through and the Stronghold impressed him. Running water piped up from an underground
reservoir was supplied to every floor of the new section. The
reservoir was filled by a stream which had been diverted
about four hundred years ago when the new section was
built.

Before this their water had come from a well. This
stretched down below ground level to a depth of four stories,
all dressed with stone, with foot and hand holds to the water
level. Tulkhan knew because he had climbed down there.

He had also instructed Imoshen to show him the main
gate defenses. Access holes had been provided above the
outer gates so that the Stronghold Guards could pour water if
potential invaders tried to set fire to the wooden gates. Reinforced with iron bands, these outer gates opened into a long
passage that ended with the inner gates. The portcullis at
each end could be dropped to trap invaders in the passage
and the holes in the ceiling opened so that the Stronghold
guards could pour scalding water or boiling oil or shoot ar-
rows into their attackers. If the invaders made it into the
courtyard this turned sharply so that they were forced to
present their unshielded right sides to attack.

Even when the new section of the Stronghold had been
built all access to the buildings had been from the second
floor, with stairs so steep attackers could easily be sent crashing to the cobbled courtyards below.

He had seen the more recent additions, the broadened
steps with stone balustrades. He had seen where lower floors
had been opened for ease of access. Tulkhan had personally
walked every passage of the Stronghold, the old, the new and
the additions to the new.

It was the same story all over Fair Isle—towns had out-
grown their fortified walls and the inhabitants had not bothered to build new ones or maintain the old. This was what
four hundred years of peace did to a people. It made them
soft.

Tulkhan's old tutor had spoken the truth when he said that all things being equal it was not the strength of the defenses, but the strength of the defenders' hearts that decided a castle's fate. If all of Fair Isle had had Imoshen's passion for freedom, his task would have been nearly impossible.

Where was she now? Ordering his Elite Guard about, no doubt.

He cursed softly. Over the past few days he had experienced a strange restlessness. Even now something that was more than hunger gnawed at him. He felt irritable, tired because he couldn't sleep at night with both moons nearly full. It was almost as bright as day, but this had never bothered him in the past.

Despite his best efforts he could not avoid Imoshen as she worked beside her people in the granaries, taking stock of what had come in, offering receipts to the farms, organizing places for the constant stream of refugees from the north. As his men returned from the harvest and the new arrivals flooded in, the plains below the Stronghold became dotted with makeshift houses. Smoke from their fires filled the sky day and night. The Stronghold had become the center of a town which rivaled the island's capital, T'Diemn.

With a sixth sense acquired through years of living with death, Tulkhan suddenly froze. He had entered a stone passage which led from the courtyard to the granaries. In the distance he could hear the people working, their voices raised in an ancient chant.

The hairs on the back of his neck lifted. There it was—a furtive step. Assassins?

Before he could back up they were upon him. Two men, one woman. From their garb, he guessed they were escaped soldiers of the Emperor's army. The nearest lunged, his dirk passing harmlessly through the thick wadding of the General's jerkin.

Tulkhan cursed himself for a fool. He was unarmed. Twisting the man's hand he kneed him in the face, tearing the knife from his fingers. The woman lunged for him with a knife, screaming a name. Her suicidal leap would have had him, but at the last instant he managed to twist from under her and felt her land heavily on the dirk. It was torn from his fingers, now slick with blood, as the third uninjured attacker leapt in with a short, pointed weapon which Tulkhan knew by custom carried poison. One scratch and he would die a lingering death.

There was no time for nicety. Grunting with the effort, he thrust the woman's body between them and saw her jolt as she took the spike in her back.

Clenching his fist, he thumped the man in the side of the head even as the first one leapt on his back. He heard the thunder of feet in the passage as his own guard arrived. They hauled the man off his back and slit his throat in an excess of zeal before Tulkhan could question him.

The last attacker turned to flee, but a dagger thrown by one of his guards caught him between the shoulder blades.

Panting with the exertion, Tulkhan looked at the bodies.

It was as he feared. The name on the woman's lips as she leapt, intent on his death at the cost of her own life, was "T'Reothe," rumored to be the leader of the rebels.

Silencing the angry comments of his Elite Guard he indicated the bodies. "Bring them into the courtyard. Send for the Aayel and Imoshen."

Imoshen knew by the smack of metal and the sharp thump of boots that this was no ordinary summoning. Kalleen ran into the room gasping something about an assassination attempt on General Tulkhan.

"What?" Imoshen's first thought was to consult the Aayel but fear closed her throat so that she could not speak. She crossed the room and knelt beside her great-aunt's chair, silently seeking reassurance.

The Aayel would know what to do.

The old woman clutched her hand. "Time has run out, Shenna. I thought we had longer. There is so much I did not tell you. I'd meant to—"

Imoshen's heart sank as the Elite Guard marched

through the open doors. Without deference they ordered
Imoshen and the Aayel out.

Their leader would not meet her eyes. He knows, she
thought. The General means to have us killed!

But she came to her feet with outward dignity, while
inside she raged at the unfairness of it. Another two days and
she could have spun her web.

Imoshen helped the Aayel to stand. She realized her
great-aunt was playing for time. The old woman walked
slowly as if weighed down by her great age.

Imoshen's mind whirled with images, half-formed plans.
Should she have warned General Tulkhan about the scrying?
It had been on the tip of her tongue so many times, but she
knew how he held such things in contempt. He might even
have assumed she knew something of the plot, or worse still,
was the instigator. In the end she had kept her own counsel.

She took a deep breath and stiffened her back. Come
what may, she would not beg.

Kalleen would have accompanied them, but the Elite
Guard pushed her aside.

They were led downstairs. Imoshen imagined the great
hall where the General would have them summarily executed.
Now she would never have her chance to seduce him, to save
her people from servitude. She should have run with Reothe
when she had the opportunity!

What? And left the Aayel to die alone?

As if sensing Imoshen's thoughts, the Aayel squeezed
her hand.

To Imoshen's surprise they were led out into the courtyard, where a sea of faces turned to them, refugees from the
north, loyal locals returned with their harvest, the household
servants and Stronghold Guard—and the Ghebites.

General Tulkhan did not meet her eyes as he leapt onto
an empty dray and signaled for quiet. He indicated the parapets where, much to her horror, she saw three round objects,
heads.

"Rebels!" he roared, and there was a hushed intake of
breath from the crowd.

Imoshen's thoughts spun. No traitors' heads had been

spiked there for hundreds of years. Nausea swept over her. These Ghebites were barbarians. Truly, she and the Aayel were about to die.

A buzzing filled her head as the General shouted something about treachery and death to all those who opposed him. He paced on the dray's boards, all eyes drawn to him.

With bravado he told how, unarmed, he had fought off three armed attackers. She realized it would become part of the mythology which surrounded him. Even the locals and her household guard were in awe of him.

Suddenly he turned to the captives and indicated they were to come forward. The men who surrounded Imoshen pushed her in the back. They would have lifted her bodily onto the dray, but she thrust their hands aside and leapt lightly up, her heart hammering.

With great deliberation she turned and helped the Aayel, steadying her as the men thrust her up. There was a concerted hush, an inarticulate moan from those loyal to the old empire.

Imoshen looked out over the sea of faces. Sections of the crowd were shifting uneasily. The camaraderie of the harvest was forgotten.

So she was to die here, slaughtered like a pig by a butcher in the courtyard of her family's Stronghold. She never imagined herself dying except with a weapon in her hand. She cursed. If the truth be told she'd never imagined herself dying!

The General was speaking, and she tried to concentrate.

". . . amongst you who would cling to the old rulers, who do not accept my right of conquest!" General Tulkhan raised one hand. "The old ways are dead. Know this."

He drew his ceremonial dagger. Someone shrieked.

The crowd surged forward. Instinct told Imoshen they were on the verge of revolt. Tulkhan must have sensed it too, because for an instant his eyes met hers in silent understanding.

Whereas this morning the locals and Stronghold Guard had worked beside the Elite Guard laughing, singing as the food was stored, now the people stood circling the dray, their work tools raised as weapons.

If the General put Imoshen and the Aayel to the sword, not only their blood would stain the courtyard stones.

Tulkhan knew it. His hold was tenuous. Here, in the packed courtyard, hand-to-hand combat would be butchery. The resentment which seethed just beneath the surface would erupt into outright rebellion. It was conceivable that he could be brought down and killed in the melée. He could lose the jewel in the crown, Fair Isle, and his very life.

Yet, all his experience told him the last of the royal house must die. He turned to the two women, one on the verge of life, the other older than he believed possible.

Imoshen's face was blanched white, her lips compressed. As the Stronghold Guard surged forward, the General caught a flicker of anticipation and realized she did not intend to let him kill her without a fight. She meant to precipitate a rebellion, and she would take him down with her. He acknowledged this with a flash of admiration.

There it was—he had to kill them both, yet the minute he raised the knife he was a dead man. The crowd would riot, the stones would run with blood. He saw no way out of this dilemma.

A withered hand pushed Imoshen aside and the Aayel met his eyes. She stepped forward, her hand extended.

Tulkhan looked from her hand to her shrewd, implacable face.

"Your code demands a death to assuage the dishonor of this attack," the Aayel stated simply.

"Yes."

"No!" Imoshen hissed as she realized what the Aayel intended. "I won't let you—"

Those old eyes turned to her. "You have no control over my actions. This is the only path and my chance to die with honor!"

Imoshen watched her great-aunt extend her hand for the knife. The General gave it to her.

The Aayel lifted the ceremonial dagger high, her thin voice carrying in the sudden hush. "I release you from all guilt and take on the guilt of those who attacked the General.''

Imoshen wanted to scream against the injustice of it. It was only with a supreme effort of will that she remained outwardly impassive. Inside she was reeling though her feet remained rooted to the spot. Her heart thudded thunderously in her ears.

In a movement too swift to anticipate, the Aayel plunged the knife up under her own ribs, committing ritual suicide.

A terrible cry, an outpouring of raw and angry pain, rose from the crowd. The Aayel had seen the oldest of them born, she had seen their parents born and buried—she was a living historical link to their communal past.

And now she was gone.

Tulkhan stepped forward but Imoshen thrust him aside, catching the frail old body in her arms. She sensed the life leave the old woman on a whisper of a breath.

How could this be? How could someone so intense and knowledgeable pass from this world to the next with so little sign?

"She died well," Tulkhan said softly.

Imoshen met his eyes and spat her words at him. "She saved your skin, barbarian."

She saw him flinch but did not care. He went to take the Aayel from her.

"No. This has to be done properly to honor the dead." Amazingly, she was dry-eyed, though inside she was weeping. Raising her voice she shouted over the rising babble of the crowd. "The Aayel must not be touched by any but one of the blood. We must honor her passing with the proper ceremony."

Burdened with the frail husk, Imoshen knelt on the dray. "Take us out onto the plain."

The General himself took the reins, urging the workhorses forward. The Elite Guard fell back and the people parted as the dray's wheels thudded over the cobbles. As they passed through the inner gates into the passage they were plunged into darkness. Imoshen blinked, momentarily blinded. She could see Tulkhan's silhouette dark against the light of the plain beyond the outer gates. It seemed fitting that he should honor the Aayel's sacrifice by taking the reins of the dray.

Golden afternoon light enveloped Imoshen as the wagon rolled out onto the well-worn road to the plain. When they were well clear of the city, she ordered a halt and firewood brought to build a funeral pyre around the dray.

As servants from the Stronghold unhitched the horses and dragged wood from nearby shacks to make the pyre, Imoshen remained seated, her arms closed protectively around her great-aunt's body. She dispatched a message to Kalleen to bring the Aayel's ceremonial robe and the sacred oils needed to perform the death rites.

Imoshen wrapped the frail old body in the robe then placed the Aayel on her funeral pyre. She would let no one else touch her kin. Awkward and stiff with grief, she climbed down.

The chill of winter came through the thin soles of her indoor shoes, sending a creeping chill through her bones. Imoshen stepped back and turned to the west to see the sun setting beyond the hills. It seemed fitting that the last of the Aayel should die as the sun set and the winter closed in on the end of the reign of the T'En.

In Imoshen's family the Aayel had held the reins of religious power, hers was the voice which had called down a blessing. Other families not blessed with a Throwback had the services of members of the T'En Church. The Aayel had never trusted the church. She would have preferred that Imoshen say the words.

Tears stung her eyes, but she blinked them away. She did not have time for grief now. This had to be done properly.

All around her they waited, the Stronghold servants and guards, the refugees, the locals and the Ghebites. They waited for her signal.

Imoshen shuddered. She was without guidance now in a world where all the rules had changed and death stalked her.

With an effort she recalled the blessing and spoke the words. From a great distance she heard her voice carry on the still evening. Then she stepped aside and retreated to stand on the rise and watch the sun.

Around her the people sang their ancient songs, songs which were old when her namesake invaded their land and placed them under her yoke of servitude. Was it human nature to take and take?

As the sun sank in a blaze of autumn glory, Imoshen stood over the pyre and sprinkled oils from the Aayel's private cabinet then raised her hand. On her signal a servant of the royal household ignited the Aayel's funeral pyre.

As the greedy flames laid claim to the pyre, Imoshen retreated, her cheeks scorched. She fingered the cupboard key in her hand. The Aayel's private medicaments were hers now. She could mix a potion to kill General Tulkhan as easily as she could mix a healing posset.

She need not continue tonight and tomorrow night to take the herb of fertility.

Cold crept up through her bones. She felt chilled to her very heart, despite the heat of the pyre. What did it matter if the Elite Guard turned on her and killed her, so long as she took General Tulkhan with her?

All around her the refugees, the harmless, blameless people of Fair Isle, raised their voices in an ancient song of lament as glowing cinders spiraled upward from the leaping flames.

Soon the skies would grow leaden with snow and these same refugees of the war would freeze in their makeshift homes on the plain. Imoshen flinched. There would not be enough wood to keep them warm. It was a terrible thing to see the old, the very young and the injured suffer, and they all relied on her.

She glanced around her at the scene, noting that the General and his men kept their distance. Perhaps they sensed that they'd had a lucky escape, saved from rebellion by the Aayel's actions.

All about her as the plain grew dark, faces were turned to the funeral pyre, its pungent smoke floating on the still autumn air as the sky faded to a pearly opalescence.

Finally, all that remained of the funeral pyre was its

glowing embers. The twin moons, male and female, met in union to flood the plain with silver light, cloaking its squalor and its desperate inhabitants.

Trembling with the effort of will, Imoshen signaled it was over. Later the royal household servants would gather the ashes and sprinkle them on the Stronghold's sacred garden.

Imoshen retreated to her rooms where she ordered hot water and placed oils in the bath. She took no food and no drink other than the drug the Aayel had entrusted her to take. And she didn't know why she took that.

After dismissing Kalleen, Imoshen sank into the hot water and stared into the flames of the open fireplace. She was numb. Without the wise counsel of the Aayel she was truly alone, and it frightened her more than she wanted to admit.

On the parapets were three round objects—the heads of those who would have killed the General in Reothe's name, in her name. She shuddered. These grisly trophies mocked General Tulkhan's claim to culture. Truly, he was a barbarian. He'd been ready to kill her.

Imoshen pressed cold fingers to her burning eyes. A soul-deep ache settled in her core. Her great-aunt was gone. How could she go on without the Aayel's advice?

But the old woman's choice of death made her smile with grim pride. She could only admire the Aayel and hope if she ever had to face the same choice, her decision would be as honorable.

Imoshen sighed. In a way death was simple. It was living that was hard. With her death the Aayel had succeeded in buying them time, but the risk was still present.

Noises came from the hall outside. Imoshen heard Kalleen's voice raised in angry denial. Heart pounding, she twisted around in the bath, looking for her robe. Before she could find it, the door to her chamber was thrown open and General Tulkhan marched in. Bounding around him like a small ineffectual puppy, Kalleen was making a valiant effort to stop him.

The General was alone, which relieved Imoshen of her immediate fear. If he meant to execute her, she sensed he would send his Elite Guards for her.

The immediate danger past, she felt a burst of defiant anger. What was he doing here? Was it not enough that the Aayel should die by her own hands? Did the man have no consideration?

When Kalleen tried to block his view the General brushed the girl aside.

"You may leave, Kalleen," Imoshen said, coolly.

As her serving maid backed out bristling, Imoshen decided how to handle this encounter. Rather than rise and attempt to cover herself she remained in the tub. "Whatever you may do in Gheeaba, here we do not invade a person's bedchamber—"

"Who is T'Reothe?"

Despite the warm water, Imoshen's skin went cold but she strove to remain outwardly impassive. Only she could feel the pounding of her heart. "Why do—"

"Answer me!" The General's voice was a whip crack.

Imoshen took a slow, deep breath to steady herself. "He was one of the Royal House, reared by the Emperor and Empress, a second cousin of mine. You must have met and defeated him in one of your battles during this campaign. As far as I know he lies unburied on a bloodied field somewhere."

"Then why did the assassin scream his name as she tried to gut me?"

So her scrying had been accurate? Reothe had sent the assassins. Didn't he realize he'd put her life at risk? Would Reothe discard her so easily? She doubted it. Maybe the assassins were zealots who had acted independently of him, but in his name.

Imoshen did not know what to think. She looked down only to find her shoulders grasped ruthlessly by General Tulkhan as he hauled her to her feet. Bath water cascaded out of the tub onto the floor, hissing where droplets hit the embers of the fire.

Tulkhan had seen the flicker of knowledge as Imoshen lowered her eyes. The Dhamfeer was hiding something.

He'd hauled her to her feet and out of the tub before he knew he meant to do it.

Now he shook her. "Look at me!"

For an instant he stared into her startled face. Her eyes were luminous dark pools, like red wine held to the candle flame. His large hands gripped her white shoulders, his fingers dark against her skin. He could feel her fine bones.

Her hands hung at her side. She was too proud to cover herself. Her damp silver-blond hair clung to her body in long tendrils. Dark nipples peeped from this tenuous covering but his gaze returned to her mouth.

She dragged in a ragged breath, parting dark lips to reveal those sharp little teeth and he was forcibly reminded yet again that she wasn't one of his race, that she was a T'En, from the mythical land beyond the rising sun.

Irritation gripped Tulkhan. He could feel the heat exuding from her body. That carnal scent he'd come to associate with her made his nostrils dilate. It called up a primal response in him, a response that went beyond rational thought—and one that must be crushed.

He shook her once again. "Who is T'Reothe? Has he been in contact with you?"

She gave a wild laugh, unshed tears glittering in her eyes.

"T'Reothe *was* my betrothed!" Her eyes narrowed, tears spilling unheeded down her cheeks. "He's probably dead like everyone else I ever loved, killed by you and your king." With a practiced flick she brought her arms up inside his guard and used his own strength against him to break his grip on her shoulders.

Her six-fingered hands curled into fists and she struck him fiercely, repeatedly on the chest, weeping freely. "They're all dead. My mother, father, brother, sister, and now the Aayel!"

The blows were not meant to hurt, but to express her frustation and anger. As they thudded into him his heart lurched, each strike slipping further past his defenses so that he felt her despair.

He caught her elbows and pulled her forward, pinning her to his chest. Her hands were caught between her breasts, her fists closed. She gasped, lifting a shocked face to him, the tears glistening on her cheeks like crystals.

As he looked into her eyes, he felt a terrible yearning. He wanted her. How he wanted her, this Dhamfeer woman. Who would have thought he would find her Otherness so alluring, so intoxicating? Yet here he was, ready to take her, to throw aside all sense and caution. Wasn't she his right of capture?

The fire crackled on the hearth. The scented oils of the bath hung on the steamy air.

Imoshen was pinned to the General's chest, transfixed by the twin flames of desire which raged in his eyes. He smiled down at her in anticipation.

No.

She was not a victim, certainly not his victim!

Her heart pounded and fury heated her blood, singing in her veins. She sucked in a breath then pulled back sharply, transferring her weight, but he anticipated in time to twist his hips so that her raised knee skidded past his broad-muscled thigh, allowing that hard male thigh to press intimately between her naked legs.

Imoshen froze.

The sudden pressure triggered a wave of unexpected heat. She gasped and saw his eyes widen as he registered her response.

He was going to rape her, here in her own bedchamber.

"That's right," she hissed, rage making her voice tight. "Take me by force, just like you took my lands by force. You haven't the wit to be anything other than a brutal plunderer."

His great arms tightened so that she gritted her teeth as the air was forced from her lungs. Star points of light danced across her vision.

He held her so close she felt his voice rumble in his chest when he spoke. "You surrendered!"

"Only to save my people." A roaring filled her ears. Each short breath was hard won. "I will never surrender to you. You can never subdue me. Not by brutality, not by forcing yourself upon me, not—"

Her mouth was covered by his and she knew a moment's despair. She was too close to wrestle, arms pinned against his chest. She had no leverage when her toes barely touched the ground.

His presence overwhelmed her senses. She registered his distinctive male scent, the heat of his body, the abrasive material of his jerkin against her breasts. His hard thigh pressed between her legs lifted her ever higher. A strange and unfamiliar sensation swamped all conscious thought. His demanding mouth overwhelmed hers, its hot velvety depths so alien, so unknown.

She was drowning in him, barely able to think.

His ragged breath filled her mouth as he groaned. The utter abandonment of the sound tugged at something deep inside her, robbing her limbs of their strength. She heard an answering moan, and realized that it was her own.

How could she feel any desire for this man when only a few nights ago she had been stirred by her betrothed? What kind of woman was she?

Tulkhan lifted his head and his eyes blazed with triumph. His expression speared her delirium.

No. She would *not* be his conquest!

She sucked in a breath and bared her teeth, lunging for his throat. He barely had time to bring his hand up to protect himself before her teeth found his flesh.

With delight she felt the small bones of his hand crack and tasted his blood. Suddenly she was released. Her feet hit the ground, but she would not relinquish her hold. She clung to him, her hands twined through his clothes, her teeth embedded in his flesh.

With a snap Imoshen registered a direct blow to her forehead. Stunned, she staggered back, colliding with a low seat.

Even as she fell, her head was clearing and she recoiled,

springing catlike to her feet. She didn't know this wild creature she had become.

Delight flared through her as she saw his eyes widen in alarm. He stood there breathing as raggedly as she, his injured hand clasped protectively to his chest. Blood seeped from between his fingers.

Fear and disgust traveled across his face.

His eyes narrowed and she knew he meant to kill her.

For the second time that day Imoshen faced death.

General Tulkhan slowly drew his ceremonial dagger. What had possessed him? he wondered.

A heady intoxicating desire still rode his body, but before him he saw a savage alien being. Even now she called to him to give up all rational thought, abandon himself in her flesh, drown in her exotic scent.

Naked and defiant, the Dhamfeer stood before him, poised for attack, her long silver hair hanging in twirling tendrils. Her intelligent, calculating eyes flashed feral red. Her lips and breasts were stained with his blood, confirming it—she was no more than a beast, with merely the outward trappings of a True-woman.

Tulkhan tried to flex his injured hand. He grimaced as pain lanced through it. He'd sustained enough injuries to know there were broken bones.

For an instant he debated calling his men to hold her, but it would demean him before them to reveal that she had injured him. He should be able to better a mere woman, a naked, unarmed female at that, even if she was a Dhamfeer.

He licked his lips. Unbidden, his mind presented him with the image of her writhing beneath him, not in agony but in abandonment.

Suddenly she straightened and the animal in her retreated to be cloaked by the regal woman. "My people venerate the old. We appreciate their wisdom, we treasure them. We would not deny our old ones medicinal herbs." Her voice vibrated with contempt and she stepped forward. "You were saved a mutiny this afternoon when the Aayel took her own life. Our people would have risen up and the stones would have run with blood."

He swallowed and watched with disbelief as she approached, making no attempt to cover herself.

The dagger stayed poised between them as he hugged his throbbing hand to his chest. Even now he could smell her distinctive scent.

She was breathing as rapidly as he, her pale shoulders lifting and falling, her lips parted. "You must kill me to be sure of your command."

He couldn't speak.

She continued. "You would have taken me by force."

"It is my right."

"Rights that make a person less than human?"

"Dhamfeer!" He made the word an insult.

Her eyes narrowed. "Barbarian!"

He gulped as she flicked her long hair back over her shoulders to reveal her pale, strong body. She stepped closer until the tip of the dagger pressed into her bare breast.

His eyes were fixed on the delicate mounds which rose and fell with each rapid breath. The sharp blade of the dagger dug into her flesh, not yet cutting it.

There was nothing but the sound of her rapid breathing and the pounding of his own heart as he raised his eyes to her face. Those intense, wine-dark eyes were fixed on him. Her skin was so unnaturally pale that even her lips were almost colorless, except where they were stained by his blood.

Something stirred within him, acknowledging the power she had over him.

Tulkhan flinched. This was his chance, one determined thrust between the ribs and he would be rid of this infuriating female, this source of rebellion—yet he couldn't move.

He could see the pulse fluttering in her throat.

She was taking a terrible gamble. Reluctant admiration stirred in him.

He didn't want to kill her, he wanted to *claim* her!

Time stood still as their fates hung in the balance.

Imoshen couldn't hear for the blood rushing in her ears. Every sense was strained, focusing on him, watching, evaluating. She could hardly breathe. Then she saw it, the slightest waver of determination.

A ragged gasp escaped her. She almost fainted with relief.

The General uttered a heartfelt groan and covered his face with his forearm in despair. He could not bring himself to kill her. Instinctively, she realized that by his standards she had shamed him.

With a cold shudder she understood she was just as much at risk this instant as a moment before. To cover his shame he might turn on her. He might call his men in to kill her.

She cleared her throat. "A great leader must know when to show mercy."

He glared at her. "A leader must know when to be ruthless."

"And when to bind her people to her with acts of kindness." She felt light-headed. "Your teacher must have studied the same manuscripts as mine."

He gave a grimace that might have been a smile. "Only my Master was not speaking of a female leader."

"Man comes from woman. She makes up half the world. Would you deny half of yourself?"

He shrugged this aside and she knew the moment of knife-edged danger had passed.

She dared to take his crushed hand in hers. At first he stiffened then he let her examine it.

"You will need treatment."

"My—"

"I have the unguents here in my chamber. Your people need not know." Imoshen led him by his ruined hand across to the window seat. She had succeeded in facing him down, now she had to win his trust.

She shivered. It had been close. If she hadn't fought him he would have raped her there and then. Imoshen knew instinctively tonight would have been wrong. The Aayel had been specific. She must seduce him tomorrow night, after she had taken the last of the brew.

With simple unhurried movements, Imoshen lifted a plain nightgown over her shoulders and knotted it under her breasts. Gathering her hair, she combed it with her fingers and tilted her head to watch him. Good, the spark was still there. She could see the desire in the tight planes of his face.

Let it simmer. Tonight was not the night.

Taking her private key from the chest on the mantelpiece, she unlocked the medicine cabinet and made her selection of herbs, powders and fluids.

"How could this Reothe be your betrothed? Aren't the females of your kind sworn to celibacy?"

Imoshen restrained the urge to respond to his mocking tone. It was a fair question.

"Normally, yes. But Reothe was granted special Dispensation by the Emperor and Empress. The Beatific witnessed the—"

"Did you love him?"

Startled, Imoshen's gaze met his. Did she love Reothe? She burned at his touch but perhaps it was her body's sensual frailty and not some deeper, pure emotion?

"I . . . I don't know. It was so long ago." She reminded herself that as far as Tulkhan knew Reothe was dead. She had denied knowledge of her betrothed's fate. "For all I know he is dead."

"So you will forget your betrothed as easily as that!" he scorned.

She grimaced, annoyed with him. According to the General she could do no right. "I have enough to worry about with a Stronghold full of hotheaded Ghebites, without borrowing trouble!"

Placing the medicants on a low table before him she explained what they were for as she worked. "This one will bring down swelling. It is used on the skin. This one aids the knitting of flesh and bones. You drink it. This one sprinkled on the flesh stops the ill-humors that cause the flesh to poison." Seeing how painful it was, she bound his hand with great care before strapping it gently to his chest with a sling. Finally she presented him with the liquid.

"Drink this."

"You could be poisoning me."

She felt a reluctant smile tug at her lips. "I had considered it."

"And decided against it. Why?"

Imoshen licked her lips, unable to come to terms with her conflicting emotions. Yet the words flowed from her. "I know you. If I kill you it will not change matters. Your Elite Guard will turn on the castle and kill as many of us as it takes to put down the rebellion and there will still be the king to reckon with."

"Honest, at least." A wry humor lit his face, eliciting a smile from her.

Still he hesitated. The General held the small cup in his hand, his dark eyes on her. Finally she took it from him, lifted it to her lips and sipped half of it, wrinkling her nose at the taste.

He accepted it from her then, turning it so that his lips touched where hers had been. Deliberately he met her eyes as he drained it.

A strange sense of fear and anticipation rushed through her, settling low in her belly, an insistent reminder of her secret plan.

The General could not know he had unwittingly shared with her one of the bonding ceremony symbols. If it was an omen, it was a good one.

Later as Imoshen lay in her bed, she recalled that moment and many other things about the evening. Her body sang with an unexpected energy and her breasts ached. Her nipples felt tender, irritated by the light garment.

Was this all part of the brew's effects?

Tomorrow night she must seduce the General. She would use the mental tricks her instructor had taught her to ensure she conceived a male child.

Imoshen buried her face in the cool material of her bedding.

Her life hung by a thread. She could only hope the Aayel had read General Tulkhan correctly. For the T'En, life was sacred, but she seriously doubted the Ghebites held life in such high esteem. Why would the General value the life of an unborn child?

But she mustn't doubt herself or the Aayel's plan. Doubt was deadly.

Tomorrow night was her one and only chance. If he rejected her, she was lost.

FIVE

THE DAY OF THE feast dawned bright and cold. Tulkhan's Elite Guard complained of the chill, which made Imoshen smile because this was mild compared to full winter.

She dressed with care, aware that tonight she would seduce the General, take his seed and begin a boy child who according to the Aayel would ensure her survival, binding Tulkhan to her.

Imoshen felt fragile and alone. She missed her great-aunt this cold morning on the cusp of the seasons.

Her breasts were tender and her head felt thick and muzzy, probably from lack of sleep, for she seemed to have spent most of last night tossing and turning, waking from fevered dreams, recalling her close escape. Just the thought of how he had forced his hard muscled thigh between hers made her heart race.

Hearing the General's voice in the courtyard, she ran to the window to observe her prey, taking in the way he strode through the throng, the way the others stepped back from him. He spoke to his Elite Guard, then suddenly turned and looked up to her window. She remained motionless, hidden in shadow. She saw his dark brows crease almost as if he could sense her plotting to ensnare him.

When the General turned his back on her to consult with his guards she felt an irrational annoyance. This was not like her. It must be the Aayel's potion that made her restless, her thoughts like quicksilver. She wanted to run down into the courtyard to taunt him, to elicit an angry response from him. She wouldn't be ignored, she wanted him to admit his attraction to her, to take her in his arms like he had last night.

She knew the General was not impervious to her. As much as he seemed repelled by her, he was also fascinated. Last night he had desired her but instinct told her she had done the right thing in fighting him off. Not only was it wrong to let him take her before the appointed time, but if he had done it in that manner the basis of their battle would have changed—and she would have lost the initiative.

She might have surrendered the Stronghold to the Ghebite General, but theirs was a personal battle which was still being fought.

General Tulkhan gestured in answer to one of his men and Imoshen stepped back from the window, released from her own spell. She called Kalleen and hurriedly finished dressing.

The day was a frenzy of activity for her. As head of the Stronghold household she had to vet all plans for the Festival of Harvest Moons, then personally oversee the decorations and aspects of the food preparation because they were part of the time-honored religious rites of this ancient festival.

Massive bonfires were being built on the plain. Normally the people would have thronged to their local villages, but because so many refugees had clustered around the keep it had become a huge township, almost rivaling the T'En capital in population, if not in size.

Homeless, hungry and fearful for their future, the people were more eager than ever to celebrate the Festival of Harvest Moons. Imoshen understood their need. The familiar feast offered reassurance. If the festival went well tonight they could expect a good crop next year. Food and shelter, that was what these people cared about, not the identity of their rulers. And who could blame them!

As was the custom, she fasted all day. By rights her great-aunt would have conducted the ceremony but her people had made it clear they expected her to do it, even though she was not recognized by the T'En Church.

One of her first and most important responsibilities was to oversee the construction of the harvest bower. It was essentially a primitive hut, decorated with fresh hay and the last ripe fruits and flowers of the season. Here the participants would consummate the union of the double moon. Usually the elders of the village chose a young man and young woman. They were singled out because they best represented the future of the village—young, healthy, ripe. After much feting they would be escorted to the bower to consummate their brief but vital bonding. Their joining in the field both ensured fertility the following spring and thanked the powers for the recent harvest.

While she dealt with practical matters, on a deeper level Imoshen fought to come to terms with what she must do this evening. If Tulkhan guessed for an instant that she was manipulating him into her arms he would resist, and she couldn't afford to miss this opportunity.

She studied the small, low-roofed hut, inhaling the scent of the fresh hay. Her cheeks flooded with heat as she imagined what would take place here tonight. Her body craved a mating and that disturbed her. She didn't like to think her actions were dictated by her body. Again she told herself that it must be the Aayel's potion that was making her feel this way.

With a word of congratulations to the eager refugees who had constructed the bower, she stepped out into the chill of late afternoon and took a deep breath to steady her thudding heart.

There he was, striding toward her. Did his step falter slightly as he caught sight of her? She hoped so. The General gestured to the man at his side, indicating the fire pits.

Food for the crowd was being prepared in great fire pits. The night before, the heated stones and coals had been raked over the meat and vegetables. Feeding the masses was a nightmare of logistics, but the Harvest Feast had to be done properly.

As she watched Tulkhan pace the plain, giving orders, Imoshen realized he was not wearing the sling she'd fashioned for him. He wore dark leather gloves and he was careful about how he used his injured hand. She understood immediately why he was disguising the injury. To explain how it had happened would diminish him in the eyes of his men and undermine his power. And, above all, he had to maintain control.

She had to admire his tactics and the force of his personality. No other leader, not even the Empress herself, had impressed her with their ability to inspire respect and loyalty the way General Tulkhan did.

Mentally she amended that. Reothe had impressed her with his courage and daring. Among all their kin only he had gone voyaging to open new trade routes, seeking adventure.

T'Reothe, last prince of the T'En.

Had she made the right choice?

A little shiver passed over her skin. Only time would tell.

It was growing dark. Imoshen left the plain and walked toward the Stronghold. A different flag flew over the battlements, but the sounds and scents were familiar enough. If she ignored the occasional Ghebite accent she could close her eyes and pretend it was last autumn and her family were inside, preparing for the ceremony.

A twist of pain curled inside her, intimate and intense. She hadn't had a chance to mourn their loss. And she was unlikely to have the opportunity now.

In the great hall a central dais had been erected to sacrifice a pig or lamb. Rumor had it that long ago the sacrifice had been more than this.

Many ancient customs and rituals had been absorbed by her people. After the initial invasion the original inhabitants had continued practicing their ancient ways, but over time their earth-close secrets had intertwined with the more formal customs of the T'En so that it was difficult to know where one left off and the other began.

Looking back over six hundred years Imoshen wondered if the original inhabitants of Fair Isle had not vanquished the T'En in the end through sheer force of numbers. Through interbreeding the pure T'En had all but disappeared. The language, customs and values of the golden-skinned locals had gradually permeated even to the highest levels of society so that now a Throwback like herself was an outsider amongst her own people.

Would this happen to the Ghebite barbarians?

She smiled at the irony of it. Six hundred years from now who would care whether Imoshen, last princess of the T'En, cemented her future by seducing General Tulkhan?

"My Lady?" Kalleen appeared at her side. "They told me to tell you that the room is ready for purification."

Imoshen felt a grin tug at her lips. The girl's tone told her Kalleen's ongoing battle with the long-established servants of the Stronghold had flared up again. They resented a farm girl being raised above one of their own to the position of Imoshen's private servant.

"Then we mustn't disappoint them." Imoshen smiled.

She followed the young woman, mentally preparing herself for the task ahead. Whatever her personal opinion of the T'En Church, the people of her Stronghold expected her to follow tradition. She could not dishonor them.

Imoshen stripped and entered the little wood-lined room. Herbs had been sprinkled over the heated stones so that when water was poured on them a heady, humid scent engulfed her.

She had fasted since the death of the Aayel, preparing her body for the purification ceremony. Her hair hung in heavy damp ropes over her bare shoulders and down her back. She cleared her mind and sought to recall each step of the ceremony, praying that she wouldn't forget a line or gesture.

In the past her parents had shared the ceremonial roles with the Aayel, right up until the final stage of the ceremony when the Harvest Feast platter carrying the ritual corn sheaf and bull's horn were presented to her father and mother, who passed it to the Aayel to ceremoniously bless the items before returning the platter to the village elders. The elders then presented these items to the chosen male and female. The young man received the bull's horn. It was a symbol of potent masculinity, associated with the beasts of the fields. The young woman received the corn sheaf, a symbol of fertility associated with the plants of the fields.

Imoshen's stomach growled with hunger but the only thing she planned to swallow was the last portion of the potion the Aayel had prepared for her and later the sacramental wine, which she had to bless during the ceremony.

To her surprise the enforced idleness and privacy did bring her a measure of inner peace and after the prescribed time she left the heated room feeling calm and restored. Kalleen escorted her to the sacred garden to fulfill the last step of the purification ceremony.

"There she is," Wharrd whispered.

Tulkhan's heart lurched. He was not spying, he told himself. He had asked for an explanation of the ceremony tonight and Wharrd had learned the details from Imoshen's maid so he could instruct his master.

That was how they came to be in the secluded balcony of the private courtyard which housed the Stronghold's sacred garden. Even through his boots he could feel the chill of the stones. The sun's setting rays no longer reached the walled garden and Tulkhan shivered in sympathy as Imoshen dropped her cloak to stand naked by the pool.

Her pale skin glowed eerily in the twilit courtyard. Kalleen took the cloak and retreated to the entrance, leaving her mistress alone. Imoshen raised her arms and her small breasts lifted, the darker tips peeping through her long silver hair.

The General felt his body stir in response. He wanted her even more after last night. His injured hand throbbed as if to mock him. What would have happened if her teeth had closed around his throat? She would have crushed it, killing him, possibly at the expense of her own life, but he doubted she would count the cost too great.

He wished Wharrd gone, he wished Imoshen's T'En religious rites were his to witness alone. He didn't want anyone else seeing her strong, perfect body. How could he have thought her too tall and scrawny? True, she was long-limbed and more slender than the women of his race but the more he saw her the more her form pleased him. It became the standard by which he judged all else.

"Leave me." The intensity of the voice that ground out

the order surprised him. He sensed Wharrd moving off through the connecting doors to the inner chambers.

Alone, General Tulkhan, leader of the invading forces, watched the last of the T'En with an intensity which ate at him. His heartbeat hastened until it was a heavy, solid drum which reverberated through his body. He was enthralled, unwilling for the moment to end.

Why was she standing there? She held something in her hands, crushed it, then sprinkled what looked like petals on the surface of the dark, stone-edged pool.

Then she surprised him by stepping off the edge down a number of shallow steps into the icy pool. Pausing to take a breath, she sank below the waters until only the swirl of her long hair remained on the surface. Then even that grew heavy with moisture and sank.

There was no sign of her presence other than the gently moving petals on the dark surface. Alarmed, his hands tightened on the stonework.

He was about to leap over the balustrade and drop the body length to the soft garden bed below when Imoshen rose from the depths. She glided up to the rim like an albino seal he had seen while making the crossing to Fair Isle.

As Imoshen surged up the steps he could hear her fey laughter. It made his skin prickle with fear and excitement. She called out to Kalleen, who ran forward with the cloak. Tulkhan could see Imoshen was shaking with cold as the little serving maid enfolded her mistress in the cloak.

"I'm glad that part's over!" Imoshen's voice carried, echoing off the stone walls of the courtyard. They hurried from the courtyard.

Ritual purification. The phrase returned to him. According to Wharrd, as the last of the T'En, Imoshen would lead the ceremony tonight right up until she was presented with the symbols of fertility for plant and beast, the corn sheaf and bull's horn.

Tulkhan shifted, staring down into the empty courtyard. Damn, he was as tense and apprehensive as a bridegroom. Her continued presence and the unspoken challenge in her eyes only made it worse. He was as bad as any of his foot soldiers. They were excited, edgy. Rumors of the excesses condoned on the night of the Harvest Feast abounded. There had been much boasting in the ranks. Tulkhan suspected even his men might be astonished at the behavior of these Fair Isle farmers.

Not much longer he told himself, not bothering to specify what he meant.

Imoshen clasped the simple white robe around her shoulders and tied the plaited belt around her waist. She wore her hair loose. It had been brushed until it had a life of its own, lifting and clinging to objects.

She went barefoot because she was supposed to feel the earth beneath her feet. Her first task was in the fields with the refugees where the stones had been raked back from the fire pits. There she blessed the feast as the Aayel would have done, barefoot, bareheaded, at one with the primitive people who surged around her, muttering eagerly. Their earthy excitement was strangely contagious. It made her stomach flutter with expectation.

Then she accompanied her own people into the Stronghold and a more complex ceremony borrowed from the ancient T'En culture followed. Blood was spilled to ensure new life. She tried to focus all her attention on the tasks at hand, to channel her meager gifts, but all the while she was aware of General Tulkhan watching her.

When she lifted her arms to signal for silence, she felt her nipples press against the material of her gown and flushed, knowing that he must have seen her traitorous body's involuntary signals. Deep inside her there was a slow burn which threatened to consume her.

The bitter aftertaste of the last portion of the Aayel's potion still lingered on her tongue. In a daze of heat from the open fireplace and the expectant press of the hushed crowd she repeated the words her mother would have said and slit the pig's throat as her father would have done. A little of the blood was mixed with red wine and presented to her in the ceremonial chalice.

When she sipped it, the tangy fluid went straight to her empty stomach, triggering a soporific feeling which spread through her limbs. The chalice felt heavy, significant in her hands. It made her think of the way the General had taken the drink from her and turned it so that his lips touched where hers had. The memory warmed her. Before she meant to, her eyes sought his face and she read the same need there.

His gaze burned with unspoken promise, threatening to banish all else from her mind. For a moment she faltered with the chant, then recalled it and went on.

The initial ceremony over and the food blessed, the revelers moved to the tables. Great platters of food were brought out, voices rose, wine flowed freely. Soon the long tables were groaning with the Harvest Feast. A heady rush of music and excitement filled the long hall.

Imoshen knew she could eat now, but she felt so tense she couldn't swallow a morsel. Instead, she looked around, marveling at the strange assortment of people gathered in the great hall for this Harvest Feast. Minor nobles who had fled the invading forces with their entourages were scattered around the hall, vastly outnumbered by the Stronghold Guard and Ghebite soldiers. There was much laughter and crude commentary from the Elite Guard.

To a casual observer the inhabitants of the Stronghold might be mistaken for convivial company as the food was shared around, and toasts drunk. Imoshen watched, feeling strangely detached. Who would have thought that only yesterday the Aayel had averted mass slaughter by ritual suicide? Violence seethed below the surface, valid anxieties warred with petty rivalries.

Imoshen's fingers tightened on her crystal goblet. In her heightened state of awareness, she felt the raging emotions, sensed how this apparently peaceful scene could change in a heartbeat to one of bloodshed. The Aayel had averted one crisis but there would be others. She needed a bargaining tool to hold over the General.

It was time to make her move.

Imoshen winced. Suddenly she felt awkward, unsure of herself. To delay the moment she lifted her wine goblet and sipped, silently vowing that she would not fail the Aayel, would not fail herself. The warmed wine slipped down her tight throat and into her belly, adding fire to the furnace below. She eyed General Tulkhan's profile. Somehow she would seduce him. After all, he was only a man.

But now that the moment was upon her she didn't know what to do. Soon the village elders would come forward to present her with the symbols of fertility. Already she could see the old couple waiting in the shadows. Once this part of the ceremony was over the refugees would retreat to the fields to mimic the rituals of the bower.

As for the Stronghold inhabitants, they would conduct a slightly more circumspect celebration of their own. Anything was condoned on the night of the harvest moons—it was a night for madness. She had always been sent to her room at this time. The untouched, untouchable T'En.

Imoshen's heart lurched as she saw the old man and woman approach. The corn sheaf and the bull's horn lay proudly displayed on the platter.

She started to rise. Her head spun. Had she drunk too much on an empty stomach, one goblet of warmed wine?

A hush fell over the hall. All eyes were on the Elders. It was clear to Imoshen that even the Ghebite barbarians understood the significance of the platter.

After licking her strangely numb lips, she said the blessing over the symbols. As the Elders waited patiently for her next move, Imoshen felt the weight of their expectation. She must not falter. Resolve strengthened her as she silently vowed she would not fail her people.

Tulkhan watched Imoshen, tension crawling through his body. She looked ethereal standing there in the simple white shift, her hair a glowing nimbus over her shoulders. She also looked slightly unfocused, as if she was having trouble concentrating. If he hadn't known better he would have said she was tipsy. The thought made him smile to himself. The Dhamfeer was young and inexperienced, despite what she might think.

He'd been watching her all day and knew she had been on her feet since dawn. It had been a day full of responsibilities for the last T'En. He also knew she'd taken no food since the Aayel died by her own hand the afternoon before. Imoshen must be close to collapse. An oddly protective urge surprised Tulkhan.

As he watched her intone an arcane T'En chant over the two objects, a premonition gripped him. Anticipation made his heart race.

When Imoshen presented the Elders with the platter the old man turned and lifted the bull's horn.

Tulkhan sensed more than heard a whisper pass through the ranks of his men. It was his own name. Then it grew to a deep repetitive chant. The chant captured his drumming heart's beat, urging it on.

This wasn't how the ceremony went. According to Wharrd, the Elder was supposed to present the horn to the most virile young man of the village, some fellow out there in the makeshift town was probably waiting right now, hard and ready.

The Elder's dark eyes set deep in his seamed face fixed on the General. Suddenly Tulkhan's mind cleared of every extraneous thought and he understood the forces at play with utter clarity. It came to him much like a decision made in the heat of battle. He knew he could seize the prize if he seized the moment. He was on his feet before he knew it.

The chanting fell away. The silence stretched, broken only by the scuff of his leather boots on the stone as he strode through the gap in the long table and out into the center of the hall. He looked down into the Elder's wise old face. Behind the man his woman made a slight movement which drew Tulkhan's gaze to her face. Devilment twinkled in the depths of her hazel eyes. They knew what they were about, this old pair. They were playing politics for the sake of their people.

Instinctively, Tulkhan dropped to one knee. There was a hushed murmur of approval. The Elder held the horn out to Tulkhan. His hands closed possessively around the cool, grainy surface. It was his and for tonight he was their symbol.

The old man placed the leather thong over Tulkhan's neck. The horn rested on his jerkin, heavy with significance.

He came to his feet and caught the old woman's eye. With an almost imperceptible flicker of his eyes he indicated Imoshen. The old woman nodded and walked across the stones. A buzz of excitement rose from the tables.

Imoshen was still standing. Two bright spots of color flamed in her cheeks, but she didn't look down. Instead her eyes flew to meet his, glittering with something Tulkhan couldn't read. They held a knowing intelligence which both frightened and excited him.

A smile almost touched her lips. If he didn't know better he would have sworn her expression held triumph, then the old woman's silver head came between them, blocking his vision.

He saw the old woman's shoulders move as she lifted the corn sheaf. The excited whispers dropped away. The moment stretched. For a heartbeat it seemed the Dhamfeer would refuse to accept the symbol.

Whatever she might feel, Tulkhan knew Imoshen had to accept. His men would take it as a personal insult if she refused him. The fragile illusion of peace would be shattered.

Then the hall's inhabitants let out a collective sigh of relief. Their sibilant whispers grew progressively louder as the old woman stepped back and bowed before rejoining her mate. Tulkhan was left alone in the center of the hall, his heart beating wildly in his chest.

He could not take his eyes from Imoshen.

She held the corn sheaf stiffly in both hands. He knew she was pinned, helpless as a butterfly, trapped by events beyond her control and the expectations of those present. But he wanted her. He'd wanted her since the first moment he saw her bloodied and defiant, restrained by his men.

Only last night she had refused him at risk to her own life—now she must accept him, or destroy the brittle peace. Already she had given much for her people's safety. Would she give herself?

Did he want her on those terms? He almost laughed.

Knowing Imoshen as he did, there were no other terms, and he vowed to have her any way he could!

Tulkhan beckoned Wharrd and quietly ordered his horse brought forth, bridled but unsaddled. He knew the next step—they would be escorted to the bower. To the people their joining was a symbol, a sign to the gods to ensure a good crop come spring. This Harvest Moon the joining would be more than symbolic. It held significance for the whole island, the joining of the conquered and the conqueror.

Intent on claiming his prize before she could escape him, Tulkhan stepped forward and extended his hand to Imoshen across the feast table. He could see the rapid racing of the pulse in her throat and for an instant he thought he caught a glint of fear in her eyes.

If she had been a Ghebite woman of comparable social position, she would have been a shy virgin, terrified by the events forced on her. A sudden pang of pity prompted him to turn his hand over in a gesture of entreaty. His action caused a flicker of uncertainty in her eyes.

A buzz of speculation spread through the hall.

He watched Imoshen lift her chin. Her nostrils flared as she took a deep breath. Her free hand rose to settle in his palm. The physical contact triggered a tug of recognition deep inside him. His fingers closed possessively over hers.

Her flesh was so pale against his coppery, scarred skin. He felt as if he were holding a rare prize just within his grasp, one wrong move and he might crush her. Yet he knew her air of vulnerability was deceptive. Imoshen had an innate, immutable strength. He'd clashed with her and experienced the force of her will on more than one occasion.

But at this moment she felt fragile to him. He had won this round and, perversely, he wanted to make her path easier. Tulkhan gestured to the left, intending to escort her the length of the table and around into the open center of the hall.

A half smile flitted across Imoshen's face. Before he could guess what she was thinking, she stepped lithely onto her chair and up onto the table. Stunned, he stared down at her slender foot and narrow ankle. Her bare toes looked in-

congruous nestled amid the platters of food. As she stepped
forward her white gown parted to reveal the long, shapely
length of her pale thigh.

His mouth went dry. He looked up into her face and saw
her smile. It was a hungry, feral smile. Imperiously, she
dropped his fingers and placed both her hands on his shoulders. Instinctively his arms lifted. His hands encompassed
her slender waist. He felt the flare of her hips, the tight muscles of her abdomen as he took her weight, bringing her
forward to him.

He held her there, her hips pressed to his chest, her feet
far from the ground. Then very slowly and with great deliberation he lowered her, letting her slide down the length of
his body. He cursed the thick jerkin which prevented him
from feeling her soft curves against his flesh.

When her toes touched the ground she smiled a small
satisfied smile and lifted her arm regally. He offered his and
she laid her forearm along his arm, her fingers over his hand.
As her eyes met his, he realized that never for a moment did
she acknowledge him as her conqueror. She considered herself his equal.

A surge of raw desire clawed at him.

His head rang with his men's ragged cheers. He knew
they had been laying bets on how long before he claimed her
for his bedmate.

He had neither admitted nor denied seducing her that
day in the forest. In that instant Tulkhan recalled the odd
sense of menace which had pervaded the clearing and
Imoshen's terror. She had seen more than he, things a True-
man could not see. She was Dhamfeer, privy to other gifts.

What was he thinking? He could not deny what he had
experienced. More than once he had felt her words inside his
head. When it had happened he had hated her intrusion because she had breached his defenses. His mind was the private bastion of his thoughts. Insidious fear curled through
him.

Tulkhan hesitated. If he were to lie with Imoshen, would
it give her even greater power over him? Would the joining of
their bodies allow her access to his inner thoughts?

He searched her face for duplicity but saw only the flush of desire mingled with embarrassment in her cheeks and the uncertainty in her eyes. She was wanton one moment, pure innocence the next, and he wanted her.

Tulkhan banished his misgivings—right now Imoshen was all woman and his by right. He had waited long enough.

Wordlessly he indicated that they should leave and she nodded. They stepped forward in unison, escorted by an enthusiastic rabble of Elite Guard and minor aristocracy into the courtyard where Tulkhan's magnificent black destrier waited, shifting nervously.

He caught the bridle firmly in his hand and leapt across the beast's back. It took a moment for him to regain control as the horse sidled away and the crowd scurried back, then he extended his hand to Imoshen.

Tulkhan flexed his booted foot. She used it like a stirrup, stepping up and taking his extended hand. With a graceful leap she sprang up onto the horse and settled into place before him.

The scent of her freshly washed hair rose around him, its silver tendrils tickling his nose. She swayed with the movement of the horse, rubbing against him, tantalizing him with her nearness, with the knowledge of what was to come.

They were through the passage and outer gates, down onto the plain before he knew it. Torchlights danced on the still air, the refugees cheered and sang as they formed a living sea around them. A primal, almost wordless chant rose from the masses as if from one great communal throat. The air was rich with the scent of roasted meat.

The bower was nothing more than a primitive hut, fashioned from thatched straw, yet it looked like a haven to him. The black horse stopped before it and Tulkhan tossed the reins to Wharrd. Swinging his weight over his mount's back he leapt to the ground then lifted his arms to Imoshen. An inner urgency seemed to animate her. The dancing torchlights reflected in her dark eyes, filling them with restless points of fire.

She swung her leg across the horse's back. When she slid forward into his arms her dress rode up so that he caught a flash of her firm white thighs. Then she was in his embrace, real flesh and blood.

This time he pressed her hips to his chest and buried his face between her breasts, eager to inhale her distinctive feminine scent. He felt her fingers lace through his hair, pressing him to her breast in an oddly protective, intimate gesture. When was the last time a woman had held him with such gentleness?

Tulkhan raised his face and looked up into hers. Wisps of her hair floated on the air as if alive, her eyes glittered and her lips parted in a gasp. Imoshen looked into his eyes, her soul naked. He felt a tug of recognition as if he had always known her and suddenly he understood she was as vital to him as the very breath he drew, or could be, if he let down his guard.

Stunned by this revelation, he let her weight slide down against his body, bringing her face closer to his. Cupping his face in her hands, she traced his eyebrows with the soft pads of her thumbs, pressing gently on his closed eyelids. Momentarily blinded, all his senses focused on touch, smell and sound, he felt her lean forward and her lips brush his closed lids, first one, then the other, in a benediction of tender desire.

Again, he was disturbed by the intimacy of her touch. He had meant to claim her body, not to lay his soul bare to her.

When he opened his eyes to look into her face she seemed to glow with an inner radiance. He wondered if when she touched her lips to his closed eyes she had laid some sort of magical charm on him in order to make herself appear even more beautiful than nature had made her.

He was mad to want her, mad to lay himself open to her tricks. Yet he had no choice. He was mad for her. He *had* to have her.

A sudden rush of desire blazed through his body, obliterating all need for thought. Caution played no part in what he felt. The primitive chant drummed on the air, seeming to vibrate on his flesh, making it throb in time to the sound. Suddenly impatient, he released her waist to take her by the hand. Without preamble he strode toward the bower's open flap, urgency driving his steps.

At the entrance Imoshen planted her feet and caught his arm, indicating he should wait. She hung her corn sheaf on a hook above the opening and looked at him expectantly. He had no idea what she wanted.

Her gaze fell from his eyes to the bull's horn which hung around his neck and he realized he was meant to remove it, to place it with her corn sheaf.

At her signal he inclined his head and she lifted the leather thong from around his neck, hanging the masculine symbol next to the feminine.

"They burn the bower afterwards, along with the symbols." Her voice was raw, bereft of all pretense.

Afterwards.

The significance of the word hung in the charged air.

Imoshen wouldn't meet his eyes and he wondered if she was suddenly shy. But she took a quick breath and stepped into the bower without any urging from him. He followed her, letting the flap fall so that they were alone in the half dark.

Tulkhan marveled. It was so strange to find himself here in a primitive dirt-floored hut, alone with the deposed princess of the mythical T'En. He had only to lay a hand on her to claim her as his prize. She had been untouchable, unattainable. But for tonight she was his. Surely the fates were playing with him, promising him heaven only to dash his hopes.

Her pale hair and white gown glowed as his eyes adjusted to the dark. He smelled fresh herbs, dried flowers.

Imoshen stepped forward into the center of the hut, under the smoke hole. The twin moons' brilliant light fell on her, bathing her in its silver glow. She lifted her hand, beckoning him. To him she was an ethereal glowing object, enticingly Other.

Tulkhan tensed. This was Imoshen, a girl not yet a woman. Why was she so matter of fact? Did she know no shame? A woman of his own people would have wept, begged him not to dishonor her. A woman of his own kind would not have accepted the corn sheaf.

Anger sparked in him. He could smell her distinctive scent, so familiar yet so unlike Ghebite women. There was no point fighting it. He had to admit her differences aroused him. But he also desired her simply because she was who she was. He had never met anyone like Imoshen of the T'En.

Tulkhan hesitated, strangely reticent now that they were alone.

She touched the shoulder clasps on her gown and the material fell to her feet in a pool of pale luminescence.

He heard his own sharp intake of breath. His body carried him forward two steps, so that he joined her in the circle of radiance. Her pale hands lifted to his chest as if to help him disrobe but he caught her hands in his.

"I don't understand. You held me off at knifepoint last night." He gestured to the bower around them, the furs on the floor. "Why does this make me acceptable?"

Silently, she placed her cheek on the back of his hand. He felt dampness, tears on his skin. Something twisted inside him and he despised himself. Was she weeping because she hated him, because he had given her no choice?

What did he want from her? Forgiveness? An invitation?

A surge of desire seized him and he had to admit it to himself. He wanted her to want him, to welcome him into her arms and into her body.

She kissed his knuckles. He felt her warm breath caress his flesh. Her tongue rasped across his skin and a ragged groan escaped him. He pulled her to him, feeling the warm curves of her body wrapped in the silken cloak of her hair.

Outside he could hear the dull roar of the people's chanting—the knowledge that they were waiting for him to lie with her before continuing their ceremony irritated him. He knew he could not take Imoshen against her will as part of a ritual, yet he could no more stop breathing than call a halt to what was about to happen.

He could not fail now.

When his hands tugged at the laces of his jerkin he found his fingers strangely numb. Her deft hands undid the ties and slid the material over his shoulders. His shirt followed.

He held his breath as her flesh pressed against his bare chest. He could feel the tips of her breasts on his skin.

Suddenly she stepped back, pressing the fingers of one hand to her chest as if she was short of breath. He could see her eyes glittering strangely. She stood just out of reach.

Heart pounding, he drew off his boots, unlaced his breeches and freed himself. Naked at last, he stood before her. The little bower was full of heated air, the heady scent of arousal. Impatience seized him.

He caught her hand and pulled her close against his hard body. She shuddered on contact, malleable but not taking the initiative. It was as if she wanted him to claim her, as if she was holding back.

He wanted her to touch him, to want him. He willed her to seduce him so that he could despise her. But she remained passive, his captive, betrayed into this. He guided her hand to cup his shaft, closed her fingers around his length, felt the outrush of her hot breath on his throat. Even so her hand remained still, encased in his.

He recalled the strangely gentle touch of her lips on his closed lids. Had it only been an illusion? Why wouldn't she touch him like that now? He craved her willing touch.

The pallet of furs was at his feet. He sank slowly to his knees, inhaling her scent as he went. Her breasts brushed his face. His lips traced a path across the silken flesh of her abdomen. His tongue dipped into the indentation of her belly button and he felt her tremble.

Lower still he sank. The soft curls of her mound tickled his face. He wanted to taste her, but was suddenly afraid to invade her so intimately. He knew instinctively that to take would negate the prize.

Sinking back onto the furs he pulled her with him, bringing her body over his, her face to his throat. Her hair spilled across his chest, a silvery blanket.

"Touch me." Naked desperation laced his voice.

She slid away from his body to lie beside him, her weight supported on one elbow. One of her thighs lay over his. He could feel the heat of her on his flesh.

He had revealed himself with that plea and he felt utterly vulnerable, afraid she would mock his need.

Cupping her cheek in her hand she peered down into his face. Her features were bathed in the upglow of the moons' twin light. Her eyes, usually so dark, were pools of silver radiance. He saw the flash of her teeth as she licked her lips. If only she would touch him.

As if curious, her warm, dry fingers caressed his face, traced the line of his eyebrows, defined the curve of his lips. Her touch was balm to him. It held a degree of intimacy, yet was almost asexual in its tenderness.

"Why do you hesitate?" she asked softly. "You chose me. For this one night I am yours."

It was enough. Desire flared into action. He felt the fragile bones of her shoulders as he caught her to him, claimed her lips. Even as he kissed her he seemed to hear her laughter in his head. Then he couldn't think for the urgency in his body.

Somehow she was under him, slender and soft, yet surprisingly strong—although this time she was not fighting him. She met his need with a need of her own which made him strive to conquer her. As their bodies joined he felt her resistance but instead of tensing, she welcomed him.

When he buried himself deep in her it was enough for a heartbeat. Then the urgency took him again.

Their limbs entwined, their breath mingled, their bodies strained against each other. Before he even realized the moment was upon him he was swept over the edge into a cascade of ecstasy so intense that when he regained control of his body he was surprised to find her beneath him, the world unchanged. He knew a moment's savage triumph. She might be T'En and sacrosanct, supposedly too pure to tolerate a man's touch, but she was still a woman.

Her body had welcomed him despite the pain he caused her.

"You were untouched."

She closed her eyes in silent agreement. When she did not open them he watched her face. She seemed to be concentrating. The air inside the bower shimmered around them. Tulkan's heart skipped a beat.

He knew that sensation all too well. The Dhamfeer was calling on her gifts and he didn't want to be a part of it. But when he tried to withdraw and roll to his feet her thighs locked around his hips, trapping him.

Startled, he looked into her now open eyes only to find they glowed with an inner radiance. The sight both fascinated and repelled him. There was a strange taste on his tongue and his head ached as if a thunderstorm were about to break.

Suddenly she gasped and tensed beneath him. He felt her inner muscles convulse around him. A groan escaped him. He could feel the tension solidify within him once more. He wanted her again.

This time he needed to affirm she was his.

Tulkhan tried to speak but she embraced him, drawing his face to meet hers. Her lips sought his, eagerly, hungrily. The strange metallic taste was strong on her tongue.

Was this the taste of T'En magic?

He couldn't think. She was in his mouth, in his head. Her scent was in his nostrils, her heat enveloped him. Her laughter rubbed across the back of his skull like velvet. His every instinct screamed *Beware* but he couldn't escape her, couldn't escape her triumph.

"I felt the flare of your son's life force!"

Her words were sensation, nonsensical slivers which barely registered in his fevered mind. His body urged him to claim her once more, yet his head warned him to stop while he still could.

He had tasted her and he was drunk to have her again. Why was she so triumphant. What had she said?

"What?" His voice was slurred.

Little ripples ran through her body and her inner muscles tugged on him so that even though he made the effort to still his urges, she drew him deeper into her.

He couldn't afford to drop his guard. A short bitter laugh escaped him. Was it already too late?

"What did you say?" He tried again, his voice harsh.

Moonlight brimmed in her eyes, illuminating her face. She answered him, so sweetly serious. "I have your son. I felt his life begin just as I was taught I would—"

"Impossible!" The exclamation was out before he could stop it.

She tilted her head curiously. "No, I would have said inevitable considering."

Stunned, he pulled away from her and this time she released him, observing him curiously.

Rolling out of the circle of moonlight he crouched defensively in the shadows, watching her.

She sat up, negligently naked, her hair draped over her body like a pale silken shawl. At that moment she was totally Other, alien and implacable yet . . . her luminous form still called to him. His traitorous body urged him to rejoin her and bathe in the radiance of the twin moons' glow.

Mouth dry and heart pounding, he clenched his fists, determined not to fall under her spell again.

This was a trick.

He knew she must be able to smell the fear on his skin and hated himself for the weakness. Tulkhan sensed that if he went to her now he would belong to her, body and soul.

"What is it?" In one fluid movement she came to her knees, flicking her long hair over her shoulder. "Why do you fear me?"

He could not answer. Had she plucked from his mind his impossible dream, buried deep behind walls of bitter denial? His shame revealed, did she now seek to manipulate him?

She tilted her face to the opalescent glow, held out her hands and bathed in the silver light. A soft laugh escaped her as she played with the moonlight.

"I can feel their power. I've never felt like this before. I have been half asleep all my life."

In her voice Tulkhan heard innocent wonder and the Imoshen he had come to know returned. He lunged forward and caught her, pulling her into his arms, out of the moons' direct light as if they were the enemy. When he touched her he knew she was only flesh and blood, distractingly beautiful flesh and blood, but real, capable of fear and pain like himself.

"What do you mean, you have my son?"

The moonlight still seemed to live in her eyes and their luminous quality captured him as she looked at him almost pityingly.

"Every act has its consequence, General. You came to me willingly, you gave him to me."

"Impossible!"

"How can you say that? You chose me for this bonding."

Tulkhan shook her, feeling the tensile strength of her body. She did not have the brute strength he had, but there was a tenacity to her flesh as if her fierce will imbued her body with an added power.

Power?

"How can you know when a life starts?" he demanded.

She tilted her head, studying him. "Don't your women know when they are with child? This is my fertile night. I felt the new life flare within me, just as I was taught—"

"You planned this, but you can't trick me!" He thrust her aside so violently that she fell back into the patch of moonlight. He sprang to his feet, rigid with fury but still unable to ignore her beauty as she crouched there in the circle of silver moonlight. He paced back and forth across the dirt floor.

Imoshen watched the Ghebite General, unable to understand his reaction. He was deeply disturbed, distressed almost. Prowling back and forth he spun to face her, chest heaving. She could see a glowing form reflected in his dark eyes like the twin moons and realized it was herself.

Why did he deny she carried his child?

He swore softly and appeared to come to a decision. Imoshen watched as he fumbled in his haste to pull on his breeches and boots. She could have sworn he was shaking with anger—or was it fear?

Had the Aayel miscalculated when she Read General Tulkhan? Apprehension settled in Imoshen's core, drowning the last warm flare of the new life she had felt quicken. Had she been mistaken? Was it simply hope she'd felt? No. That flare of new life was too intense to be misunderstood.

Why then was the General denying her?

He scooped up his jerkin and thrust his arms in, not bothering to lace it before he turned to look down at her. "Well, get up. We have to walk out there together or this thing won't have served its purpose!"

Imoshen flinched but rose to her feet. He had purposefully and cruelly distanced himself from her. As she pulled her shift over her head and tugged her hair free, letting it drop down her back, she sensed him watching her. He was devouring her with his eyes. His gaze caused a physical sensation on her flesh. She was glad the moons' silver radiance did not reveal her flaming cheeks, her tear-laced eyes. For all the world she would not admit he had hurt her.

His desire for her was like a heady drug. She could feel her body responding to his unspoken need. He wanted her, but it was her own response which surprised Imoshen. She had naively thought once the moment of conception was passed, she would be free of this distracting desire for him. But it was not to be.

"Come."

The Ghebite General stood by the door flap of the bower, a dark, brooding presence. Try as she might she could not begin to understand him. She wanted to refuse, to make a stand, but it would negate what she had achieved so far. The fragile peace must be kept and her hold on the General must be tightened.

So she stepped into the shadows by the bower entrance to join him, mentally preparing herself for what was to come.

The General caught her hand and pulled her close to him. She'd thought he meant to march straight out, but his hands encircled her waist, then slid down to cup her buttocks.

She felt him swell, pressed into the soft flesh of her belly. His need for her was like a fever, contagious, consuming him and her, consuming all rational thought.

He cursed and plunged through the flap. There was a ragged shout, which turned into a cheer and by the time they had climbed astride his war horse, the bower was aflame.

Amid a sea of celebration, Imoshen watched the bower burn, isolated, alone. Somehow it seemed fitting to her that her son should be conceived on the field like this, caught betwixt the invader and the conquered, under the twin harvest moons.

A flush of fierce determination inflamed her. In that moment Imoshen understood what she had begun. A helpless new life depended utterly on her. She knew she would do everything in her power to see that her child lived to claim his place. It amazed her to discover that without a qualm of conscience she could contemplate lying, even murder, to protect her flesh and blood.

Was this why the Aayel wanted her to get pregnant, because it would focus her will? Imoshen did not know. Suddenly she felt terribly vulnerable. How was she to save her unborn child when her own life hung by a thread?

Flames leapt high into the night sky, sparks spiraled upward. Tulkhan felt Imoshen stiffen in his arms. She turned to him. The leaping patterns of the fires illuminated her pale skin, creating shadows which haunted her features.

A shudder ran through her body and she surprised him by pressing her face into his chest. Her arms slid around his body. Wordlessly, she clung to him and he felt a surprisingly strong protective urge.

Around them the gathered refugees mingled with his own Ghebite soldiers. They watched the bower burn in almost total silence. When the roof and walls collapsed and sparks flew upward into the still air, a sibilant sigh of satisfaction traveled through the masses.

Someone struck up a tune and the dancing began.

Tulkhan knew the night would get wilder and wilder, even by Ghebite standards. He turned his beast toward the Stronghold. Imoshen rode across his thighs, her face buried in his chest. He guided the horse with his knees, holding her in one arm.

No one paid them any attention as they entered the stable courtyard. The servants had done their duty and been dismissed, and now the night was turned over to revelry. Already he heard raucous laughter and shrieks from the stables.

The anger which drove him to distance himself from Imoshen had dissolved, departing with the sparks of their bower on the still night air. The Dhamfeer had tried to trick him, but he would not be taken in. He would not allow himself to hope for the impossible.

The twin moons' light fell so strongly in the courtyard before the stables that Tulkhan cast a shadow as he swung his weight off the horse's back. Imoshen slipped down before he could help her and ran inside. Strange, he had expected another confrontation. It was out of character for her to avoid him.

He had to admit he wanted another confrontation, another reason to rail at her, to take her in his arms and . . . his face grew hot at the thought. He must have been a fool if he thought one bedding would get her out of his blood.

Impatience raged in his body but he forced himself to tend to his horse, to leave it safely stabled and rubbed down. Before he could make his way through the great hall he was hailed by several of the Elite Guard who wanted to drink to his health. Much ribald comment was directed to him concerning the Dhamfeer. They wanted to know if she was as wild as rumor had it.

Strangely, Tulkhan couldn't join in the jest. He felt as if he was watching everything happen to someone else, as if there was something he should be doing elsewhere.

He knew what it was. His blood was boiling for her. Perversely, he made himself stay in the great hall and jest with his men. He knew the value of bonding. He might be the son of the king's second wife, but he was a soldier first and they respected him for that.

Slightly drunk, though not near enough considering the ale he'd consumed, he climbed the stairs to his bedchamber. Wharrd was sleeping in the outer room, his limbs entangled with those of Imoshen's small serving maid. Tulkhan stared morosely at them.

He could remember when his life was that simple, when he thought success on the field of battle would win him his father's love and acknowledgment. Impatient with himself, he forged ahead, but in his slightly hazy state he stubbed his toe on the doorjamb. His curses woke Kalleen, who fled.

Wharrd sat up, his protest dying on his lips when he met the General's eye.

"Bedding the enemy, now?" Tulkhan asked. It was meant to be a jest, but he saw the man flinch.

Wharrd opened his mouth but thought better of it, choosing not to make the obvious rejoinder. Tulkhan gave a rueful smile, acknowledging Wharrd's unspoken comment.

"I should cut out my tongue," Tulkhan muttered and tried to make amends. "Wine?" He'd had more than enough, but it didn't ease the continuous ache that thrummed through his body. It seemed no amount of wine could dull that need.

The bone-setter nodded and accepted a mug. Tulkhan stirred up the fire and built it higher. He wouldn't sleep tonight. To lie alone, without her in his arms would be hell. He could still smell her on his skin, feel her flesh on his fingers. The silken caress of her hair haunted him.

He clenched his fist and stared into the flames, resting his forearm on the mantelpiece. He'd forgotten the older man.

"I've seen you grow from a boy to a man. I've served you all these years, but now I want to step aside. This is how I see it," Wharrd said suddenly. "I've followed the army for nearly thirty years. I was but a lad when I first saw men die. I've sewed men up, sawn off their arms and legs, watched them die in agony. I'm tired of it. I want a quiet little cottage somewhere, a wife who'll warm my bed and my heart, who'll give me strong, healthy children. And I pray to the gods they will never have to live through what I've seen." He met Tulkhan's eyes, his face an odd mixture of the defiant and apologetic. "I'm tired of fighting. I want peace."

Tulkhan said nothing. The events of the night were pressing in on him. His most trusted friend was stepping down. His father was dead, his younger half-brother had become king. He had conquered every country from the north to Fair Isle. What was left for him?

Should he return to the mainland and lead the army into the Southern Kingdoms? What purpose would it serve? His father was dead. Even after all he'd achieved in his father's name he had not won the old king's love. Why should he lead an army to conquer land for his half-brother?

What then?

Should he build some ships and sail off to the archipelago in search of wealth? The idea did not cause his blood to ignite with passion. Personal fortune had never meant much to him.

For the first time in his life he felt lost, without purpose. An emptiness and a sense of dislocation filled him.

Yet all around him through the Stronghold he could hear the shouts of revelry, the laughter and music. The only thing worse than a rowdy drunk was a morose drunk and Tulkhan did not like his own company.

Imoshen prowled the moonlit room, cat-light on her bare feet. Kalleen huddled before the empty fireplace watching her. The rest of the Stronghold had cast care aside to indulge in the revelry.

"But something is wrong, I can feel it!" Imoshen spun around, her hands opening and closing agitatedly in futile fists. She strode to the window, but the sight of the twin moons offered her no comfort. "If only the Aayel were here. She could tell me what I feel."

The little serving maid said nothing.

"Of course!" Imoshen spun to face her. "Bring me the scrying platter."

While the girl hastened to obey, Imoshen took her knife and pricked her finger, squeezing several drops of dark blood to the surface. "Here, Kalleen."

She knew she was worrying her maid and one part of her

regretted this, but she had to do something. Her T'En senses screamed a warning.

The blood fell on the silver platter. Imoshen added a little water, watching the two liquids mingle. She walked to the moonlit window seat and leaned there in the embrasure, swirling the water lightly over the plate's surface.

A scrying rarely worked for her. Tonight she couldn't focus her thoughts. Dread of what she might learn and impatience with her lack of skill warred within her. She felt as if there was something important she was missing, something she should sense.

Kalleen hovered just out of reach, breaking Imoshen's concentration. It was pointless! Dispirited, she stopped pushing for a vision and let her thoughts drift.

Too late now to flee with Reothe, she had made a commitment to save herself and her son as well as the people of Fair Isle.

Imoshen was about to throw the water out the window in disgust when something appeared in the plate. Bodies writhed, people fled in terror, women, children, horses screamed. Their stomach-churning cries filled her head. Acrid smoke from the burning buildings stung her throat.

Panic seized her.

They were being hunted through the streets. There was nowhere to run. Metal clattered on stone. Imoshen screamed. She fled with her people, her heart pounding.

One of the invaders grabbed her gown, tearing it. He trapped her arms. She was dead!

She writhed in his vicious embrace, a parody of love. She was silent, full of desperate fury.

She must escape but his grip was unbreakable.

Weeping. Someone was pleading, calling her name.

Another voice, this time masculine, pierced the screams of those around her.

"Imoshen!" The familiar deep voice was filled with concern.

She recognized the scent and realized it was the General who held her. With that knowledge the terrifying vision faded.

"Put out the fire!" he bellowed.

What fire? Imoshen strove to see through the gray mist which enveloped her.

The General was holding her against his body, her back pressed to his chest. She twisted in his arms and caught sight of Kalleen. The girl's small, nimble figure darted forward, slapping the flaming bed curtains with a blanket.

Imoshen blinked, the last wreaths of gray mist fading as her sight returned. Her bedchamber was alight?

"What happened?" Imoshen tried to sidle out of Tulkhan's grasp.

"You tell me." He swung her around to face him. "Kalleen screamed for help. We found it like this!"

Imoshen thrust his hands aside and turned to survey the damage. It looked worse than it was. Wharrd and Kalleen almost had the fire out. Who would set fire to her bedchamber?

She had no idea.

Impatient with the blank in her memory, Imoshen paced across the room. Her bare toe caught the scrying plate. It went skittering across the stone like a live thing, flashing silver, clattering sharply. The sound scraped on her raw nerves.

Imoshen gasped. Her heart jumped, then began to pound rapidly. Kalleen yelped with fright. Wharrd cursed.

Imoshen shuddered as echoes of the slaughtered innocents' screams filled her head.

What had she seen, done?

She turned to Kalleen, grabbing the girl's wrist. "Tell me what happened."

The little maid's mouth twisted with reluctance. She fixed her golden-hazel eyes on Imoshen's face, then glanced sharply toward the men and Imoshen instantly regretted her demand. The Ghebites were still their enemy. Kalleen's instincts were correct, she did not want to reveal any weakness before them.

Wharrd pulled down the last of the bed curtains and rolled them up. They were still smoldering.

Forcing herself to behave calmly, Imoshen let Kalleen's

wrist go and stepped away, turning to the men. "Thank you for coming in, General, but everything is under control now. You may leave."

He gave a short, impatient laugh. "You haven't answered my question." Abruptly he turned on Kalleen. "What happened, girl?"

She jumped with fright and looked to Imoshen for guidance, who knew instantly that the girl would lie for her.

Why? Why should she inspire such loyalty?

Imoshen put this thought aside and concentrated on rubbing her temples tiredly. The General would not be put off. He had come to her aid, saved her from something. What? She frowned. Perhaps he deserved an explanation.

"There are a dozen jumbled images in my mind. I remember standing by the window under the light of the twin moons and searching the scrying plate, but I saw nothing . . ."

Even as she spoke, the memory returned, cleaving her tongue to the roof of her mouth, closing her throat with fear.

"You began to scry," Kalleen said softly. "Suddenly you dropped the plate and screamed . . ."

"I saw genocide! Women, children running, being hunted down through the narrow streets and slaughtered. There was nowhere to run. Then I was running with them.

"One of the invaders lunged for me. His hand raked my shoulder. I tried to run between the blazing buildings toward the square. But it was a trap." Imoshen bit her lip, aware that the General was watching her closely. It would not do to reveal the extent or, in this case, her inability to harness her gift. He already feared her T'En powers. What would he do if he thought she was unable to control it?

"You ran about the room, as if trying to escape someone," Kalleen whispered.

"And then?" General Tulkhan prompted the little maid, who looked to her mistress for the signal to proceed. Imoshen nodded. A cold certainty settled in her chest. She was sure the bed curtains had not been set alight by natural means.

"Then?" Kalleen echoed, her eyes widening with terror

as she remembered. "My lady did not know me. She screamed and the bed curtains burst into flames. I went for help."

Several slightly drunk, but reasonably alert soldiers charged into the room half-dressed. One was naked except for his sword.

Tulkhan swore under his breath. Suddenly he swung his cloak from his own shoulders, to clasp it around Imoshen's. Before she could speak, he was marching toward the men.

"What drunken revelry is this?" he demanded.

"We heard a scream. We thought it was another assassination attempt!"

"Nothing like that!" Tulkhan laughed, his voice rich on the charged air. "The Princess had a nightmare. She cried out in her sleep—"

"I smell burning." One man eyed Imoshen suspiciously.

"I knocked over my candle. I'm sorry." It galled her to let them believe she was such a poor creature that she was frightened of her own dreams, but she understood Tulkhan was containing the disturbance and knew she had to do her part.

He ushered the men out and shut the door, then turned to meet her eyes across the chamber. Imoshen realized the General had given her the Ghebite equivalent of her title. Did that mean he was acknowledging her as his equal? Did he even realize he had done it?

"Explain," he growled.

"Explain what? I had a bad feeling. I did a scrying. I must have knocked over my candle."

Kalleen went to speak but reconsidered. Aware of what the girl might have revealed, Imoshen was grateful.

Tulkhan strode toward Imoshen, his long dark hair streaming behind him with the speed of his approach. Her heart leapt to her throat. She felt an instinctive fear, mingled with admiration. Even now she wanted him.

His hands sprang to her neck. She flinched but held her ground as he tore the cloak off her shoulders. "Explain this!"

He spun her around to stand before the polished metal mirror. By the candlelight she could see nail marks on her bare shoulder. The material of her simple shift had been torn, rent as if someone had attempted to grab her and she'd only just eluded them.

SIX

FEAR MADE IMOSHEN'S skin go cold. Had the vision felt so real because it was real?

But how?

She did not know. Truly, her life had been in danger. Here was the evidence. Yet . . . it had only been a scrying. Nothing like this had ever happened when the Aayel did her scryings. What had she done wrong? Why had the bed curtains burst into flames?

Confusion overcame her, robbing her of her confidence. Her heart sank. She was a danger to herself and those around her.

"By the Aayel!" Imoshen hissed. What was happening to her?

"Who attacked you?" Tulkhan demanded, his voice vibrating with repressed emotion.

Imoshen realized the General was holding himself on a very tight rein. It was clear he thought someone, perhaps one of his own men, had attempted to rape her. It was a logical assumption. She realized unless she wanted him punishing his men unfairly and causing further resentment, she would have to tell him the truth and that meant admitting her own lack of control over her gifts.

Imoshen hated to admit her weakness but there was nothing for it. She must face the consequences of her actions with as much dignity as she could muster.

"Kalleen, take Wharrd out and offer him some wine.

I'm sure he could do with refreshment," Imoshen ordered and walked to the empty fireplace. It was cold and dark, the wood laid ready to strike the tinder. She missed the fire's welcoming warmth. When had they lit the candles? Last she recalled the room was bathed in moonlight.

As she turned to confront the General she saw a moment of silent communication pass between him and the bone-setter. Yes, she must remember that as kind as Wharrd was, he was still Tulkhan's man sent to spy on her. Not that he needed to do much spying, Imoshen thought grimly, when she set her own bedchamber alight.

On his General's signal, Wharrd left with her maidservant. Imoshen swallowed. Where to begin?

She didn't want to meet Tulkhan's eyes. Surely he would despise her for her weakness? She was torn. She only had to look at him to recall his arms around her. Her body thrilled at the memory, and ached for his touch. She frowned—at this moment the last thing she needed was this physical distraction. Suddenly she felt awkward, vulnerable because he had known her body and now he would know her weakness.

To hide her discomfort she resorted to social etiquette. "Wine?"

He waved a hand as if the answer didn't matter then strode to the fireplace. Imoshen crossed to the low table and poured two goblets. Turning to offer him one, she saw him building up the flame. When had he had time to strike the tinder?

"I want an explanation now." Tulkhan straightened up. He made Imoshen feel small and she wasn't. She resented that. She enjoyed looking down on men.

Licking her dry lips, she began. "The Aayel could have explained it. She knew so much more than I. Maybe it is normal. But it never happened before. My scrying has been poor. Healing was always my gift."

"You're saying this wasn't done by one of my men?" Tulkhan asked, obviously trying to contain his exasperation.

Imoshen touched his arm. She told herself it was to ask his forbearance, but the moment she felt the hard muscle under the fine material she knew she'd touched him because she had to. The warmth of his skin went through her finger-tips, traveled up her arm and settled in her core. She felt a tingle of excitement move over her body. The intensity of her physical reaction startled her.

Her eyes flew to his and she knew he felt it too.

The General stepped away to pick up his wine. But she sensed he was using this to escape her.

"What happened tonight?" he asked. "Were you in danger—"

"Yes. Something went wrong." Imoshen flushed. She had to tell him. He deserved the truth. "You asked if it was one of your men who attacked me. It wasn't. But I think he was a Ghebite. He nearly caught me.

"I was in a narrow street. All about me the buildings were ablaze. The choking smoke . . . I couldn't breathe. It was so very real. I don't know how . . ." She heard her voice rise and bit her lip, taking a deep breath to regain control.

Someone hammered on the door. Imoshen gasped and stepped closer, clutching his arm. Tulkhan's hand closed over hers. She snatched it away, already regretting her frailty.

With exaggerated patience General Tulkhan put his wine aside and cursed in three languages, making Imoshen smile. The hammering came again.

Their eyes met and something passed between them—a rueful acknowledgment of their situation. Whatever they might feel personally their positions meant they were always on duty, at the beck and call of their people.

"Come in?" Imoshen raised her voice.

The door swung open and half a dozen of the Elite Guard staggered in with a bloodied individual between them. She felt the General stiffen. Another assassination attempt?

"My Lady T'En?" The man writhed in his captors' grasp, twisting to pin his one good eye on her.

Imoshen stepped forward. Suddenly all the unease she had been feeling settled into one lump of leaden fear in her belly.

"Put him down. Step back!"

Fear and fury made her voice ring like steel. The Elite Guard obeyed instinctively. Imoshen simply accepted their obedience, her mind on their captive. The man was bleeding freely but he was not badly hurt. She took her own goblet and sank to her knees, offering it to him. With a jolt she realized he was only a youth, not yet out of his teens.

"Lady T'En?" His fingers closed on her wrist as his eyes searched her face. "You must save T'Diemn. The Ghebite King surrounded it. Our Mayor parleyed for Terms. We laid down our arms and opened the city gates. They marched into our streets, into the palace.

"Then they beheaded the Mayor. They called for all the heads of the Guilds, bade them come to the square with their families. First they killed the leaders of the guilds, then—"

"Then they slaughtered the women and children," Imoshen muttered, understanding her vision.

"No." He frowned at her.

Imoshen shook her head. It would have taken him at least a day to reach the Stronghold. Instinctively, she knew slaughter of the innocents was happening right now. And she was helpless to prevent it.

"When I left they were calling for the firstborn son of every family. My mother wouldn't let me go. They'd already killed my father, Guildmaster of the Silversmiths. She told me to slip away to the docks, and swim down river to escape."

Imoshen sprang to her feet. The goblet fell to the stone floor, rattling in a half circle. It was all horribly clear at last. "They're killing women and children, hunting them through the streets—"

"Who?" The General caught her arm, swung her around to face him.

"Your half-brother and his army!" she hissed. "It's a massacre! If you want the rest of the country to turn against you, go join the king and murder the townspeople of T'Diemn!"

She saw the General blanch. He did not question her claim.

"We ride at dawn," he bellowed. "I want every man of my Elite Guard ready to move out. I'll select a core guard to hold the Stronghold. Move!"

The men were startled into action. They headed for the door and the General strode past her to follow them. She caught his arm.

"What are you going to do?"

His dark eyes met hers. "Save the city. If I don't make a move I'll lose the Island."

She nodded. "You may have already lost the Island. When word of this gets out the people will fight to the death rather than be slaughtered after surrender."

"I keep my word!" General Tulkhan ground out. "Hasn't the Stronghold met with a fair surrender?"

Rage flared through Imoshen. She wanted to deny him his answer, but honesty forbade it.

"You have been fair." The words left a bitter taste in her mouth.

A muscle jumped in his cheek. His obsidian eyes blazed and she suddenly realized that his honor was at stake. At that moment she had an insight into the General's warrior code. It was so alien to hers in some ways, and yet so similar in others.

"What will you do? You are not the king and people are dying."

"What can I do? I am only a True-man, without T'En gifts. Let me go!" His voice was harsh.

She realized she had been holding his arm, though he could have easily thrust her aside. Anger burned in his dark eyes. Was he angry with her because of her ability to scry, or with his half-brother for risking what he had fought so hard to gain? Imoshen could not tell.

Now was not the time for a battle of wills. For once they were both on the same side. She wanted General Tulkhan to save the townspeople of T'Diemn. She released his arm and stepped back. He swung away from her, striding from the room.

Imoshen's bedchamber was suddenly empty except for

the exhausted, bloodied youth who had lain there at their feet watching all this. She offered him her hand. "Come to the fire."

"My Lady." He clasped her hand and brought it to his lips, raising a weary face to hers. "My mother is part T'En. She said the Aayel would know what to do. But they tell me the old one is dead. Do you trust this Ghebite General? How can you? When—"

"Nothing is that simple." She stared down at his bruised face, exasperated. "We can trust General Tulkhan to take steps to hold this island. And that does not include murdering the townspeople after they've surrendered. It goes against the principles of basic war craft!" She tightened her grasp and pulled on his hand. "Now come and let me clean you up."

He staggered a little as he came to his feet. His eyes were level with hers. "Nay. It would not be right for the last of the T'En to tend me."

Imoshen almost laughed. She pushed him toward the fireside. "Sit down." Then she turned to get her medicants. He reminded her of her brother, an odd mixture of earnest and cocksure. That thought made the laughter die on her lips. Her brother was dead. Every member of her family was lost to her. She was the last T'En, struggling to survive.

Even if she were able to forge an understanding with Tulkhan, he was not the king. His younger half-brother Gharavan held the power and he was sacking T'Diemn.

Imoshen felt she understood the General on one level at least. He was an honorable man by his own standards and a statesman. But what if this King Gharavan ordered Tulkhan to raze the Stronghold, execute her and her supporters? Her skin went cold. What would he do? Would he commit treason and betray his half-brother for her, a mere Dhamfeer?

It was a while since she had seen the contempt in his eyes, but he had a lifetime of prejudice to overcome. And anyway she was not one of his people. He owed her no allegiance. He owed her nothing. He did not even believe she carried his son.

So much for the Aayel's plans!

She shivered as she poured a few herbs into the bowl and dipped the cloth to cleanse the lad's face.

"It isn't right," he said suddenly.

"What isn't right?" She concentrated on the wound above his right eye, which had swollen shut. The gash in his forehead was bleeding freely still.

"It isn't right that you should serve me."

Imoshen met his good eye then, surprised to see it was the golden brown of a True-man's, while his skin was pale like her own. He was the result of six hundred years of inter-breeding.

"You have a name?" she asked.

"Drakin, uh Drake."

She smiled. His mother would have called him Drakin, little Drake. She wrung out the cloth and pressed the wound's edges together. Instinctively, she used her gift to urge the flesh to knit and felt the warmth flow through her fingers into his skin. He didn't flinch, seemed unaware of it.

Why did the healing come so easily to her? Imoshen didn't have time to wonder.

"It is as it should be, Drake. I am the last T'En. I live to serve the people. You are one of my people. Yes?" She smiled when she saw his bemused expression. He nodded briefly. "Then let me serve you."

She took the cloth away, pleased to see the wound had stopped bleeding. Applying crushed leaves to prevent it festering, she wrapped clean cloth around his head and saw to the lesser cuts on his lip. All the while she felt his eyes on her.

"Yes?" she asked at last.

"You are very like him. You could be his sister."

Even before she spoke she knew who Drake was referring to but she pretended not to understand. "My brother is dead."

"No. T'Reothe. He came to my parents to have his silver valued when he returned from his first voyage. I was only a lad then but I was allowed to stay. He spoke kindly to me, told me tales of things he had seen while my father weighed the silver.''

"Really?'' Imoshen knew so little about the man she had been betrothed to. So Reothe had been kind to a boy who could do him no favors. The thought hurt her and she realized she would rather not know Reothe's good qualities.

"My mother has your eyes. She told me tales of T'Imoshen the First. In T'Reothe I saw them come to life and now again in you,'' Drake whispered shyly. He touched her sixth finger lightly and his gaze lifted to her hair. "I heard he was betrothed to you and I wondered. Now I see. You were meant for him, to bring back the great—''

"Hush.'' She pressed her fingers to his lips, distressed by what she knew he would say. If she wanted Drake and other young men like him to live, she must lie. Those lies sprang easily to her lips. "That was another lifetime. Reothe is dead. I have made my peace with the General.''

"Murderer. His king called the Guild Heads to the square. He had them beheaded before their families. My mother screamed . . .'' He moaned, unable to go on.

Imoshen felt his terrible pain as if it was her own. When healing she had to open herself to the other's feelings. It left her vulnerable. But to dwell on it would only bring more suffering and anger. "You did the right thing in coming here. How did you manage it so quickly?''

He gave a rueful grin. "I stole a soldier's horse, rode it then walked it and rode it again. I tried to sneak into the Stronghold but the General's men caught me. They beat me.''

"I see. Kalleen?'' Imoshen came to her feet. She'd sensed the farm girl's curious presence for some time now. Her maidservant stepped forward. "This young man has done us a great service. Would you see that he has a room, someone to see to his needs.''

He protested faintly, his cheeks burning with embarrassment, but Imoshen ignored this. With some final instructions to Kalleen about preparing a healing broth, she left him by the fire with a blanket around him.

•   •   •

Restlessness plagued Imoshen. She had followed the Aayel's plan to success only to have her peace of mind destroyed by a petty Ghebite king.

She dragged a full-length white fur cloak which had been her mother's around her shoulders and made her way to the stairs. She needed to escape the confines of the Stronghold.

It was nearly dawn and the festivities of the Harvest Feast were over. In the courtyard by the stables the Elite Guard were already stirring. Imoshen could hear their excited voices, the champ of horses, the jingle of harness.

Driven by something she did not understand she made her way up to the battlements and paced their length. She could feel the sting of the cold predawn air on her cheeks and on her bare feet, but her body was warm within the cloak.

Out on the plain below hundreds of fires still dotted its far reaches. Her heart sank with the enormity of it all. Thousands of people sought shelter down there, expecting safety on her doorstep. And she had no magical path to safety, not even for herself. Covering her face with her hands, she withdrew into the stone crevice between the battlements, tears stinging her eyes.

Her ancestors had planned well, creating little stone nooks behind the battlements so that defenders could hold off their attackers protected on their unshielded right sides. But they had not anticipated a time when the Stronghold would surrender without a fight. Shame and frustration gnawed at her. While she stood here the people of T'Diemn suffered at the hands of King Gharavan.

If only the Aayel lived! She could have asked her greataunt's advice.

A shudder shook Imoshen. She dared not attempt another scrying. Now that she was facing her darkest fears she had to admit it—the thing had gotten beyond her control. She had run with that woman who fled her captor. Unleashed by her terror, a fire had sprung up spontaneously and engulfed the bed curtains. And what of that poor woman?

She was probably dead now. Imoshen had not saved her, could not even save herself.

Scalding hot tears slid unheeded down her cheeks.

Lack of sleep made her weary, lack of food made her light-headed. As she pulled the cloak tighter about her, she caught a faint scent of her mother. She closed her eyes, seeking comfort.

But the dead offered no comfort.

Only Reothe still lived. He had known his gifts longer than her. He had healed her wrist then shown her she could do the same for him, something she had never known she was capable of. He was familiar in a haunting way, a mirror to herself. If only she could ask his advice.

She felt sleep creep up on her, making a mockery of her racing thoughts.

As she drifted the sounds from the courtyard below interwove with her dream so that she thought she was lying in a cold hollow in the woods, hearing the enemy pass by. There was no fire to warm herself or her companions for they couldn't risk one. They were rebels.

Then she recognized the identity of the person who lay beside her in the hollow, felt his warmth down her length.

"Reothe?"

His eyes gleamed in the dark woods.

"Imoshen?"

It was so real, but sometimes dreams were like that. Suddenly she wanted to unburden herself.

"The General goes to stop his half-brother the king from slaughtering the townsfolk of T'Diemn. I fear for my life, for his."

"And for mine?"

Imoshen opened her mouth to speak, then it occurred to her that she had already named him a dead man tonight.

Reothe clutched her shoulders, pulling her close to him. She felt his hard thigh between her legs. His face, coarse with its unshaven growth, scraped her cheek. His mouth was hard on hers. Yet it moved her to feel him like this—needful, urgent. She let herself go, savoring the fire of his touch, the fire created by his body's need for her. His mouth claimed hers.

Suddenly, he inhaled sharply.

"What have you done this night?" he hissed, his breath fanning over her skin. "I can taste him on your mouth, smell him on your skin. How could you give yourself to him? You were mine. Promised to me!"

His rage both frightened and aroused her. She wanted to laugh.

"You arrogant fool!" Only in her dream would she dare to speak like this to him. "The world has changed. I am a caged captive, awaiting my death sentence. You are a woodland mouse fleeing before the raptor."

"How could you do this?" he whispered, running his hands down her body. She felt the hard length of him against her, the possessiveness in his body and understood that he wanted her. "How is it that I can touch you?"

She lay there, watching his face by the twin moonlight filtering through the trees. There were other shadowy forms in the hollow with them. She could smell their unwashed bodies. The damp was seeping through her clothes.

Suddenly, Imoshen knew this was no dream.

She went to move, but he restrained her.

Reothe lifted on one elbow, his other arm stretched jealously across her. She heard him send the others on to scout the party they were tracking. They scurried away through the woods, leaving her alone with Reothe.

She shrugged out of his grasp, pulling herself up to hug her knees. He sat up to watch her. His pale face and hair glowed in the twin moonlight. It was a bad night for hunting, too much visibility.

Suddenly he smiled. "If you have given yourself to him, why did you come to me?"

She opened her mouth to speak but did not want to admit her fear.

He leaned forward, crouching before her in the deep debris of the forest. She could smell the dying leaves, taste the tang of winter on the air. But overlying all that was his scent, his hunger for her.

"You came to me because you are bound to me. We are the last of our kind. Your body calls to mine. I felt it the first time I saw you, saw it waken in you that time in the woods when you quickened at my touch. You came to me because I called you—''

''No!'' She tried to think through the rush of desire that warmed her body. Once again she did not know if what she felt was her own natural reaction to him, or some trick he used to seduce her.

Imoshen hated her uncertainty, hated feeling out of control. Confused, she rolled to her feet and stepped around him, pacing across the clearing in the dappled light of the twin moons. It was as if a thin band joined them—the further she moved from him, the more painful the sensation was.

She spun to face him. ''What are you doing, Reothe?''

He came to his feet, a pale silver figure. He exuded a menace she hadn't recognized before. Still she stood her ground as he walked slowly, almost silently, through the leaf litter toward her.

''You gave him that which should have been mine.'' Reothe's voice was low, a corrosive caress. ''I want you. Come to me now. Join with me. We will be so much more paired, than apart.''

She felt the strength of the bond which joined them, felt it tighten, drawing him to her, preparing her for him. In a flash Imoshen understood what he wanted.

Fear gripped her. Even though she had never lain with Reothe he had this ability to cloud her mind and arouse her body. How much more power would he have over her if she were to take him willingly into her arms, into her body and into her mind?

More importantly, if he had her at his side the people would see them as a viable alternative to the Ghebite invaders. All her plans would go astray. General Tulkhan would—

Reothe cursed. He sprang forward to cover the distance between them.

She knew if he laid a hand on her she would be unable to resist his strange allure. Everything slowed. Like some feral being from a nightmare he covered the distance between them. She saw him passing through the patches of moonlight, alternately illuminated and dark, his face twisted in a grimace of determination.

The realization hit her—she could not stand against him. "No!" The cry was torn from her.

Imoshen turned and tried to run.

Thud. Her head struck the stone of the battlements. Tears of pain stung her eyes. Heart still raging in her chest, she staggered to her feet, trying to take stock of her surroundings. She was alone, standing on the ramparts of her family's Stronghold.

Anxiously she searched the long walk, but it was empty. Reothe was not here, could not follow. If he was able to move as she had, he would not have had to use the secret passage in the Abbey. No wonder he wanted her to join forces with him. Yet, she had no idea how she had traveled to him. Had she really been present in the glade, or had it only been her mind which joined Reothe? Everything had seemed so real.

One thing was clear, Reothe considered their vow still stood. He wanted her. More than that he needed her to regain Fair Isle. Had she made the right choice?

Feeling the dawn breeze lift her long hair, Imoshen pulled the cloak more tightly about her. Grimly, she turned to go inside. A dark figure strode toward her. Her heart lurched. For a moment she thought it was Reothe come for her. Then she recognized the set of General Tulkhan's broad shoulders, his outline unfamiliar in full battle regalia.

"T'Imoshen," he said, giving her her full royal title. He performed something she assumed was a formal gesture of greeting in his own land.

She felt utterly vulnerable, frightened by what she had learned, afraid of being left alone for fear Reothe would find a way into the Stronghold. She was afraid for the General because he went to meet King Gharavan and possibly oppose him, and last of all she feared for her own future and that of the child she had begun this night.

If General Tulkhan was not strong enough to stand against his half-brother and win him over, her position was dangerous.

"I have come to ask something of you," the General said. She could tell he did not like to ask. "I must take most of my men to confront my half-brother. A small force will remain here—''

''You have my word we will not rise against you,'' Imoshen cut him short. She stepped forward, covering the distance between them. She wanted to feel his hands on her, feel his reality once more before she was left to deal with her fears alone. ''You will not be fighting a war on two fronts.''

She heard his ragged intake of breath, felt his rough soldier's hands on her flesh as she drew them inside her cloak. The simple shift she wore parted for him. His breath caught in his throat as she placed his palms on her flesh.

She strained against him.

''Take care when you move against your king,'' she whispered, her lips moving on his skin where his jaw met the tendon of his throat.

His unshaven chin scraped her face as their lips met, his words came in a puff of breath over her face. ''I don't fear him. He's poorly advised. Gharavan will listen to me. I taught him to ride, to fight.''

His callused palm brushed her taut breast. A moan escaped her. The material of her shift tore. It was a shocking sound, punctuated by their ragged breathing, his guttural groan.

He shuddered as she boldly cupped his arousal through the material of his breeches. Wrapped in their twin cloaks, the trapped air between them grew hot. She felt the hard stone at her back as he pinned her there.

She wanted him now, as much of him as she could have. It did not matter if this was illogical. She didn't want him to leave, to face danger alone as she would be doing. Her unspoken desperation seemed to call to something in him.

He shuddered as he stepped away from her. She followed, pressing her face into his neck. Her tongue touched his throat where she felt the tight cords of his neck, the pounding of his pulse.

She wound her fingers through his cloak. He stepped back again, though she could feel how much it cost him.

Why was he rejecting her?

He was about to ride out. Imoshen flushed. Was she so

desperate for him that she would join with him here on the battlements?

The answer was simple. Yes.

Shame heated her cheeks. What had possessed her? She must not lose sight of her real purpose here. "The rebels will look for any sign of Ghebite dissension—"

"Don't you think I know that?"

"Where do you stand on this, Imoshen?"

She sucked in her breath. Where did she stand? Not with Reothe, not with futile fighting and more bloodshed. But did she truly stand with the Ghebites?

Could she lie? No.

"I stand for the people of Fair Isle, for their right to live without fear and oppression."

He nodded once as if this was no more or less than he expected. "And you will back me so long as I follow that course?"

This time she could answer without hesitation. "Yes."

There were cries from the courtyard below, the sound of men gathering. General Tulkhan stalked to the stone work and waved down to the men. They responded with the Ghebite war cry.

"We march. Come here to my side, Imoshen."

It was a show for his men, for those of her personal Stronghold Guard who would remain here and might be tempted to take a stand. Imoshen hesitated, understanding the significance of her public support of the Ghebite General but she joined him. Whatever her personal feelings, they must present a united front.

The General's men fell silent at the sight of her at his side but those of her retinue, the servants who had prepared the food for the journey, the stable hands who had saddled the horses, gave a ragged cheer.

"Kiss me," Tulkhan whispered. "Pull me into your arms and kiss me."

She was shocked by the naked hunger in his voice and by the unspoken message he wanted to impart to those below.

"Do it," he hissed, turning to her.

Imoshen faltered. To lie with him at the Festival of the Harvest Moons when she had been chosen was one thing, but to accept him like this before her people and his was another thing entirely. Would her own people despise her for taking the invader willingly into her bed?

"I must have your support if I'm to stop the bloodshed," he whispered.

The General was right. She stepped forward, her eyes fixed on his grim mouth. She felt the breadth of his chest on her hands as she reached for him, felt the longing of her body to cleave to his. When his mouth sought hers she was ready to open for him. His broad hands found the small of her back, pulling her into him, pressing her body intimately into his.

Dimly, she heard the cheering from below, but there was a great rushing in her ears. She felt both frightened and exhilarated. There was nothing halfhearted about his response. His hunger for her had never been in doubt. It was a physical reaction which, if her own body was anything to go by, he had little control over. But whatever the reason for his need, he was certainly not above using their attraction for political gain.

Even knowing this, she longed for him as their lips parted.

General Tulkhan waved to the men gathered below and shouted: "Time to ride."

They cheered.

"Ride safely, ride swiftly," she gave him the formal reply.

Imoshen was still standing on the battlements when the sun rose and the tail end of the Ghebite General's men left the plain, entering the thick woods.

Her gaze traveled the plain, taking in the campfires, the makeshift dwellings. The land below the Stronghold walls teamed with refugees, desperate people who had come to her for safety.

A new phase in her life had begun. Whether she had

intended it or not, she had made a commitment to General
Tulkhan and she had to see it through. Just as she had done
whatever she had to ensure her personal survival, she would
do whatever she needed to ensure the survival of her dream.
The people of Fair Isle had no one else to care for their
future.

T'Reothe, the General and King Gharavan—as far as she
knew they were following their own plans for their own ends.
True, she wanted to survive, but she wanted more. Fair Isle
and its people were her responsibility.

General Tulkhan's troops were used to moving quickly and
they made good time despite a chilling downpour the following day.

The scouts spotted the desperate townsfolk on the great
eastern road out of T'Diemn. Those who were able to run
fled from the Ghebite scouts but several, mainly the old and
injured, were captured and delivered to Tulkhan. He knew the
value of information and ordered the columns to stop while
he questioned them.

He had a hard time convincing the poor wretches he was
not going to summarily execute them. They spoke of cruelty,
of mass murder. Rumor had it every inhabitant of T'Diemn
was dead.

Tulkhan's army marched on, leaving the people he'd
questioned by the side of the road. They watched him and his
men with dull eyes, seething with the hatred born of power-
less desperation.

He'd spoken to them personally, struggling with the local patois, but many of them spoke the more common language of trade. Tulkhan told them to go home, to tell the
people who had fled their farms to return to their homes and
villages, that there would be no more killing. They did not
seem convinced.

It was late afternoon when Tulkhan saw the fabled
T'Diemn for the first time. The sun was setting behind the
domes and spires, cloaking the destruction caused by the

invaders with a deceptive golden haze. Some of that haze had to be smoke hanging heavy on the still air.

The city had sprawled beyond its original fortified walls. From the rise where his party stood Tulkhan could see that it was the more recent outer buildings of T'Diemn that still smoldered in places.

As they rode down the paved road he recognized the signs of a prosperous city. Beside the road stood little shrines made of dressed stone and clearly well cared for. But as they came closer to the outlying buildings they could see the devastation.

In the steadily growing twilight the stench of smoke hung on the air, rich with the stink of death. No children ran in the burned out streets, no chickens or pigs. What buildings remained were boarded up and shuttered. Tulkhan sensed hostility and fear, as if the city were drawing its collective breath to face another onslaught.

A deep and pervading anger settled in Tulkhan's core. He knew from experience that sometimes a show of force was necessary, but he abhorred senseless cruelty and destruction. Behind him his men were silent, only the chink of their weapons and the creak of their horses' gear punctuated the steady thud of the horses' hooves.

When he crossed the bridge and approached the great gates that pierced the wall of the inner city, Tulkhan saw the heads on the pikes and his fury rose a notch. Making an example of three assassins who had attempted to take his life was one thing, killing townsfolk who had laid down their weapons after surrendering was unacceptable.

Tulkhan tried to imagine his charming young half-brother giving the order and could not. Gharavan was not vindictive. When Tulkhan had last seen the youth he would have sworn he did not have the ruthless nature required for this.

No one opposed them as General Tulkhan and his men entered the oldest part of the city and made their way up through the winding streets to the tall spires of the royal palace.

The nearer they came to the city center the less destruction Tulkhan saw. He noted men of his brother's army lying drunk in the streets. His own men rode by without answering their bawdy cries. Here not every place was boarded shut and the taverns were open doing a roaring trade. No doubt the women of the street were busy as well. But the respectable townsfolk made their opinion clear by their absence.

Tulkhan entered the main square where the rain had washed most of the blood from the stones. He paused to study the royal palace. Which building was it? A great multi-domed structure stood on the west side of the square, facing a large towered building on the east. Smaller but equally spectacular buildings faced the square on the north and south sides.

He had read of the wonders of Fair Isle. Its wealth and culture were legendary on the mainland. This was why he had launched his attack when the Lowlands negotiated a surrender without resistance and the southern kingdoms expected him to continue south on the mainland, consolidating his hold. But Tulkhan had other plans. He wanted Fair Isle. He believed if Fair Isle fell it would demoralize the southern kingdoms. Strike swiftly, strike unexpectedly, that was his credo, and look where it had led him—to the very palace of the T'En.

Triumph and contempt made him smile, for these legendary rulers of Fair Isle had not felt the need to build their palace as a defensible last stand. In their arrogance they had created a palace of fragile glass and delicate stone towers.

At that moment the clouds parted and the setting sun bathed the white stone of the building crimson with its caress. The palace blazed with a welcome glow of light against the blue-black clouds of the retreating storm.

But Tulkhan did not mistake this for an omen. He knew the real storm lay inside. Dismounting, he ordered his commanders to have the men camp in the square. They could have taken shelter in the palace or claimed any building they took a liking to, but Tulkhan wanted his men isolated from the rot he had found in his half-brother's army. He wanted to be sure his men remained self-disciplined, ready to come to his aid.

Leaving the commanders to make camp with their usual efficiency, Tulkhan entered the palace by one of the largest entrances. A young, slightly drunk Ghebite soldier straightened at his approach. Recognizing Tulkhan he blinked and tried to draw his weapon in formal salute. The General brushed past him wordlessly, too angry to speak.

He followed the bawdy music, laughter and feminine squeals down a series of long formal galleries. Hundreds of candles were already alight, filling the air with their scented wax.

His boots crunched on the smashed glass and crockery littering the brilliant mosaics on the floor. Wall hangings so rich the colors glowed hung lopsided from their frames. The destruction reminded him of animals invading a home, smashing, eating, fornicating at will, unable to appreciate the beauty of their surroundings.

How Imoshen would mock him if she could see this.

Imoshen—he felt a yearning tug deep within him, and was glad she was not there to witness this destruction.

Shame filled him, quickly replaced by anger.

Tulkhan thrust open double doors to see half a dozen Ghebite soldiers drinking and gambling. He took in their state of undress, their inebriation. Amongst them he recognized a number of the small-boned, golden-skinned males and females of Fair Isle decked out in borrowed finery. Their overbright, frightened eyes watched him carefully.

Tulkhan marched straight across to a young Ghebite noble and pulled him upright by his fancy jerkin.

"Where is Gharavan?"

The youth gasped, tried to focus his wine-dulled perceptions and blinked. "General Tulkhan?"

Startled, he plucked ineffectually at Tulkhan's hands, but his voice held a note of reprimand when he replied. "The king is in the far chamber entertaining."

Tulkhan tossed the youth back onto the ornate couch with the others. Before this campaign the young men who had associated with his half-brother had respected him. To them he was the triumphant General Tulkhan, almost a legendary figure.

In those days the young nobles as yet unblooded by war had been eager to hear stories of his battles. Tulkhan cursed softly. Now his half-brother was king and he was expected to show respect to these puppies!

"Take me to him," Tulkhan ground out, hardly able to contain his fury.

The youth stood and straightened his clothes.

"This way, *General*." He made the title an insult.

As Tulkhan entered the throne room of the T'En Emperor he was only dimly aware of the white walls inlaid with pale golden designs. His gaze was drawn through the tall multipaned windows to the leaping flames of a huge bonfire in the courtyard beyond. The hungry blaze cast bizarre moving patterns over the room's inhabitants. Leering, leaping shadows danced along the walls. Tulkhan felt as if he had entered a waking nightmare.

This room was even more crowded than the outer chamber. Hundreds of scented candles hung from ornate candelabras, crusted heavily with several days' wax, or littered the tables, guttering in their own wax puddles. The room's inhabitants were as varied as the lighting. They consisted of his half-brother, the king, and his advisors. Some were old and wily men Tulkhan recognized as advisors to his father, others were ambitious and brash, barely out of their teens. They were dressed in what he assumed was the latest fashion of the Ghebite court.

Food was piled high on several low tables. Fair Isle musicians played unfamiliar instruments. Obviously they were locals forced to appease the invader. The others, pretty young men and women of T'Diemn, suddenly stopped their revelry as they caught sight of Tulkhan. The silence spread. It was not a welcoming silence.

Sprawled on a luxurious day bed surrounded by sycophants, Gharavan's face settled into petulant lines. Tulkhan's heart sank.

News of his father's death had come to Tulkhan on the battlefield. He had sent his sworn fealty to his half-brother and continued the campaign. Now that Gharavan was no longer the boy-heir Tulkhan was ready to accord him the respect the King of the Ghebites deserved. He strode forward purposefully, his boots striking the tiles loudly in the hushed silence. He felt the eyes of the assembled elite of King Gharavan's traveling court on him. Some were amused, some openly curious.

Tulkhan tensed. He had never been a courtier, content to play lapdog at his father's side. There was no warmth in his half-brother's eyes, only wary resentment.

Where was the happy-go-lucky boy he remembered?

Tulkhan dropped to one knee; king or not, he really wanted to haul this weak youth outside and douse his head under a water pump before knocking some sense into him.

Instead, General Tulkhan placed his hand over his chest and bowed his head.

"The last royal Stronghold is taken, the people from this town to the Landsend swear allegiance to you, my King. As do I, your half-brother, General of the Ghebite army."

The relief in the room was palpable.

His half-brother straightened, pushing a partially clad girl away.

"Tulkhan!" His eyes blazed with drunken fondness and a certain sly satisfaction. "So you've torn yourself away from your campaigning at last to come and swear fealty."

Tulkhan rose and glared down at his half-brother, seeing the old familiar pettiness, the inclination to self-indulgence, written in his features. These were things he had always regarded as youthful excesses. What might have been charming and forgiven in a young boy were dangerous weaknesses in a king. But Tulkhan knew enough of human nature to understand now was not the time to berate his half-brother.

"You will wish to hear how the campaign went," he announced. "Where will we go?"

Gharavan had no such wish. Tulkhan could see his half-brother simply wanted to stay where he was. But he came to his feet, overcome as always by Tulkhan's stronger will.

"The antechamber at the far end would be suitable, my

King,'' a Vaygharian of about Tulkhan's age advised. "I will have food and wine sent through to you.''

King Gharavan hesitated, then seemed to decide to make the best of it. Swinging his arm through Tulkhan's, he ambled toward the far door, waving to the musicians as he approached. ''Continue.''

As Tulkhan drew nearer he could read fear in their faces. Though they smiled and inclined their heads in obeisance to the invading king, their hearts were closed. They hated him. His half-brother had done irreparable damage to the peace. It was one thing to capture a land, quite another to hold it.

When they entered the antechamber, a servant was hurriedly scurrying out after lighting a sconce of scented candles. The far door had barely closed when Tulkhan rounded on his half-brother.

''What were you thinking of, to murder your subjects like this?''

''To teach them respect, these townsfolk were over-proud. True, they surrendered, but they smirked behind my back, called me a barbarian king!''

''So you proved them right?'' Rage flooded Tulkhan. ''What possessed you?''

''I had to break them, to show them I had ultimate power. Only fear would bring them to their knees—''

''With hate in their hearts and a knife at the ready behind their backs!'' Tulkhan paced to the tall windows and looked into the courtyard, where embers from the fire blew on the breeze. What was Gharavan burning? A charred manuscript lay in the cinders. Tulkhan ground his teeth, knowing this evidence would only confirm Imoshen's opinion of the Ghebites.

''Now they jump to do my bidding!'' Gharavan muttered with surly defensiveness.

''Only because they fear you.''

The young king laughed, an odd, high sound, almost unsteady. ''And don't they fear you, Tulkhan the Ghebite General?''

Tulkhan turned and caught his half-brother by the shirt-front, smelling wine on his breath. It disgusted him.

"They respect me. I keep my word." He watched as Gharavan blinked uneasily. "I can't believe you gave this order. Who advised you on this mad venture? Didn't you realize you were fostering insurgence?"

"Insurgence?" a voice repeated.

Tulkhan spun to see the dark-haired Vaygharian who had suggested they use this room. He had never liked the Vayghars. In his father's youth the Vayghar nation had chosen to form an alliance with Gheeaba rather than do battle. Since then they had grown rich feasting on the wealth of Ghebite conquests and their merchant-aristocracy had infiltrated the upper echelons of Gheeaba.

Tulkhan turned to his half-brother, who made the introduction.

"My advisor, Kinraid of the Vayghar."

Kinraid inclined his head, offering the merest civility of greeting. Tulkhan felt an instinctive dislike.

"You spoke of insurgence?" Kinraid smiled. In Gheeaba it was said a Vaygharian could smile while he traded you out of your home and wives. "You, who harbors Imoshen, last princess of the T'En? Even now rebels gather in the heavily forested highlands to the south, plotting to steal back Fair Isle. The Princess will be their rallying point, a Throwback, a Dhamfeer bitch. Was bedding her worth the risk?"

Red anger blazed through Tulkhan's veins. He wanted to cross that space between them, to take the Vaygharian by the throat and throttle the life from him. He'd already taken two steps when he collected himself.

The Vayghar smiled.

The man was no fool—Tulkhan could read malevolent intelligence in Kinraid's gaze. With a start he realized this Vayghar was his real enemy. This was the man who had been whispering poison in his half-brother's ear.

Tulkhan felt them both watching him, waiting for his reaction. He ran through the options. If he were to answer the provocation now his half-brother would be justified in calling in his own guards. Gharavan could have him executed in self-defense and his own men would be helpless to come to his aid. They would be fed a pack of lies they wouldn't believe. But their allegiance was to the throne and if he was dead, what was the point of opposing their king?

All this flashed through Tulkhan's mind in less than a heartbeat and he knew he must tread warily.

"T'Imoshen has given me her word," he said, giving the Dhamfeer her title. "She will not urge the thousands of peasants who have fled to the Stronghold for safety to rise against us."

"And why should we believe this Dhamfeer bitch?" his half-brother asked, belligerence lighting his dark eyes.

Tulkhan met Gharavan's gaze and knew at that moment he trusted Imoshen, the Dhamfeer woman, more than his own flesh and blood.

He had made this boy his first wooden practice sword and taught him to fight. He had picked him up when he fell off his horse, dusted him off, soothed his hurts and loved him like a father. Their own father had been too obsessed with ruling his growing lands to take the time to father his sons.

Tulkhan lifted a hand and saw his half-brother flinch, but he laid it gently on Gharavan's shoulder. "Unless you want the whole country rising against you, you must stop this vindictive slaughter. Offer them an honorable peace. There is much we can learn from these people. Theirs is an ancient culture."

Gharavan's eyes searched his face and for a moment Tulkhan was reminded of a younger, charming youth who had listened breathlessly to tales of his campaigns.

"It is much easier to rule by love than fear. Fear must be enforced, love is given." They were old lessons, learned at the knee of his tutor who had stood in for his absent parent. Gharavan nodded and Tulkhan forged on, hope rising in his chest. "We must win back their trust, their respect. Make reparation to the families of the Guildmasters, call on the leaders of the city to help govern T'Diemn. They know the needs of the city and its people—"

"And all of this will stop the rebels?" Kinraid asked.

Tulkhan turned to him. "No, but it is better to fight on

one front than two. We need to secure the townspeople's loyalty.''

''And what of your loyalty?'' The Vaygharian strode toward them, placing a protective hand on the young king's shoulder. ''I did not see you swearing fealty when Gharavan was crowned. You walk in here, criticize his judgment and order him about! Who is king here?''

A spasm of anger gripped Tulkhan. He could already see the doubts taking root in his half-brother's febrile mind.

''My loyalty is not at doubt. I serve the king. I have secured Fair Isle for his glory—''

''Secured it?'' Kinraid remarked scornfully. ''Not when the rebels congregate in the southern highlands and prepare to make forays against us.''

''True.'' Gharavan was ready to find fault with Tulkhan. ''What of this T'Reothe? I hear he's a Dhamfeer prince, betrothed to the bitch you are so hot for.''

Tulkhan winced. He noted the Vaygharian's eyes gleam with satisfaction.

They could not know whether he had bedded Imoshen or not. It was simply speculation, but it revealed the way their minds worked. They were united against him, unwilling to listen to reason.

Tulkhan could see the Vaygharian maneuverings as clearly as if they were laid out on a chart before him, but could think of no way to avoid the coming confrontation. The man was dangerous.

''If you were truly loyal to King Gharavan,'' Kinraid announced, ''you would take those men who serve you and lead them in the service of your king. Clear out the rebel camps.''

''Yes. Wipe them out like the vermin they are,'' Gharavan's face glowed at the thought.

Tulkhan could not afford to hesitate; it would only confirm his disloyalty. Yet . . . ''The highlands are inhospitable. In places a whole army could disappear and not find its way out. The rebels have chosen well.''

''You refuse my order?'' his half-brother demanded.

''No.'' Tulkhan tried not to let reluctance tinge his

voice. "I serve my king. My advice is not tainted by personal gain. Remember that, Vanny." He'd used the diminutive, the nickname he had given his brother as a child, with the intention of reminding him of their shared background. The Vaygharian might be a clever, cunning man, but he did not have their history. "I will stay a few days and help to restore order and placate the townspeople. Then I will take my forces south and seek the rebels."

It took four days to calm the people of T'Diemn. Tulkhan lost count of the number of times he needed Imoshen's sage advice. He did not know these people, their customs or their beliefs.

Acting under vague orders from his half-brother, he saw to it that fires were extinguished, food distributed and the damaged homes were rebuilt by the king's own soldiers.

He met with the various leaders of the city, from the civil administrators and Guildmasters to the head of the T'En Church. The Beatific was a woman, which once again reminded him of the differences in their cultures. In T'En society there were many women in positions of authority. They were mature women who by Ghebite standards would have been considered non-persons. But they spoke with the weight of experience and he could not fault their advice.

He saw to it that businesses and produce markets reopened and normal services were resumed.

Tulkhan offered his personal apology to those who had lost loved ones and was abused or berated for his efforts. He took this as a good sign because it meant the townspeople did not fear him. Through it all he focused on the outcome. If he did not win over the people of T'Diemn they would be against him. Should the countryside rise against him and harbor the rebels, they would be welcomed into the capital at the first opportunity.

He could not afford to lose the support of the people of T'Diemn.

If there was an overwhelming swing against the Ghebites he was doubtful of Imoshen's loyalty. She was a pragmatist and he had to admit that if he were in her position he would side with the winning army whether it was invader or rebel. Imoshen wanted peace for her people, not years of protracted warfare.

On the evening of the fourth day Tulkhan strode into the private entertainment wing of the royal palace looking for his half-brother. He wanted to return to the Stronghold to be certain of Imoshen's loyalty but he told himself this was unnecessary. Unless other factors changed Imoshen would keep her word.

It had been a harrowing six days, six days apart from Imoshen when he had been living day and night with her. He could have used her reassuring presence and her diplomatic skills on many occasions while dealing with the towns-people, and he had even considered sending for her.

But the knowledge that he had sworn to enter the southern highlands to hunt the rebels stopped him. Much as he needed her, he could not bring Imoshen to the palace and leave her at the mercy of his half-brother and that treacherous Vaygharian. Instinct told him that once Imoshen was in Kinraid's power he would relinquish her. Let Imoshen remain safely among her own people of the Stronghold.

Tulkhan grimaced as he heard the usual sounds of revelry. The room was full of young Ghebite nobles for whom the campaign had been one good billet after another, one party after another while the foot soldiers moved on ahead and cleaned up resistance. Sprinkled amidst them were the fawning advisors who had curried favor with King Gharavan, offering him the words he most wanted to hear and nothing else. Tulkhan was surprised by a surge of hatred for them all.

Those nearest the entrance looked over at him. No one offered a friendly greeting.

He had noticed a definite change in these young men. A subtle rot had set in. They cast him sly, mocking looks, and there were barely whispered jokes about the man who lay with the Dhamfeer. His part in the Harvest Feast was now common knowledge, not that he regretted it.

Despite this, Tulkhan remained hopeful. On the few occasions he had been alone with his half-brother he had managed to talk some sense, to plan for the future of Fair Isle. Now he hoped for one last talk before he left. He had to impress his loyalty on the youth.

The smaller antechamber where he and Gharavan had had their first private meeting seemed a sensible place to look for his half-brother. Someone tittered as he strode toward the door. Tulkhan ignored them. There wasn't a man amongst them he would choose to have at his back in a fight.

He thrust the door open and stepped inside, expecting to catch his brother with one of the wenches. Instead he found Gharavan and the Vaygharian naked on the fur before the fire.

Gharavan lifted his head, visibly annoyed at the interruption. Tulkhan cursed. This was worse than he expected. It was common for young Ghebite men to take a male lover. It was encouraged in the ranks because it made a stronger fighting force. But now Tulkhan understood the hold the Vaygharian had over his half-brother. No wonder he would not listen to Tulkhan. While Kinraid was Gharavan's lover the youthful king would always give more weight to his words.

The Vaygharian raised himself on one elbow and studied Tulkhan calmly, making no attempt to cover his nakedness.

"What do you want?" Gharavan snapped.

"I ride at dawn," Tulkhan's voice revealed nothing of his feelings. "The townspeople are resigned. They will bring their disputes to your tribunal for satisfaction. It is your chance to prove just." His brother waved this aside, irritating Tulkhan. He wanted to say more, but with the Vaygharian's insolent eyes on him he knew it was pointless. "I will go to my bunk. Good night."

"So early? Why don't you take one those willing girls or boys?" Gharavan's smile was vicious and vindictive. "Ah, but I forgot, your tastes do not run that way. I'm afraid we haven't any Dhamfeer to indulge you. In my court we draw the line at bestiality!"

It was a deliberate insult, delivered with more venom than he expected of his half-brother. Tulkhan knew from the satisfied smirk on Kinraid's face that something similar must have passed his lips recently.

Seething with anger Tulkhan turned and left them, marching through the cluster of men and women who had fallen silent when he opened the door to the outer room. They watched him, amused by his disgrace. It struck him with a savage sorrow that he was watching the decline of his father's power. The old master who taught him tactics was right—a monarchy is only as strong as its king.

Imoshen finished braiding her hair and tossed the heavy plait over her shoulder. So far so good. Nothing had arisen that she could not deal with. As appointed leader of the Elite Guard, Wharrd was responsible to her. The Ghebites had responded to her orders promptly, without a grumble. They were vastly outnumbered by her own Stronghold Guard and the refugees, and very aware of it.

To keep everyone occupied and because it served a useful purpose, she had set the able-bodied adults to building a new town on the plain below the Stronghold. Sturdy wooden houses were springing up with broad paths between. If the refugees were to survive the bitter winter as well as the threat of disease through overcrowding, simple sanitation had to be observed, fresh water supplied and waste disposed of.

Already people were setting up shops to ply their trades—seamstresses, carpenters, bakers, cobblers. From the battlements yester-eve she had marveled to see the town emerging, one that would rival T'Diemn in size and population, if not in cultural accomplishments.

"Oh, Mistress," Kalleen gasped as she ran into the room. "I would have been here to do your hair but for . . ." She rolled her eyes expressively.

Imoshen did not need further explanation.

"It is nothing. I could not sleep." Imoshen rose and stepped closer to her maid. She could smell lovemaking on Kalleen's body and recognized the scent of the youth, Drake. "Should I look to find a place for Drake in the Stronghold?

We don't have a silversmith since old man Larkin died and his apprentice went off to war and got himself killed.''

Kalleen glowed and preened. ''It's not as if he has said anything yet.''

Imoshen laughed and pulled her cloak on. Even inside the Stronghold it had grown colder. The sooner they finished the shelters the better for those on the plain.

She was climbing the stairs after taking inventory of the food stores when Drake suddenly stepped from the shadows. His intense gaze held hers, their faces level. Something was amiss. His overbright eyes worried her.

Imoshen touched his forehead instinctively, checking for fever. ''What is it, Drake, are you unwell?''

When he caught her hand his trembled with energy. She assumed he had come to speak of Kalleen and nervousness held his tongue.

''Tell me what you wish,'' she urged.

''Lady T'En.'' He fell to his knees, bringing her hand to his lips. ''I am here to serve you. I know how General Tulkhan has forced you to serve him. But he is gone and I'm well enough now. I have two horses saddled. You can escape to the forests, to the rebels. I hear T'Reothe himself leads them—''

''Hush!'' Imoshen stiffened. For the moment the Elite Guard were obeying her, but she knew their ultimate loyalty was to Tulkhan. ''You mustn't speak that one's name here. The Stronghold and all who live here are sworn to General Tulkhan's service. Besides,'' she hesitated, looking into his earnest face. The bruising over his eye had faded to a greenish yellow now. He was so young, so sincere and so eager to die for a cause.

She felt immeasurably older than he, though they were about the same age. With a tug she urged him to rise. ''Who knows if Reothe lives? They say he leads the rebels, but it could be some imposter using his name. Winter will be upon us soon and the rebels will have to suffer through it in the deep woods, without shelter or safety from pursuit.'' She paused. Drake did not look convinced.

"The Stronghold needs you," she tried again. "We have no silversmith."

Servants came up the stairs eager to consult Imoshen about household arrangements. The youth uttered an impatient exclamation. She smiled and squeezed his hand sympathetically, then turned to deal with the servants' requests. When she had finished he was gone.

Imoshen sighed. Instinct told her Drake was unconvinced.

That evening as she sat before the fire calculating how to bring water from the underground caverns into the new town, Kalleen came to prepare her for bed. The young girl's hair was untidy, her face truculent and her eyes red-rimmed. Intent on her work, Imoshen didn't notice the signs for a moment.

"I need an engineer like . . ." she muttered softly as she looked up. "Why, what is wrong, Kalleen?"

The girl brushed her cheek impatiently. "He's gone, my Lady."

"Drake?" Imoshen's heart sank. She did not have to be told where he had gone—in search of Reothe, glory and death. "I offered him a place here."

"I know." A bitter sob escaped Kalleen. "It was not enough. *I* was not enough for him."

Imoshen came to her feet, hugging the girl. There was nothing she could say.

Far to the south in the treacherous highlands, Tulkhan led his mount up the steep incline. Behind him his men were scattered over the slope, also leading their mounts. The noise they were making was enough to wake the dead. Spread out as they were they offered a prime target for ambush.

He felt the sweat of fear drying on his skin. Here on the north slope of the hillside he was shielded from the cold wind, and the sun was a welcome change from the chill which crept up through a man's boots into his bones, stealing his very passion for life.

The same chill had seen dozens of his men come down

with a bone-shaking fever. He'd had to leave them in the small villages which dotted the southern highlands and trust they would not be murdered in their sick beds.

He made the crest and looked out to the south over the densely wooded ridges which stretched like frozen green waves, rolling away as far as the distant southern ocean. It was impossible to march an army through land like this. The rebel leader would find it ideal for a trap.

Tulkhan was only too aware of their vulnerability. If he'd been Reothe, instead of the hunter on this fool's errand chasing shadows, he would have harried his pursuer till not a man stood.

Only two nights ago he and his men had accepted the hospitality of one of the T'En southern nobles. It did not take Tulkhan long to recognize the signs. The man and his family were giving lip service to the Ghebites, but their loyalty lay with the rebels.

When the nobleman claimed he knew nothing of the rebels' whereabouts, Tulkhan could have had him executed. This might have loosened the tongues of his three daughters. But it would have made them hate him and strengthened their resolve to stay loyal to the old regime.

The eldest girl reminded him of Imoshen though she was only part Dhamfeer. He caught himself wishing Imoshen were with him, riding at his side. The local villagers would have answered her questions and she would have known if they were lying.

Mist clung in the hollows between the ridges. There were no visible signs of the rebels' passage, nothing to tell him he wasn't wandering pointlessly through these accursed blue hills.

Only the fact that seven nights ago one of his advance parties had been massacred to a man told him he was on their trail. He sent two commanders out with a number of his men on alternative routes in the hope of flushing the rebels out.

But his commanders could have lost the rebels since then. They had local guides who knew the paths and the caves, much good it did them.

His local guide was proving annoyingly obtuse. Not that

the man actually lied to him as far as Tulkhan could tell, but getting information from him was like extracting teeth.

Tulkhan cursed softly. "What is that slim column of smoke?"

A finger of smoke hung on the still air in one of the deep ravines. When it reached the turbulent upper air it vanished.

The guide shaded his eyes and gave a noncommittal shrug. "Could be bushfire. Lots of fires this time of year."

"Could it be the rebel camp?" Tulkhan persisted.

The guide turned burnished gold eyes on him. The man was a True-man like Tulkhan but of a baser race, one of the very old stock who had settled Fair Isle so long ago they had grown apart from their mainland cousins. His coloring, his accent all marked him. In his own way he was as alien to the Ghebites as Imoshen.

"If you were leading the rebels would you leave a smoking cooking fire to mark your camp?" the guide asked.

Tulkhan cursed. "Then it's a small crop holder?"

"Could be." His guide shrugged.

"We'll go there."

The guide shifted and Tulkhan thought he sensed reluctance. Was the man hiding something?

"How long will it take us to get there?" Tulkhan asked. It seemed only a short way, but he had learned that distances were deceptive, particularly in these dense highlands. There were two ridges between them and the deep ravine. With no paths, the ravines could prove impassable. The army could lose a whole day in backtracking.

The guide shaded his eyes and studied the terrain. "Go that way. All day."

Tulkhan frowned. The rebels would be long gone if it was their camp, but at least he would be able to tell if he was on their trail.

He signaled to the men to move out. Stoically they responded.

He should have left the horses quartered on the plains. But who was to say they would be there when he returned? He hadn't known that the southern highlands would be so impassable.

They traveled for most of the day. As far as Tulkhan could tell the guide might have purposefully chosen the roughest, most uncomfortable path for him and his men. But he could see no easier route so he held his peace.

The cold was seeping up through the ground and the sun no longer reached the deep valley floor of the ravine when they neared their destination. It was time to find a place to camp. Every night he tried to select a spot they could defend if attacked. It was not always possible.

As they advanced in the steadily growing twilight Tulkhan felt on edge. He paused and sniffed. There was a strange tang on the air and he could have sworn the valley floor was not as cold as it had been before.

He turned to the guide, only to see him making a sign across his chest and eyes.

"What's this?"

"Holy place." The guide would not meet his eyes. "Not a good place to go."

Tulkhan wondered if the guide was trying to divert him. "Move on."

He forged ahead, rounding a bend in the ravine floor to find a relatively open space where the new scent was even stronger.

A low mist clung to the stones and spindly trees, making it impossible to see more than a few feet ahead of them.

But there was a stream and it would provide a relatively safe place to camp for the night. Tulkhan strode over to the brook and dipped his hand in. His cold fingers registered the warmth of the water. It was almost hot enough to bathe in. His eyes narrowed. This wasn't mist. The place was shrouded in steam which rose from vents in the rocks. There was something wrong.

"What manner of place is this?"

But the guide had moved ahead, leaping from smooth river stone to stone, over the stream. Tulkhan followed, growing uneasy as the mist thickened and visibility dropped.

He found the guide crouched before a flat-topped stone, blackened by fire.

The guide made a complicated sign and left some of the

hard cakes he carried as part of his food supply on the stone.
"For the Guardian. We go now."

"Wait. What is this place?"

"Old. Older than the T'En, older even than my people.
Not a good place to stay."

Tulkhan was inclined to agree, but it was almost dark
and they couldn't risk stumbling about in the ravines. He'd
already lost men and horses because of falls.

"We camp here for the night."

The guide stifled an involuntary exclamation.

Tulkhan's eyes narrowed. "I'll have one of my men
leave an offering on the stone for the Guardian. Satisfied?"

The guide said nothing.

He retraced his steps across the stream to check on his
men. They filled the ravine floor. With practiced ease they
were selecting places to make campfires, places to bed down
and spots for lookouts.

Tulkhan beckoned the soldier who handled the cooking.
He chose a fine pullet hen, "donated" from the nobleman's
kitchen.

"Will this do?" Tulkhan asked the guide.

The man glanced sharply to the bird then away. He gave
a shrug.

Exasperation made Tulkhan impatient. He was trying to
meet these people halfway. Grabbing the chicken by its leg,
he stalked off with it squawking indignantly, across the
stream back to the sacrificial stone. He felt ridiculous, hungry and tired. He wished he had never come to the southern
highlands to hunt rebels. But he was determined to do this
right. He had always made it his policy to pay lip service to
the religion of conquered countries. Men who had lost everything would risk everything. Men who had scraps feared losing even those. Give the masses food and religion and it
would keep them quiet, if not content.

"Come."

The guide followed silently, almost reluctantly.

Tulkhan laid the bird on the stone and took out his ceremonial dagger. "Is there any formal observance I should
make?"

"A little of your own blood should mix with the sacrifice's."

Tulkhan grimaced. It was like other religious procedures he had witnessed. Every country thought their religion superior.

He snorted. By the gods, he had grown cynical.

Pricking the ball of his thumb he squeezed out a drop or two onto the stone.

Many was the time he had overseen an offering to some obscure deity and appeased the inhabitants. It was amazing how similar religious ceremonies were.

"Like so?"

But when he looked up the guide had backed away. The man made the sign over his eyes and again over his chest. Tulkhan grimaced. Whatever he might think of their religion, the guide at least believed in its power.

Tulkhan's stomach rumbled. He wanted to get this over and done with and have his dinner.

With one slash he sliced off the chicken's head, letting its blood flow over the stone. The stone was so hot that the blood bubbled. Hissing steam rose, obscuring everything, even the guide, who stood only a body length from him.

The hairs on the back of Tulkhan's neck rose. His heart hammered as he recognized the sensation. He could feel a tingling on his tongue, that familiar metallic taste he associated with a gathering of power.

"What's happening?" Tulkhan hated hearing the note of panic in his voice.

The guide's answer came from a great distance. He was no longer subservient, but insolent and pleased. "You have fed the ancient ones. Now they will feed on you. Feel the Guardian's power!"

The steam almost blanketed all noise, but Tulkhan could hear the guide scrambling for his life. He dropped the body of the now still chicken and turned. But a wave of dizziness swamped him.

He could not tell which way the camp lay, no sound came through the mist. An ominous sense of expectancy hung on the air. Tulkhan cursed himself for a fool.

He drew his sword, vowing to sell his life dearly, but in his heart of hearts he suspected that whatever the Guardian was, it could not be hurt by cold steel.

Blood pounded through his head, drumming in his ears. Was it really his own blood, or the sound of a drumbeat and the chanting of voices? Red, leaping shadows filled the mists.

His mouth went dry with fear.

Incongruously he saw the mists before him part to reveal a sexless, naked child of eight or nine. This apparition raised ageless, ancient eyes to study Tulkhan.

A great oppression settled on him.

He wanted to drop to his knees and beg the child's forgiveness.

Abruptly the drumbeats faded and the steam swirled behind the child, who turned as someone or something approached. Rippling opalescence traveled through the mist in expanding waves.

Then, as if the mist were a living thing, it exhaled, revealing a tall, slender T'En male who stepped from its embrace. Tulkhan blinked, shielding his eyes. The man seemed to carry his own inner illumination.

Squinting into the glare, Tulkhan gasped. He was looking at a male version of Imoshen. The man was T'En. He had the same narrow nose, high cheekbones and wine-dark eyes, and he was clad for war.

The warrior frowned at him. ''What mischief have you been working, Ghebite? Don't you know the Ancients are greedy once awakened?''

Tulkhan glanced around but the child was gone. Had that sexless creature been one of the Ancients? Was this man its Guardian? Was he some past T'En warrior bound by a curse to patrol this place?

''Well?'' the intruder demanded.

''I sought only to honor the local's beliefs.'' Tulkhan was surprised to hear the firm tone of his voice. Who would guess his heart was hammering with fear? ''Who are you, the Guardian?''

''Guardian?'' The feral red eyes gleamed and Tulkhan

could have sworn the T'En was laughing silently at him. "In a way. Who are you?"

"General Tulkhan, half-brother to King Gharavan."

This time the T'En warrior did laugh, a bitter, rueful laugh. "I should have let them devour your soul, General."

Tulkhan's hand tightened on the sword. "Who are you?"

"I am your death. You do not know it but you are a dead man who walks and talks." He executed a mocking bow. "I am T'Reothe of the T'En."

Tulkhan leapt forward, sword slashing to take the warrior in the gut. The blade traveled through Reothe's insubstantial body. The T'En's laughter poured over Tulkhan, scraping along his raw nerve ends as the momentum of his lunge met nothing and he staggered forward into the swirling mists. The uneven ground caused his boot to slip and he went down on one knee. Even as he fell, he turned and lifted the sword point between them. But T'Reothe was gone.

Shouts. He heard his men calling his name. They charged through the mist, swords drawn, carrying burning brands from their campfires.

Rising stiffly, Tulkhan favored his injured knee and tried to calm his men. They had heard him give his battle cry and come to his aid.

By the time he had settled the camp and arranged the watches, Tulkhan was not surprised to learn their guide had disappeared. He would have liked to move camp but it was after dark and he had to satisfy himself with posting extra watches.

He shuddered, knowing that mere metal would be poor defense against an attack led by this T'Reothe.

As the men settled down for the night, Tulkhan paced the length of their scattered camp along the ravine floor. Huge fern trees rose above his head, dripping moisture from the heated misty air. His men were forced to spread out because the ravine was so narrow. Once again, they were vulnerable to ambush.

How he hated this southern highland. He should never have come here. Driven by impatience, he kept patrolling, pausing to exchange a word here and there with the sentries. The spirits of his men always improved when they saw him.

But Tulkhan had no such faith in himself. He had seen his enemy in the flesh, or at least the insubstantial flesh. T'Reothe of the T'En was pure Dhamfeer. His skin crawled at the memory.

Tulkhan had experienced firsthand the tricks Imoshen could do. What more could this Reothe achieve? Even the Ancient one had fled at the T'En warrior's approach. Reothe had called him a dead man who still walked and talked and somewhere deep inside Tulkhan felt as if a light had gone out.

He had looked into himself and discovered he was hollow and he hated it. He had never felt inadequate before this. How could he, a True-man, compete with this T'En warrior when cold steel could not wound insubstantial flesh?

But there was nothing insubstantial about Reothe's existence.

What if Imoshen discovered her betrothed was more than a rumor? If she knew Reothe lived, would she feel bound to honor her earlier vows? Would she see her male counterpart as the likely victor and change allegiance?

Two days later he spotted smoke and led his men to a ravine floor where they found the remains of one of his other contingents. More than forty men dead. The lone survivor was their commander, who had been tied to a stake unharmed.

His eyes rolled in terror and then he wept and laughed when he saw them approach.

Tulkhan stepped forward as his men cut the survivor down and helped him massage sensation into his limbs.

"Leave me!" he shrieked, almost falling when they released him. The man stared at Tulkhan with a mixture of horror and relief. "He said you would come. He said I would not have to wait long—"

"Who?" Tulkhan asked, though he suspected he knew.

"T'Reothe. Two nights ago he led his people into our camp just before dawn. He left me with a message for you."

Then the commander clamped his lips shut and his body shuddered.

"What message?" Tulkhan grimaced.

The man shook his head. "The moment I tell you I will die."

"Nonsense!" Tulkhan felt the men around him stir uneasily and felt a terrible sense of foreboding ripple through his body. He had to know the message. "There is not a mark on you. No festering wound, nothing! You are a healthy man. Take heart. Give me the message."

Tears slipped from the man's eyes, falling unheeded. He pulled his jerkin open to reveal his chest, marred only by a small burn. "The T'En prince touched the skin above my heart with the sixth finger of his left hand. He looked into my eyes and he said the moment I tell you his message my life will flee my body." He dropped to his knees. "Please don't make me tell you."

Tulkhan hesitated. He could not afford to show weakness, yet the man's fear was very real. It made his own skin crawl with dread.

At last he temporized. "Is it an important message?"

The commander nodded once. He took a deep breath, came to his feet and looked Tulkhan in the eye, giving the salute a man at arms gave his superior.

"T'Reothe is going north to claim his betrothed, the Princess Imoshen." The words left his mouth in a great rush. He gasped, pressed his hands to his chest and stood absolutely still.

Tulkhan stared, unable to look away, unable to offer aid. Surely this Reothe could not kill by mere suggestion.

Tulkhan placed his arm on the man's shoulder in a gesture of solidarity. Silently the commander shook his head, clasped his own hand over his General's then frowned.

His body jerked once.

The breath left his body in a long sigh. He swayed. Tulkhan cursed. His men swore by their many gods as their fellow soldier fell to his knees and pitched forward into the dirt, dead. Not one man tried to break his fall.

Even as Tulkhan knelt down to feel for the man's heartbeat he knew what he would find. He had seen death too many times to be mistaken.

Fearful whispers told him Reothe's little ploy had done its damage.

"Get moving!" he bellowed. "I want a funeral pyre for the dead and the words said over them."

He watched as his men worked efficiently, gathering dead wood to burn the bodies. Was Reothe headed north to the Stronghold to claim Imoshen, or was he simply diverting Tulkhan?

The General had no way of knowing. How did you defeat someone who could move in mists, who could kill with a touch of his finger and the power of suggestion?

Despair gripped Tulkhan but he clamped down on it, knowing this was what Reothe wanted.

When the men lit the funereal pyre, he rose to his feet, his decision made. He would find the last contingent of his men before Reothe slaughtered them, too. Then he would return to T'Diemn and report to his half-brother before going to the Stronghold.

He needed to warn Imoshen and more. He needed her to tell him what manner of man he was fighting. Did Reothe have a weakness? Of course he did. If anyone knew T'Reothe's weak points it would be Imoshen.

Tulkhan tensed. What was he thinking? How could he confront Imoshen with the news that her betrothed still lived and in the same breath demand she tell him, the Ghebite invader, how to defeat her T'En kin? How could he ask her to betray Reothe, her betrothed?

Did she love him? Did love enter into the proceedings of a T'En betrothal? In Gheeaba a man looked for compliance and good family connections in his wife. Family loyalty . . .

Who would Imoshen choose to support, her once betrothed and near kin, or himself, the invader who had taken her Stronghold by force? Did he really want to know?

Imoshen and her mount made the crest with energy to spare. It was good to escape the confines of the Stronghold along with the constraints of her position. She turned her horse to face the distant settlement. From here she could see the great walls and towers of the Stronghold and the new town that sprawled at its feet.

Because the town had been designed, not grown, there was a broad avenue leading directly to the outer gates of the Stronghold and wide streets which fanned out to ring the outer walls. Smoke rose from the the many chimney tops. The familiar, reassuring smell of baking and humanity carried on the afternoon breeze to her.

The sky held a heaviness which promised cold, perhaps snow, tonight. She shuddered, thinking of how many people they would have lost without the efforts of the last small moon cycle. There was still work to be done. She had been busy settling disputes, while greater and lesser guilds had been formed and guildmasters elected to deal with their internal problems.

She sighed. There was still no word from General Tulkhan. But she had heard how he had calmed the townspeople of T'Diemn and despite the rumor that it was the king who had ordered these changes she recognized Tulkhan's hand in them. She also knew that he was in the southern highlands, hunting the rebels, and she was troubled.

On a purely practical level, if Tulkhan should die her position would be precarious. She would have to deal with young King Gharavan, who from what she had heard would not be easy to reason with.

With the passing of the small moon cycle she knew the Aayel had been right. She had conceived. If Tulkhan died while she carried his son where did that leave her and the child? Her hands tightened on the reins as frustration filled her. She was still a pawn in a larger game with no security.

Imoshen's horse shied and snickered. She stood up in the stirrups, twisting in the saddle to survey the woods behind her. The refugees' voracious need for timber for fuel and building materials meant undergrowth had been cleared and suitable trees taken. Consequently the woods had retreated farther from the Stronghold. She had traveled quite a distance through cleared land to reach this knoll.

Come spring she hoped to see tilled fields below the knoll, stretching from here to the outskirts of town. They'd be needed to supply food for the new township. With a shudder she realized her world was changing. Her home would never again be as it was during her childhood.

Truly, she felt as if the person who had watched General Tulkhan's army march across the rolling grass was someone else. She had seen so much since then and so many others depended on her now.

It was a relief to get away from the constant demands of the Stronghold, to be truly alone, her own person. Imoshen wondered if she would ever be as free as the child-woman who had unwittingly ridden into the woods with Reothe.

Knowing a little more now she wondered if her parents had realized who he really was. They couldn't have known the extent of his abilities, else they wouldn't have let her ride off with him. She flushed and bit her lip.

He could have had her there on the grass and she would have welcomed him. The knowledge stung her pride, stained her cheeks. But even now the memory stirred her body and she could feel the tug of like to like.

Out here away from the mundane demands of her position she could face her fears. Was it true? Did she crave Reothe because only in his arms could she know her true mate, one whose abilities meshed with her own?

Something stirred and flickered to life in the back of her mind. She swallowed, noting a strange taste in her mouth, the way her heart pounded in her chest. Suddenly, surrounding sounds and colors seemed unnaturally clear and bright.

Fear curled through her body, intimate as a lover, insistent as pain. No. She would not call on the T'En gift which lay dormant in her. She feared what she did not understand and could not control. Worse, every time she flexed her powers it appeared to make her more vulnerable to Reothe. For an instant she seemed to hear his mocking laugh echo on the cry of a bird. She shuddered and banished him from her thoughts.

Since the night of the harvest moons nothing strange had happened. She had studiously avoided any use of her ability.

She hadn't even tried to use her gift for healing. It was fear that held her back, fear of the unknown. If only the Aayel had lived!

With a sigh, Imoshen urged the horse off the crest and down into the woods behind. The path she had forged led back around the base of the rise and down onto the plain.

So preoccupied was she that she had no presentiment of danger. When the body darted from the undergrowth and grabbed the horse's bridle there was nothing she could do. Before she could aim a kick at his head, another body tumbled from a low branch onto the horse, pulling her to the ground.

She fell with his weight atop her, knocking the wind from her chest. Stars spun in front of her eyes. Desperately, she fought to drag in a breath.

Someone pulled her upright into a sitting position and she blinked, trying to focus on the face. She must catch her breath, discover who her attackers were and figure out how to escape. As yet she didn't fear for her life.

''My Lady?''

She knew that voice. ''D . . . Drake?''

He grinned, well pleased with himself. He looked leaner, scruffier. He was dressed in a farmer's practical winter furs, as were his two companions. They also smiled, pleased with themselves and with her.

Imoshen had a sinking suspicion. ''I'm glad you are safe, Drake. You know you and your friends can claim sanctuary in my Stronghold anytime—''

''No. You don't understand.'' He gripped her arm, pulling her to her feet with the strength of a fanatic. ''Reothe sent me to bring you. We ride now.''

SEVEN

HER FIRST IMPULSE was to refuse him, emphatically. She had already refused Reothe once when he had come to her, and a second time when she had unwittingly gone to him.

But now it appeared her once-betrothed had tired of waiting. Imoshen knew a moment's panic.

She did not want to spend the winter hidden away in the deep woods, snowed-in with Reothe for company. It would give him the chance to work on her, claim her physically and then try to lay claim to her will, her gifts. What kind of abilities would they have if they were bonded? Was that why Reothe had been so eager to claim her last autumn?

For an instant she had a vision of Reothe and herself—beautiful, terrible dictators ordering the lives of the inhabitants of Fair Isle. She shivered. No, she could not spend the winter in his camp, in his arms. Who knew what would be left of her "self" come spring?

But she could not explain this to Drake when it was only an instinctive suspicion. She must play for time, choose her moment.

"Drake, you found him?" She searched the young man's face for any sign of doubt. Her hands went instinctively to his own, to feel his bare flesh. But all she received in response was a flash of overwhelming certainty.

"I found him and others. More join us every day. The

whole Island would rise if it were known the last of the T'En rode together," he assured her.

"And what would happen if I left the Stronghold after giving my word? Think, Drake! Don't you care about the fate of our people there? Thousands rely on me. General Tulkhan would be justified in making an example of them. Would you have me abandon my people?"

She glanced swiftly to the other two, recognizing their origins—farmers, shepherds. They were practical people, unlike Drake, who had known the comfort of town living. It was easy to be idealistic when you had enough to eat.

Drake looked stunned.

Imoshen pressed home her advantage. "I can't abandon my people!"

"*Your* people?" his voice rose. "You abandoned them to these Ghebite barbarians. Your betrothed, the last of the T'En, waits for you, T'Imoshen. The people would rise behind the true rulers. Now is the time to think on a grander scale! What is the fate of one Stronghold when the whole Island is at stake?"

Imoshen's heart sank. The other two nodded, convinced by Drake's rhetoric. She looked down. Now was not the time to resist—she was outnumbered three to one.

"Come." Drake caught her arm. "Reothe waits. I promised I would not fail him."

One of the men led her horse. Drake held her arm in what was meant to be a courteous grasp, but in effect he restrained her.

As they stumbled down the slope into the deeper woods, Imoshen's mind spun with ideas. She had to get away before they rejoined their larger party. While there were only three of them she might yet escape. Her horse whinnied and another answered from behind the thicket. Four mounts as scruffy and ill-fed as their riders waited patiently with a fourth man holding the reins. His eyes widened when he saw her and he made the sign of obeisance.

"Truly," he whispered. "She has the same look as our leader."

Drake laughed. "Why do you think he chose her?"

"We were betrothed," Imoshen corrected.

Without warning Drake spun her around, pulling her arms behind her back.

"Reothe warned me that the Ghebite General has influenced your mind, my Lady. Forgive me." He signaled the men. "Bind her."

One of them moved behind her and she felt him tie her hands with a leather strip. Imoshen resisted the urge to struggle, instead she managed a shaky laugh.

"Is this how you deliver Reothe his bride, bound?"

"Only a precaution, Lady T'En," Drake said.

He helped her climb onto her horse and took the reins. She could have struggled but that would have reduced them to rolling in the damp leaf litter in an ungainly heap and served no purpose. No, when she made her bid to escape she would make sure it was successful. Anger flashed through her, sharpening her senses, making her aware of that strange taste on her tongue, that tingling in her body.

Drake mounted his own horse and pulled on the reins of her mount. One of the rebels rode before them and another two behind as Drake led her through the woods.

Imoshen's innate sense of direction told her they were heading away from the Stronghold. Dusk closed in early as the temperature dropped, promising snow.

Imoshen shivered. She was not dressed for this. Soon her own people would wonder where she was. Would the Stronghold Guard turn on Tulkhan's Elite Guard? Would Wharrd assume she had betrayed them? It would be his duty to report her defection to the General.

What would Tulkhan think? Would he believe she had betrayed him? Her heart sank. How could he think otherwise? He wouldn't know she had been abducted.

Imoshen ducked her head as they wove under the branches of a grove of stark trees. It was growing darker by the moment and colder. Yet they hurried on. Their destination must be nearby.

Her skin prickled with fear. She didn't want to face Reothe, didn't feel she had the resolve to resist the force of his will. She had to make a move soon.

"I'm cold," Imoshen complained. "Here I am, without even my winter cloak. I'll be wanting a word with Reothe when I see him. How much further till we reach him?"

"Not far, my Lady," Drake answered automatically. "I'm sorry, I have no cloak to lend you."

It was as she'd suspected. Imoshen leaned low on the horse, feeling the warmth of its body. Fleetingly, she wished she was an unimportant pawn like this horse.

A rush of alien images suddenly flooded her mind. Scent. Man smell. Cold, mingled with eager images of food and a warm stall, and underneath that lay a dislike of the woods, a fear of predators.

She lifted her head as her mind cleared, and she knew what to do. It was quite simple really. They were deep in the woods now with poor visibility. A light snow fell, coating everything with its soft white powder. Would it interfere with the scent? She wasn't sure. She made herself recall the rank smell of the predator which had stalked her and General Tulkhan that day near Landsend, how it had made her skin crawl and her hair lift with fear. She recalled retreating up the slope with Tulkhan at her back, her knife at the ready. Then she projected that memory.

She couldn't have said how she did it, only that by reliving it, her body reacted as if she were experiencing it again and her horse reacted to the change in her body scent and its fear communicated itself to the other horses and to the men with them. They drew closer.

"Strike fire!" Drake ordered, climbing off his mount to hand out several torches.

No one asked why.

Imoshen couldn't let them regain the security the naked flame offered. If only the snow would break a brittle branch . . .

Something snapped nearby, triggering a rush of raw energy.

From the dark undergrowth there came a muffled crack and the rapid pad of a heavy carnivore charging.

Imoshen's heart leapt in her breast. "It comes!"

Her mount reared, reacting to her terror. She clamped

her knees and leaned forward, keeping her seat despite the angle. The other horses snorted, pivoting as their riders fought to maintain control.

"Hurry with the torches!" Drake hissed.

It wasn't enough. Panic flared in Imoshen. She needed a real attack, a leaping, snarling shadow which . . .

Even as she thought it, a white snow leopard broke from the trees, all grace and ferocity.

Horses and men screamed.

The last she saw was the cat leaping for the throat of the nearest horse. Then her mount was bolting through the tree trunks and it was all she could do to huddle low in the saddle and hug the horse's heaving sides with her knees.

Behind her she heard the terrible screams of a dying horse and the knowledge that she had called forth the beast frightened her as much as the knowledge that it was real. Once again her gifts had outreached her ability to control them.

In the mad rush she did not know which way they were going. Snow fell in a thick curtain. It was so dark that the tree trunks were only darker shadows in a dark gray world.

Suddenly before her she saw tightly packed trees with no possible gap between them. Blinded by fear, her mount charged straight ahead. She tried to plunge into its mind as she had unwittingly done before but a solid wall of terror held her out. Or was it her own terror? Too late, the wall of trees were upon them.

She could only hunch down and hope.

Impact stunned her.

Her side ached, and she heard something thunder away.

Imoshen lifted her head to see the hooves of her mount disappearing into the deep shadows. She was lying on her side in the snow with no memory of how she got there. She must have lost consciousness briefly. Something blocked her vision in one eye and she blinked it away, then looked down to see dark droplets staining the snow. Blood.

She was bound, wounded, lost in the woods without a cloak in the first snows of winter. But at least she was free!

Fueled by determination she rolled to her knees, amazed

to find nothing was broken. True, she staggered as she came to her feet and there seemed to be a lot of blood, but she could still move.

Blood. It was likely to attract predators.

Exhaustion threatened to overcome her but she drove herself forward after the retreating hoofbeats. Somewhere nearby Drake and the men would be regrouping.

Imoshen looked up, trying to catch a glimpse of the stars, but they were obscured by the clouds and her head was spinning so she couldn't work out in which direction the Stronghold lay.

Her mount would know. She followed the churned snow, hardly able to distinguish anything in the gray-black world. Again she tried to call the horse, concentrating on its scent, its sense of self which she had experienced so briefly.

There, a flicker of recognition illuminated her mind. The horse had slowed to a steady walk not far away and was thinking, if it could be called thinking, of food and its stall. Relieved, Imoshen broke into a run.

Her mount was like a bright beacon in a world of silver shadows. She was so relieved to have discovered the horse nearby, tears stung her eyes.

A whinny greeted her, then it changed to a snort of fear. Icy fingers of dread traveled up Imoshen's spine. Something was hunting her, just as she had hunted the horse. She could feel it now, probing the preternatural night. She stopped and spun around, searching the woods.

Suddenly she realized the night was not inky black as it should have been. She could make out the fall of the land, the trunks of the trees, everything had a silverish-green cast.

What was after her?

Without knowing she intended to do it, her mind sent out a questing probe, following the sense of pursuit to its source.

Flare!

She met the mind which sought hers and recognized its pure essence, free of the trappings of a mortal body.

"Reothe!"

Her knees crumbled. Terror robbed her of coherent thought.

His thoughts sliced like a blade through her identity, shutting down all rational thought. Communication went beyond words. She recognized his anger and his determination. He would not relinquish her, not while he still lived.

While he held her thus she could not even lift her head, let alone flee, and now that he had located her, he was coming to claim her. She sensed his triumph.

Despair flooded Imoshen. Fool! By using her powers she had unwittingly drawn him like a magnet.

Something soft and moist touched her cheek. Horsey breath engulfed her face, making her choke. Suddenly she was free, blinded by the night but alone with her horse, kneeling in the steadily building snow.

The horse was a dark bulk. Its soft nostrils nuzzled her face. She didn't need to probe its mind to know it wanted food and thought she would provide it. Tears of relief stung her eyes as she staggered to her feet. She had to get away from here, had to be invisible to Reothe's questing talent.

She was just another gray patch, as gray as the snow which fell in the inky blackness, just another piece of the night. She pressed her face into the horse's flank, savoring its warmth, for she had grown deathly cold while Reothe held her in thrall.

Then frustration seized her as she realized that without her hands she could not climb into the saddle. Still, it was reassuring not to be alone and maybe, just maybe, she could use the animal to deflect Reothe.

Her horse shied, its animal intelligence recognizing the T'En power Reothe was harnessing to search for her. She could feel it, too. It made her teeth ache, triggered that strange taste on her tongue again. She almost wanted to answer it to feel that flare of mental recognition. Until that moment she had never known how completely alone she was.

The temptation to touch minds was insidious, startling her with its intensity. She thrust the thought aside, clamping down on it. Placing her face in the hollow of the horse's neck she inhaled its earthy scent. She would hide her presence, assuming the horse's identity. She was anxious for warmth, for her stall and food. The beast began to move and she moved with it, her booted feet already numb with cold. But the thought of what lay ahead of her drove her on, while the thought of what lay behind drove her to push herself when cold and weariness threatened to overwhelm her.

Time passed. The ground passed beneath her boots.

Walking became automatic.

Thought was a luxury she did without. The night stretched out before her.

When she raised her eyes and saw the huddled outline of the houses below the Stronghold, the smoke lifting from their chimney tops and their lights almost hidden behind the shuttered windows, she was too weary to feel any joy, only relief.

Her horse hastened and she kept pace with it, stumbling forward on numb legs.

The snow-mantled streets of the new town were empty, the houses tightly shuttered. The wide avenue that led up to the outer gates of the Stronghold stretched before her, one last obstacle. The heavy gates were open, the passage dark, its far opening lit by a glow from the courtyard beyond.

Strange, Imoshen thought. Why weren't they searching for her? Why weren't they alarmed? Where were her Stronghold Guard and General Tulkhan's Elite Guard?

She stumbled down the passage, thinking it was not that long since Tulkhan had entered these gates at the head of his army to lay claim to the Stronghold, yet it felt like a lifetime ago to her

No one challenged her. Odd.

The horse threaded its way through the courtyards toward the stable where the soft glow of lamplight told her someone was waiting. She let the horse go, deeply grateful for its unwitting protection.

Imoshen could hear the sounds of revelry in the great hall but everything sounded wrong to her ears. Why were they celebrating? Why weren't they searching for her? She felt an odd sense of dislocation, as if this weren't her Stronghold at all. Had the use of her T'En gifts distorted her perceptions so that she would never feel normal again?

She shuddered with more than cold.

Would every use of her gifts cause her to drift a little

further from True-people until she lived isolated in a trap of her own making?

She was shivering uncontrollably now, partly with delayed reaction to her ordeal.

The great hall held a crowd of brightly costumed people. Music played, but it was not her native music. It had that vivid intensity of the Ghebites. So unexpected was the scene that greeted her, Imoshen wondered if she had unwittingly transported herself to another time. She did not recognize the brightly garbed young men. They were Ghebites, that much was certain, but wearing those outlandish clothes? Then amidst the newcomers she was relieved to recognize her own Stronghold servants scurrying about to serve the newcomers.

Strange. Her people looked right through her.

Suddenly a man came to his feet and shouted for silence. The general din instantly died away. He lifted a goblet in salute to his companion, another man, a young man who reminded her vaguely of . . . Tulkhan.

"To our King Gharavan and to the jewel in his crown, Fair Isle!"

There was a shout as the others drained their drinks and called for more.

The young king rose, good-naturedly accepting their shouted comments. "To my half-brother, may he find the rebels and kill every last one!" They roared. "And to my loyal courtiers. I lay claim to the Stronghold and declare the Princess Imoshen a traitor, to be hunted down and executed without trial."

The breath left Imoshen's body in one exclamation of amazement.

The Ghebites roared, while Imoshen noted her own servants kept their eyes downcast.

This had gone far enough.

Rigid with anger, she strode forward into the center of the hall. This time her people noticed her.

"My Lady," one lad cried, dropping his jug. It smashed on the stone floor, shockingly loud.

An old woman would have come to her, but Imoshen shook her head, her eyes fixed on the young king's face. She watched his features go slack with surprise, then harden with a mixture of fear and hatred.

"Welcome to my Stronghold, King Gharavan!" She greeted him formally. "On behalf of General Tulkhan, with whom we made our terms of surrender, I bid you and your people welcome. And if someone will cut my bonds and bring me some warm food I'll tell you how I was abducted and how I escaped."

She noticed the young king cast a swift glance to the man who had first spoken and instantly recognized the power behind the throne.

"Abducted you say, yet you are here?" the dark man remarked in such a way that she could not take offense, but clearly it was designed to undermine her veracity.

She felt someone slit the bonds which held her arms from wrist to elbow and brought her arms forward. Her shoulders ached fiercely. Lifting her hands, she stared at them. They were blue, the fingers curled up like the unfurled petals of a flower. She couldn't feel a thing. It was as if they belonged to someone else.

She tried to rub them together but though she was able to move her arms and her wrists met, her hands remained useless. Would she get frostbite? Lose her fingers?

Imoshen did not know, but she understood she could not afford to show a moment's weakness here.

"I was abducted." She stepped closer to the table and held her hands out toward the king and his confidant. "Or do you think I would strap my hands behind my back and stagger through the deep woods in the snow for hours till my feet and hands went numb for the joy of it?"

"Who tried to abduct you?" the king asked. There was no more talk of doubting her word.

Imoshen went to speak but even now she could not bring herself to turn Reothe over to these self-serving barbarians. "Rebels. My horse bolted. I was knocked from the saddle. My head . . ." She tried to feel the extent of her head wound, but her hand wouldn't open and she only succeeded in starting the bleeding again.

Warmth seeped into her, melting the ice on her clothes.

Little droplets landed on the stones at her numb feet, which were beginning to burn as circulation returned. She was so hungry she could feel her body trembling at the sight and scent of food, but she couldn't use her hands to feed herself and she would not bury her face in the nearest platter of food like an animal.

Imoshen lifted her gaze from the meat on the table, aware that the gathered Ghebites were staring at her in horrified fascination. If she didn't get help soon she would fall at their feet, and she couldn't afford to do that. Unlike Tulkhan, these men had no compassion. They saw weakness as an opportunity to be exploited.

"Forgive me greeting you like this. I will go to my chambers and clean up." She stepped back and made formal obeisance, then turned and walked from the great hall.

As she stepped through a doorway her knees buckled and she sagged against the wall in the shadows, listening to the din of voices raised in exclamation.

The woman who ran the kitchen was there to meet her as well as the housekeeper who oversaw the bedchambers and galleries.

The first clutched her arm. "They arrived at dusk, my Lady. Just marched in and took over."

The second massaged Imoshen's free hand. "They ordered us about and you could not be found! We had no idea . . ."

Imoshen lifted her hand for silence. "Treat them as honored guests, of course—"

"My Lady!" Kalleen ran down the steps to join them. "I thought they'd taken you!"

Was Kalleen in league with the rebels? Imoshen frowned. Had the girl betrayed herself to the other women? But no, they were still chattering on, excusing themselves for condoning the king's behavior. A laugh escaped Imoshen. She bit it back when she heard the odd lilt to her voice. In another breath she would be crying.

Kalleen hugged her, then studied her face. I heard you'd been abducted by rebels and escaped. How—"

"I need a warm bath and food, and then I will tell you."

On the stairs her legs gave way and several of the servants who had followed her ran forward. Kalleen pushed them aside, offering her slender shoulder.

Imoshen accepted her help, amused by the girl's proprietary air.

Up in her room Imoshen waited while the hot bath water was carried up and poured into her tub. She had to clench her teeth to stop from crying out as Kalleen massaged sensation back into her hands and feet.

"We did not know what had become of you. Last anyone saw of you, you were down in the town speaking with the blacksmith," Kalleen reproached her. "Then when the king marched in around dusk you couldn't be found. Wharrd was worried but he would not admit it. There has been no word from General Tulkhan and now the king is here. What does it mean?"

Imoshen did not know, but her instincts told her it was not good.

When the tub was full she sprinkled soothing herbs on the warm waters. "Send them all away, Kalleen."

When the girl returned Imoshen lowered herself into the tub. She winced as she attempted to bathe the blood from her hair, studying her progress in the polished metal mirror Kalleen held up for her. In the royal palace they had real glass mirrors and hot running water but the Aayel had not believed in such things.

"I saw Drake today," Imoshen said, watching the girl's face closely.

Kalleen leaned closer. "Was he well? Has he reconsidered?"

"He abducted me."

"No!"

"Yes. He's with the rebels." She caught Kalleen's hand as the girl put the mirror aside to rinse Imoshen's hair. "I need to know where your loyalty lies. Do you stand with me or against me?"

Kalleen's golden eyes widened with hurt, her body stiffened. "You have to ask!"

Imoshen flushed. "I'm sorry, Kalleen, forgive me. All

about me I see enemies. That young fool the king for one, but even more so his companion. Then . . .'' She bit her lip. She feared Reothe more now than before. "Where is the General?"

"Hunting rebels in the southern highlands," Kalleen answered automatically.

Fear for General Tulkhan's life assailed Imoshen and her heart sank. Did he still live? They'd had no word from him.

How could Tulkhan compete with Reothe? Her once betrothed was T'En and his men were fanatics, while Tulkhan was a canny leader of True-men whose soldiers loved and respected him. But he did not have T'En gifts. How could he hope to stand against Reothe?

In a flash it came to Imoshen.

If she stood at Tulkhan's side, she could help him defeat the rebel leader. Was this what Reothe feared?

No wonder her betrothed would not take no for an answer. She could not be neutral. She had to take sides, had to choose which man would live or die.

Imoshen groaned.

"Do you hurt, my Lady?" Kalleen whispered. "I will call Wharrd."

Imoshen laughed. "My hurts can't be healed by a bonesetter." Morosely she watched as Kalleen laid out her night garment and warmed the bed with a pan of hot coals. Such luxury. She was sure Reothe did not have his bed warmed, if he slept in a bed at all.

But she didn't want to think of him. Thinking of him called to mind the memory of his essence when their minds touched. Imoshen shuddered. What would she give to know such a bonding? What would it be like to share a mind-touch that was bathed in love instead of fear and dominance?

She now believed what she suspected Reothe already knew, that if they were to bond, they would be able to defeat the invaders. But at what cost to the people and where would it end? Would Reothe be content with Fair Isle?

Her head hurt and her limbs trembled.

"I'm hungry, Kalleen. Find me something to eat."

"Now?"

"Yes, now!" She noticed Kalleen's expression. "I'm sorry. I spoke harshly."

"You seemed . . . strange," Kalleen confessed. "For a moment I did not recognize you. It must be the bruising."

But when the girl left and Imoshen looked in the reflective metal she knew it wasn't that. Something inside her had changed. She had lost her innocence tonight. She was no longer so naive and trusting.

Tonight she had used her T'En skills to lure a predator to kill True-men. She had faced Reothe with her naked mind and run from the pain of his knife-sharp gifts.

If she had to choose sides, and it appeared she did, then let Tulkhan be her General. Strangely enough, she did not fear him. But they were all threats—the king, his advisor, Reothe and the General. She would use whatever tools came to hand to ensure her survival.

Suddenly Imoshen realized she was thinking just like Reothe, and she shivered.

Thoughtfully she stood before the fire to rub her body dry. Apart from a few bruises she had survived the ordeal physically, but her inner certainty was gone. She knew something lay deep inside her, the buried T'En power that could surface, *would* surface in times of stress, and if it did, Reothe would know because the same ability lay in him. And he was hungry for her.

Tulkhan sat tall in the saddle despite his weariness. His men slumped, wrapped in their inadequate winter cloaks. Their land to the north would be much warmer now. The snow still fell and the lookouts he'd posted at their flanks were lost in the whiteness. They were probably so weary they hadn't the energy to keep watch.

Was it only one small moon cycle ago that he'd left his half-brother in T'Diemn and entered the southern highlands to hunt rebels with three companies of men behind him?

He had led pitifully few of those men back to the capital. Ever since they'd seen one of their own commanders drop dead two days after T'Reothe's touch, the men had whispered of black sorcery.

They spoke of haunted dreams.

While their General dared not reveal his secret fears. Reothe had said he was the man destined to kill Tulkhan. He seemed so sure . . . Tulkhan told himself it was only bluff. But his sword had passed through the Dhamfeer, while that unnatural being's laughter mocked him.

The rebel army had proved as insubstantial and impossible to catch as its leader. Even knowing that Reothe's warning about Imoshen might be a trick, Tulkhan had chosen to believe him.

So he had returned to T'Diemn with the pitiful remains of his three companies, only to find his half-brother had left for the Stronghold.

Why did that worry him?

Surely he could trust Gharavan?

But he feared for Imoshen. Was Reothe the real threat or was it the lies of Kinraid, the Vaygharian? It would not take much skill to weave a story to convince his lackwit half-brother that Imoshen was a liability.

Tulkhan grimaced. He had nearly had her killed himself. Yet now he was urging his weary men on to reach the Stronghold in an attempt to avert that very thing.

Imoshen was a focal point. The fate of Fair Isle lay in her lap and his own fate lay entwined with her choices.

Tulkhan didn't like feeling helpless. He was used to taking the initiative, not reacting to the challenges of others. Urging his horse on, he breathed a sigh of relief when he saw the tower of the original keep rising above the naked branches of the trees. The Stronghold was still distant but within reach before nightfall.

His men and their horses seemed to sense their journey would soon be over and their pace increased. When they broke from the trees and rode down into the basin of the plain, he marveled at the changes. A real town had sprung up. The steep pitched roofs were coated with snow. The same white snow hid the newness, and the bare earth he guessed he would find in the streets instead of paving. They had accomplished much in one small moon cycle but he doubted they would have had time to pave the roads. People saw him returning with his men and though he did not expect cheers or happy greetings, he was surprised to see the doors and windows being shuttered. The people anticipated trouble.

His own men muttered uneasily. Tulkhan was grateful he'd left the wounded and sick behind, taking only those well enough to travel. It had been a difficult balance to strike. If he approached his half-brother with the better part of his army at his back the young king might take alarm. Now was not the time for a show of strength. Tulkhan knew the loyalty of the army lay with him. He smiled grimly. At least he believed it did.

So he rode through the streets of the new town with a mere sixty men, all of whom had seen service in the woods fighting rebels. There were practicalities involved in his decision to bring such a small force. When he reached the Stronghold he would have to house and feed the men he brought with him. He knew how overstretched the Stronghold's resources were.

The lookouts on the battlements watched their approach stonily. Tulkhan knew news of their arrival would have been reported long ago. It galled him to think he was walking into the Stronghold which he thought of as his own, more his own than any other keep he had taken, to report failure to his half-brother who was only looking for a reason to find fault with him.

A deep sorrow gripped him as he passed through the claustrophobic passage to the courtyard beyond.

When had it changed? Once Gharavan had looked up to him, loved him.

Tulkhan swung down from the saddle weary and stiff, but he couldn't show it. Wharrd and the members of his Elite Guard who had been left to maintain the Stronghold had contrived to be present in the stables on his arrival.

Amid the jostling of horses and stable lads, Wharrd made his report. Without so much as a flicker did he betray that he was doing anything other than reporting to his General, but in effect he was passing information about their king, who had invaded the keep in the role of usurper.

Tulkhan hid his surprise. Normally he trusted Wharrd's judgment. Yet the grizzled bone-setter felt the king was a threat. Surely he was mistaken. In the time it took Tulkhan to unsaddle his horse he learned the number and nature of the men his half-brother had brought with him.

As usual Gharavan had surrounded himself with a court of young, unseasoned nobles, but he had also brought a company of men who had served under Tulkhan on other campaigns. They were seasoned fighters, loyal to Gheeaba. If it came to trouble would they stay loyal to Gharavan?

Tulkhan was still considering the ramifications when Wharrd lowered his voice and told him of the attempted abduction.

It rocked him to learn Reothe had nearly succeeded. So the T'En warrior's challenge hadn't been a bluff. Apparently only Imoshen's determination to elude her captors had foiled the rebel leader's plans. That she rejected her betrothed and returned to the Stronghold gave Tulkhan a fierce surge of satisfaction.

Why should it?

He forced himself to look at Imoshen's actions rationally.

True, she had given him her word that she would not lead an uprising of Stronghold Guards against him while he was calming T'Diemn. But at Reothe's side she might have been at the forefront of a rebel army determined enough to retake Fair Isle, aided by their accursed Dhamfeer gifts. Why hadn't she joined her betrothed?

Was it loyalty to Tulkhan or was it simply that she had weighed the odds and thought the Ghebite was the more likely victor?

He felt a cynical smile tug at his lips. At least the Stronghold was still under his control. If it had fallen and Imoshen had turned against him the king would have had good reason to doubt his general's judgment.

Whatever Imoshen's true reason for not joining the

rebels, Tulkhan could now face his half-brother secure in the knowledge that the Stronghold was behind him.

He hesitated, suddenly confronted with the enormity of it. He'd been preparing to challenge his king's authority in anticipation of a threat. No, impossible! His half-brother would never turn against him. It *must* not come to that, he told himself.

He was a warrior, trained to think in terms of battle tactics. His mind had been automatically weighing factors— nothing more. It was an almost instinctive response arising from years of campaigning.

As Tulkhan strode through the Stronghold halls, rounding the now familiar corners, he found himself thinking of Imoshen when he should have been preparing for his interview with the king. The escort led him upstairs to the Great Library where he had first met Imoshen.

A vivid memory, a flash of her beautiful white breasts stained with her dark red blood returned to him, making his body race in anticipation. He ached to claim her. Time and distance had not dulled his craving for her.

Even as he made his sign of obeisance to the king his gaze slid past Gharavan's, searching for Imoshen's familiar, tall form. For a brief moment she held his eyes, her wine-dark gaze intense, urgent. The intimacy of it made his heart leap in his chest but the planes of her face were too sharply defined, belying her supposedly composed features. After one brief instant of unspoken communication she looked away, her expression carefully neutral.

What was she trying to tell him?

He was very aware of her standing proudly behind the Ghebite conquerors. On a purely physical level the sight of her jolted him. An almost painful longing to touch her swept over him.

Tulkhan came to his feet. He had been weary beyond belief but now his body answered his commands without complaint and his mind felt startlingly clear.

"My king," he acknowledged his half-brother.

Abruptly his mind registered what he had seen and again his gaze was drawn to Imoshen's face. A great purple bruise marred her forehead, making his stomach lurch sickeningly. Instinctively, his hands flexed. Outrage flooded him. The thought of anyone hurting her was abhorrent to him. It made him inexplicably angry.

Imoshen's garnet eyes narrowed as she tilted her head ever so slightly toward the Ghebite King in what Tulkhan interpreted as a warning. His heart pounded. Imoshen was warning him against his half-brother? Why should he trust her?

She was an enemy who had vowed never to surrender to him. If he believed Imoshen only dealt with him because it suited her purposes, why should he heed her warning against his own flesh and blood?

"Well, General?" Gharavan prodded impatiently. "What have you to report?"

"When you stop lusting after the Dhamfeer bitch!" the Vaygharian muttered.

Tulkhan stiffened as Gharavan gave a snort of laughter. But the Vaygharian only shrugged when Tulkhan's eyes challenged him.

The casual insult had been directed at Imoshen as well as himself. Tulkhan swallowed his instinctive reaction. Had his preoccupation been so obvious? Offense was always the best defense.

He focused on his half-brother. "I looked for you in T'Diemn—"

"Well I am here, as you can see." The youth indicated the ancient manuscript which was opened on the table. "You advised me to study this Island and its inhabitants."

Was it a threat? Was Gharavan saying I have this Island, this Stronghold and this woman you want. I am king, not you. It is all mine to do with as I will?

Tulkhan began to doubt his own judgment. Perhaps he was seeing threat where a young man stood, merely flexing his newfound power?

Tulkhan felt the sands shifting beneath his feet.

He knew his arrival at the Stronghold had been noted when he entered the valley. His half-brother had had time to set up this meeting in the chamber of knowledge and to choose the participants. Was Gharavan planning on using Imoshen against him?

And as for the Vaygharian, Tulkhan wished him elsewhere. How was he to reason with Gharavan when the Vaygharian stood there, insolent, indolent, undermining Tulkhan at every turn?

"As you see, the Princess has been translating the history of Fair Isle for me," Gharavan remarked, indicating the illuminated vellum. He flicked a page of the heavy tome with an idle finger. "But the first chapter of a new and glorious book will have to be written in our tongue, not some long-dead script."

Another insult, or youthful bravado?

"The Island has seen many invaders. They came to conquer but stayed to become one with the land," Imoshen remarked. "Only Fair Isle endures."

Tulkhan saw his brother flinch.

Why was Imoshen drawing his brother's anger?

The young king slammed the book shut and slid it across the polished wood to the Keeper of Knowledge who shuffled off with it, stroking the offended tome as if to reassure himself it was unharmed.

The Vaygharian's hand rested lightly on Gharavan's shoulder. The youth drew a slow breath then turned glittering dark eyes to Tulkhan, who read impatience, anger and an underlying fear in his half-brother's face. "Well, General? Have you brought me the rebel Reothe's head, or at least news of his death?"

Tulkhan stiffened. He hated reporting failure but it was best to be frank. Besides, Imoshen knew the man she had been betrothed to still lived, and despite that she was here facing Gharavan with him and not in the woods with Reothe and his rebels. "Reothe escaped. The southern highlands are a death trap and the rebels know them intimately. They ambushed my men then disappeared without a trace. We weren't properly provisioned to camp out in the depths of winter. The cold was so intense our water-skins froze."

While he spoke he felt Imoshen's eyes on him. He wanted to look at her, but he disciplined himself to make his report. "If the rebels didn't kill us, cold and fever would have. My men have returned to the capital and I have decided to call the hunt off until spring."

King Gharavan came to his feet slowly. "You have *called off* the hunt?"

Tulkhan felt suddenly weary of games. Why should he explain himself to an untried youth and a conniving merchant?

"A good tactician knows when to retreat," Imoshen said, softly but forcefully.

Tulkhan noted that his half-brother and the Vaygharian both ignored her. Was it because she was female and Dhamfeer? Or was it simply because her comment, though true, was not what they wanted to hear?

"I won't risk my men uselessly," Tulkhan stated simply. "Besides, our latest information places Reothe far from the forests where we were hunting. He's come north, this way, if my informant could be believed."

He repressed a shudder, recalling the way the breath left his commander's body, taking his life with it. One touch from the T'En warrior, one word, and a man was dead.

The Vaygharian's eyes narrowed. A flash of something passed swiftly across his face and Tulkhan wondered what it meant. But his head buzzed with conflicting thoughts.

He realized his half-brother was speaking.

". . . Take fresh men into the southern highlands—"

"No. I won't risk any more men until the thaw. The rebels will go to ground through winter. We'd never find them." With a start Tulkhan realized he had interrupted and contradicted his king, spoken to him as if he was still the boy he had once been.

Gharavan rose, anger suffusing his face.

Tulkhan considered apologizing but he was right, he knew his war craft. He simply refused to obey a foolhardy order.

Imoshen moved around the table, filling the ominous silence. "I will have food prepared and see that the General's men are quartered." She stepped between the two brothers. "King Gharavan, you do not know this land. Your Ghebite

soldiers do battle with more than the cold or the rebels or the
predators in the highlands. There are ancient powers in the
deep woods, dating from a time before the dawn-people
came here. And the Ancients do not like to have their peace
disturbed.''

A flicker of something akin to fear traveled across the
young king's features, even the Vaygharian's knuckles whitened on the tabletop. Tulkhan recalled the stone circle he and
Imoshen had stumbled into on their way to Landsend and his
more recent encounter with the Ancients' powers. He shuddered.

The ancient, sexless child had fled before Reothe when
Tulkhan had unwittingly tripped the guide's trap. Could Reothe be in league with ancient evil?

Was Imoshen guessing? Or was she using basic statesmanship, bluffing to distract the attacker?

And since when had his half-brother become his enemy?
If he could only get the lad alone and talk some sense to him,
Tulkhan fumed.

"Dhamfeer bitch!" Gharavan hissed. "Do you think to
frighten me with nursery tales? Ancient evils!" He cursed
fluently, calling on their gods to exorcise such things.

Tulkhan saw Imoshen's shoulders stiffen. She did not
flinch when his half-brother strode around the table to glare
at her, his face only a hand's breadth from hers.

"Milk-faced bitch," he snarled. "Don't try to play your
Dhamfeer tricks on me. If your people had such great powers, why didn't they use them to stop my General and his
army? No. They died like the dogs they are on the battlefield,
bathed in their own blood! *Kneel!*"

When Imoshen remained frozen, Gharavan became en-
raged. He lifted his hand to strike her.

Even as she went to block the blow, Tulkhan moved. His
knee struck the backs of her knees so that she fell to the floor
at his half-brother's feet.

A gasp of surprised pain escaped her. Tulkhan winced.
She would hate him, he knew, but it couldn't be helped. His
half-brother was just looking for an excuse to execute her.

"Bow, woman," Tulkhan commanded. His fingers bit

into her shoulder, holding her there. He could feel her fine bones grinding. He knew he must be hurting her. Slowly, Imoshen's head of silver hair, topped by an intricate knot of small plaits, dipped before his half-brother.

King Gharavan's dark eyes gleamed with satisfaction. His gaze went to Tulkhan, demanding an unspoken response. The General sank stiffly to his knees to kneel at Imoshen's side.

"I swear, the rebel Reothe will be captured and executed in your name, King Gharavan," he ground out.

Tulkhan was aware of Imoshen at his side. His hand still rested on her shoulder, though not gripping as cruelly as it had before. Her profile was a perfect mask, hiding her fury.

"Very good," Gharavan purred.

When Tulkhan heard the satisfaction in his half-brother's voice, the crazy pounding of his heart began to ease. How had it come to this?

He must get his brother away from the Vaygharian. Given the chance, Tulkhan was sure he could make Gharavan see reason.

"You may go." The young king dismissed them.

Tulkhan rose to his feet, his fingers linked around Imoshen's arm, so that he drew her upright with him. He expected to see hatred in her eyes as they both bowed and turned to leave, but instead her expression was carefully guarded. Two spots of color burned high on her cheeks. Her eyes glittered and her mouth was a tense line.

When they stepped out into the hall Tulkhan was aware of his half-brother's courtiers gathered in clusters. Their conversations died as they turned, watching and weighing, awaiting the return of their king. How was he going to get Imoshen past them before her temper erupted?

"General Tulkhan?" Imoshen's voice was an imitation of itself, but only he knew that. She offered him her arm. "Allow me to show you to your chambers. I had them prepared when your party was sighted. A bath has been drawn for you."

He laid his arm along hers and closed his hand over hers. Avid, unfriendly eyes watched them. He searched his mind for a neutral topic. "The buildings surprised me. There will be a thriving town on the plain in no time."

As they walked the length of the gallery, maintaining their innocuous conversation, Tulkhan sensed their every word was being memorized, every gesture observed and cataloged. He hated it.

Now that the threat was passed, his heartbeat returned to normal and weariness fogged his brain.

They turned the corner to enter the wing where he had slept the last time he was here. Several Stronghold servants scurried past with empty buckets.

Imoshen opened the door to his chamber, inspected it and dismissed the rest of the servants. Tulkhan watched her, waiting for the outburst, willing it to come. He found the tension unbearable.

There was a bath already drawn before the fire. She stepped toward it, her back to him. "Strip. You smell of horse sweat and death. And your brother hates you."

He lifted his hands. "I had to do it. He was only looking for an excuse to have you executed."

She spun to face him, eyes blazing, chest heaving. "Do you want me to thank you for saving my life? Very well. Thank you!

"My knees will be bruised for a week. I should have knelt faster but my stupid pride wouldn't let me. There! Are you satisfied?"

He could see a sheen of unshed tears shimmering in her eyes and he longed to take her in his arms but he suspected that if he took one step closer she'd pull her knife on him.

She drew a deep, ragged breath and blinked fiercely. "How does it feel to kneel to a brother who hates you?"

"*Half*-brother," he corrected. "And he doesn't hate me, at least he didn't. He's been led astray, badly advised by that Vaygharian—"

"Is that what you call it?" She laughed bitterly, then seemed to hear the hysterical edge to her voice and clamped her mouth shut.

There was a sudden silence in the large chamber. Imoshen shivered, then moved closer to the fire. Tulkhan watched her. True, she was one of the Dhamfeer, but he could not regard her as less than a True-woman. She was a challenging mix of vulnerable and fragile yet she exuded an inner tensile strength which he could not ignore.

Today she was ornately dressed in an elaborate embroidered gown which was laced under her breasts and fell in heavy brocade folds to her knees over a fine underdress of soft white material. Strands of her pale hair were plaited and threaded with small, semiprecious stones into a crown. She looked every inch a T'En Princess, regal and somehow older than he remembered her.

Suddenly he felt awkward. Imoshen had changed since they were last together. Was this the girl-woman who had clung to him on the battlements?

"Why are you looking at me like that?" she demanded.

So many things threatened them both, so many things stood between them, suddenly he wished he was simply a soldier and she a camp follower who had come to bathe him.

"I don't trust that smile," she whispered, an answering smile lifting her lips.

By the gods, he wanted her. "Why are you here?"

She indicated the bath. "Strip. The bath is going cold. I'm here to speak without being spied on."

"You're going to watch while I bathe?"

"Does it bother you?"

"What will they think?" He gestured to the corridor, his tiredness suddenly gone.

"Since they already think that I warm your bed, what does it matter?"

Her reply held an odd tinge of defiance and despair. Tulkhan could not understand why this troubled her. From what he had seen the women of Fair Isle took lovers with impunity. Their men didn't mind and since the Ghebites despised all women, what did it matter if they thought Imoshen was his bedmate? They might even despise her less. But he wisely chose to keep this observation to himself.

He had yet to find his way with this new Imoshen. He had been finding his way since the first time he confronted her. The memory of that meeting made his body quicken.

"If you're staying you might as well help me undress."
He waited, watching for her reaction. He wanted her to touch
him, wanted to feel her hands on his skin. Any excuse would
do. "You've dismissed my servants."

She laughed, then stepped forward. "What barefaced
brass! I suppose you are waited on hand and foot while on
campaign, a hot bath drawn every night and food served on
golden plates?"

He laughed. It felt good to laugh.

As she spoke, her hands moved deftly across his chest,
unlacing his vest. She tossed it aside and turned back to him.

He sat and lifted one booted foot imperiously. Her reaction was just what he'd hoped. Amusement and fury mingled
in her face as she stepped astride his leg to work his boot off.

It slid over his foot and she dropped it, turning as he
lifted the other leg.

She snorted. "I hope you're enjoying this—"

"Immensely!"

A flash of fire lit her eyes, igniting a surge of dangerous
desire in him.

Wordlessly, she stepped astride his other leg and worked
his boot off. It fell with a thud.

He rose, standing in nothing but his breeches and undershirt.

She stepped back.

If he hadn't known better he would have said she was
suddenly shy with him. A silence hung between them, heavy
with unspoken questions.

"You should know," she told him. "That yester-eve
when I could not be found, without sending out a party to see
if I had been thrown from my horse or lost my way, your
half-brother had all but declared me a rebel and authorized
my execution. I *was* abducted." Her fingers indicated the
bruise on her forehead. "And I was lucky to escape."

Tulkhan peeled off his undershirt, aware of how the material stuck to his grimy skin, and tossed the garment aside.
Her gaze flew to his breeches and color suffused her pale
cheeks. Suddenly she seemed very young and uncertain.

It amused him, but the amusement vanished when he

noticed that the flesh around the wound on her forehead was already turning green as though the bruising had happened days ago. She must have been treating herself. A prickle of wariness traraveled across his skin. He must not forget she was Dhamfeer—and all that this implied. This hastened healing was all the evidence he needed.

But instead of sensible wariness, he felt a deep anger. It annoyed him to think anyone had raised a hand to Imoshen.

Her eyes widened as he lifted his hand to touch her bruised face. "What did they do to you?"

"My horse bolted and ran into a tree. That was how I escaped the rebels." Her offhand comment was at odds with the tension in her body.

He wanted to break through her defenses. Some devil prompted him to take her hands in his, guiding them to the laces at his belly. "The bath is going cold. Undress me."

Startled, her lashes lowered as she glanced down to his breeches and the arousal they could not hide.

Her face was a comic mixture of reluctance and curiosity.

He nodded, unable to speak, his heart hammering in his chest. This battle of wills was more testing than any encounter on the battlefield.

"Very well," she whispered.

He let her hands drop. She stepped closer and in that instant retrieved the knife he now knew she wore strapped to her upper thigh. Her hand emerged from the slit in her undergown, armed with the naked blade.

His heart missed a beat as the knife's wicked, polished edge moved close to his loins. He swallowed. She caught the waist of his breeches in one hand and pried the knife blade under the lacing. With a snap, snap, snap the laces gave, falling aside.

"There." She stepped back, her voice unsteady.

He took a deep breath as if relearning how to breathe and dropped the breeches, stepping out of them. Her eyes widened and he realized that she had not seen him this way before, not in the brightness of a candlelit chamber.

He untied the leather thong which held his hair and

stepped forward. Before he could reach for her she darted around the far side of the bath and he had to smile.

When he'd lain awake shivering in the snow, waiting for the rebels to spring from their hideout and slaughter them all, he'd thought of Imoshen, imagining her in his arms, pliant and willing. But when had she ever been like that? She was a firebrand, deadly one minute, sweetly unsure the next and he wanted her desperately. But for now he was willing to enjoy the chase.

At fifteen he'd wooed and tamed one of the wild ponies of his homeland. He knew when to feign disinterest. So he sank into the tub and reached for the soaping sand. It was scented with sandalwood and something else he didn't recognize.

"Did you mean what you said about Reothe and the powers of the deep woods or was it just a ploy to divert my half-brother's thoughts?" he asked.

She didn't answer, but he sensed her coming closer and hid a smile when she knelt behind him. Lifting the ladle she poured warm water over his neck and shoulders.

He could see the fingers of her other hand. The knuckles whitened as she gripped the rim of the bath. "You risked death in the woods."

He laughed softly. "I've risked death every day since I was seventeen—"

"Don't you know what Reothe is?" she demanded abruptly.

Startled by her intensity, Tulkhan twisted to study Imoshen's face. "He's Dhamfeer, like you."

She rolled her eyes. "You don't know what that means. I didn't either, not until . . ."

Seeming to recollect herself, she didn't finish what she'd been about to say but lifted her hand to indicate he should pass the bath scrub.

He gave it to her, watching as she rolled up her sleeves, then worked up a lather. His skin tingled in anticipation. "Explain what you mean about Reothe."

On her knees she moved around the side of the tub next

to him. "You can't defeat him in the woods. And you can't trust your half-brother at your back."

He gave a grunt of amusement. "And I can trust you?"

"Yes," she hissed.

"Why should I believe that? You surrendered the Stronghold, but you've made it clear you never surrendered to me." He waited. What did he want from her, some admission of commitment? Ridiculous, she wasn't even one of the True-people. Yet . . .

"I want to survive," she said with simple sincerity. "I don't want to see Fair Isle reduced to years of civil war. You can trust me because I'd rather deal with you than your half-brother and that Vaygharian. At least you listen to reason and see beyond your own immediate goals."

"What of Reothe?" He had to know. Her reasoning was logical, exactly the path he would have taken in her position. Sometimes an enemy you could trust was better than a friend who might betray you. But where did that leave the man she'd been betrothed to?

She looked down.

"He was your betrothed, the last prince of the T'En," Tulkhan pressed. "And now you know he still lives . . ."

She sighed and he thought she was going to lie to him. Instead, she stroked the lather along his shoulders consideringly. Her fingers massaged his tense shoulders, manipulating the slabs of muscle, working wonders. When she moved behind him to run her fingers up the nape of his neck he did not object. No one had ever pampered him like this.

He felt the knots of tension and tiredness seep from his weary body. When her fingers worked through his scalp, lathering his long hair, every sensation was somehow intensified. Her fingers were magic, he could lose himself in her caress.

"You are a wonderful witch," he whispered, his voice hoarse.

"If I am a witch then Reothe is a warlock."

There was a tremor in her voice. It chilled him despite the warm bathwater. He tried to twist his head so he could see her face, but she wound her fingers through his wet, soapy hair so tightly it was almost painful.

"Listen, General!" Her breath tickled his ear, making the little hairs on the back of his neck rise. He sensed her whispered words were torn from her at great personal cost. "Reothe has powerful T'En gifts, things I am only just discovering. He . . . he nearly trapped me out in the woods and if he had I would not have been able to fight him."

She was afraid of one of her own kind? "I don't—"

Abruptly, she tipped a ladle of water over his head, indicating the conversation was over. Warm water cascaded over his shoulders, bringing with it the scent of the soap.

So Reothe was a sore point with her. Biding his time, Tulkhan let Imoshen rinse out the soap. When she'd finished he rubbed the water from his face and caught his long hair to wring the excess from it.

He looked across the bath to where she now knelt opposite him, watching him warily. Imoshen was not telling him everything. He knew he should pursue it, yet he was so weary he found it hard to concentrate. The only thing he could think of was how beautiful she looked despite the bruise over her troubled eyes.

He indicated the puckered skin. "You'll have a scar."

"I'd rather be interesting than pretty."

He laughed. "You are nothing like the women of my homeland."

She looked at him as if she didn't know what to make of his comment. The damp heat of the bath had made the short elf locks around her face tighten into ringlets. Even her eyes looked bruised. Fear gave them a shimmering quality. He wanted to erase that fear, to know that she trusted him for himself, not because she had no choice.

The thought of someone striking her face so hard that it split the skin and drew blood was physically distressing to him. Was this wound the reason she feared the male Dhamfeer?

"Did Reothe hit you?"

She made an impatient gesture. "I told you. I was trying

to ride a bolting horse with my hands tied behind my back. No, if only it were that simple. Since . . .''

She looked down to lather her hands once again. Shifting to the side of the tub beside the fire she prepared to soap his chest. He sensed she wanted to speak but couldn't.

Tentatively, he touched her arm. ''If we are to be allies, you must trust me.''

Her eyes met his. Then her pale hands began to work their magic again, slowly circling the skin across the broad planes of his chest, working deeper and deeper. The sensation was so intense he had trouble concentrating on what she was saying.

''You call me Dhamfeer, we call ourselves the T'En,'' she whispered. ''Six hundred years ago there were several hundred of us. We were blown off course far across an ocean thought to be too broad to traverse, so my namesake claimed this island for the T'En. She took it by force, but in the end the island has taken us.

''Reothe and I are the last of our kind, Throwbacks born because of inbreeding in the royal line. There is no one to teach me how to use the gifts the T'En knew.

''Since that night with you something has wakened in me. It stirred to life, quickened by our joining.''

The glance she cast him was swift and unsure. It stirred something deep and primal within him. He caught her hands before they moved lower on their self-appointed task. Her touch was too intoxicating, confusing. He wanted a clear head.

''Is that . . . normal?''

She shrugged. ''The Aayel is dead. I don't know. I know only that certain things happened the night of our joining which frightened me—''

''The scrying, the bedding bursting into flames?''

She ducked her head and nodded as though ashamed to admit a weakness, which he supposed it was from her point of view.

''I don't know how to control what has woken so I've chosen not to use it, even when I felt it stir like a restless beast in the dark caverns of my mind.

"But yester-eve when they captured me I was frightened. They said Reothe was nearby. I knew once he had me in his power . . ." She glanced quickly at Tulkhan. "I don't know how it is with your people. But Reothe and I were betrothed. There was a bond formed that day. And he uses it to draw me to him."

"I don't understand." Tulkhan was afraid he did and he didn't like what he suspected she meant.

She rinsed the lather from her hands and straightened. "Hold out your hand and close your eyes."

It was a strange request, yet Tulkhan complied without question. He realized it was a measure of how far he had come since taking the Stronghold. He felt her fingers lace through his. Her hands were soft, still damp from the bathwater. He wondered what it would be like to taste her skin, to run his tongue up between her breasts, inhale her subtle feminine perfume. He wanted to see her eyes darken with desire, hear her gasp of appreciation.

"Well?"

"Well, what?" he asked, hoarsely.

"What were you thinking of?"

This time he felt his face grow hot. "Nothing. Why, what was I supposed to think of?"

She looked closely at him. Her fingers went to the laces which held her overdress tightly cinched beneath her breasts. With deft fingers she undid the lacing, letting the stiff material drop away to the floor.

His mouth went dry and his breath seemed to falter in his throat. Next her fingers tugged on the string which held the neck gathering of her underdress. His blood drummed in his ears as she loosened the material, letting it fall from her shoulders to reveal her perfect small breasts, the nipples puckered.

Unable to look away, he watched her fingers circle those tight nipples. "This is what you were thinking."

His mouth went dry with fear, not desire.

"How?" One word escaped him.

"Good. I haven't tried that before."

"Damn!" He sprang to his feet, dragging her upright.

Bathwater slopped over the rim onto the floor. On contact with his damp body the material of her underdress clung to her body. Her bare breasts brushed the dark matted hair of his chest as he held her. He could feel her warm flesh, as good as naked next to his.

Anger and desire warred within him. "Keep out of my head!"

"How do you think *I* feel?" She jerked as if to escape him, but he wouldn't release her, not while there was still breath in his body.

Pain traveled across her face, shadowing her eyes with fear. "I hated it when Reothe invaded my mind. At least I admitted it to you. He played with me, manipulating my senses without thought for my feelings! How do you think I feel knowing he can do that?"

"Reothe manipulates you?"

She nodded, and stepped back as he released her. Tulkhan hated to acknowledge the terrible feeling of foreboding stealing over him. The rebel leader had stood and laughed mockingly as Tulkhan's sword sliced through insubstantial mist. Reothe vowed he would be the Ghebite General's death, had even called him a dead man who walked and talked.

Somehow the Dhamfeer rebel leader had evaded Tulkhan's army in the highlands, yet killed or wounded half his men. And then there was the inexplicable death of the commander.

Reothe had arranged for Imoshen to be plucked from the land around her Stronghold in broad daylight and nearly succeeded in abducting her.

What manner of man was T'Reothe?

Dhamfeer. Other and dangerous.

If so, then so was Imoshen. The knowledge that she had invaded his mind still rankled Tulkhan.

He caught her shoulders, drawing her near to search her face.

"You were betrothed to him, destined to be his bedmate." The thought of another man planting images of seduction in Imoshen's mind incensed Tulkhan. He wanted to strike out. Imoshen had freely given her vow to Reothe, while Tulkhan had to admit he had laid claim to her body through trickery. He had no real hold on her. His throat closed with bitterness, choking his voice. "What does it matter if he seduces you with mind tricks, surely it is his right?"

He watched her eyes widen, knew he'd hurt her and cursed himself because suddenly he didn't want to cause her pain.

"You don't understand!" she hissed, pulling away from him as if she had been stung. If he hadn't been standing in the bath Tulkhan suspected she would have kicked him. "I'm afraid he'll seduce my mind. If joining with you that once gives me this much access to your thoughts, can you imagine what joining with Reothe would do? He wants to use me to regain Fair Isle!"

"And I want to use you to hold Fair Isle," Tulkhan ground out. "What is the difference?"

She stiffened, her face beautiful and masklike in its stillness. She was shocked beyond pain.

He had pushed her till she reacted but this resistance was a hollow victory.

"Choice!" The word fell from her lips, startling him with its force. "I *choose* to ally myself with you."

"But you were betrothed to him, promised—"

"In another time, before the old empire fell!" Her voice was low and intense. "You must understand, for all our sakes. Reothe tried to use the betrothal as a lever on me and I refused him. Now he has tried force. If he gets me in his power I will have no defenses against him. I don't know how to use the T'En gifts and he does!" The confession was torn from her. "How do you think I feel, knowing he can manipulate my mind?"

"How do you think I feel knowing you can do the same to me?" Tulkhan demanded raggedly.

She blinked, and he could have sworn she was surprised.

"But I'm not going to hurt you." Her sincerity was obvious.

He almost laughed. "As long as I'm useful to you, as

long as there are other threats like my half-brother and his lover, or your once-betrothed, Reothe.''

Tulkhan could hear the mockery in his own voice. He didn't want to stand here arguing with her. Suddenly nothing mattered but his desire for her, his need.

He had missed her presence while in T'Diemn, missed her advice while in the southern highlands dealing with sly locals. More than that he had yearned to feel her warm, compliant body next to his at night, to sleep with her in his arms. He blinked. Where had these thoughts come from?

Furious, he turned on her. ''Damn you Dhamfeer. Are you playing with my mind now, planting suggestions?''

Imoshen blinked, startled by the General's sudden savagery. His face conveyed such anguish that she longed to convince him his thoughts were his own, but how?

''Of course not!'' She snapped. But why should he believe her? ''It wouldn't be right—''

''You deny tampering with my thoughts before?''

''No. But that was done to prove a point. To tamper with your thoughts to change your mind wouldn't be right.'' She drew herself up, not deigning to cover her breasts. The damp undergown clung to her thighs and abdomen. ''If you were having lustful thoughts they were your own—''

''Ha!'' He stabbed an accusatory finger at her. ''How did you know they were lustful thoughts?''

She bit her bottom lip to hide the smile which threatened to undo her. Now was not the time to mock him. Wordlessly she pointed.

He hastily covered himself with the drying cloth.

As he stepped from the bath, the cloth held securely in place, she couldn't help but admire his long flanks and the curve of his taut buttocks as he turned his back, pointedly ignoring her.

His coppery, battle-scarred hands rubbed the cloth firmly across his chest. She wanted to feel those hands rub as firmly across her flesh, wanted to feel him clasp her with a passion that would ignite them both, banish all fear and doubt.

''You are angry with me.''

The firelight danced on his tall frame, illuminating the many small scars where old wounds had healed. She hated every one of those scars because they were evidence of his life before she knew him.

He wanted her, that was plain enough. What did she have to do?

Imoshen licked her lips. When she spoke her voice was almost hoarse. "I would not mock you."

He gave a single grunt. It conveyed a world of meaning.

"General Tulkhan?" she breathed his name, her heart hammering with tension as she released the material of her underdress. It fell at her feet.

Mortally afraid he might reject her, she closed her eyes, unable to meet his. Naked physically and emotionally, she held her breath, heard his sudden intake of breath and braved his gaze.

The planes of his face were taut with need, his eyes twin fires of dark desire. Yet he stood there, rigid with contained urgency.

Did he want her to beg? Unable to speak, she took a step and put her hand tentatively on his chest. The fevered hammering of his heart leapt beneath her palm. With her other hand she caught his wrist and lifted his hand to press his palm over her own raging heart.

"Please." The word was a whisper. It hung on the supercharged air between them.

"Why?" Desire and despair warred in his voice. "So you can control me as Reothe seeks to control you?"

Imoshen shook her head. "I wouldn't . . . couldn't do that."

"You expect me to believe you?"

She could only nod.

With a groan he caught her to him.

EIGHT

I MOSHEN'S HEART SANG. She felt light-headed with relief. A delicious anticipation tingled through her limbs. The length of his hard thighs pressed on her legs, the heat of his arousal melted into her belly. His hands circled the small of her waist, lifting her to him.

Tears stung her eyes.

Blindly she searched for his lips, felt the graze of his unshaven beard on her cheek, then the heat of his mouth on hers. There was nothing tentative about his kiss. It was totally possessive, demanding. She reveled in it, in the knowledge that he wanted her despite his better judgment, because it was the same with her.

What did the rational mind have to do with this? It went beyond thought to a primal source deep within.

Her fingers wound through the damp silk of his long, dark hair. His mouth parted from hers. When he spoke his lips grazed hers, his breath caressing her skin. "Is it true?"

What was he talking about?

She shook her head, blindly seeking his lips only to have him clasp her face between his hands. His fierce obsidian eyes searched her features, as if to probe her soul.

"Is it true?"

"Is what true?" She wanted him at that moment more than life itself, could hardly think.

"Are you with child?"

She blinked, surprised by the question. "Of course. I told you so."

A flash of something that might have been anger traveled across his face, then he bent to kiss her and she was lost in sensation. This time his passion was bruising but she met it with the white hot fury of her own.

When he raised his head she twisted out of his arms and stepped backward, wordlessly lifting her hand to draw him after her to the bed. But he stood unmoving, watching her as she slipped under the down-filled covers. Hugging the cool material to her chest, she looked at him expectantly, her body alive with anticipation.

Silent, unable to speak, she waited for him to come to her.

He prowled across the room, lean and dark, urgent. "Have you no shame? You were untouched when I took your maidenhead."

A shiver ran through her body. She didn't understand his anger.

A nervous laugh escaped her. "I want you. Why should I deny it?"

"Why indeed?" He gave a strange laugh and stepped toward her.

Relieved, she held the covers back to welcome him, drawing him down to her. The long length of his body met hers. Their legs entwined. Impatience gripped her. Feverishly, she guided him into her.

There was a sudden flash of pain but she ground her teeth rather than admit it.

"I hurt you?" He seemed startled.

She denied it. "No. Not much. Don't pull away."

He lay still in her, supporting his weight on his elbows. She wriggled under him, experimenting with the extent of her discomfort.

It was nothing compared to the thrill of having him like this.

But when she reached for his face and her lips met his, his manner had changed again. This time he was tender and she reveled in it, relaxing so that the pain of accepting him faded until it was swamped by the ever increasing excitement of her impending release.

This time he lingered with her, bringing her slowly to her peak. She forgot everything in the moment of their joining, forgot herself in him.

The power of their meeting left her breathless and dizzy. It was frightening to be so vulnerable to someone she didn't really understand or know, someone who only recently was her enemy.

She watched as he slid from her embrace and knelt above her, inspecting the bedding. She sat up, not surprised to see that she'd bled again.

"It didn't hurt as much as the first time." She tried to reassure him.

He seemed stunned. "It's true then. If you carry a child it's mine."

She looked at him curiously. "Of course it is."

"How can this be?" His eyes searched her face.

She almost laughed. "A child is usually the consequence of what we did, unless the woman uses—"

He caught her shoulders. "You don't understand. I've never fathered a child. I thought I couldn't!"

Imoshen felt her skin go cold. So this was what the Aayel had seen—his secret shame, his one weak point. How cunning of the wise one not to tell her, for she might have doubted her ability to conceive.

Now the babe was a foregone conclusion.

He placed a tentative hand on her belly. "You are sure?"

She covered his hand with hers, touched by the wonder in his voice. She had meant to steal this child as a bargaining tool, but now she understood it was much more than that. It was the greatest gift she could give him.

He seemed so hopeful but the healer in her had to temporize. "You will see your son born, unless I miscarry."

The fire had fallen down to ashes. Imoshen lay nestled in the curve of the General's body, listening to the soft rise and fall of his breathing. At that moment she felt tender toward him but more than a little indignant. He had suspected her of trying to pass off another man's child as his own!

Now she understood his private bitterness.

Stretching against him, she felt him harden and nudge into the crease of her buttocks. He made an appreciative noise in his throat and she smiled. She was sure if she were to . . .

A ragged shout made her heart falter. The sound came from the corridor, followed by the repetitive thud of booted feet. A woman shrieked.

Imoshen sat bolt upright, her heart thudding.

The General lifted his head, his dark eyes startled, hair wild over his shoulders. "What is it?"

"I don't know." She licked dry lips. "Soldiers in the hall outside—"

The door to the chamber flew open, crashing against the stone wall. Armed men poured into the room.

Tulkhan rolled out of the bed, running naked for his sword. Imoshen knew her dagger lay discarded by the cold bath. There was no time to reach it and they were outnumbered. Violence would not free them from these Ghebites. She did not recognize any as Tulkhan's men.

Several men drew their weapons, preventing the General from reaching his. He cast a quick glance to her. Their position was hopeless and they both knew it.

Tulkhan straightened. "This is my private chamber. Explain the intrusion."

The Vaygharian stepped forward, his eyes alive with malicious triumph. "Arrest these two by order of the king. They were plotting treason."

"*No!*" General Tulkhan roared. But whether it was to deny the accusation or the knowledge that his half-brother had ordered their arrest Imoshen did not know.

"On what evidence?" she demanded, pulling a soft blanket from the bedding and wrapping it around her. Fear pounded through her veins, but she refused to show weakness as she stepped from the bed to confront her accusers. "There can be no evidence because the accusations are untrue!"

"You were convicted by your own words, both of you."

The Vaygharian was enjoying himself. She could sense it oozing from him. He strode toward Imoshen but not near enough for her to jump him, or to fall within Tulkhan's reach.

"The Dhamfeer withheld information. Her former lover, Reothe the rebel leader, was in the woods. Had she told us, we could have sent men out to capture him and his followers. His head would have been sitting on a pike on the battlements even now!"

Imoshen went cold with fear. Yes, she had withheld information which Tulkhan had unwittingly revealed, implicating her.

"I knew only that rebels had captured me, not how near their leader was," she lied. "And you're lucky you didn't venture into the woods after Reothe because if you had, not one of you would be here to tell of it!"

The men stirred uneasily. Her conviction carried weight.

"A groundless charge!" Tulkhan stepped forward. Though he was naked the mantle of leadership was still visible in the set of his shoulders. Imoshen admired his assurance. The General was used to giving commands. Men were used to obeying him. Perhaps there was hope.

"Release the Princess. She is innocent of treason." Tulkhan was firm but not strident. "As am I."

"You deny you refused a direct command of your king?" the Vaygharian cut in swiftly, stilling the voice of reason. "King Gharavan ordered you into the highlands to hunt rebels—"

"And I refused," Tulkhan agreed. "To go would have been to murder my troops. I gave a commitment to hunt the rebels in the spring—"

"Convicted by his own words. Arrest him!"

The shouts of Gharavan's men drowned Tulkhan's voice. Goaded on by the safety of numbers and weaponry against an unarmed, naked man, they surged forward.

Imoshen stiffened. She refused to fight them, but as it was they pawed her body on the pretext of subduing her. The blanket she held was torn from her so that she was clad in nothing but her long, pale hair. She refused to cower or plead when they pulled her toward the Vaygharian.

The General received worse treatment. Though he did not resist, their sheer numbers bore him down, arms were raised and the flat of their swords struck him. She wanted to cry out, but she held her tongue and ground her teeth.

It was just as well. She found the Vaygharian's eyes on her, enjoying her anguish, feeding on her distress.

"Enough," he said finally and they drew back, hauling Tulkhan to his feet.

The General was bleeding freely and barely able to stand. Even so, he straightened with painful dignity. "I demand to speak with my half-brother—"

"The king does not wish to be disturbed," Kinraid cut him short. "Take them below and secure them."

Someone shoved Imoshen between the shoulder blades so hard that she staggered forward, falling to her knees at the Vaygharian's feet. The pain in her already bruised knees was sharp and immediate.

"You see," he purred. "It grows easier to kneel before your masters."

Hatred surged through her. What she wouldn't give to hold a knife in her hands right now. He would be dead before his next breath. But then so would she and where would that leave the General?

Imoshen's mouth went dry. What was she thinking?

It startled her to realize she had put Tulkhan before her people. They were her priority. She had to survive for the sake of Fair Isle and the child she carried, though in truth the babe seemed unreal to her at this moment.

The Vaygharian seized her arm, hauling her to her feet. His fingers caught in her long hair, pulling it so that tears of pain stung her eyes. She blinked them away, fiercely determined not to let him see even the slightest weakness.

He released her arms and, with his black-gloved hand, tilted her face to study her features. His eyes were level with hers and as she watched she saw his gaze darken with desire. Instinctively, she knew this was a man who liked to inflict pain, that it aroused him.

"Is it true what they say about the 'pure' Dhamfeer women?" he purred. "Well, General, is this celibate bitch as hot to bed as rumor has it? No sniveling pleas, no martyred silences, just hot thighs and eager lips."

She would have pulled back but the men behind her pinned her arms.

Smiling slightly, the Vaygharian lifted his free hand and caught the leather covering the tip of each finger in his teeth, tugging until the glove slipped off his hand.

Imoshen stiffened as his warm, dry fingers brushed her breast, delicately tracing her nipple. To her shame her body responded and his smile broadened.

She hated him with every fiber of her being. Rage flooded her, blotting her vision. She wished him dead.

Sparks flashed before her eyes as if she were about to faint, but instead she realized they were the sparks of a raging fire. She saw the Vaygharian spin to face her, the flames at his back. He could not escape.

Panic flashed across his face, sheer terror. Then his features hardened. He turned and with a shout of despair leapt into the roaring fire.

A cry of horror escaped her and she stiffened, panting.

Her vision cleared to see the Vaygharian's pleased face. Imoshen suddenly realized that he thought she was afraid of him and she smiled with the foreknowledge of her vision.

"Why do you smile?" he snarled.

"You will die by your own hand, in flames of agony," she told him.

It was very satisfying to see fear tighten the planes of his face. His hand swung in an arc which she tried to dodge but her captors restrained her. His balled fist caught her in the side of the head.

Dimly she heard Tulkhan roar as everything faded.

Cold clawed its way into her bones. Imoshen shivered and fought the need to wake. Her head hurt. Fear slept like an unwelcome twin in the back of her mind. To return to consciousness would mean a return to the real world of pain and . . . treachery.

It came back to her in a rush—the king, Tulkhan's own flesh and blood, had betrayed him.

She lifted her head and winced. Mercifully it was dark, but terribly cold. Shivers wracked her body. Nausea roiled in her stomach. Fighting the waves of pain, she tried to focus on a dim gray shape in the darkness and felt around her.

Her fingers encountered cold stone. She was lying on a floor lightly sprinkled with stale straw. Something scurried away and she knew she'd had company.

A soft laugh escaped her—how ironic! She was a prisoner in her own dungeon. She must remember to have the place cleaned, the rat-dogs released and fresh straw sprinkled. It was even more ridiculous when she did not know if she would escape this trap.

"Imoshen?" the General hissed.

She stiffened. A wave of longing enveloped her. She wanted him to hold her, to tell her everything would be all right, even though she knew it wouldn't.

"Imoshen, are you all right?"

She snorted.

And when he spoke she heard the answering smile in his voice. "Come closer."

She crawled toward the sound of his voice, but her fingers met cold, ancient wood. Dragging herself upright she found metal bars and saw a dim shape beyond. They were separated by a passageway. So she would not have the luxury of warming herself in the General's embrace.

"What time is it?" she asked, when she could trust her voice not to betray her.

"Near dawn," he answered.

Something in his tone warned her. "What are their plans? A trial first then execution, or simply execution?"

She heard him chuckle softly.

"Imoshen?" Dimly, she made out his outline, pressed against the bars opposite her, and saw his hand waver in the space between them.

By thrusting her arm through the bars of her own prison

she could just touch his fingers. Her shoulder ached abominably. Then she remembered how he had forced her to kneel to his petty king. Even that had not saved them.

His fingers were cold but gripped hers firmly.

"They will hold a trial. I am the king's half-brother. He couldn't have me executed without the formality of a trial."

"And me?"

He hesitated.

"I see." Her throat was tight with anger. "When will they come for me?"

"Dawn."

"So little time?" Her heart wrenched within her.

She had dodged death so many times in these last few moons, how ironic it was to die like this at the hands of a petty king and his vindictive lover.

Would her people revolt? What would General Tulkhan's Elite Guard do? Would they remain loyal to their rightful king or to the man they had served so faithfully?

She'd been right. Gharavan was not to be trusted.

Rage warmed her. Would she have a chance to take that spiteful tyrant with her? If she did, she would only have the one opportunity.

Imoshen considered her chances. Hopefully they wouldn't bind her. Seeing how contemptuous they were of a mere female they probably would leave her arms free. Then if they let her get near enough to King Gharavan, she would go for his throat. A killing blow would crush his windpipe and he'd suffocate even as his men gutted her.

She smiled, that was a pleasant thought.

"Imoshen?" General Tulkhan interrupted her reverie. "I . . . I should have heeded you when you warned me not to trust him."

She knew it was true. What did he want from her, absolution? Strangely enough, she felt compelled to give it.

"You loved him."

"Yes." The word was torn from him. "Even though he was my half-brother and destined to inherit what I could not earn."

Her arm ached, but she didn't want to release the General's hand. That contact was her one point of humanity. Without him she would be nothing but a weapon primed to kill. She was glad he would not see her die. Once she had killed Gharavan there would be confusion. Tulkhan's Elite Guard would surely revolt. The General was next in line for the Kingship. If the Elite Guard turned on the king's Vaygharian advisor . . . Was that the meaning of the fore-telling she'd seen?

Imoshen's heart raced in anticipation. She would like to have a hand in his death. Of course, it meant her own and that of the child she carried. A cold chill ran through her body. Did she have the right to decide the fate of her unborn child? A black laugh threatened to escape her. What was she thinking? She was as good as dead anyway.

If only she had let Drake take her to Reothe, but what then? She would be his captive as surely as she was King Gharavan's. What did it matter if the cage was stone or silk? It was still a cage.

Imoshen sighed, the Aayel had been right. There were no simple answers.

The sudden pressure of the General's fingers on hers recalled her to the present.

"The first time I saw you, your breasts so pale, your eyes so fierce, I wanted you," he whispered.

Imoshen swallowed. "I hated you."

"I know."

She could tell he was smiling.

"But you proved an honorable enemy and . . ." her voice grew thick, "a true friend."

She wanted to tell him that he had become so much more to her, but the words stuck in her throat. She did not want to weep before him. She had to remain strong, to focus her will on killing Gharavan.

There were muffled footsteps, voices, the glow of an approaching torch.

"So soon?" Imoshen whispered, flinching as Tulkhan's fingers tightened their grip on hers.

"Imoshen?" he hissed.

She could see the outline of his bruised face, his mouth

and throat stained with dry blood. She knew she must look as battered.

Suddenly a group of the King's men strode into the narrow corridor. Their two torches blinded Imoshen and their cruel laughter seared her soul.

Through a blur she saw one of them dart forward, weapon drawn ready to slash her extended arm. Though stiff and sore she pulled back, only too aware how easily her arm could be broken even with the flat of the sword. She needed the use of her limbs if she was to carry out her plan.

Several cloaked figures blocked her view through the door's grate but she could hear them shouting insults at General Tulkhan.

"Lady T'En?" a soft voice whispered.

Imoshen looked to see Kalleen restrained between them and her heart sank. What were these barbarians planning? The girl was innocent.

One of them moved forward to unlock her prison door. Stiffly she stepped back.

Kalleen gave a soft cry of distress. "What have they done to you, my Lady?"

Imoshen tensed at her tone. The Kalleen she knew was not so weepy. Had they been brutal with her?

The youth who had opened the door was barely out of his teens, richly dressed, out to conquer the world on a great adventure at the king's side. Imoshen saw it all in his face, and knew instinctively that he had never shed blood in anger or fear.

He flinched when Kalleen turned on him.

"How could you mistreat my lady so? She is the last of T'En, a princess in her own right. Get out while I help her dress!"

Shuffling, his face hot, he backed out.

Imoshen caught a glimpse of the others pressed against the far prison door, taunting General Tulkhan, then her door swung shut.

"My Lady," Kalleen whispered and Imoshen found the girl pulling her into the shadows.

"It's all right." Meaningless words, but she said them

anyway. The girl hugged her fiercely. Once released, Imoshen indicated the basket. "So I am to die dressed, they allow me that much dignity."

Kalleen stepped back and tugged at her cloak, dropping it to the stones.

"What are you doing?" Imoshen asked uneasily.

"I'm here to take your place."

"No. I won't do it—"

"My lady," Kalleen said sternly, her voice a fevered whisper. "They will behead you at dawn. If you leave now, you can slip away from the Stronghold, run into the forest and contact the rebels."

Even as she spoke she was pulling on Imoshen's rich fur cloak. Urgently, the young woman dragged the poorer cloak over Imoshen's shoulders.

"They will kill you," Imoshen croaked.

Kalleen blinked, her face barely visible in the spears of light which came through the grate.

"They will be angry, probably beat me. It does not matter."

Imoshen's heart twisted within her. They both knew Kalleen was lying.

"I am taller than you, fairer—"

"Pull the cloak up, hunch down." Kalleen gave a start as the door shook on its hinges. "They come."

There was no time for more. It was a trick they were sure to expect. Yet, hope fluttered in Imoshen's breast. If she managed to escape she could turn on the king, rouse the Stronghold Guard. She had to succeed.

Too much was at risk to fail.

Her captors must believe she was the serving maid. They must perceive Kalleen as the captive Imoshen.

The girl proudly turned away from the door, acting a role. Someone tugged on the back of Imoshen's cloak. Her heart pounded with urgency. What should she do? She'd never tried to befuddle the minds of men before.

If only the Aayel had lived long enough to help her to understand and harness her T'En gift. Panic threatened to steal her wits then, like a fog lifting, her mind cleared and only ice cold determination filled her.

She would be Kalleen, the faithful servant distraught because her mistress was to die. A thousand stinging ants picked their way over her skin.

The youth dragged her away from the proud, fur-cloaked figure.

"My Lady!" Imoshen wept and thumped the youth. He caught her hands and looked down into her face. It seemed she was smaller than she had been. Fear flickered in the back of her mind, but she was Kalleen and words leapt to her tongue. "Ghebite barbarian!"

He laughed and pushed her through the open door. "Get out, or you can stay and keep your mistress company with the headman's axe."

Imoshen dared not glance in Tulkhan's direction and risk breaking her concentration. She was Kalleen the former farm girl, an unimportant creature in the scheme of things.

With every step she took out of those dank, oppressive chambers terror warred with elation. The guards jostled her in their eagerness to escape the dungeon. Any moment now she was sure they would look into her face and see through the illusion.

At the entrance to the kitchen wing they marched off, talking amongst themselves. Imoshen sniffed and scurried away into the warren of storerooms and then into the great kitchen itself, where the woman who ruled this domain was already up, preparing fresh bread and warm broth for their first meal of the day.

Imoshen paused to catch her breath. How long did she have? Dawn could not be far away.

Running lightly through the empty corridors, she headed for the wing she had put aside to house the Elite Guard. Wharrd was pacing the floor, arguing with several of the men when she entered.

A man grabbed her as she ran into the room, lifting her off her feet.

"Kalleen, what are you doing here?" Wharrd rounded on her. "Have you a message from Tulkhan?"

As she slid from the man's grip Imoshen remembered Kalleen and Wharrd had had a falling-out over Drake and, as far as she knew, they had not made up their difference. But she was no longer Kalleen. She must resume her own identity now.

At the thought her skin crawled with a thousand pin-pricks of pain.

She must take control of the Stronghold defenders, trap Gharavan's men, convince the Elite Guard to . . .

Wharrd swore softly and made the sign to ward off evil. Several men turned their faces away, others went for their weapons.

By their reaction Imoshen knew the change must have taken effect, she felt like herself again. The cloak did not brush the ground as she drew it tightly about her.

"Princess." Wharrd made a soldier's attempt at a bow.

"Dhamfeer!" someone hissed behind her. She ignored him.

"I need clothes, breeches, boots and a jerkin. Kalleen has taken my place. I won't let her die in my stead. And I won't let them make a mockery of the General's devotion to his king. Tulkhan is innocent of any treason."

"I know," the grizzled campaigner muttered. "We all know that."

Imoshen moved toward the bone-setter. He flinched as she approached though he tried to hide it. She didn't have time to reassure him. "The Vaygharian poisons Gharavan's mind with lies. The king is weak, not half the man General Tulkhan is. Where does your loyalty lie?"

Wharrd did not hesitate. "With Tulkhan—"

"Aye, the General."

"General Tulkhan!"

Their voices joined the bone-setter's, gaining conviction. Imoshen's hand closed on Wharrd's arm. "Will you fight beside my people?"

"What would you have us do?"

She smiled. "First find me some clothes."

                •   •   •

Tulkhan shivered. He had called to Imoshen repeatedly but she would not answer. She was going to die at dawn and the knowledge was bitter. He would also face the headman's axe once they were through with the mockery of his trial. And he had only himself to blame. He had thought he could reason with his half-brother, wean him from the influence of the Vaygharian, but he'd overestimated his own influence with Gharavan.

On the battlefield you could not afford to underestimate the enemy. But this was not the battlefield and backroom politics was not his style.

He had thrown away Imoshen's life and his own, as well as Fair Isle, which should have been his. He had won it while his half-brother and his army had ridden on his coattails, mopping up survivors, swaggering through crushed villages.

He had misjudged his man and must face the consequences.

Shivers wracked his body. He despised himself. But it was the empty cold ache within that troubled him most. They would lead her away, proudly defiant to the last, and he would never see her again.

Tulkhan did not believe in an afterlife. How could he when he had seen too many religions in too many countries to hold on to the faith of his Ghebite homeland? But just this once he wished he were a believer, that there was some way he could ensure they would be reborn and meet again in another life.

Contempt seared him. It was this kind of woolly thinking that had led him astray. He should have assessed his half-brother's character flaws and recognized his weakness for what it was. A stronger mind could lead Gharavan to great things, but it could also lead him to evil.

Booted feet struck the stones.

"Imoshen, answer me. They come!"

But she stubbornly refused. Was she frightened? Tulkhan longed to offer comfort. Yet he dared not. She probably despised him for leading them into this. Self-disgust seared him. What right had he to offer her anything?

Knowing they would taunt him, he moved back from the

grill, but not too far. He wanted to catch sight of her face this one last time.

"Let's see this Dhamfeer Princess," one of them growled.

"See her die like any other woman. Where is your Dhamfeer magic now, Princess?"

They flung the door open.

Tulkhan could see nothing but their backs. The after-image of flickering torchlight danced on his night-blinded eyes.

Why the silence? He had expected cruel mockery.

The king's men staggered back. One of them cursed.

Between their shoulders Tulkhan saw Kalleen's trucu-lent, frightened face as she walked determinedly out of the cell.

The men broke into a gabble of accusations and counter-accusations. They swore the switch was impossible.

One of them grabbed Kalleen and shook her. "She's real."

"The last one was real too, remember I held her, looked into her face," the youth cried. "Dhamfeer magic!"

They swore and called on their gods to protect them. Not surprisingly, their greatest fear was who would tell their king.

Tulkhan rejoiced. Imoshen was free. But he dared not draw attention to himself. The men were angry and fright-ened. They would turn on anyone.

One of them grabbed Kalleen, twisting her arm so that she cried out. They dragged the girl away and Tulkhan knew there would be no mercy for her. Gharavan would be en-raged.

In the same breath fierce joy coursed through him. Imoshen was free.

What would she do?

What could she do, an outlaw in her own Stronghold? The servants would be on her side, unless his half-brother had them all cowed by fear. No, he doubted if they would betray her.

What was he thinking? He had seen the king's men lead

Kalleen away twice and he had not known one of them was Imoshen. He'd had no idea she could change her appearance. She constantly surprised him. He shuddered as he remembered how she had described the Vaygharian's death.

Was she using foreknowledge? She had said it with the same certainty that Reothe had spoken of his own death!

Tulkhan repressed a shudder.

What was the extent of Imoshen's Dhamfeer heritage? Could she retake the Stronghold on her own and leave him to rot down here?

Self-loathing filled Tulkhan.

She didn't need him. She had said herself she only took him as an ally for practical purposes.

Why had she taken him to her bed then? He flinched. Was that quicksilver passion of hers an incandescent coal ready to leap into flame for any man who knew how to ignite it?

Imoshen had admitted Reothe moved her.

Even now she was probably far from the Stronghold. Why shouldn't she flee into the woods and take Reothe's side? If this was but a glimpse of her T'En gifts, how much more powerful would the two Dhamfeer be when joined?

No wonder she had abandoned him. He had proved himself incompetent so she had cast him aside.

Despair cut through Tulkhan. He was a fool.

It was love for his half-brother that had undone him. Love had clouded his vision. That would never happen again, he vowed. He only wished he might live long enough to see his half-brother brought low by Imoshen's hand. A grim smile tugged at his lips.

King Gharavan had made a bad enemy in the Dhamfeer woman. Tulkhan knew as surely as the Vaygharian's days were numbered that Gharavan would meet death before his time.

Marching feet sounded on the stones again and he tensed. Surely it was not time? They couldn't have summarily executed the little maid already.

Three different king's men approached his cell. Tulkhan wondered grimly what had happened to the others. These men flung the door open and hauled Tulkhan out. He tried not to flinch but the torchlight hurt his eyes. Chilled to the marrow by the cold, he tried to walk with dignity down the length of the dungeon chambers.

He expected them to be rough with him but they were circumspect. Still, a pair of breeches wouldn't have gone astray. If he was to meet death he'd have preferred to do it clothed.

He was sure the oversight was deliberate. But if they thought to cow him they would discover they were wrong.

The upper floors of the Stronghold were abuzz with activity and suppressed excitement. Servants scurried about but he could not see his own men or the Stronghold Guard. He understood why when the men marched him into the great hall.

His own man, Wharrd, stood behind the king's chair, flanked by the Elite Guard, who it appeared had sworn allegiance to Gharavan. Tulkhan's gut twisted at the thought. He had believed his men, especially the Elite Guard, were bound to him through years of service, years when he had sweated in the sun, shivered in the cold, slept on rocks and faced death at their sides.

Did it count for nothing? Fury made him stand taller. He would not flinch before his own half-brother. He would meet his end with dignity.

He met Gharavan's eyes and something traveled between them, some acknowledgment of his humanity. Was there a chance he could reason with the youth?

Then he noted the arrogance in the Vaygharian's eyes, saw the way his hand rested on Gharavan's shoulder. The hopelessness of his situation threatened to overwhelm Tulkhan. His brother had sold his soul to a soulless man who wanted only power.

Tulkhan surveyed the hall. The king's men were gathered around in clusters, some still buckling on their weapons, adjusting their cloaks. He was right—he had been called prematurely.

Little Kalleen was a miserable creature. Unbound, she knelt at Gharavan's feet. Where was Imoshen now? Halfway into the woods, running to Reothe, no doubt. He felt anger on Kalleen's behalf. She had been willing to give her life for her mistress, only to be abandoned.

"The Dhamfeer has escaped, thus confirming her guilt. What say you, General?" Gharavan asked.

Tulkhan wondered why his half-brother felt it necessary to prolong this mock trial.

"I knew nothing of it. I ask one thing only. Spare the maidservant."

His half-brother stiffened and glanced down at Kalleen, who ducked her head as if expecting a blow.

"If she is so eager to take her mistress's place, she can die in her place."

"No!" It was out before Tulkhan could stop himself.

"No?" Gharavan stiffened in the seat.

Tulkhan ground his teeth. His own life was forfeit but he might yet save the girl.

"It was I who taught you to ride. I made your first wooden practice sword. If you have any memory of the love we once shared, grant me this one request. Release the girl."

"What of yourself?" Gharavan asked. "What do you ask for yourself?"

Tulkhan ignored the glittering eyes of the Vaygharian who was relishing every moment of this.

"Nothing?" pursued his half-brother. "Do you deny you refused to obey my command?"

Stung, Tulkhan looked past his shoulder, to his own Elite Guard behind them. He knew he must look a pitiful sight in their eyes, naked, almost blue with cold, bruised and bloodied. They had followed him because they respected him. It irked him to lose their respect.

"Well?" Gharavan prodded.

"I would not lead my men to certain death in the southern highlands in the depths of winter. I've given a sworn undertaking to hunt Reothe and his accursed rebels come the thaw. But why continue this? We all know it is a mockery. You . . ." His anger threatened to choke his voice. "You, who had my father's love, who always was his chosen heir, why do you fear me? I've served our father in his army as a youth and eventually as his General. I rose to that position through skill, not favor. Never once have I done other than served in his name. I would have honored you with the same service—''

''Say you!'' hissed the Vaygharian. ''But what of the Dhamfeer Princess? You took her to your bed. The country is behind her. You could have taken Fair Isle for your own. Admit it, that was what the pair of you planned!''

Tulkhan was stunned. What the Vaygharian said was true, he could have used Imoshen to unite the people. But it was never his intention to take the island for his own.

''You twist my words—''

''Enough!'' The Vaygharian strode forward. ''This man calls me a liar because he lies. He plots to further his own ambition.''

Rage gripped Tulkhan, ridding him of the last shreds of despair. To be unjustly accused of the very crimes the Vaygharian was committing was the ultimate irony.

Giving the formal signs he challenged the Vaygharian. ''I call you liar, you are dishonored!''

Kinraid laughed. ''I won't accept a challenge from a condemned prisoner. There is no honor in that!''

He was loudly seconded by the king's men, making Tulkhan wonder how many of them owed their position to the Vaygharian.

Gharavan came to his feet. ''Who says General Tulkhan can't challenge Kinraid, the Vaygharian?''

It was a strange question, one that surprised Tulkhan and made the king's men hesitate. They looked to each other.

''Who says he is a dog without honor and should be beheaded?'' roared the Vaygharian.

His shout was taken up by the king's men, who followed his lead eagerly. Tulkhan noted the silence from his Elite Guard, the silence from the rest of the Stronghold servants and guard scattered through the great hall. They were unwilling witnesses to his trial and execution.

Quickly he scanned the room, once again in familiar territory. This was a battle with the odds against him, but one which he recognized and understood. Now, he knew where he stood, who was loyal and who would stab him in the back given a chance. Now he could see for himself where his half-brother stood. Gharavan's expression caught his attention.

Odd, it was almost sympathetic.

The young king stepped forward, pulling Kalleen to her feet. ''Go home to your people.''

She stared at him, her mouth open with disbelief.

Kinraid started and strode toward Gharavan, obviously about to disagree with the king's order. Tulkhan heard a shout from the back of the hall.

His half-brother gave Wharrd a signal. ''Arrest the Vaygharian.''

''No!'' Kinraid spun. ''What manner of—''

''Impostor!'' A scream echoed to the vaulted roof as someone charged through the throng by the kitchen door. Someone who . . . Tulkhan stared. It was his half-brother, disheveled, frantic to reach them.

The Vaygharian spun to face King Gharavan. ''Then who? You!''

He drew his sword and lunged toward the false Gharavan who thrust Kalleen aside and drew his own sword.

Even as Tulkhan watched, his half-brother's face wavered and slipped to reveal Imoshen in breeches and jerkin, her hair tightly bound at the nape of her neck. She parried Kinraid's wild thrust.

The hall reacted to the sight with gasps and curses.

Wharrd darted forward with a bundle for Tulkhan. He found clothes and a sword thrust into his hands even as the great hall erupted. Men screamed, servants ran or turned on their oppressors.

It was the Stronghold Guard and his own Elite Guard against the king's men. The outcome was inevitable. But Gharavan's men were well armed and desperate. They rallied around their king.

Tulkhan discarded everything but the breeches. He dragged them on and laced them in record time, then leapt forward to engage the Vaygharian.

Before he could reach him, one of the king's men staggered into him. The man went down to his knees, dragging

Tulkhan with him. Imoshen brought the hilt of her sword down onto the man's head and offered Tulkhan her arm. A wild, fey smile split her face. Her wine-dark eyes were alight with battle fever and he shivered, recognizing it for what it was. Once he had wielded a sword in an ecstasy of killing. When had he lost that thrill? Now he hated bloodshed, hated death.

Wordlessly, he took her arm and pulled himself up. Where was the Vaygharian? Bodies obscured his vision, threatened to overwhelm them both. Men were dying all around them.

Turning, he plunged into the fray with one aim in mind.

His half-brother fought desperately, his back to the wall, his men going down around him. Tulkhan swept through, hitting with the flat of his sword, kicking men aside as they went down.

At last he faced his half-brother who stood, chest heaving, blinking with shock. Gharavan wore nothing but a nightshirt. Tulkhan could only suppose Imoshen must have surprised him in bed, subdued him, then made the switch.

The king dragged in a ragged breath and lifted his sword point in the defense position as Tulkhan had taught him.

Years of training on the battlefield guided the General's sword. The blow sent the young king's weapon flying from his numbed fingers. Then Tulkhan's sword tip pressed at his half-brother's throat.

"Tell them to put down their arms," Tulkhan said.

"Surrender!" His half-brother swallowed, his Adam's apple bobbing close to the sword point. "Lay down your arms!"

The terror in Gharavan's voice communicated itself to those around him and the swordplay ceased. There were repeated scrapes of metal on stone as the king's men were disarmed or voluntarily downed their weapons.

Tulkhan stepped back. "This way."

"What will you do?" Gharavan whispered.

Tulkhan had no idea.

He didn't want to kill his half-brother. Yet his instinct and all his experience told him letting Gharavan live could be a fatal error. The youth's death was needed to consolidate his position.

When had it come to this?

Tulkhan turned his back on his half-brother and walked away. Would Gharavan attack him from behind? Was he hoping Gharavan would? Then he could strike the lad down in self-defense and remain guiltless of his half-brother's murder. Tulkhan did not want to carry that burden.

He saw Imoshen stride toward him.

"Kill him!" she hissed, her face feral with the heat of battle.

Tulkhan touched her cheek sadly and searched her eyes looking for something, though he could not have said what it was.

"If I took life as easily as that, you would be dead," he told her softly.

She blanched, recoiling as if he'd slapped her.

"Tulkhan?" Gharavan pushed through his kneeling, wounded men. "Tulkhan, blood kin—"

"Don't tempt me, Gharavan!" Tulkhan ground out.

"He would have killed you!" Imoshen's eyes were dark pools of anger. Tulkhan knew he had hurt her, and after she had saved him from being executed by his own half-brother.

The enormity of what the Dhamfeer had done hit him. How she must be laughing at him! She had held them all in the palm of her hand during that masquerade. He shuddered at the thought. How could he trust Imoshen when he would never know what she was capable of?

"Tulkhan?" Gharavan seized his arm. "It was Kinraid's idea, he—"

"Where is the Vaygharian?" Tulkhan yelled and thrust his half-brother aside. But though everyone looked for him, Kinraid had escaped the great hall.

Gharavan did not seem surprised.

"Wharrd?" Tulkhan turned to his Elite Guard, grateful to know that they had been loyal all along. "Send men out to the stables. Kill him if he resists, but I fear he has already escaped." He turned to his half-brother. "As for you. I renounce all kinship with you. To me you are as one dead. You may take that which you can carry on your back, a horse and your wounded. Make haste to Northpoint.'' He named the port where he knew his half-brother's ships had made landfall. ''Never set foot on this island again. If you do your life is forfeit.''

He knew Imoshen would object. His half-brother was about to speak but Tulkhan overrode them both. ''Go now. My Elite Guard will escort you. Stay clear of the capital, T'Diemn.''

The king's men were eager enough to flee, knowing they would escape with their lives. They hurried out of the great hall, escorted by the Elite Guard.

At last Tulkhan turned to Imoshen, visibly seething at his side.

''He would have killed you!'' she repeated.

''He's still my half-brother—''

''You're sending him back to rule an empire seven times the size of this island, seven times as wealthy. Do you call that punishment?''

The Dhamfeer stood there questioning his judgment as if she was his equal, as if it was her right! A strange double vision overcame Tulkhan. He saw Imoshen as a Ghebite male would view her. Once he would have thought her an ignorant female who had no right to question his authority. Now he knew she was not only trained in matters of state and battle tactics, but her T'En gifts gave her the ability to manipulate True-people.

Fear of her Dhamfeer powers rippled through him. Why did she even bother to argue? When would Imoshen stop arguing and simply wrench control from him? A bitter smile made him grimace.

But he answered her question. ''Gharavan is going back to an empire made up of conquered nations. My father held it together by the sheer force of his personality. It will take only one uprising for the whole house of cards to come crashing down. If I am lucky Gharavan will spend the rest of his life losing the countries I annexed since I became General of my father's army.''

He watched her face, saw her assess his words and nod slowly. "Very well."

So she was convinced, for now.

He was banishing one weak enemy, but he still faced internal threats, Reothe and his rebels and . . . he watched Imoshen as she absently cleaned her blade and resheathed it.

Dare he trust her? No, after this night he dare not turn his back on her.

It galled him to see how, unlike him, his own people turned to her. Even his wounded men limped or were carried to the Dhamfeer for treatment. She simply accepted this as her duty, sending Kalleen for her medicants.

Broodingly, Tulkhan watched Imoshen go about her self-appointed task as healer. She was as much a threat to him as Reothe. Other, unknowable, she could befuddle his mind, plant thoughts in his head, even confuse a hall full of people with her shape-shifting.

She was a dangerous enemy but a good ally. It was wiser to keep her close, to observe her.

He realized with a jolt that Gharavan had been right. While Imoshen stood at his side the island would remain behind him.

Wharrd returned to report no sign of the Vaygharian. Tulkhan shrugged his shoulders, easing his bruised body and tried to concentrate. There was so much to do. Events had forced him to lay claim to Fair Isle for himself.

Grim determination seized him. All his life he had served his father as the first son of his second wife. He had taken pride in his skills as a general. He had sought to win his father's respect by his service and what had it led to? This debacle. Now he served no one. He was his own man. His hands tightened on his sword hilt. This island was his, and what he took—he held.

Imoshen tended the wounded until she was so weary she could hardly think. Each time she closed a wound she exerted a little push to help the skin knit, adding a little warming glow that would close off the bleeding and fight infection. It was instinctive, something she had done in the past with an effort. One part of her mind marveled at the growth in her gift, or at least in her ability to control it.

But she was also physically exhausted after lying awake all night, shivering with cold and dread. The mental effort to maintain the deception in Gharavan's form had taken every fiber of her being. Numbly, she regretted the lost opportunity. She might have won them over, fooled the king's men and had the Vaygharian executed all without bloodshed if Gharavan hadn't escaped.

She should have had him killed. But the fact that he was General Tulkhan's half-brother had stayed her hand. The General's loyalty was sadly misplaced but it sprang from his true heart and she'd had to respect that.

Her hands trembled as she straightened and sensed Tulkhan's piercing eyes on her. He looked distant, brooding. Suspicious, even?

The thought was unwelcome. Why should he be suspicious of her? Hadn't she stood by him? Hadn't she proved more trustworthy than his own flesh and blood? Why then, was he standing there in the shadows tight-lipped, the planes of his face taut with tension?

She tried to put herself in his place, not literally since she knew he didn't like her invading his mind, but figuratively.

In one night General Tulkhan had lost his half-brother, his generalship, his very place in the world. But he had laid claim to Fair Isle. That gave him a purpose, yet the freshly taken island was seething with rebellion. His hold was a fragile thing. Was he capable of holding Fair Isle?

For one terrible moment Imoshen again wondered if she had made the right choice. After all, Reothe was one of her own kind. True, his T'En gifts were greater than hers and she feared his single-minded determination. But he had never threatened her personally. Back before this invasion he had been kind to her when she was nothing but a gauche child-woman out of her depth in the Royal Palace.

Reothe had even risked his life to rescue her from the Ghebite army at Landsend Abbey. He did not know she did not want to be rescued. Her choice to stay at Tulkhan's side for the sake of her people still seemed the right decision. But was it?

It was the old dilemma. If only the Aayel were here to advise her!

"That's the last of them, my Lady," Kalleen said, her voice breaking with weariness. But she would let none other stand at Imoshen's side.

Imoshen felt guilty. She took the girl's small golden brown hand in her own. "You saved my life this night and I won't forget it. Is there anything I can do for you or your family?"

Imoshen winced as Kalleen stiffened, offended.

"I did not do it for gain, Lady T'En!"

"I know." Imoshen smoothed her hand absently. "But we can't eat principles. Give it some thought. You're tired, so am I. Tired beyond thought. We'll rest now."

"No." Tulkhan stepped forward. "Send warm water to your mistress's room, Kalleen. See that she is dressed as befits her station."

Imoshen was made aware of her men's breeches, the grime and blood on her hands and clothes. She stiffened. If Tulkhan didn't approve of her that was his problem! But what was he planning? "Why can't I rest?"

"I must ride to the capital. The army awaits and if I don't lay claim to it my half-brother or that Vaygharian may well stir up trouble."

"Kinraid is probably riding the fastest horse he could steal to the coast." She grinned. But Tulkhan was right. The army was leaderless and probably rife with rumor. Now was the moment for him to take command. "Very well. You go to the capital and secure the army."

She felt him study her face and wondered what he was looking for.

"You're coming with me," he said.

"But there is work for me here. The township is still being built. As the winter tightens its grip more people flock here every day looking for food and shelter. I cannot leave my people when they need me." Imoshen saw his closed expression. "You must go to T'Diemn and assume command of the army, see to it that they are settled in for the winter, that there is enough food for everyone and the soldiers are occupied so they don't cause trouble for the townsfolk during the idleness of deep winter. But you don't need me to—"

"I do."

Imoshen laughed. "What for?"

Wharrd returned to tell his General that the king and his men were about to leave.

Tulkhan nodded. His hand slipped around Imoshen's upper arm. "Kalleen, go fetch your lady's white fur cloak. And I'll need my cloak, too. Wharrd, have our horses saddled—"

"What are you doing? We can't leave yet." Imoshen planted her feet and twisted to free her arm, instinctively breaking his hold at the weakest point, the thumb.

Casually, the General stepped behind her. She could feel him undoing the leather thong which held her hair. The skin on the back of her neck prickled as his fingers brushed her flesh. She ached for his touch, and hated herself for this weakness.

Turning a little to face him, she could see the bruises on his chest overlying the old scars. Was he badly hurt by the beating?

His distinctive male scent came to her. It was intoxicating. Like strong wine it went straight to her head, clouding rational thought. Her body urged her to take that one step which would bring her into contact with him. She wanted to feel him down the length of her, to tuck her face into the crook of his neck and taste the salty tang on his skin. A shudder of longing ran through her.

Surely he could sense her reaction to him? Yet he remained unmoved. Shame stung her.

It startled Imoshen to admit that her body's needs could almost override her good sense. She knew the General had withdrawn from her, though she didn't know why. Tulkhan should have been grateful for her help but instead he stood grimly behind her, his dark eyes impassive as he unbound her long hair. He lifted the tangled tresses to run his fingers through the knots, freeing them.

If she were to lean back she could press her shoulders to his chest, feel his arms around her. Instead she felt the insistent little tugs on her scalp as he unraveled her hair.

Kalleen returned, breathless, with their cloaks. Imoshen didn't know how long they had been standing there. For her, time had stopped as she battled against the force of her body's need. It was an unwelcome complication when she needed her wits about her.

She should have felt relief now that King Gharavan had been dispatched and banished to his own lands, but instead she found General Tulkhan had once again become her enemy.

Weariness and something else made her breath catch in her throat. She was so tired, physically and mentally. Would she ever know a safe harbor where she could let her guard down, where she could be accepted for herself?

Tears flooded her eyes. She blinked them away fiercely, despising her weakness.

Calling on her reserves of strength, Imoshen lifted her chin and stood tall while Kalleen adjusted her cloak, spreading the mantle of her hair across her shoulders.

She watched Tulkhan swing the deep red of his cloak around him. The Ghebite cloak was not warm enough for this southern winter. His hair hung in long matted strands down his shoulder, dried with caked blood in places.

Irrationally she longed to tend him as she had done last night. The words sprang to her lips, but she contained them. She wanted to order a hot bath prepared so she could sponge the dried blood from his hair, see to his wounds. She ached to do it. Instinct told her the General needed a tender touch, but his manner was so forbidding she knew it was impossible. She was not welcome and the knowledge hurt.

Wharrd handed Tulkhan his helmet.

She watched as the General wound his hair into a knot and pulled the helmet over his head, wincing.

He was once again the distant barbarian invader, his eyes

hooded beneath the helmet's ridge, his height increased by the feathered crest which arched across the top.

He offered her his arm and she took it—understanding at last.

He had banished his half-brother the king and laid claim to Fair Isle in reality, but not yet officially. This was a show of strength. He had to look the part and she was playing her role at his side.

He needed her to bolster his position. Not by so much as a glimmer did he reveal anything as they walked from the great hall. The corded muscles of his forearm were like bands of steel under her fingers.

Before she knew she meant to do it, Imoshen used the physical contact to probe. She had to know why he deliberately distanced himself from her. But she met a blankness, a wall of iron will which held her probing gift at bay.

Startled, she looked at him and saw only the grim line of his jaw, the chiseled tip of his nose and broad angle of his cheekbone. The General had not consciously resisted her, yet he had excluded her from his mind.

This was interesting, and daunting. It meant she could not dip into his mind at will to gauge his mood and motivations. Not that she would have done it, she amended hastily. But honesty forced her to admit the temptation would always be there. Uncertainty had prompted her to try dipping into his thoughts just then and how soon would she have slipped into the habit of monitoring his mind?

The thought frightened Imoshen. She did not want to become so removed from Tulkhan and those around her that she thought nothing of stealing into their thoughts to gain leverage on them.

It was just as well Tulkhan did not sense her subtle probe. Or had he? Was that why he stepped back from her so stiffly now? But no, he offered her his hand. She swung into the saddle of her horse then watched him mount. Only she saw his slight grimace of pain, and her heart contracted.

He was such a magnificent creature. Only she knew how bruised and sore he was as he sat astride the black destrier.

Under that red cloak his chest was naked and he was clad in nothing but breeches and boots.

If he was in pain or cold he would not show it to the others.

At General Tulkhan's signal the party moved out. Gharavan and his men wore cloaks, and their horses were heavily laden with clothes and stores. They were escorted by a select number of the Elite Guard. Tulkhan urged his mount forward, signaling Imoshen was to ride beside him.

It was a crisp early morning. They moved down the slope away from the Stronghold at a slow walk and the inhabitants of the township lined the broad street's edge, staring and silent. Rumor would have kept them informed of what had passed. King Gharavan had invaded the Stronghold and tried to execute the General and the last T'En princess. In less than a day he had been vanquished and was being banished from the island.

Imoshen could sense the relief of the crowd and their animosity toward Gharavan. With a start she realized that if she and Tulkhan had not been there to add dignity to the escort, the townspeople might have picked up clods of snow or refuse and thrown it at the deposed king and his men.

She had to admit Tulkhan was wise, far wiser than any other Ghebite.

They left behind the last of the rude shelters which had been hastily built by the recent arrivals and came to a halt on the empty snow of the white plain. A finger of winter sunlight found its way through the sullen low clouds, illuminating them with its cold brilliance. A thousand diamonds of light sparkled on the cold snow. Their breath hung in clouds on the still air. Their horses snorted and shifted, steaming in the cold.

Tulkhan nudged his mount forward. At his signal Imoshen followed. Light reflected off the snow and off her white cloak so that it felt as if she was bathed in a cold silver brilliance. The moment had a timeless quality that seemed to stretch forever. The significance of the night's events struck Imoshen, stealing her breath for a moment.

They were living history.

On this bitterly cold winter's morning General Tulkhan had faced death, routed his half-brother and laid claim to Fair Isle, all with the aid of the last princess of the T'En.

What would Reothe say if he knew how instrumental she had been in this night's events?

Imoshen squinted and scanned the line of the woods. Like benevolent giants the massive evergreens rose above the bare deciduous trees. Scattered through the forest they stood head and shoulders above the bare black branches, defiantly green still. In deep winter they would be cloaked in a protective layer of snow which insulated their foliage from the cold.

A horse snorted and her mount shifted uneasily.

Was Reothe himself watching this tableau from the safety of the woods? Would Gharavan ever reach the north-western port and his ships?

The words exchanged between General Tulkhan and his half-brother washed over her. She heard only their tone, resentful on Gharavan's part, cold and uncompromising on Tulkhan's. Then the General raised his hand and Wharrd gave the cry to move off.

Tulkhan's horse shied and would have joined the others but he held it back, wheeling the beast around to rejoin her. Side by side they sat their mounts, he in his barbarian battle finery, resplendent in red, purple and black, she in white—white-tipped fur and silver hair.

What was General Tulkhan thinking? Imoshen wondered. Was he mourning his dead father, his half-brother, or his Ghebite homeland lost to him forever now? Or was he thinking of warmth and food, like she was?

When they could no longer see the banished men and their escort, when they had become one with the dark trunks of the woods, the General turned his horse and she followed suit. She was cold under her cloak and she knew he must be colder still. But they rode solemnly into the township, down the main street. People had drifted out to watch the king leave and now followed them back through town in a mass.

The place seemed pristinely beautiful coated in snow,

glistening in the pale sunlight. You couldn't see how hastily it had been cobbled together. Snow coated the scarred earth which had so recently been rolling grasslands.

Everything was so beautiful Imoshen's eyes stung with unshed tears. Perhaps it was her. She hadn't expected to see this day dawn, so suddenly she found life very precious.

They had almost mounted the rise to the Stronghold when someone gave a ragged cheer. As if this was a signal the townspeople took up the cry. It was a mixed babble—some called on General Tulkhan, others called on the T'En, but the meaning was clear.

Not only had the General and Imoshen delivered themselves from death this last night but they had delivered the people from persecution.

At the outer gate General Tulkhan slowed and turned his mount to face the populace. Imoshen followed his cue. Her heart swelled with an emotion she didn't try to name and the tears she had been holding back flowed freely down her cheeks, scaldingly hot on her cold skin.

She told herself the people were weary of war, that they wanted peace and prosperity, not oppression. She and the General had shown that they could maintain peace and deal fairly. Was it more than self-interest that prompted this show of loyalty from her people? Imoshen did not know. Her head might hold doubts but her heart could not help responding, soaring with their cheers. She felt a rush of comradeship for her people who had suffered under the Ghebite invasion. Lifting her hand in salute she smiled through her tears.

At last Tulkhan turned his horse and they entered the passage, moving through the inner gates to the courtyard where the servants, remaining Elite Guard and Stronghold Guard greeted them enthusiastically. It warmed Imoshen's heart because she knew these people personally. Fresh tears made her vision swim.

She was so tired. She wanted nothing more than a warm bath and food, then to crawl into bed.

The General swung from his saddle and turned to her, holding out his arms.

She wanted to feel his hands on her waist, to feel the length of his strong body as he lowered her to the ground. She wanted to lay her head on his chest and know that she had nothing to fear, but she couldn't afford to lower her guard.

Disdaining his help, she swung her leg over the saddle and leapt to the ground.

Tulkhan caught her arm, his fingers biting sharply into her flesh. He raised their joined arms to acknowledge the greetings of the Stronghold. She knew he was annoyed with her show of independence. They had to present a united front. Their every move was being assessed, watched by servants, petty nobles and members of the Stronghold and Elite Guards.

When the cheer died down General Tulkhan raised his voice. "I thank you for standing true. I will not forget this night, or your loyalty."

Again they cheered and Imoshen grimaced to herself. Other than the Elite Guard, the Stronghold's loyalty had been to her and Tulkhan had benefited from it. By relieving them of Gharavan, the General had become a hero. And what of her?

As they moved toward the steps to the great hall the people surged forward, jostling to get near her. They stroked her hair and touched her sixth finger.

"T'En," they whispered reverently, proudly. "Lady T'En."

But they wouldn't meet her eyes.

Then Imoshen understood. She had become their talisman—a creature to be revered and feared, the T'En of nursery rhyme!

It stung her to the quick, but it also amused her because she was the same person today she had been yesterday. Only their perception of her had changed. A rueful smile tugged at her lips. She glanced at General Tulkhan expecting him to be amused as she was, but instead she read suspicion in his obsidian eyes, quickly masked.

Imoshen couldn't fathom his reaction. Her head spun with weariness. Rest, that was what she needed. Later when she could think clearly, she would deal with General Tulkhan and his suspicions.

He took her arm. "Prepare yourself. We ride for the capital within the hour."

Imoshen's heart sank.

NINE

BUT IT TOOK longer than an hour to prepare to ride out. Imoshen had to speak to the Stronghold staff and the Guildmasters of the township. A representative had to be elected from the townsfolk to make requests on behalf of their people.

Several officers of the Stronghold Guard loyal to Imoshen volunteered to accompany them to T'Diemn, along with a large force of Tulkhan's Elite Guard. A small contingent of Ghebite soldiers remained at the Stronghold to serve as Tulkhan's eyes and ears. The good behavior of the Stronghold inhabitants was ensured by Imoshen's presence at the General's side.

Imoshen did not want to leave her home. All her instincts were against this hurried departure and the weather suited her mood. The sun had given up its unequal struggle with the advancing mist and the sky hung heavy with snowladen clouds. The air was still and charged with foreboding.

The immediate threat to her life had passed, and Imoshen felt exhausted. A strange lassitude enveloped her, making conversation impossible. Voices echoed in her head and everything seemed to be happening at a great distance. Dimly, she realized she had overextended herself by assuming the young king's form.

But the events of the last few days were too fresh to think on. She felt only a mild irony. She had never expected to make her way to the capital at the side of a Ghebite conqueror.

This was very different from her first visit to T'Diemn and the Royal Palace. Riding into T'Diemn two seasons ago for her first Midsummer Festival she had been so eager. She could remember her excitement, her anticipation of the delights offered by the sophisticated town. At barely sixteen she had been impatient to grow up.

The memory was easily recalled, but Imoshen felt distanced from her younger self as if that Imoshen was another person. Her family and their retinue had taken two days to make the journey, traveling at a comfortable pace. In midwinter, in heavy snow, the journey could kill.

For the second time that day the townspeople escorted them out of the township. Despite Imoshen's foreboding, the attitude of the Elite Guard, her own Stronghold Guard and the townsfolk was positive.

In better times the route to the capital had been a well traveled road with a serviceable inn at the halfway point. Imoshen doubted if they would find it standing now.

As they pushed on through the snow the sky darkened and Imoshen slept with her eyes open, hardly aware of where she was. The General ignored her. She felt despised, less than human. It would have hurt if she could have felt anything beyond brain-numbing weariness.

Snow fell lightly at first then with gathering intensity. It was clear that despite their fresh horses they would not reach the inn or what was left of it before darkness closed in on them. Imoshen roused herself from her lethargy, rising in the saddle to look around. They must find shelter for the night.

If only they were near one of the hot springs—even during the coldest winter they did not freeze over. The simple folk worshipped these places as sources of ancient power. But only someone in direst need would camp there overnight.

With a sudden surge of inner certainty Imoshen knew that Reothe was sheltering his rebels at one of the hot springs. Knowing him, he would dare to flout convention. It was an ideal winter hideout, shunned by the locals and protected from the worst of the weather.

Should she tell the General what she suspected? Instinct told her it was true, but it was still only a guess and there were many hot springs scattered over Fair Isle, especially in the highlands to the south.

Imoshen pulled the white fur close around her and peered from under the hood resentfully, seeing the snow-dusted shoulders of the man in front of her. This was typical of the General's style of leadership. He made snap decisions and moved fast.

She understood Tulkhan wanted to seize power by filling the vacuum of leadership in T'Diemn. But what if Reothe was hiding in the forest, his scouts observing them even now? A concerted attack could see their escort slaughtered, Tulkhan's life at Reothe's mercy and herself faced with a bitter choice—join Tulkhan in death or take her place at the side of her betrothed.

A bitter smile pulled at Imoshen's cold lips. She shuddered. Could she live as Reothe's tool? A caustic laugh welled up in her. Hadn't she chosen to live as Tulkhan's tool, his tolerated oddity? But at least with the General she was not merely his tool. He needed her as much as she needed him.

She tried to make out the dim outlines of the tree trunks through the thick curtain of falling snow. Soon it would be too dark to choose a good camp for the night. They were exposed, vulnerable.

Fighting a wave of nausea caused by sheer exhaustion, Imoshen urged her mount forward to catch up with the General. She had intended to convince him to stop, but when she caught up he was already ordering his men to make camp.

Imoshen huddled in her furs to watch them build a basic shelter. Her Stronghold Guards all knew the tricks of surviving in the open in winter. They chose a protected overhang and built a crude snow wall. While they worked the Elite Guard gathered wood.

They had food and warmth, but not peace of mind. Imoshen slept deeply, troubled by threatening dreams where Reothe accused her of treachery and she begged his forgiveness.

Waking with tears on her cheeks, she found the General sitting across the fire from her, a silent sentinel in the cold predawn. Despite his suspicion of her she found his presence reassuring. Was he regretting his hasty actions?

"Do your dreams trouble you?" he asked softly.

"No."

"How can you deny you dream of Reothe? You weep for him."

She flinched.

One of the men stirred and Tulkhan rose to walk the perimeters of the camp, leaving her to her cold, unhappy thoughts. Anger stirred in her.

If Reothe didn't attack them, capture her and kill Tulkhan he was not the tactician she thought him to be, she thought sourly, rolling over to sleep. But when dawn arrived they were still alive, unharmed. The camp broke up stiffly, leaving their crude shelter for other travelers, as was the custom.

While mounting up Imoshen marveled at their lucky escape. Possibly Reothe had elected to follow the young king and had already killed that party. Maybe their group would reach the capital unharmed.

Her only comfort was the knowledge that Reothe and his rebels would find it as hard to move about as they, and that his people were underfed, underarmed and short of horses.

In the late afternoon of the third day out from the Stronghold they spotted the towers of T'Diemn. Imoshen strained in the saddle, peering across the icy air to see if the town had changed much since her last visit.

She noted the blackened bones of buildings, the result of Gharavan's torching of parts of the town. She could not see any signs of revolt but that meant nothing. The townsfolk could have murdered the Ghebite army while they slept and thrown their bodies into the river for all she knew.

Or perhaps the army had seized control of the town. Had they panicked without their king? Even now they could be lying in wait behind shuttered windows, ready to spring on the General's small party, trap them in a blind alley and slaughter them all.

Imoshen shuddered. She was being morbid, letting her imagination run away with her.

The General was right. The capital had to be secured. It was the center of trade, the source of wealth. If she was to help General Tulkhan hold Fair Isle, T'Diemn had to swear fealty to him and she had to be at his side when that happened.

Imoshen felt a quiver of fear. She was not well known here. She had been the third child of a minor branch of the royal family, her only outstanding feature the luck, good or bad, of being born a Throwback. As the first pure T'En to be born in her branch of the family since the Aayel, her parents had never ceased to be slightly surprised by her. She was an embarrassing blessing, a potential liability.

Her family had not wished to be social outcasts, unlike Reothe's parents who had joined precisely because they had many of the T'En traits. His parents had been eccentric historians who were shunned by the more modern members of the royal family. They had produced only one child, who arrived late in their lives when they had given up hope of children. Reothe was their joy, pure T'En. Yet their end had been so tragic.

Imoshen frowned, recalling the mocking rhyme she'd learned about them as a child. Only when she grew older had she understood its significance. It told how Reothe's parents had taken their own lives. No one really understood why. They had become recluses, abandoned by the royal family, served by one faithful servant. This servant found them both dead by ritual suicide, with ten-year-old Reothe at their side, their silent sentinel.

Reothe had inherited their combined wealth but not their lifestyle. He hadn't been a recluse. The Empress had been appointed his guardian so he spent his teenage years in the royal palace, where he'd charmed the servants and learned the intricacies of protocol.

Driven by his restless nature and relentless ambition, he found court life too restrictive. He had invested his capital in ships and men and had sailed south to the archipelago looking for wealth and fame, or so the story went. He forged new trade alliances with the prosperous island nations and recouped his investment so handsomely that he could finance an even more audacious voyage to find his ancestors' homeland, which was rumored to lie to the east of the archipelago.

He had not discovered the legendary homeland of the T'En but a rich land eager to trade. The prestige and wealth Reothe gained from his enterprise ensured him a place in minstrel songs and stories which carried his name to every corner of the island.

Reothe was relying on that popularity to help him escape the Ghebites. Imoshen shivered. How would the townsfolk of T'Diemn react if it was Reothe at the head of a rebel army about to enter the city?

Imoshen studied her companions thoughtfully. As with their entry to Landsend, General Tulkhan ordered them to stop and don their battle dress for their arrival at T'Diemn. The Elite Guard wore Tulkhan's vibrant colors and her own Stronghold Guard wore the more subdued and familiar royal colors of her family. What kind of welcome could they hope to receive?

The townsfolk of T'Diemn might see her as a reminder of the T'En Emperor and Empress who had failed to protect them. They might direct their anger at her. Of all Fair Isle the T'Diemn townspeople had borne the brunt of King Gharavan's destructive vengeance. They might give lip service to the T'En Church but how would they react to a Throwback like herself?

The General rode down the ranks inspecting their party with a critical eye. Galloping back to the lead, he met Imoshen's gaze. She might have doubts about her welcome, but she would not reveal them. Sitting tall in the saddle, she dropped the hood so that her face was not hidden. She would not cower before the townsfolk.

"Ready?" General Tulkhan asked.

Imoshen nodded and adjusted the folds of the ornate ceremonial gown she'd changed into and settled the fur cloak around her shoulders. In white fur and red velvet she was dressed for effect and she noted with some satisfaction that it had not been lost on the General.

The Ghebite battle regalia was also designed for effect—and to show off the might and muscle of its soldiers. However, as impressive as the combination of heavy armor and bare skin was, it was hardly practical in the depths of a Fair Isle winter. She knew he must be cold but there was no hint of this in his proud bearing. His men also bore the chill stoically, setting aside their borrowed furs to make a good impression on the townsfolk. Her own Stronghold Guard wore thick woolen padding beneath their battle gear.

Satisfied, the General gave the signal to move out. Imoshen urged her horse forward. She was sure their party must have been sighted from the town gates. The people of T'Diemn had opened those same gates and surrendered to the invader only to be betrayed. She was grateful the General was a man of his word. Otherwise the people of the Stronghold might have suffered the same fate.

People lined the street, silent and sullen. Had they heard about King Gharavan's defeat? It was unlikely. The trail to the far northwestern port veered before T'Diemn so, unless someone had slipped away from the Stronghold or the town and rode ahead of them, the townsfolk could not know their persecutor had been vanquished by General Tulkhan and herself.

Imoshen searched the faces of the crowd. They had been a prosperous, almost smug town before this, basking in the patronage of the royal court. To find themselves at the mercy of invaders would have shattered their peace and complacency forever.

She saw people pointing in her direction. Someone called out the ritual phrase for T'En blessing. A little girl tried to break free from the crowd, presumably to touch her sixth finger for luck, but a woman pulled her back.

It felt wrong to ride through the gathered townsfolk without making contact. But she noticed children watching her wide-eyed and realized fear was not far from their minds. A horse snorted and shied and those nearest stumbled back. A small boy yelped in fright and was comforted. Imoshen felt a sudden rush of gratitude and relief that her own people had not suffered at the hands of King Gharavan.

As General Tulkhan's party walked their horses slowly up the rise, Imoshen gradually dropped behind. She slowed her mount and let her own Stronghold Guard move on ahead.

Searching the faces of the townsfolk she tried to understand their position. These were still her people and she felt personally responsible because her family had failed to protect them.

She stiffened—there, in the front row was an elderly woman, wrapped in nothing but a shawl. Her paper-thin skin stretched over her twisted knuckles as she pulled the material tightly around her stooped shoulders. It was poor protection from the bitter cold. The old woman reminded Imoshen fleetingly of the Aayel, who had stood so proudly to receive the terms of surrender. Her wise counsel had prevented Imoshen from taking rash action. The Aayel had saved them from disaster.

Before she knew what she was doing, Imoshen swung down stiffly from the horse and crossed the snow-covered cobbles to greet the old woman who stared uncomprehendingly at her.

"Grandmother, you are cold." Imoshen unclasped her white fur cloak and shrugged it off, swinging it around the old woman's shoulders. "Take this."

As Imoshen kissed the withered cheek tears stung her eyes.

The old woman lifted a cold, clawed hand to hers and grasped her sixth finger.

"Bless you, Lady T'En. Bless you."

In a blur Imoshen found herself surrounded by curious townsfolk. A small child tugged on her hand and she picked him up, feeling his fingers twine through her hair which hung loosely down her back. Others stroked her hands or her clothing. Voices were raised around her in exclamation. She lost track of what they were saying but tried to answer them, to reassure them. Theirs were the eternal questions of hope and fear for their families, their homes.

Yes, she assured them repeatedly, the wicked king was gone, banished by his half-brother.

They could hardly believe it.

Tulkhan wheeled his horse, tension stiffening across his shoulders. He had been only too aware of the resentment emanating from the townsfolk.

What was that disturbance? The crowd muttered, watching him uneasily. He glanced along the column of his small escort, automatically counting heads. Imoshen was missing!

Fear closed a cold hand around his heart. Had she been dragged from her mount, abducted, murdered?

Cursing fluently, he urged the horse back between the column of his men.

"Crawen, where is your lady?" he demanded of the leader of the Stronghold Guard. The woman flinched at his tone.

"Right behind me, General."

But when she turned Imoshen was not there. "I don't understand—"

"Come." Tulkhan had no time for the guard's excuses. He rode on with the Stronghold Guard at his back until he saw a knot of people growing larger by the minute. At its center was Imoshen's tall, fair head.

They'd tear her apart.

Even as he thought this, he realized the crowd's voice was reverent, excited—almost hungry—as they surged eagerly toward Imoshen.

There was no menace, as yet, Tulkhan thought grimly. But all it took was one disgruntled individual with a knife and a grudge to settle with the T'En who had abandoned them, and Imoshen would be lying in the snow, bleeding to death. The image flashed through his mind, spurring him on.

Anger flooded him. What was she doing risking her life pointlessly like this? What if there was an assassin in the crowd, someone who was loyal to King Gharavan? They had too many enemies!

Furious, Tulkhan urged his horse into the crowd. They pulled back, stumbling in their haste to escape his battle-hardened mount. He saw nothing but Imoshen's fair head, rising above their heads. His heart pounded, his hands ached to grasp her. He would throttle her, he would . . .

Swinging down off the horse, he thrust the last person aside. "Imoshen?"

She turned, surprised. The smile died on her lips as she took in his expression. He noted her cheeks were flushed and if he hadn't known better, he would have sworn she'd been crying. She held a small, golden brown child in her arms.

Soothingly, she returned the boy to his mother, touching the tip of her sixth finger to his forehead in T'En blessing.

Tulkhan breathed a sigh of relief. Imoshen was perfectly all right. This time. Even now he could sense the crowd's resentment of him and all he represented.

"Come." Tulkhan felt like an interloper. He grasped her arm, pulling her toward his horse. Where was her mount?

As his hand closed around her upper arm he realized Imoshen was wearing nothing but the rich red gown she had donned to enter T'Diemn.

"Where's your cloak?"

She glanced over her shoulder and he noticed an elderly woman wrapped in the white-tipped fur. What was Imoshen thinking?

"Yours?"

She caught him as he went toward the old woman. "Stay. The old woman needed it more than I."

He caught a flicker of warning in her eyes. The crowd was muttering, drawing back, women pulling children behind the ranks of the able-bodied men.

Tulkhan cursed softly. With one action, Imoshen had won over the townsfolk of T'Diemn, then he had come along and undone her good work.

"You could have been killed." He kept his voice low. "One assassin with a knife—"

"I know." Her voice was as soft and intense as his.

They had lost their entire escort now. The Stronghold Guard were cut off from them, surrounded by a sea of townsfolk. Even if they were to try to come to their aid they would have trouble forging through the packed streets. Tactical training told Tulkhan they were hopelessly vulnerable.

"Take me up on your mount. Mine must have followed the others," Imoshen whispered. "Wrap your cloak around me."

He focused on her face, on her compelling wine-dark eyes and, almost in a daze found himself swinging into the saddle, hauling her up after him. As he settled her across his thighs and pulled his cloak about them both he sensed the crowd's mood change.

There was a tentative cheer. Imoshen waved then swung both her arms around Tulkhan's neck and kissed him. The impact of her hot lips on his mouth broke the daze which had gripped him. He experienced an intense, overwhelming physical desire for her. It went beyond conscious thought. It was the call of her body to his. His hands slid inside the cloak to pull her toward him. All the frustration and rage which had engulfed him spilled over into his instinctive response to her.

Roaring. There was a roaring in his ears.

The crowd was cheering them. It could just as easily have torn them to shreds.

Trust me. He heard her voice distinctly in his head, yet her lips were melded to his.

Suddenly he understood what had happened. She had manipulated him with her T'En gift, clouding his mind, prompting him to act the way she wished. Somehow she had slipped past his guard. When had he become so susceptible to her?

A shudder of alarm swept through him.

What had she said? She feared the power that lying with T'Reothe would give him over her? Tulkhan flinched. Surely then, in joining their bodies he had given her access to him, placed himself in her power?

Furious, Tulkhan broke the kiss, and found his hands gripping her face. He could feel the fragile bones of her skull cupped in the merciless cradle of his hands. One twist and he could break her neck.

The thought horrified him. Yet with one action he could be free of her creeping power over him.

Fear flared in the depths of her eyes. Had she read his mind, again?

"Get out of my head!" The words were torn from him. Barely audible, they grated from between his clenched teeth.

She grimaced, whether in shock or annoyance he couldn't tell, and took his hand, prizing the thumb from her throat. To the watchers it could have been a fond touch, but he knew she was releasing a death grip.

"You're choking me. Ride on, while we still can, General."

Her advice was sensible, as much as it galled him. He urged the mount forward. She did not have to tell him to wave as the crowd saluted them.

The goodwill Imoshen had won surged forward with them, changing the mood of the people as they rounded the bend, flanked by the Stronghold Guard. Suddenly his entrance to the capital had become a triumphant welcome and he had Imoshen to thank for it.

He felt the sway of her body against his and the scent of her hair filled his nostrils. She had invaded his mind again, albeit to save them both when the crowd threatened to turn hostile. But he knew he had no protection from her and the knowledge ate at him like an insidious poison.

Even now as they rode she waved, smiling at the crowd, who responded eagerly. He could not be sure how much of their response was natural, how much might be trickery. After all, she had convinced everyone in the great hall that she was his half-brother. Mass hallucination—what next, mass mind control?

Tulkhan shuddered. He hated not knowing the extent of his enemy's power . . . That thought pulled him up sharply. When had Imoshen become his enemy?

Rather, he thought grimly, when had she ever been anything but? She had allied herself with him to ensure her survival, nothing more. He must not forget that. She was Other, not True-woman at all.

When they entered the square before the royal palace it was filled with milling men-at-arms. Those loyal to General Tulkhan were standing in ranks. He could identify his commanders in particolored cloaks which named them Ghebite first, his men second. Those loyal to the king who had made the shorter journey with him to T'Diemn were congregated in a resentful mass.

Imoshen stiffened as she took in the scene. There might yet be bloodshed. What if King Gharavan's men refused to swear allegiance to his half-brother, the General?

She felt Tulkhan tense and would have slipped from her perch across his thighs, but his grip on her tightened. She had an excellent view of the gathered army as he walked his mount between the orderly ranks of his own men. He paused here and there, speaking softly to individuals, inquiring after an old wound from one, a toothache from another. It confirmed what she had come to believe. General Tulkhan's men loved him, and he knew every one by sight if not by name.

Then they crossed the sludgy snow to Gharavan's men. Several men of rank stepped forward and Tulkhan greeted them with quiet dignity. Would he order their allegiance or death? How would he resolve this standoff? Imoshen tensed as she saw the unfriendly faces of the young king's men. Tulkhan was mistaken to keep her with him. They feared and consequently hated her.

The General cleared his throat. "Well men, you know me. I served my father the king since I joined the ranks as a youth. Some of you have served under me on other campaigns, others of you worked with me when we settled the town recently. I am a fair man."

They muttered and nodded.

"King Gharavan is on his way to Northpoint. I've claimed Fair Isle for myself."

There was a stunned intake of breath and a torrent of exclamations. The muttering and grumbling from the ranks grew louder. Tulkhan let them vent their surprise and outrage before calling for silence.

"If you feel you can't stomach serving me, you can take the clothes you stand up in and your kit and walk to Northpoint, under an escort of my men. You have until dusk to make up your mind. By dawn tomorrow those who won't swear allegiance to me must leave the town."

A grizzled commander stepped forward. "I don't need till dusk to make up my mind, General. You served your father, but Gharavan's half the king he was. I'll take an oath of allegiance to you and my men will follow suit.''

Tulkhan thanked him. ''By tomorrow I will have the allegiance of the townsfolk and an army loyal to me.''

He wheeled the horse. It rose on its hind legs. Imoshen clutched his chest to steady herself. He secured her, one arm pressing her to him. With a start she realized the horse was trained to rear and walk on its hind legs. Though she felt precarious she sensed she was quite safe. She was also aware of the striking sight they made as his own men broke into a spontaneous roar of approval.

Now she understood.

By keeping her with him, the General had sought his men's acceptance of her by unspoken demand. And they had given it.

At Tulkhan's gentle command the magnificent black destrier gave voice, then settled and pranced toward the stables at the rear of the palace almost as if it had enjoyed the display and approval.

When they finally arrived at the palace, exhausted as she was, Imoshen knew no peace. The town was far from secure and there was much to be done. She left the General speaking to his men in the stables and headed inside the palace, flanked by her Stronghold Guard.

She had known this building as an infrequent visitor, a minor member of the extended royal family. The first time she came here was during the Midsummer Festival before Reothe and she were betrothed.

That was the first time she met him. Although they were second cousins and the only Throwbacks of the last two generations, their paths had not crossed before because her parents had not thought her mature enough to visit the court. Even if they had, Reothe would probably not have been there. He had spent the better part of several years at sea with only a short interval in T'Diemn between his two voyages.

That midsummer the huge formal rooms had been decorated and the public hall was open to the townsfolk. There had been impromptu dances, poetry recitations, musical performances and plays. The flower of T'En culture had been present.

Barely sixteen, Imoshen had been overwhelmed by the sophistication of the palace and its occupants. She had longed to remain in the background but already she stood as tall as most men and her coloring marked her as T'En.

Everywhere she went, people stared.

For Imoshen that festival had been a prolonged period of excruciating tension and formality, as she was escorted by various family members to different venues and introduced to the members of their extended family. She had been formally presented to the Emperor and Empress and listened in on several sessions of government, where the nobles met to formalize alliances within their own island and trade agreements with the mainland and the archipelago.

How different it was now. The long corridors were filled with fearful milling servants and the debris of the young king's occupation. Imoshen stepped over smashed crockery to enter one of the formal rooms.

"Crawen, you may take your people and settle in. Send the cook and the master of the bedchambers to me."

Left alone in the room Imoshen stared unseeing at the opulent surroundings. Memories crowded her, making her face flame with shame as she recalled the first meeting with Reothe. She had been sent to collect her brother from a performance in the forecourt of the palace. Only she had taken a wrong turn and found herself in a group of the young royals and minor nobles who were watching a poetic duel.

The first duelist had to create a rhyming quartet about something topical, then the other would take an idea from that rhyme and create another quartet, often turning it back on the originator.

She and her brother and sister had played a similar game as children. Being proficient in courtly speech was considered an important tool of etiquette.

Unfortunately for Imoshen, her arrival threw one of the duelists off his speech and, to recover himself, he chose her as his subject. Or perhaps it was simply a comment about the T'En.

At any rate, she stiffened as every eye in the room turned to her. It was a cruel jest at the expense of the T'En, but it was clever—and the audience applauded him for that with their customary subtle little finger clicks.

Eager to outdo her opponent, the other poetic duelist chose the T'En again and this time made a more intimate reference to Imoshen.

She stood stranded, under unbearably intense scrutiny and unable to flee because her pride would not let her, but not sufficiently versed in the game at this level to produce a quartet of her own. She did not know the duelists by name or reputation.

As the female duelist wound down and everyone clicked their appreciation, Imoshen saw the first poet take a breath and knew he was about to use her as a topic. His eyes glistened with anticipation, making her heart sink and her cheeks flame.

But from the seated ranks Reothe came to his feet. He was as ornately dressed as anyone there and as graceful when he gave the formal sign to show he was entering the duel, but he radiated a lethal quality which she now recognized. It stemmed from years of command. Then she had known instinctively that he was different from the others.

Reothe wasn't playing—he never played.

The first part of his quartet shifted the emphasis from her to the first T'Imoshen. It was not offensive but clever. It mocked those people who resisted change. Then he turned the rhyme back on the two poets themselves, likening them to their ancestors.

He rounded it off so neatly that even the two poets clicked their appreciation.

Imoshen had met Reothe's gaze across the crowded room. His identical wine-dark eyes silently mocked her, angering her more than the poets' comments had. She could see he expected her to be grateful to him for coming to her rescue.

The two poets challenged by Reothe's skill were eager to reply. In the ensuing three-way duel Imoshen slipped away.

Her brother wasn't even where he was supposed to be. She didn't find him that day. But Reothe found her. He might have been waiting on the landing between the wing of guest chambers and semiformal chambers for her to pass, but she refused to believe he would lie in wait for her.

Seeing him there, she stiffened her shoulders and prepared to walk past but he caught her arm. "What, no word of thanks?"

His assumption irritated her, yet good manners told her to thank him. She flicked her arm free using a simple escape break she had polished through childhood bouts with her siblings. Few of her peers bothered to maintain the skills of unarmed combat but she took pride in hers.

"Thank you, but I would have extricated myself—"

"That's not what it looked like."

She stiffened, knowing he was right. True, she had been out of her depth socially but her etiquette training told her Reothe shouldn't have reminded her of it. She studied him, surprised that he should overstep the boundaries of formal court etiquette.

What she read in his narrow intelligent face did not reassure her. She knew instinctively etiquette was a tool he used and discarded when it suited him. There was an intensity about him which could not be contained by propriety.

The enigmatic expression in his dark eyes was too intimate. She felt as if he had looked into her heart and knew all her failings, and she hated the sensation.

"Thank you for bringing my deficiencies to my attention. I will make a point of not attending poetic duels!" she retorted angrily and spun on her heel, dizzied by her sudden about-face and the implication she had read in his expression.

"You're running away," he called softly, as she forced herself to walk up the broad staircase with what she hoped was stately dignity.

She tensed and turned, looking down into a face so like her own that they could have been brother and sister.

"She who runs away, lives to fight another day!" she

said, using High T'En speech, not the bastardized version of the old maxim.

Reothe's eyes widened and she knew she had scored a point. No one used High T'En nowadays, few people even read it. Only those church priests who made a study of law were proficient in it.

Imoshen gave a start, suddenly recalling where she was as the clatter of approaching palace servants interrupted her. Drawing a deep breath, she prepared to deal with them. She was no longer a gauche sixteen-year-old. She'd had a birthday since that midsummer, been betrothed, seen her world destroyed, lost her family and escaped death more than once.

Entering the palace as part of the conquering force, she could have retreated to her room and expected to be waited on. But that did not suit Imoshen. She was used to taking control. She knew how much organization was needed to run a large establishment, though the Stronghold was not as complex as the palace.

If, as she suspected, the palace staff were in disarray after serving the king and his men, they would need firm guidance. Imoshen insisted on speaking with the servant responsible for each aspect of the palace administration. She inspected every state room and many of the informal rooms. She spoke with the cook and inspected the kitchen and storerooms. They had plentiful supplies of food, spices and wine.

Finally, the master of the bedchambers reported to her for an inspection of the double wings of sleeping quarters. As she surveyed the chambers disgust filled her. King Gharavan and his men had been living like pigs, wallowing in their own filth, surrounded by debauchery. She threw out the whores, male and female, then ordered the serving men and women to scrub the rooms.

She was relieved the servants acknowledged her natural authority and responded well. The master of the bedchambers promised to restore order. She knew he feared for his position. A little fear was good, but she preferred her people to serve and strive to please her because they loved her.

It was dark and the candles lit before she was satisfied that the task of running the palace was under control.

Imoshen was so tired her hands trembled but she could not afford to let herself rest. There was still the evening meal to get through. She selected one of the semiformal rooms where she had the tables arranged in a U-shape. It pleased her sense of order and beauty to watch the well-trained servants spread out pristine white cloths and arrange the fine silver, delicate china and crystal.

When Tulkhan entered she could tell by the tense set of his mouth that he had been busy shoring up lines of support within the ranks. A rush of purely physical relief swept her body and she fought an urge to go to him. It was as if an invisible thread united them, drawing her ever closer to him.

At that moment he looked across the ornate room to her, across the table with its sparkling settings and scented candles. His expression was carefully controlled. She searched his face for a hint of softening but his obsidian eyes were unreadable.

She felt excluded.

Though the room was quite plain compared to some of the other formal rooms it was more ornate than anything in the Stronghold. Was that the problem? Did the General find the opulence of this setting repellent? Did it disgust him as a symbol of the rot which had led the T'En empire to collapse? Did she disgust him as a remnant of that richly decadent regime?

Imoshen could not tell. She only knew that she longed to go to him and must not reveal her weakness for a moment.

"General." She acknowledged him and the men who had accompanied him, recognizing several as members of his Elite Guard. Others she did not know and she marked their faces. They must have held positions of responsibility in Gharavan's army. Could their loyalty be trusted? "Gentlemen. The meal is almost ready if you will be seated. There is warmed wine and fresh bread."

It smelled delicious. Imoshen had discovered in the cook an artist forced to serve the barbarians and the woman had responded to Imoshen's overtures with a feast. Confronted with a T'En who understood the preparation of food and presentation of dishes the cook had outdone herself. Imoshen was pleased.

But it had taken time and energy. She was not as good at Reading people as the Aayel had been. By surreptitious touch and careful questioning the Aayel had Read people's needs and found the Key which showed her how to win them over. Support freely given was much better than support gained by coercion.

It was exhausting, mentally and emotionally. And now she had to sit down to a meal she felt too nauseated to eat while mixing with these men, many of whom must resent her. But she would do it. She would do whatever she had to do to survive!

Imoshen took a deep breath and lifted her chin. The U-shaped table created an intimate dinner setting which was still loosely formal.

"Wine, General?" She tilted the steaming jug. Her gaze ran over the lines of the vessel, instinctively enjoying its elegant shape. Candlelight glistened on its polished surface.

That midsummer long ago she had discovered that the simple act of eating in the royal palace could be a sensuous experience, and now she was here, serving these barbarians who probably would not even know how to use the cutlery. A shiver ran over Imoshen's skin.

Life was strange—strange and cruel.

General Tulkhan's hand gripped her wrist. When his dark, scarred fingers closed around her white flesh she felt the strength in him.

"You would serve me?" His piercing eyes held hers.

She felt color steal into her cheeks, very aware of the men who were taking their seats. It occurred to her with the instincts schooled by diplomacy that the table needed women, but she could not call in the whores she had banished.

They needed the wives and daughters of the minor nobles to normalize the situation. She suspected the Ghebites would act less rashly when there were women present, women they respected.

Tulkhan's fingers tightened on the tender bones of her

wrist. "I said, would you serve me like a common kitchen maid?"

She stiffened in silent fury as the truth of it hit her like a physical blow. Her position was tenuous at best, relying on his goodwill. Here, away from her own Stronghold she had simply assumed command of the palace servants, but if he chose the General could undermine her position. She could be relegated to the role of a menial servant.

"What place do I have, General?"

He grimaced. "Sit at my side."

She balked, the memory of King Gharavan's whores filling her with dismay. "Am I to sit at your side as your equal or your whore?"

He flushed. She saw the rising tide of anger stain his skin. The knobs of muscle at his jawline gleamed in the candlelight as he ground his teeth.

"Now is not the time—"

"On the contrary." Blood rushed in her ears as she felt all eyes turn to them. Conversations stopped. "I have spent all afternoon soothing the cook's feelings so that she could produce this meal, working with the master of the bedchambers to throw out your brother's whores. Even now the servants are stripping the beds to make them fit for your honest men. I would like to know where I stand!"

He glared at her.

Though her heart was pounding, Imoshen did not flinch when he lifted his hand. Before she could protest, she found herself swept off her feet. In a rush, he lifted her with him as he climbed onto his chair. Suddenly towering above the table, Imoshen clutched the General as they balanced precariously on the chair. Its slender legs creaked ominously.

"Fill your mugs, men, I give you a toast. A toast to Fair Isle, my new land and to Imoshen, my wife."

Cold shock doused Imoshen. But, of course, it was the next step!

Tulkhan had laid claim to her and the land in one sentence. Reothe had wanted her because of what she represented. Tulkhan could not afford to let her remain unbonded.

He would legitimize his claim to the land by binding her to him.

The knowledge that she had played into his hands filled Imoshen with shame. Once enslaved as his "wife" what bargaining power would she have? The implications swamped her.

Tulkhan's men echoed his toast as the servants hurried forward with more heated wine. Someone thrust a warm goblet in her numbed hand.

"Drink and smile, damn it!" Tulkhan hissed. His arm circled her waist, pressing her to his side.

Imoshen lifted the wine and sipped as the room swayed around her. Here she was standing on a chair in a lesser dining room of the royal palace, claimed as a prize of war by the barbarian who had murdered every member of her family.

It was too much.

She felt utterly numb. An almost hysterical urge to laugh threatened to overcome her as she recalled the last time she had eaten here, during the midsummer feast.

Only the Emperor and Empress's immediate family, about forty people, had been present. It was her first private-formal evening since she had arrived and Reothe had been present. With their argument still ringing in her ears she had been careful not to notice him during the excruciatingly long dinner and the entertainment which followed. But when she was sure he was not looking she had watched him avidly.

How dare he pity her!

He was as exotic as she was. With his silver hair and his slender rangy form he exuded male strength. He made the more civilized men of the Emperor's table seem like fat, lazy tabby cats. He reminded her of a snow leopard she had seen once in the deep woods. Beautiful, deadly, unattainable but fascinating.

He must have sensed her scrutiny because he looked across the room and met her eyes. Of course she stared back, secure in the knowledge that he would not cause a scene here before all their relatives.

Despite their rivalry she felt a kinship with him. Of all

the inhabitants in that room only she and he were pure T'En. Had he experienced the veiled taunts she had known? Did he curse the differences which made him remarkable?

Then he had lifted his wine and offered her a silent toast, which she had chosen to acknowledge. For a moment when she lowered that goblet and met his intense wine-dark eyes all else faded. It had seemed to her that they were alone amid a swarm of bees and heat moved within her.

Had he been trying to influence her, even then?

If he had, it had not been successful because she had smiled and deliberately turned her back to him so she could converse with the person beside her.

It had been her sister. They hadn't been close. Yet at this moment Imoshen willingly recalled her sister's face, the sound of her voice. Suddenly everything shifted. She felt as if she was seated at the formal tables. She could see her mother and her father. As always her brother was showing off.

Pain lanced her.

"Dead, they're all dead—"

'Who's dead? My people?" a deep voice demanded, shaking her.

Superimposed over her laughing relations she saw the Ghebite barbarians watching her, and General Tulkhan's keen dark eyes.

"Your people?" A bitter laugh shook her. "No, *my* people, my family!"

She could even see her mother's small scar which she tried to hide by wearing her hair forward on her forehead. The curl had fallen aside. Imoshen fought the urge to let mother know. It would be so easy to slip away from the cold, dangerous present, into a fragile moment from the past . . .

"Imoshen!" Abruptly, Tulkhan swung her into his embrace. Her wine cup flew from her slack fingers to clatter on the delicate mosaic floor tiles. She resented his warm strength and was disoriented by the abrupt change as the world of the T'En was lost to her, lost to rapacious, unforgiving Time.

The General was flesh and blood, immediate and impatient. He made her intensely aware of sensation as she felt the rasp of his bristly chin on her cheek, the coarse pads of his fingers on her face and the strength in his arms.

Then his lips found hers and she was utterly confused, lost in the heat of his passion. This was General Tulkhan, self-styled ruler of Fair Isle. She knew he had claimed her for political reasons but she knew with a woman's instinct that when he took her to his bed it would be because he wanted her.

Dimly, she heard the catcalls and whistles, the thumping on the tables. It was so different from the refined finger clicking of the royal courtiers.

Revulsion filled her—these Ghebites were barbarians. The absurdity of her current situation, contrasted with the restrained elegance of the setting and her intense memory of that last formal yet intimate evening with the doomed royal family of the T'En.

Her mind went blank.

It was too much. For the first time since the Stronghold fell she allowed herself to feel the loss of those people she loved and she couldn't bear it. While they lived she had taken them for granted, dead they became precious. She couldn't live with that pain.

Desperate to escape it, she concentrated on sensation, willing herself to blot out all thought, all memory. The immediate pressure of Tulkhan's lips on hers elicited a physical response which she didn't bother to disguise. She was hungry for him, hungry for the oblivion his passion promised.

The General released her, his obsidian eyes glittering with a savage male hunger which she knew would not be easily sated. He lifted his crystal wineglass, threw back his head and gave the Ghebite battle cry. The bloodcurdling challenge shattered the restrained elegance of the formal room, reverberating down the corridors and through the heart of the royal palace.

With sudden clarity Imoshen knew the past was dead. General Tulkhan was the future.

Despite everything she was drawn to him. Her heart swelled with the intensity of his passion. He had it all now,

Fair Isle, the royal palace and herself, the last princess of the T'En.

The Ghebite barbarians had triumphed.

A fey mood was on Tulkhan and it didn't leave him as they took their seats and the food was served. She observed him as he steered the conversations with the leaders of his army. Each man vied to prove his loyalty. The Ghebite commanders saw General Tulkhan as the source of all power. Imoshen understood that to them, she was about as significant as the palace—beautiful, useful, but without will or choice.

The knowledge galled her.

As for General Tulkhan, she watched him eat his food with the same vigor he applied to everything. He would take her as fiercely and freely later tonight. Then what, throw her aside as he threw aside the bone he had just finished with?

What was a Ghebite wife but a possession, a convenience!

Imoshen tensed, hating the General at that moment because he held her life in his hands and hating herself because when their eyes met, she felt the insistent tug of her body to his. She ached for his lovemaking.

But she would not be a convenience. If he was taking her to bond for life, to consolidate his hold on Fair Isle, then he must abide by the laws and customs of Fair Isle. He must abstain from touching her until they took their vows! She smiled because she knew he would not like that.

The servants cleared away the main course and there was a lull as they carried the sweets from the distant kitchen.

Imoshen leaned closer to Tulkhan, lowering her voice. "You have Fair Isle, General. But can you hold it?"

His dark eyes met hers, weighing, wondering.

Good. She had his attention.

"The townsfolk are nervous. They fear your army which has inundated the town. To consolidate your victory, you need to win over the people of T'Diemn."

"I was going to call on the Guildmasters and the town leaders to swear fealty tomorrow—"

She nodded, pleased. "You think they will come willingly, considering what happened when King Gharavan did that? I suggest we stage a feast, declare a holiday, invite the Guildmasters and their families. When you have them present, praise T'Diemn's prosperity. Promise that you won't interfere with the administration of the town. The townsfolk will only revolt if threatened. Let them feel secure under your leadership.''

''Why are you doing this?''

She felt his suspicious eyes on her. Why was she smoothing the transition of power?

Tulkhan caught her hand as she reached for her wine.

''Answer me, Dhamfeer?''

The use of that word told her all she needed to know. He felt alienated from her. Why? Because they were in the palace which was so obviously constructed by the T'En race. Because it represented a richer culture than his own?

With a deft twist she slipped her hand from his grasp and raised her wine goblet, watching him over the rim as she sipped. Should she try to minimize the differences between True-man and T'En? Anger seethed in her. She would not pretend to be less than she was!

''You have claimed me as you bond-partner, wife in your language. As bond-partner my role is to aid you, and yours is to aid me. According to T'En custom you are my equal, my other half. So if I help you, I help myself.''

General Tulkhan looked down at his own hand where it lay resting on the tablecloth.

Imoshen noted the coppery skin crisscrossed by tiny scars. His broad, strong hand looked so out of place on the exquisite lace cloth. She knew how those callused hands felt on her delicate skin. A shudder of longing swept her body and she despised herself for it.

Here tonight, and over the ensuing weeks she would need all her wits about her, yet she was finding it difficult to separate her physical needs from the logical paths her mind told her she should take. Abstinence would give her a chance to overcome this weakness.

''The ways of the T'En are new to me,'' Tulkhan confessed, his voice like deep honey, so rich she could almost taste it. "We are to be partners? Then the sooner we are wedded the better. Tomorrow—"

"Tomorrow would be too soon." Despite her best intentions, she laid her hand over his because she wanted to feel the strength in him. A slow burn of desire ignited in her core. "True, the ceremony should be soon. But this must be done properly. The T'En Church is very powerful, its leaders can influence how well your rule is accepted. They hold great wealth and the minds of the people. If we woo them to our side we will have their support.

"For the people to recognize our joining the T'En Church needs to be involved in the ceremony. And what of your own religious leaders?"

Tulkhan shrugged. "I'm a soldier. I've little time for gods."

"Your men?"

He rubbed his chin thoughtfully.

She nodded to herself. "Your men might feel more at ease if you observe the rituals of the Ghebite religion." She paused as his eyes flew to hers.

A smile lurked in their obsidian depths as he ruefully acknowledged she was right. That smile did more to threaten her resolution than anything else. With a shock, Imoshen realized she liked the General. She liked his ready understanding, his rueful humor.

"Why do you smile, General Tulkhan?"

He shook his head slowly. "Is it all a game of tactics to you?"

She wanted to deny it but she couldn't disclose her weakness. The General did not trust her so he wouldn't believe her. It would be an agony to admit her feelings only to have them spurned, so she merely smiled.

"I play to win, General. There's no point otherwise." Imoshen let him believe that if he chose. It was safer for her. "Now it will take time to negotiate the cooperation of the religious leaders. The people of Fair Isle have a feast on the shortest day of the year. Declare the Midwinter Feast the day that we make our vows and you are officially crowned ruler of Fair Isle. It will allow time for the minor southern nobles to come in from their estates.

"They need to see that you are a fair man, they need reassurance. They need to know that you will not confiscate their estates—"

"I want to reward my loyal men."

"There are empty strongholds and estates to the north. Reward them with those and with bond-partners. Marry them to the eligible daughters of minor southern nobles. Blood ties are much stronger than the bonds of fear."

The General's eyes flickered over her face then away and Imoshen knew she had lost him. What had she said?

Tulkhan shifted in his seat, leaning away from Imoshen. The Dhamfeer's vivid, intense face was like a magnet drawing him in. He wanted to look on her forever, to drink in her features. Her intelligence glinted behind her eyes, brilliant as sunlight on water. Then, just when he thought he understood her, she revealed another facet. And he feared he would cut himself on her sharp surfaces.

Now this. *Blood ties are stronger than the bonds of fear.*

How true. He had loved his half-brother almost to his own death. And look at Imoshen. She had tricked him, seduced him. No . . . that was not fair. He had chosen her and now she carried his child—the child he thought he could never have. Imoshen was the key to Fair Isle and to the future.

But could he trust her? Dare he trust her?

Dare he not? Her words of advice were true, even if they were motivated by self-interest. He almost laughed. Of course they were motivated by self-interest, what better motivation?

Selfless interest? He pushed that thought aside as irrelevant.

Imoshen was his captive, willing to work for his good because it benefited her. By what right did he, the slave master, wish for love as well as devotion?

She came to her feet. "You will excuse me, General. There is much I must organize for tomorrow—"

"Leave it." He caught her around the waist, drawing her

between his thighs. He could feel the gentle swell of her hips, the rise and fall of her ribs as she drew in a sharp breath. He had to tilt his chin to look up into her face. She was so much taller than the women of his own people. And proud. He liked the way she met his eyes, liked the way she would not defer to him.

She was Dhamfeer, Other and dangerous. She was possibly the instrument of his death, but he wanted her and he would have her. He'd laid claim to her.

"I want my bed." His voice was a low growl. He tightened his hands on her waist, felt the tension in her. She heard the spoken words and he knew she understood his meaning. He wanted her in his bed, under him, preferably with her thighs wrapped around his hips. A shaft of desire flamed deep within him.

A wicked smile lifted the corners of her mouth and played in the depths of her garnet eyes. It should have warned him.

"I will show you to your bedchamber, General," she told him. "Then I will go to mine. It is customary for betrothed partners to practice abstinence until they take their vows."

"To hell with abstinence!" The thought was abhorrent.

She laughed. The throaty peal was like velvet rubbing across his skin. He sensed more than saw every head in the room turn to them, and knew instinctively that every man there desired her, whether he would admit to it or not.

She ran her fingers over his head, down the line of his jaw, lingering on the hollows of his throat. He could see the candlelight reflecting in her eyes, twin flames of desire. He wanted to immolate himself in those flames.

"As leader of your men, you set the tone for your army," she purred. "Your half-brother set no example."

The truth of it hit him. If he wanted to take Imoshen to be his wife by his own laws he must observe the rituals, which it would appear were similar to the customs of her people. Abstinence.

"Damn."

He caught a gleam of triumph in her eyes and told himself to be wary. After all, this was a political wedding even if by good fortune it promised to soothe the physical ache which was driving him to distraction.

He studied Imoshen and she tilted her head, returning his gaze. How much of what he was feeling was his own body's response to hers? Was she planting thoughts in his head, manipulating him? She had sworn she wouldn't do it, said that it would be wrong, yet he could count the instances when she had invaded his mind.

"General?" She leaned forward, peering into his eyes, unconsciously giving him a view of her high, firm breasts barely contained by the neckline of her gown. Desire flared through him again. Useless, potent flames of lust seared him from within.

He pulled her onto his lap, burying his face in her soft flesh, inhaling her womanly scent.

How long until midwinter? He tried to think, but could not recall the dates. It had to be at least five weeks.

"Six," Imoshen whispered.

Anger lanced his mind, cutting through the cloud of desire. She had been in his head again, Damn her!

Their gaze met.

Even as anger flared in him, he saw her eyes widen as she realized what she'd done.

"Please!" she hissed, pressing his face to her breast. He felt her strength, her soft curves on his cheek. The rapid pounding of her heart thundered in his ear.

He turned his head away, almost overcome by her physical presence.

Abruptly, Imoshen slipped from his lap and dropped to her knees, kneeling between his thighs.

"I didn't mean to," she confessed, whispering to escape their curious company.

He saw the truth in her eyes and the knowledge both repelled and fascinated him because at that moment he realized Imoshen's ability to touch his mind was an instinctive reflex.

Could he live with that knowledge?

Tulkhan didn't know, but for now he would maintain a

distance between them. So far she had invaded his thoughts only when their bodies were touching. It seemed safe to assume Imoshen's ability weakened with distance or only worked on contact.

A grim smile warmed him. His body might crave hers but he didn't want to pay the ultimate price for his lust and become her instrument.

It was just as well their customs required abstinence.

Tulkhan pushed his chair back, coming to his feet. Imoshen also rose, withdrawing from him and gathering her dignity about her like a cloak.

With a formal bow, he bid her good night. Tulkhan knew by her rigidly controlled features that he had hurt Imoshen, and it galled him to admit that it hurt him to see her pain.

From dawn until midafternoon the following day Imoshen was frantically busy. Messengers ran from one end of the palace to the other delivering her orders, tallying information and coordinating the efforts of the army of servants.

Imoshen vowed that this time when the Guildmasters, the town dignitaries and their families met the Ghebites they would not be greeted by treachery but with familiar entertainment. They would see General Tulkhan was not like his uncouth, uncivilized and treacherous half-brother.

The people of T'Diemn were not surrendering their city, but greeting their deliverer from oppression. It was a fine distinction which Imoshen hoped to impress on them.

The day was bitterly cold, too cold to hold the ceremony in the square. She elected to open the public rooms of the palace, which necessitated cleaning, heating and lighting them. Food had to be prepared and seating arrangements organized for several hundred guests. At her insistence the leaders of Tulkhan's army were to be scattered through the civilian guests. All weapons were to be left at the door. It would not be a welcome request, but if both parties cooperated it would go a long way toward reassuring the townsfolk.

At short notice she had sent messengers to scour the town for the skilled performers who had fled the palace.

Original T'En forms of entertainment would be staged as well as the more robust Ghebite entertainments provided by the army's camp followers. Her aim was to blend the two cultures—a symbol, she hoped, for the blending of people.

Shortly before midday she tracked General Tulkhan down and reported her plans to him for approval. He had to agree to disarming his men or the townsfolk's gesture meant nothing.

She watched the General anxiously as he gazed through the tall window of one of the palace's entertainment rooms which faced onto a formal garden, lightly dusted with snow.

"All weapons at the door?" he muttered, casting a swift glance to the men who had remained at the table when he left it.

"To reassure the townsfolk," Imoshen insisted.

Tulkhan read the list. "Six jugglers, a set of balladeers, seventeen acrobats, two storytellers, and a pair of dueling poets?"

She smiled at the tone of his voice. "A T'En custom. You'll see. The entertainment is to give the formal ceremony a festive air, to make it less threatening."

He nodded, glanced back to the table where his commanders waited, then down at the list again. "This ceremony will take hours."

"Up to six hours, yes. It will be a great occasion."

"Pomp and ceremony," he sighed. "Very well. I will put my work aside for the rest of the day."

Imoshen stiffened. It wasn't as if she had been waited on hand and foot, her every wish catered to. She hadn't eaten a scrap since dawn and her head spun with details. "Pomp and ceremony has its place, General!"

He gave her a long-suffering look and she realized with a shock that he was teasing her. It was a new sensation, not unwelcome just . . . different.

When the church bells of the great domed basilica across the square struck two, Imoshen was ready to play her part. She greeted each of the leaders of T'Diemn personally, before passing them along to servants who escorted them to their seats.

The Church was represented by the Beatific, its temporal leader. She was a handsome woman in her early forties with eyes that saw too much. She made Imoshen feel gauche. Determined to be as regal as the Empress who had impressed her so deeply when she was sixteen, Imoshen greeted the large retinue of priests and priestesses in their formal finery. She made a point of leading them to their seats personally. Soon she would have to deal with this woman to negotiate the church's approval of Tulkhan's coronation and their bonding.

Something told her it would not be easy. The Beatific was young to have risen to this post so she must be a skilled negotiator.

Imoshen returned to her post and continued with the greetings. The townsfolk were all seated before any of the Ghebites appeared and then it was General Tulkhan himself, alone and unattended, who arrived first. He surprised her by entering from the square.

Imoshen stepped back as she took in his appearance. He was dressed in full battle regalia, looking magnificent in his red, purple and black. She was startled by his choice of apparel since he had agreed they would not bring weapons.

But understanding dawned on her when, after the formal greeting, he unclasped his weapons and handed them to her. Piece by piece, he discarded his battle regalia till he was dressed in nothing but his tight-fitting breeches, boots and a simple white undershirt.

She had to admire his sense of timing. Divested of his cloak, breastplate and helmet, he stood before her simply a man, though no one could accuse Tulkhan of being a mere man. Even divested of all his finery he carried himself like the leader he was.

He gave her a formal bow and whispered, "Satisfied?" Imoshen had to smile.

"Very effective," she replied as she returned his formal bow of greeting. "But won't you be cold?"

"I can live with it and so can my men."

As he straightened, she saw his loyal commanders all waiting to greet her as their leader had done. She went forward to greet them.

While she did, she was aware of the General making his way slowly toward the rear of the public hall. As he did, he paused to speak to certain people. They appeared to know him and look on him favorably. Imoshen deduced they were the Guildmasters he had dealt with when King Gharavan had been in charge of the city and he had to repair the damage his half-brother had done.

Imoshen greeted each of General Tulkhan's commanders and their trusted men. They handed her their weapons and were escorted to their seats. So far it had gone well. Her mind ran through the plans for the next step.

When everyone was present Imoshen turned and saw that Tulkhan had not taken his seat on the dais before the High Table. He was waiting for her. Instinctively she understood—he wanted to consolidate his position with the people by having her at his side when he took his seat.

A now familiar stab of sadness pierced her. Once again she was reminded of Reothe. Both he and General Tulkhan wanted her for what she represented. Still, she had her part to play and she would not falter!

Imoshen moved lightly down the length of the hall, lifting her hand to meet Tulkhan's as he waited.

A rueful smile lurked in his eyes and she felt an answering smile on her lips despite her somber mood.

He kissed her fingers. It was unexpected. She felt his warm breath dust her skin and a stab of desire surged deep within her.

"I thought you had a soldier's hatred of pomp and ceremony?" she whispered.

"I do, but someone once told me, there is a time and place for it." His words were meant only for her. They charmed her, as they were meant to. She ground her teeth, telling herself she had to steel herself against him.

Imoshen placed her hand along his raised arm, recalling that this was how he had led her from the great hall of the

Stronghold the night of the Harvest Feast. That reminded her of their joining and her cheeks grew hot. She silently cursed her betraying fair skin.

Together they mounted the two steps onto the dais. As she looked out at the sea of faces below Imoshen reflected that at least she had no painful memories of the great public hall. The Midsummer Festival's formal ceremonies had been held outside in the square and in the gardens of the palace grounds. But these town dignitaries would have memories. Were they comparing the Emperor and Empress with the Ghebite General?

Imoshen listened to Tulkhan give his speech of welcome but her concentration was focused on the inhabitants of the hall. She was trying to weigh the reaction of the town's leaders and of his own men.

The townsfolk had already met General Tulkhan when he repaired the damage his half-brother's cruelty had caused. She could tell they were relieved with the General's reasonable tone. His own men must have been privy to the contents of his speech because they were not surprised by any of the concessions the General was making. It was for the best. T'Diemn was an orderly, prosperous town and it would remain so if the town's leaders were allowed to go about their business without interference.

Then Tulkhan called for the leader of each guild to step forward and swear loyalty to his rule. Imoshen did not doubt that they would. They were a practical people, intent on trade and wealth. There was a murmuring and shuffling as chairs were pushed back and people rose, moving forward to congregate before the dais. They were men and women of age and distinction, leaders in their own fields.

A finger of pure winter light found its way through the clouds. Its silver rays plunged through the high, ornate stained-glass windows so that the area surrounding the dais was bathed in multicolored patches of light.

The town's leaders congregated and after whispered consultation the first couple stepped forward to kneel and swear fealty. Imoshen knew they would be the representatives of the largest of the greater guilds. She smiled. Even within the guild system there was a pecking order.

The man was ancient. To Imoshen's healer-trained eyes, he looked as if he normally walked with the aid of a cane, but had done away with it out of pride. The woman was a stout matron with intelligent eyes. Imoshen deduced she must be in training to take his place as Guildmaster. She suspected the old man had been called out of retirement to groom her after the previous Guildmaster had been murdered by King Gharavan.

As the old man stepped from the dimness into the multicolored light he faltered. The woman, possibly blinded by the transition into the light, did not notice. Imoshen saw the old man lift his hand, feeling for the woman's shoulder, and miss.

Her healer's instincts took over. If he fell on the hard tiles he could break a brittle bone. Before he could miss his footing, she ran down the two steps and caught his outstretched hand.

He seemed startled to find her there supporting him and instinctively moved to pull away.

"Let me be your cane, grandfather," she whispered.

"T'En?" He stared, bemused.

She smiled and placed his hand on her shoulder. When he knelt, she knelt with him. There was a hushed, collective sigh from the crowded tables.

She saw that the General had come to his feet and started down the first step. Now he stood above them. She found his expression unreadable. Would he think she was currying favor with the townsfolk? Anger flickered through her. Would he rather she let the old man fall?

It did not matter what she did, he could interpret her actions negatively if that was what he chose to do.

The old man and his assistant gave the oath of fealty and General Tulkhan formally accepted it, giving in return an oath which bound him to fair treatment of all their guilds and their members.

The oaths finished, Imoshen rose to her feet with her

hand cupped under the old man's elbow so that her assistance appeared minimal, but she was there ready to offer him help if he faltered.

He lifted his eyes to hers. His bald pate came only to midchest on her. He raised her hand to his withered cheek and as they stepped apart he kissed her sixth finger for luck. The woman thanked her softly, taking her hand to stroke her finger.

As the next couple moved forward, Imoshen sensed movement behind her and found General Tulkhan had descended from the dais. He joined her.

Why? Was he annoyed with her?

She had not felt comfortable seated up there while her people bowed and swore their oaths.

Standing before the dais, the General linked his arm with hers. She liked the feel of his strong body next to hers, but she told herself he was only aligning himself with her to bolster his position with the townsfolk. It was a political move.

Imoshen knew she could not let down her guard, there was so much to bear in mind. As yet, she had not approached the church representatives to ask for their oath of fealty. That would require delicate negotiation.

It was a long process. Each of the greater guilds and then the lesser guilds swore their oaths. The last to make his oath was the elected administrator of the city and his cabinet of six people.

The mayor rose from swearing fealty and took Imoshen's hand. ''Welcome T'En. The city has been too long without an Aayel.''

Imoshen was so surprised she was speechless. Did he think to flatter her? The title Aayel was not something given lightly. He moved off before she could speak.

The formalities over, the food was served and the entertainment begun. Much later as the guests broke into patterns for the dances Imoshen found a gray-haired woman waiting at her elbow, obviously anxious to speak with her.

Imoshen's whole evening had been a series of intense

conversations as people sought reassurance. She turned, ready once again to shore up the General's position.

But when the woman caught Imoshen's hand her face was tight with tension, her wine-dark eyes glistening. With a jolt Imoshen recognized the T'En trait, though the woman bore none of the other signs.

"My son? Do you know what became of him?" she whispered.

Imoshen searched her mind for the identity of this woman. She was Guildmaster of the silversmiths.

"You must be—?"

"Drakin's mother." The woman nodded.

Imoshen felt her mouth go dry. She did not want to be the deliverer of bad news. "You should be proud of your son. He came to the Stronghold. His word convinced General Tulkhan to ride to T'Diemn. It was Drake's intervention which brought aid to the city . . ."

"But what of my lad?" the woman asked.

Imoshen's fingers closed over the woman's. She gripped her hand. Slipping away through the clusters of guests, she lowered her voice.

"Drake left my Stronghold to join the rebels."

The woman groaned. "Then his life is forfeit!"

"No. I have told no one. He could yet return and if he does I will never tell."

"Tell what?" General Tulkhan asked.

Imoshen felt the woman flinch. She slid her arm around the Guildmaster's shoulders. "Tell how relieved I am it is you who have claimed Fair Isle and not your half-brother."

Tulkhan met her eyes and she realized he knew she was prevaricating.

"General," she said quickly. "Let me introduce the Guildmaster of the silversmiths."

The woman's gaze flew from Imoshen to the General and back. If General Tulkhan had been a man like his half-brother one word from Imoshen could see the Guildmaster's position lost, her property confiscated and her family imprisoned or executed.

Gharavan would not have hesitated to use Drake's family

as hostages to prize Reothe's whereabouts from them. Would the General stoop to the same tricks?

Imoshen did not believe it, but she had no intention of testing him.

With a start, she realized she did not want Tulkhan to fail her.

TEN

THERE THEY GO AGAIN!'' Kalleen exclaimed, rolling her eyes. ''I've never met a town so keen to listen to bells!''

Imoshen looked up from her papers. Was Kalleen jesting? No, being a farm girl she had marked the passage of her day by the rising and setting of the sun. ''Those are the bells of the basilica. They ring the hour and the half hour for the convenience of the townsfolk.''

Kalleen laughed. ''No wonder the townspeople of T'Diemn rush about with such worried faces. Life's too short to mark each half of the hour as it slips away!''

Imoshen felt a smile tug at her lips. Kalleen was good for her.

With an impudent grin, the girl darted out of the room, intent on some mission of her own. For a lady's maid she spent precious little time in Imoshen's room and was very quick to give her opinion on any and every subject, but Imoshen would not have it any other way. Things were said in Kalleen's hearing which would not have been said in hers. The girl was a font of information, not all of it welcome.

Sighing, Imoshen went back to reading. Her morning had been devoted to studying the documents from the palace library, searching for a clue as to the extent of the church's autonomy. She suspected that the Beatific was trying to assume more power than the church previously had claim to. It was what she would have done in the same position. As yet

Imoshen did not have the woman's "key" and it frustrated her.

She read until the convoluted grammar of the High T'En tongue turned her thoughts to nonsense.

Arching her back, Imoshen stretched and wandered to the window. Looking out over the spires and towers of T'Diemn to the blue-white hills which ringed the capital, she tried to clear her head. Only a few weeks had elapsed since they had arrived in the capital but already she felt hemmed in. If she felt trapped how did the General feel?

He spent much time in the town itself inspecting its fortifications and seeing to his men. Although she had vowed to keep him at a distance, when he made no effort to be with her and seemed to prefer the company of his men, Imoshen found she was perversely irritated.

She told herself it was better this way. Her negotiations with the head of the T'En Church required a clear mind and just being in the same room as the General distracted her. Somehow his voice rang clear above every other man's. When he laughed something deep within her stirred with unspoken longing—not that she would ever reveal this to Tulkhan.

Kalleen's spirits had improved markedly with the return of Wharrd and his small band of Elite Guards who reported that Gharavan had sailed eight days previously without trouble.

Meetings with the T'En Church did not go so smoothly. Not that voices were ever raised. The Beatific was all smiles and polite interest, but her position was solid. She knew General Tulkhan wanted the church's approval.

Of course, the General could raze the T'En basilica and confiscate the wealth gathered over six hundred years of devotion but that would destroy the people. He had to win the populace over to hold the island.

Imoshen and the Beatific knew he would not use force. Unfortunately Tulkhan's religious advisor was a relatively young man whose zealous devotion to his own faith made him intolerant of the T'En religion. Cadre Castenatus had the arrogance of youth armored with pious righteousness.

Imoshen wished he was a battle-hardened realist like Wharrd or Commander Peirs, who had offered the General his allegiance so willingly when they entered T'Diemn. It was not going to be easy to find common ground.

The basilica bells pealed again. Imoshen cursed. Despite the reminder of the bells, she was running late for yet another meeting with the Head of the Church. Luckily she was already dressed for the formal meeting. Head down, she slipped out of her chamber and ran lightly along the long corridor, grateful there were no servants to report her behavior. Her poor mother would not have approved of her running down the halls of the Emperor's palace even if she was late for a meeting with the Beatific.

She was almost at the formal wing when she remembered she'd meant to bring a critical document with her. If she could cite decrees by her forebear and provide written evidence of the extent of the church's power the Beatific's advisors would have to retract their stipulations.

It paid to have a working knowledge of the language of law and Imoshen was glad she had kept up her study of High T'En. With a muttered imprecation she spun on her heel and this time ran in earnest.

Her supple dress boots hit the floor with a soft thud, thud. She flung open her bedchamber door and darted across to the worktable. Intent on riffling through the scattered documents, it was only when the vital scroll was in her hand that she heard an angry voice coming from Kalleen's antechamber.

Imoshen's mouth went dry. She listened but could not detect a second voice. Still, she could not walk off knowing Kalleen was in distress. She hated to witness another's hurt, even a stranger's. It had always caused her physical discomfort, but even more so since her gifts had been awakened.

Stepping lightly across the rugs, she pushed the connecting door ajar. It looked as if Kalleen had flung herself across her bed. Even as Imoshen took in her silent despair the girl noticed the open door and rolled off the bunk, silently wiping her face on her sleeve. Meeting Imoshen's eyes with a steady gaze, she almost dared the T'En to accuse her of crying.

Instinctively Imoshen's hand reached out to touch her, but Kalleen jerked away.

"I won't have you seeing my thoughts, Lady T'En," she explained stiffly.

A shaft of pain stabbed Imoshen. Kalleen, too?

No, she was certain the girl trusted her, which was more than could be said for most of the palace servants. She'd overheard the whispers, talk of how she'd assumed Gharavan's form to save General Tulkhan. She'd seen the hastily averted eyes, experienced the sudden absence of conversation when she entered a room. Since the night they had deposed Gharavan, Imoshen had noted the shift in her people's perception of her.

"I would never do anything against your wishes, Kalleen." Imoshen was surprised to hear how reasonable her voice sounded despite the pain. "I sought merely to comfort you."

"So you say." Kalleen sniffed, wiping her nose inelegantly with the cuff of her sleeve. "You'd do it without thinking. Ten times a day I've seen you anticipate what people are going to say."

Imoshen's heart sank. Was Kalleen right? Was she unconsciously alienating the palace servants? She licked her lips, forced herself to face this unwelcome revelation.

The girl took a step closer, very obviously placing her hand on Imoshen's arm. "I do trust you, my Lady, no matter what *they* say."

Imoshen smiled wryly. Kalleen was a friend in the truest sense of the word. Who else would speak the unpleasant truth? "I'm glad to hear it. So, if you trust me, tell me what's wrong."

A tremor rippled through the young woman's features and she broke contact. "Wharrd has asked me to bond with him, to be his *wife,* as he calls it, his."

So she was to lose Kalleen. Imoshen said nothing.

The girl drew a shuddering breath. "I told him no."

"Why? If you care for him, surely—"

"I love him! But I won't be his slave."

Imoshen's eyes widened.

Kalleen walked to the small window. The exterior of the thick glass was crusted with ice crystals glistening in the direct sunlight. "Wharrd says the General will give him an estate and a title. I have nothing. I can already see it happening. I will be his wife-slave, part of the estate." She spun to face Imoshen. "I might only be a farm girl but I am not stupid. I've been asking questions. Ghebite women don't own their share of the family property. They are *part* of the property." Kalleen shuddered, visibly revolted. "They *belong* to their men!"

Imoshen stepped closer, pierced by ready compassion. "Of course, I see your dilemma!"

Kalleen's golden eyes blazed. "No matter how much I love him, I won't be his slave. I told him I'd rather stay here and serve you!"

Again a smile tugged at Imoshen's lips. So she was an acceptable alternative to slavery.

She could understand Kalleen's decision. As long as the girl's mistress retained her position, Kalleen ranked above almost all other palace servants.

Imoshen had no trouble empathizing with Kalleen. If the girl bonded with one of her own people she would be an equal partner—half owner of a farm was better than the kept slave of a nobleman.

Imoshen took Kalleen's small, golden brown hand in her own. "Simple. I will gift you with an estate. I wanted to find some way to reward you for taking my place in the dungeon. I'll make over the Windhaven Estate to you and your heirs . . . damn!" Imoshen dropped Kalleen's hand and strode into her own room, her cheeks hot with frustration.

Windhaven was no longer hers to give. It lay to the north and had probably been gutted by the Ghebite Army. But the lands would still be good. She would have to ask General Tulkhan to release it to her so she could gift it to her maid. She hated to ask him for anything. The thought galled her.

Imoshen was aware of Kalleen watching silently and turned to her.

"General Tulkhan took that estate when he took Fair Isle. I will have to speak with him." The words left a bitter taste in Imoshen's mouth. Kalleen's golden eyes held ready sympathy.

Pacing the room, Imoshen tried to come to terms with her position. It infuriated her to know she had so little control over her own life. In truth, even the Stronghold was no longer hers. She had surrendered it to Tulkhan.

As long as she strode the corridors of the palace and advised the General it was easy to forget that she was his captive, a prize of war.

She needed a lever on the Ghebite General.

The Aayel had indeed been wise.

She had to maintain her hold on the General, and what better way than through his own flesh and blood! She would see to it that her children held the reins of power, made the decisions of government. Fair Isle would not slide into barbarism in one generation.

"My Lady?" Kalleen whispered. "Even if you gift Windhaven to me, the moment I give Wharrd my vows he will own everything including me. Ghebite women have no rights. I know what will happen." Her top lip curled contemptuously. "The Cadre has been most helpful. According to him I don't even have a proper soul!"

"Absurd!" Imoshen looked down into Kalleen's indignant face and had to smile. The girl was right. She could not let that happen, not to Kalleen, not to herself. "True, you would lose everything if you *married* by their religion, but what if they were to recognize our church and its laws? Bonding is another thing entirely."

Suddenly Imoshen understood what she had to do and she was sure if she handled it correctly the Beatific would comprehend the benefits for the T'En Church. Imoshen's greatest opponent would become her ally!

Delighted, she hugged the smaller girl. "Don't worry, Kalleen. I will see to it. You will own your own home and yourself. Every female of Fair Isle will retain her dignity."

Kalleen searched Imoshen's face, hope warring with despair. "We surrendered, my Lady. We have nothing but what they choose to give us."

Imoshen chewed her bottom lip. It was true. They were

fine words, fine sentiments, but how realistic was she being?
Yet possession was nine tenths of the law. As of this moment,
by custom she and Kalleen possessed the rights of ownership
and self-determination. Imoshen vowed she would not give
up these rights without a fight!

The basilica bells sounded again.

"Wait and see. I must go, I'm terribly late for my meeting."

Imoshen tucked the document within the brocade vest
she wore and strode off, her mind racing with ideas.

As the last of the royal family she was the titular head of
the church, a position she found bizarre. Since the Aayel had
opened her eyes she had been observing the T'En Church
officials. It was clear to her now that the current religious
leaders gave lip service to her status but jealously guarded
their positions of power within the church structure.

Maybe long ago the T'En race had been regarded as
being touched by the gods, but as the T'En began to die out
the church had gained more and more control over the temporal world. Imoshen could understand why the religious
leaders resented anything which rivaled their position. She
was an anachronism, an embarrassing reminder of the spiritual side of the church which had lost significance as the
church's hold on temporal matters of law expanded.

Imoshen frowned. She had to have the church's blessing.

It was a powerful, multilayered beast whose fingers of
influence spread into the smallest isolated village, but here in
the city the greatest power lay in the basilica. This served as
the religious and administrative center for the church's many
branches. In her elected position the Beatific held the position for a term of five years. Imoshen suspected much maneuvering behind the scenes had gone into securing that
position.

The Beatific rose as Imoshen entered the semiformal
private room, her attendants rising with her. If the woman
was annoyed by Imoshen's late arrival she did not show it.

Etiquette demanded Imoshen make a formal apology.

Commander Peirs hardly let her finish before opening
the inner doors to a circular table laid with food and drink.

"Everything is ready, Lady T'En," the grizzled commander announced. At his side Cadre Castenatus resumed a heated discussion with one of the high ranking T'En priests. For once Imoshen understood Peirs's impatience. The Cadre could be trusted to irritate a saint.

Imoshen offered the formal invitation to the table and the group moved into the inner room. The correct ceremony had to be observed. It was only after warmed wine and sweets had been consumed that Imoshen was able to broach the real subject of their meeting and she did it tangentially.

"Beatific, before we begin our discussions I thought the Cadre might like to tell us a little about his homeland, Gheeaba."

The woman's sharp, golden eyes fixed on Imoshen. This was off the subject. The Beatific had been holding out for an increase in church powers before agreeing to officiate at the wedding ceremony or give the church's blessing to the crowning ceremony which followed.

"Tell me, Cadre Castenatus." Imoshen turned to the northern priest. His righteousness was so ingrained that she hoped he would speak without considering his audience. "How many sisters do you have and which positions do they hold in the governing council of your country?"

He blinked at her. "I have three sisters, but they hold no official places. Their husbands sit on the council."

"How then do they use their education to mold the laws?"

He laughed. "They have no education in such matters."

Imoshen turned to Commander Peirs. "You, sir. Will you take a wife and settle here?"

He was startled by her sudden change of subject. Imoshen caught his worried eyes. He knew she was up to something but not what it was.

"I don't know," he began slowly.

"Commander Peirs could take several wives. His position allows him up to four," Cadre Castenatus explained.

Imoshen sensed the stiffening of all the women present but did not allow herself the luxury of looking at the Beatific.

Instead, she turned to the old commander. "Surely that is a Ghebite custom. You would abide by our customs here?"

He hesitated, obviously aware that his answer could be detrimental to the negotiations. "I am a simple soldier—"

"If women do not sit on council then they must serve their country in some other way," Imoshen remarked ingenuously, turning to the Cadre. "What do they do, administrate the townships or disseminate information through schooling? Or do they officiate at the religious ceremonies?"

He laughed. "Everyone knows a woman has but a poor weak soul which cannot sustain itself without guidance." With the conviction of absolute certainty he launched into a long speech about the learned doctrines on the weakness of a woman's soul and the female's need for protective guidance. Imoshen had no trouble translating this into a justification for the males of Gheeaba to dominate the women of their society. It was clear every other woman present had come to the same conclusion.

It was only at this point that Imoshen allowed herself to meet the Beatific's eyes. For a fraction of a heartbeat the handsome woman's political mask slipped and she exchanged a knowing look with Imoshen. It was underlaid with pure fury.

Neither the Beatific or Imoshen could afford to let secular differences divide them when their enemy was so obviously determined to grind them down.

Sitting back, Imoshen let Cadre Castenatus win her argument for her.

When he paused to draw breath, she remarked, "I am a little lost. Your system is new to me. If a man were to die, which of his wives would inherit the property?"

"The man's eldest son by his first wife, of course."

"Not the first wife?"

"None of the wives. The property belongs to the man."

"But surely the women—"

"No woman can own property."

The Beatific rose suddenly. The movement was at odds with her usual stately grace.

The Cadre fell silent as her assistants also rose. His expression of surprise revealed how little he understood his companions.

Imoshen came to her feet. Stepping around the formal table arrangements, she placed a hand on the Beatific's arm. "I feel we have a great deal in common, Beatific. I think we could work for the good of Fair Isle, particularly the women of Fair Isle."

It was a simple, honest statement but the Beatific only gave Imoshen a sharp look before formally taking leave of those present.

Imoshen was sure she had convinced the Beatific to give her support but could not understand the woman's suspicion. Of all the people she had met since coming to the palace, the Beatific remained elusive. Because she could not find the woman's Key Imoshen could only wait and hope her ploy had worked.

In the late afternoon she received a communication from the leader of the T'En Church. Heart pounding, hardly able to let herself hope she opened the brass cylinder and unrolled the vellum. Feverishly, she read the covering missive.

A surge of triumph flooded her. The communication contained two copies of a formal agreement in which the Beatific offered to host the ceremonies on Midwinter's Day on the understanding that the church's current systems of law, particularly those pertaining to ownership and inheritance regardless of sex, would remain in place. It meant General Tulkhan's position had the support of the church, but in acknowledging the church he had to give credence to their laws.

It was exactly what Imoshen was hoping for.

Returning the documents to their brass cylinder Imoshen left this on the table. She felt very pleased with herself as she went looking for the General to give him the good news. The servants sent her to the stables where the Ghebites had organized entertainment. Trudging across the courtyard, Imoshen heard the throaty growl of the crowd and tensed.

She stopped, undecided.

Rumors of the Ghebites' penchant for bird-baiting had swept the palace. But her workload had been so heavy she had not had time to investigate and Imoshen had to admit she did not want to know the full extent of the Ghebites' barbarism so she had avoided the stables. She'd heard that the birds were reared especially for this fate, bred winner to winner. Their only purpose in life was to die at their owner's whim.

It was a typical example of the Ghebite mentality! Everything must serve their purpose and damn the feelings of lesser creatures, be they female or dumb animal. To the Ghebite way of thinking they were probably one and the same. Imoshen smiled wryly—she felt an unwilling sympathy with the birds.

It was no good. She wouldn't ignore the cockfighting. Everything that happened in the palace set the tone for the city. The townsfolk would take their cue from her and if she condoned this barbarism what else might she condone?

Gritting her teeth, Imoshen strode toward the closed double doors. Her excuse to consult the General was legitimate. He could not accuse her of prying. She would just take a casual look while delivering her good news. Perhaps it was all exaggeration.

Imoshen slipped unobtrusively inside the stable. The sound and stench hit her like a physical blow.

The long barn was crowded, filled with strident voices. Men bellowed as they placed their bets, competing with the music to be understood. The Ghebite musicians who had traveled with the army as camp followers were set up in a stall playing their rowdy, raucous excuse for music.

Wine flowed freely, as did the opinions of those who considered themselves experts. They argued over the skill exhibited in the previous match and the likelihood of the surviving bird beating the new contender.

As Imoshen forged through the thickly packed crowd of sweating bodies, disgust and frustration filled her. The Ghebites thought nothing of inciting birds to kill each other, feeding their own blood lust with the male bird's frenzy.

Deep within her, Imoshen felt an innate sense of injustice. The cockerel was only doing what nature intended it to do. How could these men take perverse pleasure from so pointless a death?

She wanted to banish them and their sordid entertainment from the royal palace. At the very least she wanted to confront General Tulkhan. How could he condone this?

But she was frustrated, unable to join him, because though she could see him standing on the far side of the fighting pit, she knew she couldn't simply march over and upbraid him.

Like herself, the General was treading a fine line. He had to retain the support of his commanders and she could not afford to undermine his position. His men would resent it if she didn't show the General proper deference. Tulkhan would have to retaliate by treating her as he would treat a Ghebite woman. If he didn't, he would lose the respect of his soldiers.

Imoshen drew a short, tight breath. Frustration welled in her. She looked around, tried to be fair. Was she overreacting? Was this only harmless entertainment?

It worried her to see so many of her own people present. There were male palace servants, stable hands and entertainers. No women, she realized. But the men of Fair Isle were obviously enjoying the spectacle. It concerned her to see how quickly they forgot themselves. They were only too happy to immerse their senses in mind-dulling violence. Was the beast so close to the surface in even the most civilized male?

Were they really closer to the animal than females? Was it only the strength of the women of Fair Isle that maintained their society's level of civilization? It was a sobering thought!

She noticed the Cadre in the thick of it. Blood flecked his tunic from the last bird's death, staining the religious symbol of purity. How dare he claim Ghebite women had lesser souls than men? A sharp surge of anger flared inside Imoshen. She clenched her fists, trying to control her rage.

Densely packed bodies heated air which was heavy with the scent of horses, men, wine, blood and . . . A prickle of insight danced across Imoshen's skin as she identified the last ingredient—crude, eager excitement! It was so thick she could almost taste it. How dare they sully the palace's rich culture with their Ghebite barbarism!

When the new bout started an expectant, hungry hush fell on the crowd. Imoshen's heart pounded. Fury boiled inside her. A strange taste filled her mouth, making her teeth ache and her skin itch. She felt a rush of feverish hunger, as though the blood lust which lay so thick on the air was a dainty morsel she could inhale. It made her body sing and her head spin.

Across the crowd, beyond the fighting pit, she met Tulkhan's obsidian eyes. Why was he watching her so intensely?

The crowd roared. Dimly, she was aware that the fighting birds had drawn fresh blood.

Imoshen's nostrils stung. Her very flesh vibrated with the deep-throated growl of the crowd—a magnificent rage empowered her. The rush was so intense she felt weightless, as if she might rise off the dirt floor and draw it all into her.

The birds in the pit caught her attention. One was weakening. She could feel its life force slipping away. With every ebb the flood of joyous rage welled greater in her, but one part of her mind remained crystal clear. With a start, she realized that the spilling of life, even a life so insignificant as the cockerel's, could be channeled to empower her T'En gifts. It was enticingly, achingly sweet.

One by one, the men stopped shouting. Those who'd had their backs to her, turned, eyes widening, lips pulling back from their teeth. She could smell their fear, taste it on her tongue. It was also sweet, tempting.

Acting on instinct, the triumphant fighting bird attacked its weakened opponent, tearing out its throat. The shrill death screech sounded obscenely human in the sudden silence.

Imoshen knew the moment the bird's life left its body.

The combined life forces of the crowd and the bird joined within her, flooding her. Fingers curling, teeth aching she caught her breath as her vision blurred and swam, filled with pinwheeling sparks.

But she would not give in. The urge to manipulate this power was overwhelming. Instinct told her it would be too sweet and far too easy to grow dependent on it. How long before she began to crave this heady rush?

Fear was her anchor. It was the rock to which she clung in the tidal flood of newfound power.

But the buildup demanded release. Imoshen sensed if she didn't channel it, it would consume her. She had to release this.

Brilliant white light engulfed her. Blinding her.

Dread raced through her. She had lost control, immolated herself!

No.

The light consumed the birds. With an ear-numbing absence of noise they exploded in a ball of flame and feathers. Men ducked for cover. Shards of burning flesh and feathers sprayed over the crowd, burning skin, hair, igniting straw. People screamed. Horses screamed, sounding just as human and terrified.

Imoshen staggered back, nearly overwhelmed by the rush of those escaping the stables. The stench of burning feathers made her gag.

Disbelief warred with an instinctive knowledge that went bone deep. She had done this.

Aayel help her! But the old woman couldn't. Imoshen was alone.

She clutched the edge of a stall and retched, tears stinging her eyes. The crackle of greedy flames added to the confusion. When the retching had stopped, she dragged a trembling hand across her lips and ran, fleeing with the last of the others.

In the press of bodies she was swept out of the stable into the courtyard. Those around her were so shaken they didn't notice her. Could it be they didn't realize she was to blame, or had fear of the greedy fire overcome their fear of her?

Her mind reeled and nausea clawed at her.

Like swarming bees the terror of those around her stung her senses. It was too immediate and raw, too easily tapped. She had to escape them.

Abruptly she changed direction, shoving her way

through the bodies. Her footsteps took her away from the others into the bowels of the palace. Though Imoshen ran she knew there was no safe harbor, for the enemy was within her. Tears blurred her vision. It wasn't fair. She'd been so careful. She hadn't once tried to use her gifts. Until now she'd had no idea they could be triggered by violence and death. Blood roared in her head, thudding in her ears in time to her pounding heart.

She had nearly lost control. Only a reflex action had saved her at the expense of the birds.

What must the General think of her? Would he assume she'd done it intentionally?

Others had turned to her, sensing something as it built. The Cadre's suspicious face remained imprinted on her mind. She snorted, seared by self-disgust. The tale would be all over the palace by evening.

Now Tulkhan's men, the palace servants and even the stable boys—all of them would fear her. If only there was someone she could ask. Someone she could trust to help her with this!

Imoshen rounded a corner and met up with a group of women plucking chickens. Downy feathers hung on air made humid by the kitchen ovens. Death, blood and heat. It was too reminiscent of the stables.

In her quest for privacy Imoshen had fled to the kitchens, the place she always chose as a child. But this was not her childhood home. Even the Stronghold was no longer hers! Tears flooded her eyes.

There were too many witnesses here, too many people ready to watch and judge, to condemn. She ran down another long corridor. Then she came to the door she knew led into the gardens and the lake with its mock forest. She craved the peace and solitude of the silent snow.

Wearing nothing but her thin boots and a formal dress with a brocade vest she ran out into the open. Cold cut into her bare skin, through the thin gown and boots. Her throat and chest burned with each breath of chilled air. But it was good to escape the confines of the palace and all it represented.

To clear her head Imoshen scooped up a handful of snow, crunching some in her mouth, rubbing more on her cheeks, her closed eyes. It stung, but it was invigorating and cleansing.

Wiping her stinging palms on her thighs, she ran on, not thinking, knowing only that she needed to escape. Her feet carried her into the hollow to the edge of the frozen lake. One year when she was too young to attend the Midwinter Festival her sister had returned with tales of an ice ballet on the lake.

Midwinter was still a small moon cycle away but now she would never see an ice ballet. All the beauty of the old empire was dead, consumed by the crude hunger of the Ghebites.

Without stopping, she ran out onto the ice. Her boots had no grip, their soft soles skidded and her momentum carried her forward awkwardly. She careened with her legs locked, arms wavering to keep her balance.

Letting her body go limp, she hit the ice and went with the skid. Imoshen felt her momentum slow until she came to a stop.

All was utter silence. Cold, uncaring quiet.

The folly of her mad run struck Imoshen. It was freezing, too cold for what she was wearing. And who knew if the ice was safe.

She tried to get to her feet, but her legs went out from under her and she dropped in an undignified heap, sliding across the ice on her backside.

"Imoshen!"

General Tulkhan's furious voice startled her. Heart sinking, she looked over her shoulder to see his dark form on the edge of the lake. The indignity of it seared her.

Did he have to witness her every indiscretion? Couldn't he leave her be?

"Go away!" Anger flooded her. With sudden insight Imoshen knew it could happen again. The power of her T'En gifts seethed just below the surface. She could lose control, hurt someone.

Cold fear cooled her rage. It was demeaning to admit

she couldn't trust herself. Today she had discovered she was but a child with an adult's weapon.

Pressing icy fingers to her heated cheeks, Imoshen closed her eyes and took a deep, shaky breath. There was nowhere to run. She had to admit her failure and face the General. He deserved an apology.

Besides, sitting in a puddle of melted ice while Tulkhan looked on was not doing anything for her dignity. With a sigh, she rolled over onto her knees and rose carefully to her feet.

Tulkhan watched as Imoshen stood up and straightened her shoulders. He was going to tear strips off her. How dare she try to intimidate his men with careless displays of her T'En gifts. That he had been as startled as his men hadn't helped. He hated being at a disadvantage. Not to mention the damage she'd caused. Luckily the fire hadn't spread, but the rumor would and with it the damage to Imoshen and himself.

Imoshen lifted a hand and acknowledged him with a wave. She took one step forward and went through the ice.

Her disappearance was so abrupt that Tulkhan stared, too stunned to move.

Then he was running across the slippery surface, his heart pounding in his head. He didn't even remember moving. His boots thudded on the ice, striking chips. One part of his mind told him he would go through the ice into the freezing lake with her if he wasn't careful.

Tulkhan slowed his mad dash and looked up, trying to judge the distance and the thickness of the ice. Frustration filled him. This wasn't his land. He came from the steamy north. He'd be no help to Imoshen if he ended up in the lake with her.

He tried to stop, but his boots wouldn't grip and he went down on all fours, skidding across the ice.

Ahead of him he saw Imoshen's head break the surface of the icy lake, her mouth open in a silent scream. She lunged for the ice lip, trying to lever herself out. But the ice gave way, dragging her under the choppy lake water again.

His mouth went dry as his momentum continued to carry him toward the weak ice.

Imoshen's head broke the surface. Her hair clung to her skull like spilt milk. Seeing him, she shook her head furiously.

"Stay back!" Her voice was a frantic, breathless cry.

He came to a stop. Fear sank its icy hand into his gut. To advance might mean his death but to hesitate would be her death. He couldn't let her drown.

It was a cruel choice.

Frozen with indecision. Tulkhan watched as Imoshen pulled her weight onto the ice lip. He was close enough to see skittering cracks race across the surface of the ice.

Though he hadn't grown up skating on frozen lakes he understood it would precipitate both theirs deaths to approach her now.

Wordlessly she looked across to him, deliberately not calling for help. Her silent struggle to ease her weight onto the precarious ice tore at him. His heart swelled to choke him. No, he couldn't leave her to struggle alone.

He crept forward on his hands and knees.

She looked up and saw him coming.

"Stay back!" Fury ignited her face.

It made him smile.

Creeping laboriously forward, he watched the ice for cracks. His bare hands stung with the cold, then burned until they felt nothing.

"No further!" she hissed.

This time her tone stopped him. Her eyes were dark pools in her white face. Shivers wracked her body. She could hardly speak for the chattering of her teeth.

He crouched there, impotent and hating it.

She was just a body length from him, trapped from her waist down in the lake, her upper body pressed to a cracked ice slab. Tulkhan knew if he returned to the palace for help Imoshen would be dead before he could come back.

"Where are your men when we need them?" she hissed.

A painful grin escaped him. "I told them not to follow."

"Wh . . . why?"

It seemed ridiculous now. "I wanted to confront you. What possessed you? Why incinerate the birds?"

She rolled her eyes and shook her head then grew very still. He was afraid she had lost her strength and, with it, all hope. But abruptly she kicked with both legs, lunging up onto the ice.

His breath caught in his throat. Would the ice crack?

It held.

She was closer, almost within arm's length. If he could only pull her off that weak ice . . . Tulkhan edged toward her. She watched him, hope warring with desperation. Her arm stretched out to him, fingers splayed.

Only a little further.

He lay on his belly, thrusting one arm forward. Their fingers touched. Convulsively hers closed around his. Chilled as his hands were, hers felt colder.

She smiled, her blue lips parting, teeth chattering. "You f . . . fool!"

He grinned and flexed his arm, but he had no leverage and she was weighed down by her soaked clothes. The cold lake still claimed her from the thighs down.

With quiet desperation she raised her knee up, shifting her weight onto the ice lip.

Tulkhan's grip tightened. "Now the other . . ."

She nodded, clenched her chattering jaw, and eased her second knee out onto the ice. He dragged her toward him. The strain made his muscles protest.

Trembling with a combination of cold and effort, he drew her toward him until they were face-to-face, belly down on the ice.

Imoshen clutched his shoulders, panting with relief. He felt her bury her cold face in his shoulder. Even her breath seemed icy.

"S . . . so cold!"

She was. Tulkhan realized she could still die.

He had to get her back to the palace, get her warm. "This way."

With painstaking care they slithered across the ice on their bellies. As soon as the ice appeared more solid they clambered onto their hands and knees to crawl across it. Imoshen fell behind. When Tulkhan looked over his shoulder she was struggling to keep up with him, her head down, trying to lift her shoulders. Her faltering efforts frightened him.

Furious, Tulkhan lunged back to her, knelt and pulled her into his arms. He shook her. "Keep moving!"

She nodded but clung to him, great spasms of shivers wracking her body. When he looked into her face her eyes were dull, her concentration turned inward. He was losing her. *No!*

Instinctively he caught her head in his hands and kissed those cold lips, willing the desperate passion that warmed him to animate her.

At first her mouth remained unresponsive under his. He could feel only her reflexive shivers shaking him with their intensity. He pulled her hard against him, ignoring the icy cold of her clothes which seeped through his already damp clothing.

A shuddering sigh escaped her and suddenly he felt her respond, an unmistakable sign that he had reawakened her fierce will to live. Desperately, she returned his kiss, her lips like cold liquid satin on his. The sensation was so potent he caught his breath. Now he felt her body's instinctive move to meet his.

She held nothing back.

His long years of battle experience told him Imoshen's response was a reaction to her narrow escape from death.

"General?" voices called, worried voices.

Tulkhan detected frantic figures in his peripheral vision. Stunned, he lifted his head, peering past Imoshen's shoulder. The dark figures shouted and capered on the lake's shore. They insisted he acknowledge them.

He groaned and felt Imoshen tense as she registered the change in him. It took a determined effort to release her from his embrace.

He indicated the people on the bank.

Imoshen turned, grimaced then sighed. "Now, they come? What are they yelling?"

There were so many voices all shouting at once that the individual words were lost.

Imoshen went to stand and staggered. Tulkhan came to his feet, catching her before she fell.

"Damn! I'm so weak," she complained.

"Stop!" someone called from the shore. "Don't move. The ice is not safe!"

Tulkhan looked down at Imoshen. Laughter rose inside him. He could see the same impossible laughter igniting her face. He threw back his head and roared.

A peal of fey delight broke from her lips. The sound brushed across his skin like silk. He wanted to wrap himself in it.

Imoshen clutched his arm, grasping for breath. "Don't laugh. They'll think you're touched like me."

That sobered Tulkhan.

He judged the distance they had yet to travel. "Can we walk to the shore from here?"

She nodded.

Together, hands clasped for balance, they walked gingerly across the ice to the lake's shore. Men were just returning with planks of wood when they made the bank.

"My Lady!" Kalleen panted, a party of palace servants scurrying up behind her. "You're soaked. You'll catch your death!"

Imoshen went to climb the bank but slipped. Tulkhan caught her before she could land in the snow. He swept her up in his arms.

She stiffened. "Put me down!"

He ignored her, plowing up the bank as the servants, men-at-arms and Stronghold Guard milled around them.

Imoshen stiffened in his arms, furious but unwilling to cause a scene in front of the others.

"Put me down!" she hissed, twisting to escape his arms. "I'm too heavy for you. I'm as big as an ordinary man!"

"And I'm bigger than most men. If you struggle I might drop you in the snow." Tulkhan smiled when she stopped wriggling. Would he have dropped her in an ungainly heap in the snow? Yes. She knew him well.

He realized he was enjoying this.

The servants and men-at-arms shot questions at him. He

answered them all with an edited version of the accident. Finally they fell silent, dropping away to accompany them in small groups.

Imoshen's arms slid around his neck. "You risked a dunking in the lake to save me."

He heard the serious tone behind her facetious words. He had risked his life to save her.

"I must be mad," he muttered. "I can't even swim!"

Her arms tightened compulsively around his neck.

"Mad, indeed," she whispered. Then her tone changed. "You can put me down. You must be getting tired."

His arms were beginning to ache but she wasn't the only one who could be stubborn. He was glad he'd inherited his grandfather's build. It had been a nuisance as a boy. At twelve he'd stood as tall as a man and been expected to act like one. At sixteen he'd been a head taller than most men. He'd discovered his size influenced the way people treated him.

"You know," he said softly, pitching his voice so only Imoshen could hear. "When I was younger people used to think I was stupid because I grew so big. Tulkhan, the dim-witted giant!"

He glanced down and saw her sharp, wine-dark eyes on him. With a jolt he sensed her Otherness. What was she learning of his past from this physical contact? Once again he was reminded that she was not like him, she was T'En.

Imoshen studied the General, surprised by his admission. "I never thought you stupid. An arrogant barbarian, yes, but never stupid." She saw him grin and lightness filled her. How sweet it was to know that she had driven those bitter memories from him.

They walked on, nearing the bulk of the palace. Tulkhan's admission about his youth made him seem more real to her. She felt compelled to share something of herself with him. "Ever since I can remember people have feared me because I'm a Throwback."

He looked down into her face, his dark eyes alert but unreadable. He had closed himself away from her. She was glad she hadn't added that she was beginning to fear herself now.

Their return caused a great commotion. Imoshen suspected that many of those who wished her well were secretly wishing the treacherous ice had done its job more thoroughly.

Kalleen would have had her bathed and tucked into a warmed bed, but no sooner was she dressed than she sent for the General.

"As for you, you can go, Kalleen. I won't sit by the fire with a blanket around me like some old grandmother!" Imoshen snapped, pacing up and down.

"What's so important that you must see me now and not go to bed like a sensible person?" the General's familiar voice demanded.

Imoshen wanted to run to him. Instead, she channeled her energy into achieving her goal and darted to the table where the Beatific's terms were waiting to be read. Unable to stop herself, Imoshen lifted the brass cylinder and waved it triumphantly.

"The T'En Church will recognize our bonding and coronation, which means the rest of Fair Isle will follow suit. And you have me to thank for it!"

"Let me see." General Tulkhan strode toward Imoshen. She opened the cylinder and slid out the scroll, passing it to him. He turned it to the light of the scented candles. Dusk fell early this close to midwinter.

He frowned. "What manner of chicken scrawl is this?"

Imoshen bit her lips to hide a smile. "The language of all official documents is High T'En."

He held it out to her. "Read it to me, word for word."

"If I am to translate it shouldn't the Cadre be here, too?" Imoshen suspected the Ghebite priest intended to dismantle the T'En Church once General Tulkhan was officially recognized as ruler of Fair Isle.

"Why?" Tulkhan snapped. "I make the decisions."

She took the scroll from him and turned away so he

wouldn't see her smile. The General's dislike of the Cadre's company had not been lost on her.

She went closer to the fire, eager for its warmth, and prepared to read, then translate. General Tulkhan settled into her chair with his long legs stretched out before him. Propping one elbow on the table, he cupped his chin to watch her thoughtfully.

She tried not to let her gaze wander to him as she read each sentence, then translated it. This manner of delivery made the meaning rather disjointed as the grammar of the High T'En tongue was very different from its daughter language.

The General's keen dark eyes never left Imoshen's face and she wondered if he was having trouble comprehending the ornate prose. When it came to the paragraphs pertaining to recognition of T'En Church laws Imoshen's heart pounded. She willed him to accept what she was interpreting. The General's expression did not change. Either he was keeping his reaction close to his chest, or he did not understand how civil laws and church laws intertwined.

Imoshen felt no guilt withholding this information. If he had asked, she would have explained. But he didn't. Finally she came to the end and indicated where the Beatific had signed and placed her seal of office.

"Two copies, one for the Beatific to keep, one for us. This is where you sign, and I sign here."

"You?" His gaze flew to hers.

She tilted her head, surprised by his reaction. "By recognising your position the Beatific strips the rebel leader Roethe of his rights. As the last legitimate member of the T'En royal family I become titular head of the church. Do you want a translated version of this before you sign?"

"Why? You read it word for word, didn't you?"

Imoshen nodded. She had read it word for word as he requested, though the meaning would have been clearer had she paraphrased it.

When his stomach grumbled audibly the General shifted in the seat. Reading the scroll had taken a good while. He held out his hand. Imoshen passed the document to him, aware of her heart hammering in her chest. She had gambled that if she did provide him with a translated version he would have been too busy to read it thoroughly before signing. But it appeared he was ready to sign now.

After all, the Ghebite General was a man of action. Yet, she reminded herself how he had taken the trouble to learn her language before bringing his army to Fair Isle. He was a strange mixture of the primitive and sophisticated.

His obsidian eyes scanned the ornate pages of the document.

"What you translated is what is written here?" he asked again, watching her closely.

"I translated it word for word." But she omitted to add that a literal translation did not make for a clear translation of meaning.

"So if I sign this now, the Beatific retains control over her church and will back me in controlling Fair Isle?"

Imoshen nodded.

"Have you ink and wax?"

Imoshen noted that her hands did not tremble as she indicated her own ink and wax, then sharpened the scriber.

"You first," he said, when she offered it to him.

Imoshen swallowed and dipped the tip in the ink.

"You think this is a fair agreement?" Tulkhan asked.

She paused as she tapped the excess ink from the tip of the scriber. "I do. The terms are fair to all inhabitants of this island, whether they are Ghebite or native.

"General, you have enemies on the mainland, an unruly army of ex-soldiers, reluctant southern nobles and a competent rebel leader in Reothe. Any support from an entrenched body like the Church must be useful."

He laughed. "You think like a Ghebite soldier."

She stiffened. Was he attempting to insult her? No, she read only genuine amusement in his eyes.

"Statesmanship was one of my best subjects," she temporized.

He nodded and gestured for her to sign. Imoshen wrote her full name and title. Then she melted the wax and, instead of using an official seal, she adopted the ancient T'En method, dipping the tip of her sixth finger in the puddle of hot wax, ignoring the flash of pain.

It hurt more when she did the same for the second document. Her teeth grew chilled as she sucked in her breath.

Tulkhan's eyes met hers. She stepped back. "Now you."

Businesslike, he signed and placed his official seal on the document, first one then the other.

Imoshen went to Kalleen's door. The maidservant looked up, the remains of her evening meal on a tray on her lap.

"Give the Beatific's assistant this copy of the document, which has been signed. Place the second copy in the palace library and please have our meal delivered."

"And then you'll go to bed?"

Imoshen sighed. "There are a dozen palace servants who would be eager to take your place."

Kalleen grinned. "I wouldn't trust them to feed the pigs!" With that she scurried off.

Imoshen smiled as she shut the door. Kalleen was right. She dare not trust anyone else.

Weary though she was, she had to speak with the General. This was a perfect opportunity. The Ghebite Commanders had been excluding her by monopolizing their General's time. And today she and Tulkhan had shared a common threat. He'd risked his life to save her . . .

An unwelcome thought struck Imoshen. Would it have been more accurate to say that he risked his own life to save the child she carried, his only chance for a son?

Imoshen shivered. She didn't want to know the answer to that. It was enough that Tulkhan needed her for political necessity and desired her. She could hardly ask for more.

"Will you stay and eat with me, General?" she asked formally.

He looked at her, his face inscrutable. "After that will you go to bed?"

She laughed. "Yes. Kalleen would be honored to know you agree with her!"

He smiled fleetingly. "Then I will share a meal with you."

So they ate sitting before the fire in strangely companionable silence. When the last of the servants had departed and they were savoring the remains of their meal Imoshen looked across the hearth to him. "There is something I would discuss with you."

He put his wine aside. "What now? I've agreed to a formal dinner tomorrow night to celebrate the signing."

She knew he was teasing her and it filled her with a warm glow which she found hard to ignore. "Roasted nuts?"

He selected a handful and tossed the lot into his mouth chewing vigorously. He ate with the same voracious hunger he tackled everything in life.

After a sip of wine he reached for more. "They don't have nuts like these on the mainland."

"No. They come from the archipelago." Imoshen found she was strangely loath to disturb the peace of the moment. And she had to admit she did not want to ask the Ghebite General for a favor, even if it was for her maid.

Observing Tulkhan surreptitiously, she thought he appeared relaxed. Strangely enough, he had said nothing to her regarding the incinerated birds. Imoshen had decided that if he did broach the subject, she would have to apologize but she wasn't going to offer an apology unnecessarily. This might entail an explanation and she didn't want to go into details which would reveal her weakness.

Tulkhan accepted his wine. It always amused him when Imoshen played hostess. She had such regal bearing and used what appeared to be formal High Court manners, so that she made the simple act of pouring wine almost a ritualized dance.

It secretly delighted him to know that beneath her formal exterior she was all woman, and his touch could ignite her. He swallowed and felt his body quicken with need.

He had avoided being alone with her but this had only exacerbated his need for her. Midwinter could not come too soon.

Imoshen sipped her wine.

"Yes?" he prodded, watching her over his wine goblet.

He could sense her reluctance, could tell she wanted to broach a subject she found distasteful.

Was it something to do with Reothe? His gut tightened.

She placed her wine on the table and turned to Tulkhan, obviously ready to face him no matter how unpleasant she found it. No, it could not be Reothe, he decided. She would have simply told him and faced his anger.

Tulkhan was intrigued.

"I ask a boon," Imoshen announced.

So that explained it. He knew she hated asking for anything. "Ask. We are to be wed. I would be making you a wedding present."

"This is not for me." She licked her lips and grimaced. "The estates to the south are still held by their nobles, but the estates to the north lie in ruins. Their rich lands are your prizes of war."

Tulkhan chose not to remind her that the whole of Fair Isle was his. Two thirds had been taken by force, and the other third had surrendered by omission.

Imoshen continued, "I own an estate. Or rather I used to own an estate to the north. It is not large, but—"

"It is yours once more." He anticipated her.

She flushed as he knew she would. "Thank you."

He smiled. He could tell how much it hurt her to say those words. "Why just one estate? Are you planning to flee the capital?"

He couldn't let her do that of course.

"No. I'm going to gift it to Kalleen."

"What?" Tulkhan's wine slopped on the floor as he thrust it aside.

Imoshen lifted her chin and met his eyes. "Have you forgotten that it was her bravery which allowed me to escape the dungeon and Gharavan's axe? You sit here soon to be crowned King of Fair Isle because she took my place at risk to her own life!"

He rubbed his chin thoughtfully. "You would give her an estate—"

"And the title that goes with it. She would be the Lady Kalleen of Windhaven."

Tulkhan was reminded that he had meant to assign estates and titles to his commanders. If they owned land it would ensure their loyalty to him and Fair Isle. A mercenary fights for money but a man who fights for the land under his feet, fights with fire in his belly—it was basic war craft.

"Very well." Tulkhan nodded, relieved her request had been so simple. "I will have the papers drawn up."

"You might wish to gift the neighboring estate to Wharrd," Imoshen told him. "I know you were planning to reward him and since you have recognized the T'En Church, Kalleen can bond with him."

"Wait. Why couldn't she marry him before?" Tulkhan felt he was missing something.

Imoshen simply looked at him, her face a beautiful mask. "Kalleen refused his offer of marriage because it would have been unequal. When people are joined by the T'En Church they become bond-partners, equals. I explained all that to you the night you claimed me for your bond-partner."

The room swayed around Tulkhan and blood rushed in his ears, filling his head with a roaring noise. Now he understood the significance of everything that had passed between them this evening. He had just signed a document recognizing the laws of the T'En Church. To bring the people of Fair Isle behind him he had to marry Imoshen and have their "bonding," as the T'En Church put it, recognized by the people's church.

Fair enough, for once political necessity happily coincided with his private desires. The prospect of taking Imoshen to wife made the cool political marriage his father had arranged pale in significance.

But because he'd recognized Fair Isle's church laws, as soon as the Beatific formalized their joining Imoshen would legally be his equal. Half of everything he owned would be hers.

He had signed away half of Fair Isle to his captive!

Her face was turned away from him, presenting the curve of her cheek and the hollow under her jaw. Her perfect porcelain skin and profile were so pure he could not imagine a cruel conniving thought ever crossing her mind.

Unaware of his scrutiny, Imoshen twisted to face him, her hand cupping a bowl. "More nuts?"

"No." He saw her start, surprised by the harsh tone of his voice. He watched her face closely for duplicity. "You know what you have done?"

She turned away from him to place the roasted nuts on a low table between them.

Yes, she knew exactly what she had done. Manipulative, traitorous Dhamfeer! Anger hardened his heart against her beauty, her false innocence.

"When the people are secure they are happy," she lectured with calm precision. "By signing that document you have ensured their prosperity. They will not be open to Reothe's cunning tongue. News travels fast. Soon all of Fair Isle will know you have recognized the rights and laws of the people's church. You cannot hope to hold what you have taken if the people do not support you." She met his eyes, daring him to object. He could have drowned in those deep wine-dark depths. "I have helped you hold Fair Isle, General Tulkhan."

Burning with anger, he longed to denounce her for what she was, but on another level he knew she was right. A charged silence fell between them.

With deliberate care he caught her hand and drew her from her chair, to her knees. She waited compliantly between his thighs as though she hadn't just maneuvered him into signing away half his kingdom.

"That is not all," he told her.

"No." She lifted her chin in that now familiar gesture. "I have taken the first step to ensure the women of Fair Isle will not be reduced to slaves like your Ghebite females."

"You've ensured half of Fair Isle for yourself!"

She stiffened, her eyes flashing. "I belong to all of Fair Isle. If I didn't, I would have escaped with him when I had the chance at Landsend!"

What?

Imoshen stood abruptly. "Have you sent the Midwinter Feast invitations to the southern nobles?"

"And the ambassadors of the mainland kingdoms and the princelings of the archipelago," he answered automatically. Escaped at Landsend? Did she mean she'd planned to escape from there to the islands of the archipelago? If so, when? Before she surrendered her Stronghold to him? He doubted it. Then when?

Abruptly the answer came to him. She could have escaped when they were at Landsend together in the first weeks after he took the Stronghold.

But escaped with who? Reothe. Who else?

A flare of pure anger ignited Tulkhan. To think the rebel leader had dared to infiltrate the abbey while the Ghebite General was there. The Seculate, all of them . . . how they must have been laughing at him!

But Imoshen hadn't escaped him when she had the chance.

"Why?"

She started at the tone of his voice, then calmly went on cleaning away the remains of their meal onto the trays the servants had left behind.

"Why what?" Her tone sounded so deliberately innocent he knew she was prevaricating.

"Why didn't you run away with Reothe when we were at Landsend?"

A flush inflamed her pale skin and he had to smile grimly. She hadn't meant to reveal that she'd had the opportunity to escape. Knowing Imoshen, she was probably cursing herself.

Very slowly, Imoshen turned to meet his eyes. "To abandon you there would have meant a bloodbath. The people would have revolted, the southern nobles would have turned and forced you to defeat them. Besides," she sighed tiredly, "I had given my word."

Since the Stronghold had fallen and Imoshen had become Tulkhan's prisoner she had constantly opposed him, forcing him to confront his beliefs. He had seen evidence of her tactical training and her consummate statesmanship but until this moment he had not personally experienced its effect.

After the assassination attempt he had confronted Imoshen, demanding to know who Reothe was. She had admitted that he was once her betrothed but she had given him up for dead. He was said to have been killed in battle. Yet she had known all along that Reothe lived because he had offered her a chance to escape with him at Landsend Abbey. She had refused and because of this had faced death at Tulkhan's own hand, averted only by the Aayel's sacrifice. How she must have hated him, her Ghebite captor.

He had underestimated T'Imoshen, last of the T'En. She had risked death because she had given him her word. She had stayed and risked her life rather than betray the people of Fair Isle who trusted her to look after their interests. He would never again compare her with a Ghebite woman.

Tulkhan watched as Imoshen collected the trays then carried them to the passage for the servants to take away, even though the servants would have cleared the remains of the meal later. She was keeping him at a distance.

Why?

It was obvious she didn't want to discuss this with him any further. She had chosen to stay because she had given him her word and for her that meant everything.

But she had also given her word to the rebel leader.

A cold ball of certainty settled in Tulkhan's belly.

"You gave your word to Reothe. The pair of you were betrothed." It was out before he could stop himself. "Are your vows worthless?"

Her lips twisted in a painful smile. "I was barely sixteen. The betrothal promise was a vow sworn on a dying empire."

"Reothe is not dead." He had to pursue it, had to hear her say the deposed prince of the T'En was nothing to her. It ate at him.

She said something in an ancient language which made the little hairs on his body rise. Magic? Once he hadn't believed in the T'En gifts. But he had seen what Imoshen could do.

He sprang to his feet, heart thudding. "What was that, a curse?"

She shrugged. "It is a line from an old T'En poem. It translates something like . . . Dead man walks and talks, but doesn't know he's dead."

A shiver moved over Tulkhan's skin. Reothe had quoted the same poem when they met in the mists. A curse escaped Tulkhan.

Imoshen looked up at him, startled. "What is it, General? My vow to Reothe is dead. I have made a commitment to you—"

"For the good of Fair Isle."

"Exactly. You can trust me."

Tulkhan itched to shake her, to wipe that reasonable look from her face.

"Actions speak louder than words. Why did you incinerate the fighting birds?"

She flinched and he felt better, then perversely despised himself for picking at what he knew was a painful memory for her.

Imoshen turned and padded to the window. She picked up a plate of half-eaten fruit she'd overlooked.

"Leave that. The servants can do it. God knows, there are enough of them!"

She replaced the plate but hesitated with her back to him, fiddling with something on the table below the window. "I must apologize—"

"I said *leave it*!" He'd strode across the room before he knew he meant to. When he spun her around to face him he could feel the firm flesh of her upper arms pinched cruelly between his fingers. "I asked why you felt it necessary to stage that display for my people! You could have burned down the stables, killing people and trained battle horses."

With a liquid-quick movement she broke his hold on her, swinging her arms up against his thumb and down again so fast he couldn't compensate, couldn't hold her.

Her lips drew back from her sharp teeth and her wine-dark eyes blazed with an inner feral light which both frightened and fascinated him. He had pierced Imoshen's armor. Tulkhan was pleased.

"Why must your men act like barbarians, bringing their foul ways into the lives of my people? Fighting cocks, blood sports! What next? Bear baiting?"

Since this wasn't far from the truth Tulkhan remained silent.

Imoshen ground her teeth then shrugged past him disdainfully. She prowled the room angrily before finally settling in front of the fireplace. "You have inherited an ancient culture, with a legacy of knowledge rich beyond measure, General Tulkhan. Don't destroy it simply because you don't understand it."

The fire's glow behind her bathed her body in light, illuminating her long legs through her gown, and creating a halo in the strands of her long hair. He wanted to run his fingers through that pale, silken mane.

The ever-present need to touch her was overwhelming. He could feel it drawing him across the room to her. He wanted to step close enough to inhale her scent and grow drunk on it. He needed to feel that quicksilver response in her, to know that his touch ignited her body as she ignited his. He needed her. On the lake he had been ready to make the ultimate sacrifice to save her.

With a jolt he realized he would throw away everything to have Imoshen in his arms and in his bed. She was a drug he craved. Yet like the drug-crazed priests of an obscure sect he had seen immolating themselves, would his need for her destroy him?

Cool, rational thought made Tulkhan hesitate.

Already tonight she had outmaneuvered him by tricking him into recognizing the church. No, to be truthful he'd had little choice. He needed the church behind him. And in some ways he could see Imoshen's point of view.

Why should she give up her right to make her own decisions, own property? Had the Ghebite women he had known during his youth despised the men they loved because they were slaves of their fathers and sons?

Tulkhan's head spun with the implications. He could sense Imoshen watching him, studying him. He must not let her guess how deeply she disturbed him. Would she use it against him? In her position he would have.

Cold certainty gripped him. The more he saw of Imoshen the more she drew him. The more she knew of him the easier she would find it to manipulate him. No matter what it cost him he must keep her at a distance. Bed her, yes, but welcome her into his heart—never!

He caught her watching him. Her faintly calculating expression confirmed all his fears. Furious with himself for ever thinking there could be trust between them, he advanced on her.

Imoshen stood her ground before the fire, proud but wary.

Despite his vow to keep her at a distance he caught her in his arms, felt the curves of her strong body against the length of him. He wanted to hurt her as much as she had hurt him, wanted to leave her needing him as much as he needed her.

Her lips parted in a sharp gasp and he felt a tremor run through her body. An answering tremor ran through his as his body responded.

"Marriage or bond-partner, it's all the same to me. It means you're mine to have. Kiss me," he demanded.

"No! Not like this. Not in anger—"

But he caught her face between his hands and captured her lips, drawn tight in a grimace of anger. The force of her fury ignited him. Her foot came down sharply on his instep but she was only wearing soft indoor slippers and it wasn't painful. He laughed.

She cursed him, her knee surging up between his thighs but he twisted, deflecting the blow.

"Tulkhan, I—"

The moment her lips parted he had her. He could already feel it, the surge of need building between them. He knew the moment her kiss became voluntary. The gentling of her touch called to him. He wanted to drown in her.

A groan escaped him. Her breath fanned his cheek.

"Damn you, General!" Her lips moved on his. "Why must you take when a gift is more precious?"

Her words confused him. He could think only of his need.

Why should he wait? They'd publicly announced they were to wed. He'd already known her body twice.

"No!" Her voice cut through his thoughts.

Sharply, she twisted from his grasp. Darting back two steps, she ducked down and snatched a brand from the fire.

Holding it by the blackened end, she thrust the flame between them.

"One step closer and I'll put out your eyes!"

For a moment he believed her. Then he saw the sheen of unshed tears which masked her anger.

"You wouldn't. You want me. If I persisted I could have you now and you'd end up welcoming me!"

She gave a bitter short laugh. "Is force all you Ghebites understand? You take my land by force. You claim me as a prize of war. Do you think you can take me by force?"

"Your fingers are burning."

"Good! I'd rather burn than be defiled by you!"

"Defiled? You're no celibate Dhamfeer priestess. First, you broke your vows to your church by accepting Reothe as your bond-partner. Then you broke your vows to your betrothed because it suited your purpose. You bedded me because it suited your purpose. You're no better than the Ghebite women you despise."

"Get out!"

"I'm going."

"Good!"

They stood there panting, the air charged with the force of their emotion.

Imoshen jerked the burning brand, indicating the door. The pain in her hand was nothing compared to the pain in her heart. She'd thought Tulkhan was different from the other Ghebites.

"I'm going," he repeated and she could see him distancing himself from her. "But mark this, Dhamfeer. I know what you are and I won't forget it!"

Contemptuously he turned his back on her and strode out of the room.

When the door closed after General Tulkhan Imoshen flung the brand back into the fire and ran to the window, opening it to thrust her fingers into the snow on the ledge.

A wracking sob of despair shook her.

"Fool, fool!" she hissed, not sure whether she meant herself or Tulkhan.

When her fingers finally grew numb she returned to her seat by the fireplace to put salve on her burns. Hugging her throbbing hand to her chest, silent tears of despair slid down her cheeks.

She should heal her hand as Reothe had taught her, but perversely she felt she deserved this pain and besides, every muscle in her body ached. She was exhausted. The drenching in the lake had shaken her more than she cared to admit.

Kalleen was right—she should have rested. But she could not have taken to her bed when she did not know whether the General and his advisors were perusing the church document without her.

Now the document was signed, sealed and delivered. The Aayel would be pleased. She had achieved her goal, but she didn't feel elated. She had paid a bitter price. It had cost her Tulkhan's trust.

While she had won for her people, she had lost for herself. But she could not think of herself, too much was at stake.

Leaning her head against the tall chairback, she groaned with pain. She wasn't strong enough for this. If only the Aayel had lived to advise her. Exhaustion, emotional and physical, had made her slip tonight. She hadn't meant to let the General know about her opportunity to escape with Reothe at Landsend.

Tulkhan might be angry with her, but in recognizing the T'En Church he had secured the church's support and with-

out it he could not hold Fair Isle. She had taken the first step
to ensuring that her country wouldn't sink into barbarism.

Weary beyond words, Imoshen dropped her good hand
to her lap and peered into the flames. Her fingers splayed
across her belly protectively. Had the General only been
thinking of his child when he risked his life to save her? The
child hardly seemed real to her. It was too early to feel anything, too early to show. There was no visible evidence to
confirm that brief flare she'd felt when the new life began.

Since that night she had lain with Tulkhan—a shudder
passed through her as her body quickened with the memory—so much had happened. Her T'En powers had grown
with frightening rapidity. In her mind's eye she saw the fighting birds engulfed in a fiery ball of flames and feathers. Her
hands tightened into painful fists and she groaned, lifting her
burned hand to her lips.

How could she admit to General Tulkhan that she had no
control over her gifts when he already despised her T'En
side?

What did she expect? He was Ghebite.

What did she want from the General? Trust? Love?

What did he expect her to do? Deny what she was?

Imoshen ground her teeth in frustration. She had done
everything she set out to achieve. The Aayel would have been
proud. Fair Isle was hers and one day her son would rule the
island.

Yes, she had won the battle, but the war was far from
over. Too many factors could upset the balance of power. The
southern nobles, Reothe and his rebels weren't the only
threats. She sighed. It would be only too easy for Tulkhan
and his Ghebite army to make one wrong move and destroy
their fragile alliance with the people of Fair Isle, then they
would welcome Reothe. And what of King Gharavan? What
if he swore revenge and returned with a fresh army?

Imoshen shuddered. She may have reclaimed Fair Isle
but now she had to hold it. And to do that she needed General Tulkhan's support. But it had to be willing support. He
would not take kindly to manipulation and, besides, she did

not want to dishonor him with trickery. He had signed the church agreement because it benefited them both, and united the population of Fair Isle behind him. Now that he understood the full ramifications of property ownership he was angry with her, but the General was a fair man. He would come round. She was sure of it.

Her hand throbbed and she turned it over to the light. The blisters were already beginning to form. She would have to heal the burn. Concentrating, Imoshen reached inside herself for that one T'En skill she felt secure enough to call on. But strive as she might, she could not find it. The familiar taste did not settle on her tongue and her teeth did not ache with the buildup of tension.

She was drained. Exhausted by the bone-chilling dip in the frozen lake and the shattering outpouring of strength she had directed at the fighting birds, she felt just as she used to feel when the gift first came to her and she had tried to heal at the Aayel's bidding. Her gift had limits. It would do well to remember that.

She unfolded her legs and padded to the window, plunging her hand into the snow again to ease the pain. With a sigh of relief she let her mind drift.

A movement in the shadows of the courtyard attracted her attention. It was Tulkhan. She would know those broad shoulders and that proud bearing anywhere. He stood alone, staring up at the twin moons. The smaller moon was full while the larger waxed more slowly. It would not be full again until winter's cusp. The night was so clear that she could see the larger moon's dark face silhouetted against the stars.

What did the Ghebite General see when he looked up at the twin moons? Did he see two brothers forever in conflict, the son of the first wife trying to outshine the son of the second wife and win his father's love?

Or was he remembering what she had told him about the role of the twin moons in the mythology of Fair Isle—man and woman, different but complete in themselves. For a while one would be in the ascendancy then the other would dominate, but they were at their brightest and strongest when both shone together. Had he understood her unspoken message?

She looked down at him thinking, we are different you and I, from different backgrounds, different as a man and woman can be, yet for the good of Fair Isle we must not burn ourselves out in pointless conflict.

But was it possible for a Ghebite male to overcome barbaric ways and his prejudices? Could Tulkhan accept her T'En self?

Reothe would. The thought came unbidden. Reothe was her other half. She might fear his superior T'En powers but at least he would never despise her for her innate gifts.

He believed that together they could unite Fair Isle and drive the Ghebites out. Would the sum of their gifts be greater joined? For a moment she let herself contemplate standing at Reothe's side leading an army across the fertile plains of Fair Isle, driving the arrogant Ghebites into the sea and restoring T'En rule.

But she couldn't. Her people had seen too much death. They wanted peace. They needed to know that if they planted a crop they would live to harvest it for their children. They had the right to the simple dignity of their lives, lived without fear of being called upon to serve their rulers in a war not of their choosing.

She could not condone more fighting, and joining Reothe would inevitably ensure more death with no certainty of success. Besides, she hardly knew the man who had once been her betrothed. The General, for all that he was a Ghebite, was more familiar to her. She knew Tulkhan was an honorable man.

Imoshen had to believe that she had made the right choice when she rejected Reothe's offer of escape.

Suddenly the General looked up. His face was in shadow but she could imagine his dark eyes, broad cheekbones. What was he thinking?

He stepped into the patch of light and raised his hand in a silent salute, acknowledging an equal. She returned the gesture. Then Tulkhan strode from the courtyard.

Imoshen flexed her fingers. The snow had numbed the

pain at last. She sighed and closed the window. So much depended on her but she would not falter.

She was no man's puppet, neither Reothe's nor Tulkhan's. She was T'Imoshen, last of the T'En, and the future was hers to shape. The last princess of the T'En would bow to no one.

Don't miss a moment of the blazing passion
and heart-stopping peril as the battle for Fair Isle
and the story of General Tulkhan and Imoshen,
Last of the T'En, continues in

DARK DREAMS

by Cory Daniells

Coming from Bantam Books in Fall 2000.